D1443525

THE TRADING POST AND OTHER FRONTIER STORIES

A FIVE STAR ANTHOLOGY

EDITED BY HAZEL RUMNEY

THORNDIKE PRESS
A part of Gale, a Cengage Company

GALE
A Cengage Company

Farmington Hills, Mich • San Francisco • New York • Waterville, Maine
Meriden, Conn • Mason, Ohio • Chicago

The Trading Post and Other Frontier Stories: Copyright © 2018 by Five Star™ Publishing, a part of Gale, a Cengage Company.
The Trading Post © 2018 by Michael Zimmer
Coffin Nails in Callaway County © 2018 by Lonnie Whitaker
The Judgment Tree © 2018 by Johnnie D. Boggs
Wren's Perch © 2018 by Vonn McKee
Rider from Bordeaux © 2018 by John D. Nesbitt
An Hour Before the Hangman © 2018 by Michael R. Ritt
The Prairie Fire © 2018 by Larry D. Sweazy
Old Gun Wolf © 2018 by Frank Leslie
Dirty Old Town © 2018 by Greg Hunt
A Small Thing © 2018 by Matthew P. Mayo
Little Cheyenne © 2018 by Ethan J. Wolfe
My Brother's Keeper © 2018 by Bill Brooks
To Ride a Tall Horse © 2018 by L.J. Martin
Halfway to Hell © 2018 by Gregory J. Lalire
Thorndike Press, a part of Gale, a Cengage Company.

LIBRARY OF CONGRESS CIP DATA ON FILE.
CATALOGUING IN PUBLICATION FOR THIS BOOK
IS AVAILABLE FROM THE LIBRARY OF CONGRESS

ISBN-13: 978-1-4328-4508-7 (hardcover)

Published in 2018 by arrangement with Five Star™ Publishing, a part of Gale, a Cengage Company

Printed in the United States of America
1 2 3 4 5 6 7 22 21 20 19 18

This book, Five Star's first anthology of Western fiction, is dedicated to a man who personified the spirit of the West. Through a lifetime devoted to writing and promoting Western literature, Dusty Richards mentored and inspired many writers. He and his wife, Pat, became beloved friends of Five Star.

Ronald "Dusty" Lee Richards
1937–2018
Patricia Ann (Donahoe) Richards
1940–2018

TABLE OF CONTENTS

■ ■ ■ ■

THE TRADING POST
BY MICHAEL
ZIMMER

■ ■ ■ ■

The old man was fleshing a hide when movement on the southern prairie caught his eye. He paused to study the distant horizon, twisting his head slightly to the side to avoid the cataract haze that blurred his straight-on vision. A faint smile lifted the corners of his mouth when he recognized the man riding out front. Well, not the man, not yet, but the white mule, for sure.

"Woman," he called into the nearby doorway, leading into the side of the hill at his back. He kept his scraper pressed firmly against the wolf's pelt, stretched tightly over a willow frame braced against one knee. "They have come."

The sounds from within ceased, and a moment later he heard her at the dugout's door, could picture her standing there with one brown hand propped against the frame, watching the line of approaching carts. "They are late this year," she said in Cree, the language of her people.

"Late or early, they're here now." He straightened slowly, ignoring the ripple of twitching muscles along his spine. "There looks to be half a dozen of them," he added after a moment. "Better put some more meat in the pot."

"Do you think I do not already know this?" she replied, turning back into the dugout.

The trader chuckled and went back to his labors. The little caravan was still a few miles away. There would be plenty of time to finish the gray wolf's pelt before they arrived.

He worked the hide with practiced ease, scraping away the excess fat and meat until only the milky underside remained. He was putting away his tools when the man on the mule splashed across Cutbank Creek and trotted his white jenny into the hard-packed dirt yard fronting the tiny trading post.

"Ho!" he called in greeting.

"Ho, yourself, old friend," the trader replied, tossing aside the thin antelope hide he'd used as a rag to clean his scraper before walking out to shake the agent's hand. "You had a safe trip?"

"A quiet trip," the agent replied gratefully, his gaze wandering past the old man's shoulder to take in the condition of the post — the unlocked door to the storeroom, the empty corral down by the creek.

Although the trader didn't speak, he flinched inwardly at the agent's silent appraisal. He knew the trading post made a poor impression when compared with the fur trade company's larger forts farther to the west. There wasn't much to Cutbank Post anymore, just the trade room and living quarters for him and the woman, hollowed out of the side of the hill, and the storeroom to the west, also a dugout, although with its own entrance. In front of these burrows was a crude fur press held together with rawhide and hand-carved wooden pegs, and a cottonwood fleshing beam for the larger hides, like buffalo and elk, that sometimes found their way downstream.

At one time, Cutbank Post had handled a good portion of the robe trade among the eastern Cree, and even some from the Ojibway and Santee, but those days were long past now. The buffalo had been drifting steadily westward for decades, away from the pressure of the Red River hunters. In recent years it sometimes seemed like it was hardly worth the effort to keep the place supplied.

The trader supposed it only made sense to shift the Company's satellite posts in the same direction, moving them farther west with the migrating herds, but he'd lived on the Cutbank for nearly thirty years by then. He'd seen his children play among the towering cottonwoods along the creek, had watched them learn the skills not only of their mother's people, but of his own — reading and writing, conquering the complexity of numbers so that someday his sons could manage posts of their own. His daughters were even now married to other traders, living along the far-off Milk and Musselshell rivers, while his sons hunted for big outfits like Hudson's Bay and American Fur.

The trader's life here had been a good one, and he was happy with the way it had played out. He cared deeply for the woman who had shared his robes these many years, and still had good friends among the Cree and Ojibway, old men like himself who had stayed when others moved on. The trader wanted to stay, as well, but he knew the decision wouldn't be his to make. Or the agent's, for that matter. Cutbank Post's future rested in the hands of the Company's superintendent at the big fort on the Missouri, a decision based in no small part upon the agent's yearly assessment of the post and its profitability.

The old man's lips thinned in quiet despair as he reflected upon the nearly empty storeroom. He'd taken in fewer than a hundred buffalo robes over the summer, along with fifty or so wolf pelts, and not even enough beaver, muskrat, and other furs to run through the press for baling.

The heavy carts rolled ponderously into the yard, spokes dripping from the shallow waters of the Cutbank, ungreased hubs squealing like frightened hags in the act of being robbed. One of the *engagés* came up to take the agent's mule, while others lifted heavy maple yokes from the necks of their oxen and turned them loose to graze. The woman appeared at the dugout's entrance, and the agent swept his hat from his head. "M'lady," he said graciously, then switched to Cree. "It is good to see you again."

"There is food for all, if food is sought," she replied simply, but the trader knew she reveled in the agent's gallantry. It was often lonely along the Cutbank. Especially now, with their children gone.

"I will see to my men first, then clean up at the creek so that I don't offend your table," the agent promised, eliciting the flash of a smile from the woman's dusky features.

She turned back into the dugout without further comment, and the agent's expression sobered. "I have heard from your sons," he told the trader.

"They are well?"

The agent nodded. "The youngest sent a letter. I'll fetch it from my kit before we eat."

The trader didn't reply. He was watching a stranger standing to one side of the carts, holding the reins to a leggy sorrel horse, several cuts above the average Indian pony one usually found at fur trade posts; an expensive, double-barreled rifle was cradled against his chest with his free arm. He was young, with a neatly trimmed mustache and sideburns, and wore a new, hooded green capote, although the temperature hardly seemed cool enough to warrant such a heavy article of clothing.

"The factor's nephew," the agent explained, following the direction of the older man's gaze. "He was sent along to learn the ropes."

The trader turned a curious eye on the agent. He didn't ask the question he most wanted to. Instead, he said, "Maybe someday the boy will take over your job, eh? So you can be given your own fort to manage."

After a pause, the agent placed a gentle hand upon the older man's shoulder. "Come along," he said. "We can talk while I wash up at the creek."

It was well after dark, but the trader couldn't sleep. He'd tossed and turned atop his rope-sprung mattress long after the others had retired to their robes. He'd muttered and kicked and ground his teeth, until the woman finally jerked at their blankets in exasperation.

With an uncharacteristic curse, he rolled out of bed, dressed in the cavern-like darkness of their living quarters, then pushed aside the blanket that served as a door between home and store. He paused at the dugout's single window to peer through the thick, wavy glass. The *engagés* were scattered around their carts, oblong forms in the moonlight. A faint red glow marked the location of their evening fire.

The *engagés* had eaten on their own, a stew of tender buffalo from the trader's kettle, with carrots, squash, and onions from the woman's garden, and bread from the last of their flour. Only the agent and the factor's nephew had shared the makeshift table the trader had set up in front of the dugout, eating off the woman's best bone china.

They had talked of many things that

evening. The agent wanted to know about the summer's trade, and why it had been so poor, and his brows had furrowed in concern as the trader explained how only the older men had come in to trade.

"The younger men want guns and whiskey, and go to posts that give them these things."

The agent knew about the whiskey, but the superintendent refused to use it in the Company's bartering. Not because of its impact on the tribes, but because it was illegal, and the superintendent didn't want to risk the Company losing its license to trade with the Indians along the Missouri.

The agent had asked about the empty corral, too, and his scowl deepened when the trader told him about the Santee's raid in the Moon When the Grass Turns Brown. The agent hadn't seemed impressed when the trader related how he thought he'd wounded one of the thieves.

"You should have horses," was the agent's curt response. "Get some when the Cree and Ojibway come in to trade."

Their talk moved away from business after that, the woman hanging on the agent's every word as he told them what he knew of their children, all of them safe and healthy, the last he had heard. He'd shared what news he had from downriver as well, of the growing unrest in Kansas and Nebraska over slavery, of rumors of gold being found in the Beaverhead Valley, and of Fremont's efforts with the newly formed Republican Party.

Neither the agent nor the trader had mentioned the plans for the factor's nephew to the woman. The trader had intended to do that later, when they were alone, but he hadn't been able to find the words when the time came, nor the courage to answer the questions he knew she would ask.

The *engagés* had unloaded their carts before sunset, exchanging crates of trade goods for the meager piles of robes and furs in the storeroom. The trader had seen the disappointment in the agent's eyes as the summer's take was heaped into the carts. There had been no need to stomp the loads down tight; when the *engagés* were finished, the carts were barely a third filled.

Standing alone and discouraged at the dugout's solitary window, the old man rubbed tenderly at his watery eyes. He told himself that he should go back to bed, so that he could be sharp and on guard when the little caravan pulled out the next morning for its return journey to the big fort. But he couldn't face the darkness of the post's living quarters, the guileless presence of the sleeping woman, and after a while he took a new blanket off the shelf behind the counter and made himself as comfortable as his old bones would allow on the trade room floor.

He told her after the caravan had left the next day, the three of them standing in front of the dugout, watching the carts struggle up the far bank before striking out to the south. It was not his decision, he explained in Cree, strangely relieved that the factor's nephew couldn't understand what they were saying.

"He is the factor's nephew," the trader emphasized. "The second-in-command. His sister's son. The factor wants his nephew to learn the ways of a trader's life, here, where the tribes are not as hostile as they are farther west. It was the superintendent, the Company's chief, who insisted that we take the boy in and train him over the winter."

"He is trouble," the woman said simply.

The old man nodded. He had sensed as much himself, but his hands were tied. It was what the superintendent wanted. He didn't mention his fear that he was training his successor, that someday the kid in the green capote would take over Cutbank Post, and that he and the woman would have to find somewhere else to live. He thought he would rather see the post closed permanently than have it taken away like that, turned over to someone else.

That afternoon, the nephew saddled his horse and rode out to the west. The trader was in the storeroom, sorting inventory, while the woman puttered over the evening meal in her kitchen. He had ordered the youth to help him as he broke open crate and box and barrel, but the boy had ignored him.

"We need fresh meat," the nephew had declared, pulling his double rifle from the little stack of personal belongings the *engagés* had piled beside the dugout's entrance.

"We have plenty of meat," the trader countered firmly. "I want your help here, so that you can learn the ropes."

But the nephew had turned his back on the older man. "I will return before dark," he stated confidently, thumping his heels against the sorrel's ribs.

The trader watched him go, eyes glinting with anger. Then, quietly, he returned to his chores. Darkness came without the boy's appearance, but they didn't wait for him. They had their evening meal, and afterward sat outside and smoked their pipes, talking about the children, happy that they were still safe on such an uncertain frontier. They left the nephew's gear, his sacks and satchels and a heavy cowhide trunk, outside, and when the youth returned well after dark, knocking on the door and demanding his supper and a place to sleep, the trader went to the window and told him the evening's meal was finished, and that there was only the one bed in the post's cramped living quarters.

"There is a hut in the trees where our children used to sleep in the summer," he said. "I'll show it to you tomorrow, and let you fix it up for your own quarters."

"Where did your kids sleep in winter?" the nephew demanded.

"They slept on the floor beside our bed, but you'll have to sleep in the hut . . . unless you want to dig your own shelter." He smiled, picturing the boy hacking at the unyielding soil with pick and shovel. "I can show you how to do that tomorrow, too, if you prefer."

"No, don't bother," the nephew replied. "I'm sure a bed will turn up soon." He walked away, laughing derisively.

The trader returned to his bed, but his smile had disappeared.

"What did he want?" the woman asked as

he slid under the blankets at her side.

"He wanted to be fed."

She started to get up, but he pulled her back. "The boy is not ours. He can find his own food, or be here when a meal is served."

He sensed the woman's reluctance to let someone go away hungry, but kept his hand on her shoulder until she finally relaxed. He found an odd measure of accomplishment in that. He was still in charge of this post. The woman knew it, and the nephew would have to learn. Either that or return on his own to the big fort.

They settled into an uneasy truce after that. The factor's nephew moved his gear into the children's hut after rechinking the cracks with a batter of mud and grass from the creek bank, then adding a fresh layer of sod over the roof. The trader and his woman returned to the life they had known before the boy's arrival, preparing for the coming winter while readying themselves for the flurry of late-season trading that always preceded the heaviest snows. Soon, small parties of Cree and Ojibway would descend upon the post, bringing with them the furs and robes they had held back in the spring. Luxuries like sugar and tea and chocolate would fetch a commanding price in robes, and the trader placed those items prominently on his shelves. Blankets for the coldest months, along with powder and shot for the hunters' *fusils,* would also be eagerly sought. The trader would dicker hard for these items, but he would be fair, and next summer, in the Moon When the Ponies Grew Fat, the Indians would return with their winter's catch of prime plews and fresh robes.

For a while, the nephew's presence was like a gentle breeze — there, felt, but seldom acknowledged. After that first day, when the trader had ordered the boy to help in the storeroom and he'd refused, the trader seldom approached the youth. The nephew seemed satisfied with the arrangement. He came and went as he pleased, hunting regularly and bringing back fresh venison or pronghorn that he shared freely, accepting bread and vegetables from the woman in return, coffee and tobacco from the trader. But after a few weeks, the trader began to sense a change in the youth's demeanor, a growing arrogance in his stride. The woman noticed it, too, and commented on it one night in bed.

"He is becoming bold," she said.

"What do you mean?"

"I mean that he is becoming bold," she replied, but would say no more.

After that, the trader began keeping a closer eye on the factor's nephew. Soon, he noticed it, too. The boy was young. No doubt he missed the companionship of others his own age, especially the attention of the opposite sex — a young woman's coquettish look, the sweet fragrance of her perfume. Uneasily, the trader began to look at the woman differently, to see her as others must. He remembered the appreciative glances of the *engagés,* sitting around their fire while she ladled stew into their wooden bowls, and the charming formality of the agent, the way he removed his hat when she came near, or remained standing until she was seated.

He still remembered the day he'd gone to her father's lodge to leave a trio of fine horses hobbled outside, along with several blankets and a new Leman rifle. Not to purchase, as some thought, but to prove to her family that he was a capable provider, and could support a wife and children. He'd been a trader even then, a catch in any Indian woman's eyes; his trading post, with all of its European imports — its kettles and beads and good Sheffield knives — was like a mansion compared to a hide lodge.

He'd been thirty-seven at the time, she twenty years his junior. He tried to recall how many years ago that had been. Twenty-five, at least, and maybe even more than that. She was no longer young, but it occurred to him that she wasn't old, either. And she was still attractive. A shapely figure, long black hair only lightly sprinkled with gray, a willowy grace as she moved about the yard or tended her garden.

The trader's anger began to simmer as he observed the nephew watching her with hunger in his eyes, following her every move from the shelter of the trees surrounding his log hut. He confronted the youth the next day.

"We are getting low on meat. We need to hunt."

The factor's nephew appeared startled by the older man's declaration. "We have plenty of meat," he protested. "You tell me that every time I go out after fresh game."

"Now we need more, to dry, and for pemmican for the winter, when we can't hunt because of the deep snows. Tomorrow we'll go out together. You can follow the Cutbank downstream. I'll go upstream. We'll be gone two days, and use your horse to pack in the meat we harvest."

A smile crept across the boy's face. "All right, you'll go upstream, and I'll go downstream." His grin continued to spread, and the trader turned away before the youth spotted the motive in his eyes.

Tomorrow, he grimly promised himself. *Tomorrow, I'll know for sure.*

That night he cleaned his rifle before the crackling flames in the fireplace. The woman was piecing together a pair of mittens from scraps of leather she kept in a small box beside their bed; the smoked deerskin gleamed richly in the pulsating light.

"I did not know I needed a new pair of mittens," the trader said quietly.

"These are not for you. These are for the boy."

A frown creased his brow.

"He is young and inexperienced, and did not think to bring along a pair from the big fort," she explained.

"Is he paying you for your work?"

She glanced up in vexation. "He is young, and does not always think ahead, but he will learn."

"He is bold. You said so yourself."

"His eyes are bold, but his hands will be useless if they freeze."

"Maybe that would be for the best," he murmured.

She smiled in response. "Not if you had to care for him until the agent's return in the spring."

He let it go after that. He trusted the woman, and knew she would have made mittens for anyone the superintendent sent to them if they didn't have a pair of their own. It was the nephew he didn't trust, but that would soon change. By tomorrow he would know the youth's intentions, and if they were bad, then the boy would learn. It was why the superintendent had sent him to Cutbank Post — to learn.

They left shortly after dawn, the trader walking because the Santees had stolen his horses, the boy riding because the Santees had not yet returned to steal his.

Upstream from Cutbank Post was northwest, toward the divide that separated the Missouri River drainage from that of the Saskatchewan. It was higher ground, although not by much. Yet by following the ridge above the creek, the trader was able to keep an eye on the factor's nephew for a good long ways, the boy's bright green capote standing out sharply against the late autumn tans. The nephew kept his sorrel to a walk, following the meandering course of the creek's left bank until the timber farther down seemed to close in around him like a shroud.

With the youth out of sight, the trader

dropped over the far side of the ridge, into a ravine that would take him back to the post. He hurried now, knees protesting the rough terrain, lungs straining over ground he had once been able to fairly leap across. Despite the cool temperature, he was sweating by the time he reached the rear of the hill where the dugouts were located.

He crossed the brow of the hill in a crouch, then dropped heavily to one knee when he spotted the sorrel tied firmly to the hide press. Up until that moment, he hadn't realized how much he'd privately doubted the boy's intent. It couldn't be denied now, though, and his jaws tightened as he ran a callused thumb over the rifle's lock, checking the cap he'd placed over the nipple the night before. It was still there, and he rolled the hammer back to full cock as he closed the gap to the dugout's entrance.

The trade room was empty, but he could hear them in the post's living quarters, behind the worn blanket door. He eased along the empty space between the front wall and the wide trade counter where he received his customers' furs and robes. His moccasins barely whispered over the hard-packed dirt floor, but there was a deep roaring in his ears, and the blanket's colorful stripes seemed to blur even more than his cataracts could account for. The harsh, eager grunts of the boy and the sharp cries of the woman seemed distant and unfamiliar as he stretched his trembling fingers toward the blanket. Then the youth cried out in pain and panic. There was a loud crash from within, followed by a clatter of tin and iron.

The trader froze, one hand stopped mere inches from the heavy curtain, the other holding his rifle level, its muzzle centered on the door. He jumped back when the blanket was ripped aside. The factor's nephew stood before him, wild-eyed and panting, his left hand pressed tightly against his side. Blood flowed through his fingers, soaking the dark green wool of his capote.

Lunging forward, the boy slammed into the trader's chest, sending the older man down hard, the wind gushing from his lungs, the rifle dancing free of his grasp. He saw the boy stumble outside, but was too weak to go after him. He lay where he'd fallen, one arm and shoulder squeezed against the front of the trade counter, his free hand flat, covering the hollow curve between his stomach and chest. The flesh there burned as if on fire, and he gritted his teeth and closed his eyes shut until the pain gradually subsided.

With effort, the trader rolled onto his hands and knees, then struggled to his feet. His rifle lay on the floor nearby and he scooped it up on his way to the door, checking that the cap hadn't been jolted loose in the fall. Sidling up to the door, he eased an eye past its frame. It was midday and the sky was clear and bright, but the yard was empty. He inched out a little farther, until he could see the trees along the creek, the hut barely visible between the thick trunks.

It was there, also, that he spotted the boy, crouched behind a waist-high fallen log just inside the timber. The log's bark had long since been stripped for kindling, its wood a smooth, pale gray. The boy saw him in the same instant and raised his rifle, but the trader jerked his head back before he could pull the trigger.

Leaning back against the inside wall, the trader sucked in a deep breath to steady his nerves. He could hear the woman in the other room, muttering darkly as she began cleaning up the wreckage. He considered going to her, asking if she was all right, but knew she wouldn't appreciate his concern. She was too angry yet. Besides, he couldn't leave with the boy lurking outside, waiting for him to lower his guard.

He moved to the window, where he could

just make out the deep forest green of the youth's capote, the lad's hunched shoulders where he knelt behind the log. The twin muzzles of the double-barreled rifle stared back dully, like the empty black sockets of a sun-bleached skull.

Returning to the door, the trader cautiously poked his head around the frame, then pulled it back when the boy moved his rifle to cover the entrance. Raising his voice so that it would carry into the trees, he said, "You cannot stay out there forever."

"Nor can you stay in there forever."

The trader smiled at the boy's skewed logic. "We have plenty of food, and the water keg is full. You have nothing but the creek, and you'll have to leave your hiding place to go to it."

"I'm not thirsty," the boy shouted.

You will be, the trader thought fiercely, then moved back to the window to stare at the distorted patch of green, showing among the bare trunks of the cottonwoods. He thought briefly of firing through the window, but decided the target was too small, the odds too great that the thick glass would deflect the muzzle loader's round ball just enough for him to miss. He didn't want to do that, not yet. The trader didn't care about the youth, but he didn't want to break the window's expensive glass.

The hours passed slowly. Although the nights had been cold recently, often with a light frost by morning, the afternoons were still comfortable. Inside the dugout, the air grew warm as the day progressed. Bees buzzed at the door, and a fat black fly explored the shelves against the rear wall. The trader ignored these tiny distractions and kept his attention focused on the patch of trees along the creek. From time to time he would move from the door to the window, then back again, and each time the youth's rifle would shift just enough to cover him.

The boy's vigilance began to annoy the trader. More and more as the afternoon waned, his gaze would shift to the sorrel, hitched snugly to the fur press with a length of sturdy cotton rope. Toward evening, the horse began to nicker longingly, its big, soulful eyes on the Cutbank's purling waters. The animal was thirsty, but the trader couldn't do anything about it. Finally, he shouted, "Take care of your horse, damnit!"

"And get a bullet in my back when I try?"

"I won't shoot."

The boy laughed. "You go take care of it. I promise I won't shoot."

The trader cursed loudly, and the youth laughed harder.

"I can wait here all day if I have to," he told the trader. "All week, if that's what it takes."

Moving swiftly to the door, the trader cocked his rifle, then stepped brazenly into the opening. The boy yelped when he saw him, and ducked out of sight. Then he popped up again, the double rifle shouldered, its single front sight like a stout finger poking at the old man's chest. The trader hesitated only a moment, then jumped back out of sight.

"Hell will freeze over before you win this one," the factor's nephew bellowed.

"Hell and heaven both," the old man vowed.

Darkness came, but the trader remained alertly at his post. He could hear the kid moving around in the trees, the crackle of dried leaves like scratching rust. Yet when dawn arrived, the green patch of the youth's capote was still visible. The trader tipped his head past the door, thinking the boy might be trying to fool him, but the twin muzzles of the kid's rifle followed him out and back, and the trader's lips thinned in frustration.

It went on like that for the rest of the day,

the old man moving from window to door, door to window, the boy staying low behind the fallen log, yet never failing to have his sights on whatever location the trader chose to peer from. From time to time the trader would hear the woman in the other room, the clang of a pan or the scrape of kindling pulled from the wood box, but she never came to check on him, and he was afraid to abandon his position even long enough to look in on her. He could tell she was still angry, though. There was a harshness to the sounds emanating from their living quarters, like she was throwing the wood on the fire, or the spoon in the kettle. He knew she must be growing as weary of this standoff as he was, yet she would also understand that his hands were tied, that it wouldn't end, couldn't end, until the boy surrendered.

The trader thought the scales might tip in his favor when the Indians showed up. There were three of them, Ojibways from the north, although coming from the south, from the buffalo lands along the Missouri River. He recognized Crow's Beak and Standing Bear, both of them old friends, and cried out a greeting. He didn't know the third man, but hoped he soon would. More important was the dust that feathered the horizon, the women and children and old ones. The whole village was coming in to trade, before moving on to their winter camp in the Turtle Mountains.

A smile lit the trader's face at this unexpected aid. He moved quickly to the door, although he didn't dare step through it. When he peered past the frame, he saw the Ojibways halted on the far side of the creek, staring uncertainly at the trading post.

"Be careful, my friends," he called to them. "There is an enemy in the trees."

The kid immediately popped up, but this time his rifle wasn't pointed at the dugout. It was aimed at the Ojibways. "Get back," the factor's nephew ordered sharply.

He spoke in English, and the trader could tell that the Indians didn't understand him, yet the boy's words and his intimidating gestures with the double rifle had an immediate effect. They pulled their horses around and started to ride off, throwing quick, frightened glances over their shoulders every few rods, as if afraid the kid might come after them.

"Don't go," the trader shouted in a panicking tone, but the Ojibways only slapped their heels harder against their mounts' ribs, the ponies' hooves kicking up little clouds of dust that the wind carried away. When they were gone, the old man stood in the doorway, trembling with rage.

Chortling gleefully, the boy said, "No help there, old man."

"They'll be back," the trader replied, but in his heart, he knew they wouldn't. He feared no one would, once word of what the Ojibways had encountered spread to the other villages.

The breeze strengthened as the day wound down, and the temperature began to plummet. The trader could see the sorrel's breath in the star shine, until clouds rolled in from the northwest to obscure the light.

There was snow on the ground by morning, and the sun remained hidden behind an overcast sky. Wind snatched at the falling flakes, swirling them through the air like tiny dancers. Despite the snow and the cold, the boy remained alert and on guard, his gaze seemingly never straying from the dugout's door and window. The trader knew this couldn't go on forever. Sooner or later, one of them would have to make a move. But he also knew that the odds would favor the man with the most patience, and that he would need all the help he could get against the youth's speed and agility, and especially the sharpness of his vision. As he rubbed at his tired eyes, the trader softly cursed the boy's stubbornness.

The snow continued to fall all day, drifting in front of the dugout like mounds of the purest cotton, and in the timber, a tree split from the subzero temperatures with a sound like a gunshot. As time wore on, the trader began to experience a grudging respect for the youth's tenacity, his endurance against such frigid elements, but after a few days the weather changed once more. The sun came out and the snow melted. The trader tipped his face to the sun's warmth, although he was careful not to expose himself to the boy's rifle.

The grass turned unexpectedly green in the snowmelt, and a faint, emerald mist clung to the bare limbs along the creek. The trader was standing at the window, brooding and cranky, when he heard a sound from the prairie. Moving to the door, he felt a mixture of dread and relief at the sight of an ox-yoked caravan approaching the post. The agent rode out front on his white mule, a red-headed clerk astride a scrawny buckskin at his side. From the trees, the factor's nephew hooted cheerfully.

"You're in trouble now, old man," he shouted. "They're going to close this post for good after this, and turn you out to feed the wolves."

There was a crash from the living quarters, followed by the sound of slamming skillets and pieces of flying firewood. The trader's shoulders slumped as he turned away from the door and put his back to the wall. The rifle sagged in his hands. He knew the kid was probably right. The superintendent had sent the boy here for training. Instead, they had become embroiled in a feud that had driven away their customers.

Hearing the devilish screech of ungreased hubs from the yard, he squared his shoulders and returned to the door. But he didn't venture outside. The kid was still standing in the trees, grinning broadly with his rifle clutched in both hands. Eyes narrowing in suspicion, the trader remained where he was. He noticed the agent and the clerk staring at the sorrel's feet.

"It's a damned shame," the clerk was saying. "That was a good horse."

"We'll pull the saddle," the agent said as he dismounted. "We can replace what's rotted and still use it."

The carts were circled in the yard, the *engagés* milling nervously, their eyes shifting from the trader to the nephew. The clerk made his way through the trees to the boy's hut, bending at the waist to peek inside, while the agent came toward the post in measured strides. Observing the granite-like cast of the man's face, the trader moved behind the counter. The agent paused in the door, his gaze resting briefly on the floor in front of the counter, and his expression darkened. "You damn fool," he snarled to the trader, then moved on to the living quarters.

The trader didn't reply to the agent's words, sensing that now wasn't the time. He would speak up later, after the agent's rage had lessened.

Brushing the blanket to the living quarters aside, the agent peered inside for only a moment, then spun on his heels and stalked back outside. The trader moved to the window to watch.

"Found him," the clerk said, coming back to where the buckskin and the white mule were standing ground-tied in front of the trading post, tails switching lazily at summer flies.

"In the hut?"

"No, hiding behind that log over yonder. Still has his rifle, too." He tipped his head toward the dugout.

"Yeah, they're still in there," the agent acknowledged gloomily.

"You know we've got to shut it down, don't you? The tribes will never come back after this."

The agent spat. "Just as well, I suppose. The place has barely broken even the last couple of seasons." There was sadness in his words, though. Cutbank Post had been one of the Company's earliest efforts to stretch its wings beyond the immediate vicinity of the big fort on the Missouri. There was history here that even the thickest-skinned employee had to appreciate.

"The *engagés* won't go into the trade room," the clerk said.

"That's all right," the agent replied. "I'll take care of that. You get them started emptying the storeroom. I want to pull out of here as soon as we're loaded."

The clerk's lips thinned to a hard, razor-sharp line. "You feel it, too, don't you?"

"Let's get to work," the agent said curtly.

He came back into the trade room, and the old man moved out of his way. He started to speak, but when the agent looked at him, the words died in his throat. The agent went into the living quarters first, coming back a little later with an armload of bedding and cooking utensils. He was almost to the door when the woman slammed a pot to the floor with a loud bang. The agent jumped and whirled, his eyes going wide.

"She didn't mean it," the trader said quickly, but the agent wasn't listening. Didn't even seem to hear him. He went outside, and the trader followed as far as the door. He could see the kid down by the fallen log, standing with his rifle butted to the soil between his worn boots. He was watching a pair of *engagés* digging a hole in the dirt. Others were scurrying back and forth between the storeroom and the carts, practically throwing the untraded goods into the vehicles.

The agent returned and began emptying the shelves behind the counter. The trader hung back, feeling utterly worthless. It seemed to take only a few seconds to strip the post clean. When he was done, the agent ordered one of the *engagés* to bring up a team of oxen.

"You're going to leave them there?" the clerk asked, his brows furrowing.

"It's their home," the agent replied. "I doubt if they'd want to leave." He pried the window from its frame and handed it to the clerk. "Glass is too expensive to leave behind," he added, then ran a length of rope through the opening and out the front door.

After securing the rope to the center ring, the *engagé* shouted for the oxen to move out. The large beasts leaned into the yoke, the rope tightening until it seemed to hum. The front wall of the trading post bulged toward the straining cattle, and the trader cried out in alarm. As he darted behind the counter, he caught a glimpse of something familiar lying on the floor, pressed firmly against the footboard as if it had been there a while. But he was moving too fast to get a good look at it, and wasn't sure he wanted one.

There was a dull, rumbling groan just before the ceiling caved in, filling the empty trade room with a suffocating cloud of dust. The trader huddled against the rear wall with his arms over his head, his eyes squeezed shut. He didn't look up again until the dust began to settle. Rising awkwardly, he made his way to the front door. A scowl formed on his face as he watched the little caravan crawl out the far side of the Cutbank, moving south toward the big fort on the Missouri. He wanted to call after the agent, to ask what he was supposed to do, but then he spotted movement in the trees, and jumped back just in time. He went to the window, staring through the thick glass to where the kid stood behind the log, his rifle held firmly in both hands.

Picking up his own gun, the trader returned to the door, peering cautiously around the frame. The kid had ducked back behind the log, but the twin muzzles of his rifle were still visible, and in their living quarters, the angry clatter of the woman's spoon banged against the rim of a kettle. The trader's gaze went to the green prairie, but the caravan was gone, swallowed by the empty distance. Like ghosts.

■ ■ ■ ■

Michael Zimmer is the author of seventeen novels, including *The Poacher's Daughter,* winner of the prestigious Wrangler Award from the National Cowboy and Western Heritage Museum. His novel, *City of Rocks,* was chosen by Booklist as a Top Ten Western for 2012. Zimmer resides in Utah with his wife, Vanessa, and their two dogs. His website is www.michael-zimmer .com.

■ ■ ■ ■

Coffin Nails in Callaway County
by Lonnie Whitaker

■ ■ ■ ■

Justin watched as Wendell Benton peered over his steel-rimmed spectacles at the five cards shrouded by his brawny hands. His hands were not those of a gambler — but his mind was.

It was a mind that had vexed and mentored Justin for more than a decade. First, when he apprenticed and *read the law* in the elder attorney's office, and later as his associate.

Wendell's ample jowls folded upward into a grimace, pushing his eyes to a squint and tilting his cigar sideways. He removed the cigar, tapped the ash on the floor, and cast a penetrating stare across the table. Even at seventy-five, the old man could still tell when Justin was bluffing.

He knew it in 1860 when a skinny, eighteen-year-old Justin Davis marched into his law office holding a "Scrivener Wanted" sign and proclaimed he had completed the eighth grade. He knew it in their countless two-man poker games when Justin was an apprentice in his office on Court Street in Fulton, Missouri. And he knew it at this moment, nine years later.

"Counselor, I'll see your bet and raise you a dollar. I don't think you made that straight." The game was draw poker and Justin had only drawn one card.

"Well, Wendell, that's too rich for my blood. I guess you get the pot."

"All right, Counselor, are you ready to tell me why you really stopped by my house? I know it wasn't just to play cards with an out-to-pasture old lawyer."

Before looking up, Justin gathered the cards together and shuffled them like a postmaster sorting envelopes.

"Judge Thompson called me into his chambers yesterday and said he was appointing me to represent Lemuel Griggs for the murder of Cyrus Mosby."

"What did you tell him?"

"I told him I didn't handle criminal matters."

"How far did that excuse get you?"

"He told me it was a privilege to practice in this circuit and if I wanted to give up my Admission Order to the bar, he'd let me off the hook. If I refused, he would disbar me."

"Well, Counselor, it looks as if you will have to bone up on the criminal statutes and cases."

"But does he have that authority? The Sixth Amendment only provides right to counsel. It doesn't guarantee it."

"It isn't a battle you want to fight. Judges are the nearest thing we have to royalty in this country. For a change, however, I am in accord with His Honor. If a defendant is charged with murder, he ought not be denied counsel because he is indigent."

"That's only part of the problem."

"Now, we finally get to what's really stuck in your craw. Spit it out."

"I think Lem Griggs is guilty as sin and ought to be marched up thirteen steps to a noose."

"Counselor, sometimes you try my legal patience. Lem Griggs may be worthless as tits on a tomcat, but whether you like it or not, he is as innocent as you or the judge. The Constitution guarantees that presumption."

"But, Wendell, Mosby's wife, Sarah, saw Griggs standing over her husband's dead body holding Mosby's pocket watch. And most of his ear had been bitten off."

Wendell chopped down on his cigar and talked through his clenched teeth. "I don't care if he was standing over him with a bloody axe, he is entitled to a fair trial." He spit the cigar out on the floor and continued, "And it's your job to represent him zealously within the bounds of the law. Didn't you learn anything from me, *scrivener?*"

The demotion stung Justin. He hadn't been called that since he was admitted to the bar. He felt puny and ashamed, like always, when the old man chastened him. But the sad matter of fact was that the thought of going to trial on anything — let alone a murder trial — made him sick to his stomach. He made his modest living preparing deeds and wills and reviewing titles.

Wendell wasn't finished, but in a softer tone said, "Don't let old Phinny Thompson intimidate you. He didn't have a pot to piss in until he got elected judge. Hell, none of the successful lawyers wanted the job."

"You know I'm not a courtroom performer, and frankly, he always makes me nervous. He's got a colonial pillory standing next to the witness chair just to intimidate folks."

"Thunderation!" Wendell pounded his fist on the table. "You're never going to be worth a damn as a trial lawyer until you develop a poker face and a healthy disrespect for judges."

After Wendell's tirade neither man spoke for a moment, but Wendell's eyes stayed on Justin.

When some of the tension eased, Justin said, "And to complicate matters, at his arraignment, Griggs claimed he had seen ghosts the night of the murder. So Judge Thompson ordered Defendant Griggs committed to the lunatic asylum pending trial."

"Horsefeathers! If the defendant knows right from wrong, he's not insane. That's been the law since the McNaughton case. Don't bank on insanity giving you a free way out."

"There's one more thing."

Wendell arched his eyebrows and exhaled an exasperated sigh. "Finally, we get to the truth."

"Wendell, I hate to ask, and I know you —"

"Ah, quit stumbling all over yourself."

"Will you be my second chair?"

"You mean, will I sit with you in trial and hold your hand?" Wendell sighed again. This time more gently. "Son, I'm going to do you a favor and say *no.* Half the people on a jury wouldn't like me, and the other half that might favor you will think you are riding my coattails. The sad truth about juries, in an even-money case, is they side with the lawyer they like better."

"You think this is an even-money case?"

"Hell, no. It is an uphill battle all the way. Mosby was a popular man, and Griggs is a ne'er-do-well. The prosecutor and the jury will want revenge. You've got a serious fight on your hands, and you don't need an anchor like me."

"I suppose you're right."

"Of course I am. But if you need some backdoor help, you know where to find me."

He had gone to Wendell looking for sympathy and should have known better. He might as well have shared his dilemma with his hound, Rufus. Justin was a bachelor, so Rufus was his only other confidant. Both Justin's parents were dead and the woman he loved had married another man — Cyrus Mosby, the victim in the murder trial he was being forced to defend.

Word traveled fast in a small town. On the way to the asylum, a man whom Justin had never met told him he should be ashamed for representing a guilty murderer. From the looks of other townspeople, he was beginning to feel shunned and avoided.

The Missouri Asylum for the Insane stood

as an imposing three-story structure. An attendant met Justin at the entrance and ushered him to the room where Lemuel Griggs was held. The accommodations were spartan with few amenities: a cot, washstand, and a single chair. But it was clean and smelled of lye soap. The only source of light was a single barred window.

Griggs sat on the cot and looked up as Justin entered. At six feet tall, Justin towered over the smallish man, who was maybe forty years old, with a thick head of recently shorn brown hair. Griggs needed a shave, but a razor around a lunatic could be dangerous. Otherwise, he looked clean as a scrubbed child.

"Mr. Griggs, I'm attorney Justin Davis, and I have been assigned by the court to represent you in your murder trial."

"Yes, sir. I know who you are." Griggs was calm and did not look deranged.

"But do you know why you are here?"

"When I said I'd seen ghosts, the judge sent me here and not back to the jailhouse."

"Where, exactly, did you see these ghosts?"

"They was riding off on horses when I came on Cyrus Mosby."

"Had you been drinking that night?"

"No, sir."

"What were you doing on Richland Creek that night?"

"I was going fishing and frog'n."

"What time?"

"It was about dusk. That's the best time for fishing. And it was nearly a half-full moon, so it was a good night for frogs."

"Did Mosby give you permission to be on his property?"

"Not exactly, but a creek don't belong to anybody."

"What do you mean by *not exactly*?"

"He'd seen me fishing there before and never said anything, so I figured it was all right."

"Did you kill Cyrus Mosby?" Justin regretted the question as soon as it was out of his mouth. Many lawyers said intentional ignorance of guilt was the best way to defend the guilty.

Griggs shook his head and looked Justin straight in the eye. "I did not kill him. He was dead when I came on him."

"Tell me what you saw."

"He was lying in the weeds next to a trail that runs about a half-mile from his house to the creek. He'd been stabbed in the chest and his ear was bit off."

"Anything else?"

"Weeds were mashed down all around

him like he had been wrestling with whoever killed him. And I picked up his watch."

"You were robbing a dead man?" Justin shook his head in disgust.

"No, I saw something shiny in the weeds and picked it up. And I opened it to see what time it was. It was a quarter to six."

"You made a difficult job tougher. You've given the prosecutor and jury a motive. Then what did you do?"

"I heard a scream and looked up. It was Mrs. Mosby. I dropped the watch and ran."

"Is that all? You've not given me much to go on."

"I saw a man in the brush where the horses were."

This opened a new line of inquiry, which Justin pursued for another hour. Finally, he said, "I think I've heard enough for now, but I will be back in a day or so."

After leaving the asylum, he mounted his horse and headed to his small farm two miles west of town. He had a lot of thinking to do, and no place better to do it than in a saddle.

Things didn't add up. Ghosts on horses. A mystery man. And what was Sarah doing out there? Had she heard something? Why had she gone to look for her husband? Was Griggs just making up a tale to avoid the gallows? One thing he knew for sure — Griggs would not be taking the stand to talk about ghosts.

Mosby's funeral, two days after his death, looked to be the biggest gathering of folks since the Fourth of July. A special edition of the *Callaway Observer* covering the murder included the time for visitation and services at the Mosby farm.

Out of a sense of duty, Justin put on his only suit of clothes and saddled his horse to go pay his respects to Cyrus Mosby's widow, Sarah.

The sun was mid-sky and August hot. Justin's black felt hat shaded his eyes but collected heat like an oven. After fifteen minutes he was sweating, and the wool suit was itching like the devil. He removed his coat and hung it from the saddle horn. Maybe the air would dry the sweat from his shirt.

Heat waves in the distance blurred the dusty road, and his mind wandered. Three years before, on this same road, he had courted Sarah. Back then, she was Sarah Smith, a seventeen-year-old girl he had hoped to marry one day.

But when Cyrus Mosby came home from college to inherit a prosperous, one-hundred-acre farm on Richland Creek, Sarah's interest in Justin waned. A lanky lawyer's apprentice, with an uncertain future, couldn't compete with landed gentry. And he didn't try. When she told him of her choice, he walked away slump-shouldered and buried himself in *Blackstone's Commentaries on the Law.*

A quarter mile from the two-story white house, Justin saw a dozen horses and several wagons hitched under two post oak shade trees. Other mourners had already arrived. The burial wasn't for another hour, but funerals, like revivals, were a cause for social gathering.

Reverend Floyd Simpson, pastor of the Faith Church, greeted Justin at the front door with a tight-lipped smile. In another hour, the pulpit-thumper would stand at the family gravesite in his black suit and string tie, intoning over the dearly departed Mosby.

"Attorney Davis, we're so glad you could come and support Mrs. Mosby in her time of grief."

Justin removed his hat, shook the reverend's extended hand, and stepped into the center hallway.

The reverend gestured to an adjacent

room. "Mr. Mosby is lying in repose in the parlor."

Sarah wore a black mourning dress and stood with one hand on the walnut-stained coffin and greeted consoling neighbors. She looked tired, but in Justin's eyes, she was still the pretty girl he had adored.

The casket sat on two sawhorses draped with muslin. Condensation was forming on the pine box from the ice blocks that had been placed inside to slow the decomposition. The coffin lid, which would be nailed on before burial, sat upright in a corner.

Mosby was in full display in a Sunday-go-to-meeting suit. Justin noticed the new undertaker in town had fashioned a wax molding to replace the lower portion of Mosby's right ear. The prosecutor was keeping the original in a jar of alcohol as evidence.

As Justin approached, Sarah stepped forward and extended both hands, which he took in his.

"Justin, I didn't know if you would come, but I'm glad you did." She gave him a wan smile. "Will you be a pallbearer?"

Justin, suddenly as awkward as a schoolboy, looked at his boots and then around the room before answering. "Well, I don't know . . . given all the circumstances."

"What do you mean?"

"Well, it might look odd, me being a pallbearer, since I am defending Lem Griggs in the murder trial."

"You're what?" Her voice was incredulous. "How can you do that?"

"Judge Thompson ordered me. I didn't have any choice."

"Choice? I obviously made the right *choice* when I chose Cyrus over you."

Reverend Simpson hustled to her side. "Are you all right, my dear?"

Nodding toward Justin, she said in a trembling voice, "He's defending that murderer Griggs."

Simpson put both arms around her in a comforting embrace and gave Justin a forced smile. "I think you should leave. You are upsetting Mrs. Mosby."

Without speaking Justin turned and went outside. He lingered on the porch, wrestling with the thought of going back and making amends. Something about the reverend's smile had seemed odd. He heard the coffin lid being nailed down and decided it was best to leave.

As he rode home, the sound of the nails echoed in his head like the tolling of a church bell. It was over. Sarah's words were just the last nail.

He had wanted to be admired and loved by her, but all he felt was rejection and blame. And with a defenseless case, the future looked to hold more failure and humiliation. Once again, he would have to console himself with *Blackstone.*

Judge Thompson set the trial for late September when the weather would be cooler. He said it was too hot to confine a jury and too hard to empanel one until after the crops were harvested. Still, a month wasn't a lot of time for Justin to prepare for his first murder trial.

Three days after Mosby's funeral, Justin visited the prosecuting attorney, John McIntire, at his office. The prosecutor, a feisty, banty rooster of a man, was quick to show his attitude.

"Why don't you just let Griggs plead guilty and get this over?"

"If he pleads guilty, he'll hang."

"If you don't waste my time, I might be willing to recommend a lesser offense to the court."

"I didn't come to bargain." Justin jerked his thumb at the glass jar on McIntire's desk. "I came to examine the ear."

"It's a gruesome thing, but a relevant piece of evidence." McIntire peered at the ceiling as if pondering something odd. A crooked smile came to his face. "Funny thing. The widow wants it buried with Mosby after the trial." Refocused, he handed over the jar.

Justin held the pint jar up to the sunlight coming through the window. The lower third of the ear had been severed, not cleanly, but as if gnawed off. He used his thumb as a measuring tool to gauge its size.

"So, you figure to use this in the prosecution."

"I do. It shows the savageness of the attack and the intent to do grave bodily harm."

"Of *someone,* perhaps, but my client is not a vicious sort."

"The evidence dictates otherwise." McIntire stood up from his desk. "Unless you have something else, I have other business that needs my attention."

Justin returned to the asylum to see his client. Griggs still appeared to be sane and rather enjoying the clean sheets and regular meals afforded by the state of Missouri.

However, Justin was shocked to learn that Reverend Simpson had visited Griggs the day after Mosby's funeral. He tried not to show his aggravation, but God only knew what Griggs might have said that could be used against him. After all, it wasn't the case of a priest and a penitent — whatever Griggs said would be admissible in evidence.

"Just what did the preacher say to you?"

"I'm not supposed to say." Griggs fidgeted with a button on his hospital-issued shirt as he spoke.

"What? Unless you want to have your neck stretched and die a horrible death, you better damned well tell me." There was no mistaking the anger in Justin's voice. First, an arrogant prosecutor, and now a preacher tampering with his client.

Griggs's lower lip trembled. "He said anybody who claimed he'd seen ghosts would go to hell. That I'd better repent and pay my debt. Said it would be better to hang than go to hell."

"That psalm-singing bastard! Was Simpson the man you saw in the shadows the night Mosby was killed?"

"I couldn't say for sure. It might have been him."

"Well, you better think long and hard about it."

Justin stepped to the door. "I'm leaving now, but don't talk to anyone about your case. I'll tell the asylum warden not to allow visitors without my presence. I'll get a court order if necessary."

Justin wasted no time getting to Wendell's house. He needed some of the backdoor assistance that had been promised.

Wendell puffed on a briar pipe as Justin briefed him on the developments since their last meeting. Pungent smoke wreathed around his face and filled the room with the odor of leaves burning in the fall. He removed the pipe and directed it at Justin.

"Counselor, you've got a can of worms. You need to find out who that stranger was. But you can't put Griggs on the stand. The prosecuting attorney would crucify him and convince the jury he made up the mystery man and the ghosts to save his own neck."

"I know, but without evidence of a third party, there's no basis to attack the prosecutor's burden to show guilt beyond a reasonable doubt."

The fire was extinguished in Wendell's pipe, but not the one in his mind. "It's ironic, but it's the ghosts that make me believe Griggs. I don't think that he conjured that up — he's not that clever."

"By your logic, if he didn't make up the ghosts, he didn't make up the mystery man, either. But you don't think he actually saw ghosts, do you?"

"Absolutely not. He's not Ichabod Crane. Ghosts don't ride horses . . . but men in white sheets do."

Justin's eyes narrowed. "The Ku Klux Klan? But why would they be at Mosby's?"

"Maybe because Mosby was Catholic."

"I thought the Klan only tormented black folks."

"They don't much cotton to Catholics either, and if that preacher is involved, I can see it. I once heard a sermon of his, and he ranted about the Catholic abomination of *sprinkling* instead of regular baptizing."

Justin stroked his chin with his hand, thinking, and then blurted. "Mosby was Catholic, but Sarah Smith wasn't, and they were married in a protestant church — Simpson's church."

"Now you're using your head. However, we may have solved part of the mystery, but you can't mention the Klan either. You don't know who on the jury — or if the judge — might be a member. The Kingdom of Callaway is full of southern sympathizers."

Frustration showed on Justin's face, and an ugly picture was forming in his mind. One that he would not have believed only an hour before.

"Wendell, are you thinking what I'm thinking — that Sarah and the preacher have their hands in this?"

"Looks that way to this old man."

"Why didn't I see this before?"

"Love is blind, Counselor. Put that behind you. Now, your duty is to your client. You're the only thing that stands between him and a rope."

"I'm open for suggestions."

"Your only chance is to show that Griggs didn't bite off the ear. If Griggs didn't bite off the ear, then the only reasonable inference the jury can draw is he didn't kill Mosby."

"I agree. That would insert reasonable doubt and offset the testimony of the sheriff and Sarah Griggs."

"Counselor, I don't think the prosecutor will need the sheriff's testimony — it wouldn't add anything. He's got the widow and the ear."

"But how do I prove somebody else bit off the ear?"

"First things first. Did you check Griggs's teeth?"

"Yeah, I looked, but not like I was trying to buy a horse. He has some teeth missing, and the rest don't look too good."

"You need an expert witness who could offer opinion testimony that someone other than Griggs chewed the ear."

"Who could I use? The only dentist in town is a drunk."

"I've heard about this dentist in Columbia who actually went to dental school back east. The rumor is he got drafted by the Confederacy and deserted after one of the battles in Lexington."

"What's his name?"

"Jake Grogan."

"How did you hear about him?"

"Rollins, that lawyer in Columbia, used him in a case. I figure if Rollins used him, he's got to be good."

The next day Justin rode all day to Columbia and met Dr. Grogan. He agreed to testify for $30 and expenses, which would pinch Justin's meager savings. Griggs had promised to sell his mule to pay the attorney's fee and expenses, but if Griggs was hanged, the undertaker and the state of Missouri would get first crack at the few assets of his estate.

On Monday, September 20, 1869, the Callaway County Courthouse was overflowing. Dozens of people milled around the steps and in the street. The local newspaper and those in Jefferson City and Columbia had written about the trial for weeks. The editorial pages were of a like mind: Guilty. One even predicted the defendant would be lucky to live through the defense counsel's closing speech before justice prevailed.

With all the pretrial publicity, Justin had moved the court for a change of venue, which the judge denied. But he ordered Griggs back to the jail as a safety precaution, recalling that in 1853 an angry mob in neighboring Boone County had dragged a defendant from the courthouse and lynched him.

Wearing a black robe, the judge entered the courtroom.

"All rise," the bailiff ordered. "The Circuit Court for Callaway County is now in session, Judge Phineas Thompson presiding."

The judge pounded his gavel for order. After successive raps and threatened jail time for disruptions, the courtroom became churchlike. After preliminary charges to the jury and the attorneys' *voir dire* questions, he called for the prosecutor's opening speech.

McIntire faced the jury and began slowly, thanking the jury members for doing their civic duty, but soon he began pumping his fist and spewing fiery rhetoric. His voice blared a staccato cadence equal to any backwoods Pentecostal preacher. The folks wanted a show, and he was there to give them one.

He pointed at Griggs sitting next to Justin at the defense table. "Lemuel Griggs, the defendant, who sits here dripping with culpability, has the blood of your esteemed and beloved neighbor on his hands."

Justin leaned over to Griggs and whispered, "Take it easy and don't react."

The prosecutor continued. "The evidence will prove beyond any reasonable doubt that said defendant murdered Cyrus Mosby in cold blood, with malice aforethought and premeditation. And while perpetrating this heinous crime, the defendant bit off part of Mr. Mosby's right ear."

He pivoted to the prosecution's table and picked up the glass jar containing the portion of Mosby's ear. "I direct your attention to the only earthly remains of your neighbor, which has been marked as State Exhibit No. 1."

Without taking his eyes off the jury, McIntire placed the jar back on the table and paused for dramatic effect. He drew a deep breath and exhaled with an audible sigh, deftly removed a handkerchief from his vest pocket, and dabbed his tearing eyes.

He pointed at Sarah Mosby sitting in the first row of the spectator gallery and said, "With his evil deed, Griggs made Mr. Mosby's wife a widow . . . before there was an heir to carry on his name."

"Hang him!" a juror yelled.

"Objection!" Justin was on his feet. "I demand that juror be removed."

"Sustained. Bailiff, take that juror to the jail. I'll assess a fine for contempt later. The first alternate juror will take his place. Court is in recess for thirty minutes."

After the recess, Judge Thompson called for defense counsel's opening statement.

Justin strolled in front of the jury and smiled, attempting to display confidence he did not feel.

"Gentlemen of the jury, during the *voir dire* examination you pledged to decide this case based only on the evidence adduced and not any preconceived notions. Nothing that the learned prosecutor said is *evidence.* I submit that he will not be able to prove his allegations beyond a reasonable doubt as required by the Constitution and that you will be obliged to find Mr. Griggs not guilty."

Justin pointed toward Griggs. "Unless and until such evidence is produced, under the eyes of the law, Mr. Griggs is as innocent as any of you on the jury." He waited a moment for the jury to consider his statement before continuing.

"We will present the expert testimony of Dr. Jake Grogan that will prove that Mr. Griggs did not bite off part of the decedent's ear. With such proof, the only logical inference you can draw is that someone other than Mr. Griggs killed Mr. Mosby."

Justin thanked the jury and sat down.

"Call your first witness, Mr. McIntire."

Justin rose to his feet. "May it please the court, Your Honor. I invoke the witness rule and move that Reverend Floyd Simpson be removed from the gallery pending his testimony."

McIntire jumped to his feet, his face contorted in suspicion. "What's the meaning of this?"

Justin was ready. "Your Honor, our esteemed prosecutor is well aware that the defense has subpoenaed Reverend Simpson and that the long tradition of the common law supports segregation of witnesses prior to their testimony to ensure it won't be affected by hearing other witnesses."

"But, Your Honor," McIntire said, in his most mellifluous voice, "I see no reason this should apply to a *man of the cloth* who will swear on the Holy Bible to tell the truth."

The judge leaned forward with a grin on his face and said, "Now, Counselor Davis, I don't think there's any need to be so technical in this instance." His tone was that of a schoolmaster correcting a precocious child.

Justin did not want Reverend Simpson sitting in the courtroom watching other witnesses and tailoring his testimony. The judge was dodging the motion and in the back of Justin's mind he could hear Wendell's voice. *Healthy disrespect for judges.*

"Your Honor, I would like a ruling on my motion."

The judge's grin was replaced with a look of imperial indignation. "Very well. Motion denied."

"That's outrageous, Judge."

"Counselor, your outrage is falling on the deaf ears of the court."

"Judge, I know justice is blind. I didn't know it was deaf, too."

"Another remark like that and I will fine you for contempt."

"How much is the fine?"

"Five dollars for each occurrence."

Justin reached in his pants pocket and pulled out two gold half eagles and slapped them on the table. "Then you better give me two in advance."

The jury was a chorus of laughter. The judge pounded his gavel.

"Order in the court! Both counsel in my chambers! Court is in recess for thirty minutes. Jurors, do not leave the courthouse."

In chambers, after a fierce rebuking and obsequious apologies, the judge retreated from his threat to incarcerate Justin.

To Justin's surprise, the judge said, "I admire your zeal, Counselor, but I will not tolerate impugning the integrity of this court. When we are back in session, you will publicly apologize to me, the prosecutor, and the jury. But I will, without a formal ruling, direct the bailiff to segregate the preacher — I don't much trust preachers myself."

"But Your Honor —" McIntire started to complain.

"Mr. Prosecutor, unless you want me to find you in contempt, I suggest you keep quiet."

Back in the courtroom, after Justin's apologies, the prosecutor stood up and addressed the court. "The state of Missouri calls Sarah Mosby to the stand."

He strutted to the banister that separated the court from the spectators, opened the gate, and escorted Sarah to the witness chair, where the bailiff swore her in.

The prosecutor returned to the counsel table and began his direct examination. After covering the preliminary details of her relationship to the deceased, length of marriage, and various embellishments about the impact of her loss, he moved to the heart of his case.

"Directing your attention to Friday, August 13, 1869," he said, "how did you come to be at the scene of your husband's murder?"

"Objection. The prosecution assumes a fact not in evidence and draws a conclusion that Mr. Mosby was *murdered.*"

"Sustained."

Justin knew it was a technical objection, but it was important to plant the seeds of doubt as early as possible and come across as a force to be reckoned with.

McIntire scowled at Justin, obviously annoyed, but said, "I'll rephrase, Your Honor." Refocusing on the witness, he continued. "Mrs. Mosby, how did you come to be at the scene of your husband's death?"

"Cyrus had told me he was going to the creek to search for a knife he had misplaced. When he didn't come back in thirty minutes, I went to look for him."

"What did you discover in your search for your husband?"

"I found him lying on the ground with a knife stuck in his chest." She began sobbing and covered her face with both hands.

"Take a moment to settle yourself, Mrs. Mosby," the judge said.

After a brief moment, she regained her composure and nodded at the prosecutor.

"What else did you see?"

"I saw Lemuel Griggs standing next to him holding my husband's watch."

"And is that man in the courtroom today?"

"Yes, he is. Sitting over there." She pointed at Griggs.

"What happened next?"

"I screamed and Griggs took off running." She sniffled, but kept talking. "And part of my husband's ear was lying on the ground. It looked like it had been chewed off." Her sobbing resumed.

"I have no more questions. Your witness, Mr. Davis."

By the time Justin had finished writing a note on his tablet and stood up to begin his cross-examination, Mrs. Mosby had calmed down. Indeed, she had more than *calmed down.* Her face had become rigid and challenging, a lioness daring him to come into her lair.

He had to be careful or he might inflame the jury for insulting a widow. He would be brief, gentle, and try to escape without being clawed.

"Mrs. Mosby, you didn't see Mr. Griggs stab your husband, did you."

"No, I didn't . . . but who else could have? He wouldn't have stabbed himself." A few snickers gushed from the jury box.

Although Wendell wasn't in the second chair, his voice resounded in Justin's mind. *Poker face, Justin.*

"Isn't it also true, Mrs. Mosby, that you did not see Mr. Griggs *chew off* your husband's ear."

She gave him a defiant glare but did not respond. Justin met her stare and waited for her to answer.

"I did not see him chew off my husband's ear . . . I saw him spit it out!"

The jury erupted in an outburst of groans and laughter, requiring the judge to call for order.

Gut-punched. Justin felt the blood draining from his face. He had not seen it coming.

"I have no more questions of this witness, Your Honor." He scuffed back to his chair with his head down.

"Redirect, Mr. Prosecutor?"

"None, Your Honor."

"Court will be in recess for two hours."

Justin remained seated, looking down at his notes, as Sarah stepped down from the witness chair. He glanced up as she passed his table and cringed at her gloating look.

He gathered his papers and checked to see if the gallery had cleared and saw Wendell seated on the back row. He dreaded the critique, but lumbered over to him.

"How long have you been here?" Justin asked.

"Since the beginning. I didn't want you or the jury to notice me. I think you are still in the race."

"Didn't you hear that last answer?"

"I did. You stepped into the trap they set. It was an obvious question, but one the prosecutor anticipated and prepared for. You gave in too easily."

"But the widow directly tied Griggs to the severed ear. What could I have done at that point?"

"Her testimony was inconsistent. You could have challenged her veracity, but Dr. Grogan's testimony will do that. Once a jury gets a whiff that a witness lied, it will even turn against a widow. Make her into a *black* widow — one that kills its mate."

"You're right, as usual, Wendell."

"One more thing. When you've been dealt a losing hand, you need an ace up your sleeve. Go to your office and prepare Dr.

Grogan. I'll meet you there. I need to stop by my place."

Justin returned to the courthouse with Dr. Grogan. The doctor sat on the first row behind the attorneys' rail, and Justin proceeded to the defense table carrying a leather satchel. As he sat down, the bailiff ushered in Defendant Griggs. Moments later the jury members were seated.

"All rise."

Judge Thompson entered the courtroom and advised everyone to be seated. "Does the prosecution have any more witnesses?"

"The state of Missouri rests."

"Mr. Davis, call your first witness."

"The defense calls Dr. Jake Grogan to the stand."

The Columbia dentist, tall, erect, and handsome in a gray frock coat, strode to the witness chair. His full head of black hair curled softly at the top of his shirt collar.

Justin began with questions designed to establish Dr. Grogan's qualifications as an expert: graduation from the country's first dental school in Maryland, service as a surgeon in the War Between the States, and years as a practicing dentist.

"Now, Dr. Grogan, have you examined the portion of Mr. Mosby's ear in the glass jar, which has been admitted into evidence as State Exhibit No. 1?"

"Yes, I have." Dr. Grogan, with his dark Irish eyes, faced the jury as he spoke, following Justin and Wendell's earlier coaching.

Justin turned toward the judge. "Your Honor, may I approach the witness."

"Proceed."

"Dr. Grogan, I am handing you what has been marked as Defense Exhibit No. 1." Justin handed him a three-inch square slab of paraffin wax, about the thickness of a man's thumb. "Can you identify it?"

"Yes, this is a wax model, an imprint of Mr. Griggs's upper incisors."

"In shirtsleeve English, if you please, Doctor."

Dr. Grogan showed an easy smile. "Surely. His upper front teeth."

"What is the purpose of incisors?"

The prosecutor, with exaggerated labor, rose to his feet. "Your Honor, I question the relevance of this desultory exposition about teeth."

Justin was quick to respond. "Your Honor, the prosecution has gone to great length to make an allegedly chewed-off ear relevant, and the defense should be afforded great latitude in responding. I submit the objection was dilatory and designed to interrupt the flow of the witness examination."

"Mr. Davis, your response is well taken. Objection is overruled. Proceed."

"Doctor, if you recall, please respond to my last question."

"Yes. The upper incisors are primarily used to cut, slice, or tear."

"What, if anything, abnormal does the wax impression of Mr. Griggs's front teeth reveal?"

"He is missing both canine incisors — his eyeteeth. They are the longest and most pointed of the upper front teeth. I'll show you." He opened his mouth and pointed to his own, and turned for the jury to see.

"What effect would missing canine teeth have on the ability to chew off a human ear?"

"Objection. There is no basis —"

"Overruled. Doctor, you may answer the question."

"A missing canine incisor would impair the ability to cut and slice into tough material such as the cartilage, gristle that is, of an ear. Moreover, Mother Nature favors canine teeth where difficult chewing is involved. For example, a dog chewing a bone turns its head sideways to take advantage of its canine incisors."

81

"Doctor, directing your attention to State Exhibit No. 1 — Mr. Mosby's ear — were you able to form an opinion on the cause of the severance?"

"The severed edge appears to have been bitten and chewed."

"Now, Doctor, have you, within a reasonable degree of medical certainty, formed an opinion as to whether Defendant Griggs was the cause of the dismemberment?"

"Yes, I have."

"What is that opinion?"

"Objection."

"Overruled. Proceed with your answer, Doctor."

"In my opinion Lemuel Griggs did not bite off the decedent's ear. His missing teeth argue against that. Furthermore, the residual bite marks are consistent with chewing from uniformly spaced teeth."

"Your witness, Mr. McIntire."

The prosecutor stood up. "No questions, Your Honor."

The judge glanced at the pocket watch that he kept on his dais. "Mr. Davis, how many more witnesses do you have?"

"Just one, Your Honor."

"Call him. I'd like to finish this today. And I'm not interested in any long-winded closing speeches from either counsel."

"The defense calls Reverend Floyd Simpson."

The bailiff retrieved Simpson from the anteroom. He took the stand and was sworn in.

"Reverend Simpson, isn't it true you wear false teeth?"

"I most certainly do not," Simpson said with an indignant tone. "I'll prove it to you."

He spread his mouth open, showing both rows of front teeth and then chomped them up and down to prove his point.

"Are you satisfied, Counselor?"

"I apologize, Reverend. I was mistaken. You have a truly fine-looking set of teeth."

The reverend beamed at the compliment. "Yes, I have been blessed with strong teeth. I can crack a walnut with them."

Justin casually scanned the jury looking for any reaction and trying to communicate an unspoken message.

"You're the preacher at the Faith Church, aren't you?"

"Yes, I'm the *pastor* there."

"Is that a Catholic church?"

"It absolutely is not. The theology of Faith Church can be traced back to the Reformation."

"I gather you have theological differences with Catholics. Is that a fair statement?"

"That is correct."

"Then would it also be fair to say you wouldn't conduct a Catholic wedding?"

"That is true."

"Objection. I fail to see the relevance of this line of questioning."

Judge Thompson frowned in apparent agreement. "Mr. Davis, I will give you some latitude, but you are beginning to test my limits."

"Yes, Your Honor."

"Reverend Simpson, you said you would not conduct a Catholic wedding, yet you presided at the wedding of Cyrus Mosby, who was a baptized Catholic, and his betrothed, Sarah Smith. Isn't that true?"

"I didn't find out until afterwards."

"In your view, after you found out, the marriage must have seemed illegitimate. Is that true?"

"It was legitimate in the eyes of the law."

"But was it compatible with your faith to conduct a Catholic's funeral?"

"I did that for Sarah, I mean, Mrs. Mosby."

"Reverend Simpson, are you a married man?"

"No, I am not so blessed."

"Do you have any children?"

"Objection! Your Honor, the defense is

conducting a wild goose chase and slandering a good Christian man."

"Sustained. The jury will disregard the last question. Counselor, I will not warn you again."

"Yes, Your Honor."

"Reverend Simpson, where were you at the time of Mr. Mosby's death?"

"Why, I believe I was at home reading the Bible."

"Was anyone with you?"

"No."

"So there was no one to witness that you were at your home at the time of Mr. Mosby's death."

"No."

"But there were witnesses to your presence at the scene of Mr. Mosby's murder. Isn't that true."

"That's not true!"

Justin opened the leather satchel and pulled out a white sheet and hood and displayed each in his outstretched hands.

Simpson looked stunned. Jurors, to the man, seemed confused.

"Objection! This is some kind of stunt, Your Honor."

Justin didn't flinch or wait for a ruling. Still holding the sheets, his eyes were riveted on Simpson.

"Preacher, my next witness will put you at the scene of Cyrus Mosby's murder. Is your answer still that you were at —"

"I was there, but I did not kill Cyrus Mosby — it was Sam Jones."

"He's a liar! Mrs. Mosby was his lover," a bearded man yelled from the jury box.

A collective gasp arose in the courtroom.

Griggs jumped to his feet and shook his fist at Simpson. "You're a son of a bitch!"

"Order in the courtroom." The judge kept pounding his gavel.

In the din of the commotion, Justin felt detached from the courtroom, as if he were out of his body looking down at the proceeding. The gavel pounding was an echo of the coffin nails hammered at Mosby's funeral, which seemed distant in the past.

Suddenly, he was aware of the silence, and that all eyes in the courtroom seemed to be staring at him. He laid the sheets on the table and faced the judge.

"Your Honor, I move for an Order of Acquittal for the defendant."

The judge leaned forward over the dais. His face was stern. "Certainly, a mistrial is in order, but given the evidence that has come to light, I am inclined to grant your motion, Counselor."

The judge rapped his gavel and turned

toward the bailiff. "Take Mr. Simpson into custody." Shifting his focus to the prosecutor, he said, "Mr. McIntire, I believe you have sufficient grounds, at a minimum, to charge this man as an accessory to murder, until we get to the bottom of this matter. I would expect other charges might follow."

Judge Thompson remained seated but rose to his full height as he surveyed the courtroom. "This case is dismissed and the jury is excused." He banged his gavel for the last time in *State of Missouri v. Lemuel Griggs.*

Later that evening at Wendell's, Justin and his mentor sat at their poker table, this time with a bottle of Kentucky sour mash between them instead of a deck of cards.

"Wendell, I'm curious. How did you come up with that idea about using the sheets?"

"I heard about a case Abe Lincoln tried over in Illinois when he was a practicing lawyer. He used an out-of-date almanac to trick a witness."

Justin smiled. "I wasn't sure it would work, but it put the fear of God in the preacher. He must have thought one of his conspirators was going to rat him out and wanted to save his own skin."

"I expect you're right."

Justin took a sip of whiskey and lapsed into silence as he stared at the glass. After a moment he said, "What puzzles me is we still don't know for certain what happened, or who bit off Mosby's ear and killed him. And what were Sarah's and the Klan's part?"

"Well, Counselor, we won't know until Simpson's trial, but I'll bet the prosecutor will probably cut a deal with Widow Mosby for her cooperation. I suspect she and the preacher were carrying on, and he wanted to get the husband out of the picture. So he gets his Klan brothers riled up, and they go out to scare him. But instead of burning a cross, they find Mosby outside and decide to rough him up. Only, by then, Mosby must have found his knife and the situation turned lethal."

Justin smirked. "The preacher should have heeded the warning in the Good Book about not coveting thy neighbor's wife."

"That's true, Counselor, but there's something more important to take from this case."

"What's that?"

"You've finally learned how to run a bluff."

■ ■ ■ ■

Lonnie Whitaker, a retired federal attorney, works as a freelance writer and editor. His novel, *Geese to a Poor Market,* won the Ozark Writers' League Best Book of the Year award. His nonfiction articles and short stories have appeared in regional magazines and anthologies, and a personal essay was published in *Chicken Soup for the Soul.*

■ ■ ■ ■

THE JUDGMENT TREE
BY JOHNNY D. BOGGS

■ ■ ■ ■

I

"So . . ." Boone pauses, studying the dashing man sitting before him. Dark-skinned, dark-haired, all French, Don Charles Dehault Delassus dresses in the finest silks, brocades, and linens, but the lieutenant governor looks in envy at Boone's ripe-smelling, greasy old hunting shirt. "What exactly is it that a syndic do?"

Boone scratches the ears of one of his hounds as the question is relayed in French to Don Delassus.

Crazy country, Boone thinks. *I be American. The Don be French. And we be conversing on politics in Spanish territory.*

The question is answered, and Boone's son-in-law, Will Hays, translates: "First, you will have authority to grant parcels of land to various individuals."

That might appeal to Boone's son, Nathan, probably even Will Hays, but Boone got his fill of managing land back in Kentucky.

"Also, you will command the military district where we live," Hays says.

Course, Hays likes that idea, probably so he can commission hisself a major. I still ain't sure how he come to be captain. But I've seen enough war. Makes my ankle hurt, damn that Shawnee, damn his musket ball, and damn the Year of the Bloody Sevens. Old man like me don't need to shoot no more folks and sure don't need no more folks shooting at me.

"And you will . . ." Hays struggles. "Well . . . I guess it's kind of like being a justice of the peace."

"Like bein' a judge?" Boone asks.

Captain Hays and the Don resort to French again, while Boone considers the offer.

"Yes," Hays says, "but for minor offenses only. If the case before you is of a more serious matter, then you may send the defendant to St. Charles."

Standing beside Hays, Nathan grins. "Yeah, Pa, remember back when you served as one of those that fall in Harrodsburg?"

"Back *home,*" Will Hays adds, stressing the last word. Will Hays didn't want to leave Kentucky, Boone knows, but Boone was bound west, and wherever Daniel Boone went, his family came. Will Hays was part of the family now.

Not a bad sort, usually. After all, Hays is an educated man — just can't hold his liquor — and the "captain" has helped Boone improve his reading, his ciphering. Better yet, Hays knows how to do surveys, which will be mighty handy if Boone gets this land grant.

But *home*? Boone shakes his head at that thought. Home for Will Hays, maybe, but not for Boone. Not anymore. Not after the lawsuits, but mostly all those crowds of people, ran him west to St. Louis. They've lured him with the promise of new land, near the rolling Missouri River. And now he might even get a title. Boone stops himself from sniggering. A gentleman like the Don probably wouldn't know what to think of a buckskin-clad vagabond snorting like a wild boar and stamping his moccasins on the marble floor.

"I see." Boone rubs his jaw. "So, do I need to read me a bunch of law books?"

He waits for the French words to stop, for his son-in-law to look at him again.

"Don Delassus says he would be honored to present those to you . . ."

Boone's laugh silences the room. So much for his showing the proper decorum before the Don. The three dogs he isn't scratching lift their heads and yawn. "In French or Spanish?" His head shakes and his eyes sparkle.

As Hays begins talking again to the Don, the dogs go back to sleep.

"Don Delassus says that reading laws, ordinances, and legal rulings are not necessary," Hays reports after a while. "You may rule by common sense. You are, his Excellency says, a hero of worldwide renown. But for the Don, you remain a man of honor, and soon to be a new landowner in the Femme Osage . . . and, if you will accept the position, syndic of the district."

"Common sense." Boone scratches the back of his left ear. His eyes rise to study Don Delassus. "And just what do this job of syndic pay?"

He waits for the answer, which causes him to lean back in the cushioned chair.

"You gonna pay that much for *my* common sense?" He laughs hard and loud again, waking the dogs, and causing the officers and ladies and gentlemen in the back of the room to stare. "Well, I'll give 'er a whirl, Governor. Had I knowed you liked me that much, I'd have walked to this Missouri country a long time ago."

He wishes he were hunting. That Don neglected to tell Boone how much time being a syndic takes, but Boone carries his rifle as he leaves the farm and heads for the elm.

The big tree stands in a field being cleared for crops. Nathan wants it removed, but Boone still commands. The tree is something to behold, worth more than the stalks of corn that would take its place. Here, he can sit under the shade, lean his back against the thick trunk, and listen to the evidence presented on both sides.

Besides, he has found no better place to leave the kids, the troubles, and his family than underneath the big tree, where he can sit under the shade, and lose himself in Jonathan Swift.

But today, he must be syndic of the Femme Osage.

Two men, one named Godfrey and the other Phillips, rise, and start brushing the dirt and leaves from their clothes. Boone looks around, but finds no witnesses, just Phillips with his swollen lips and Godfrey with his left ear bandaged and part of his scalp ripped off. Dried blood stains what's left of their shirts. Their knuckles are scarred, swollen, or starting to scab over.

The Frenchman who has brought both men to trial appears bored.

Will Hays reads the charges. Boone shakes his head, and sits beneath the elm.

"You two broke up the churchin' the parson was holdin' at the Meetin' Hall?"

They answer.

"On the Sabbath?"

They answer.

"Over what year this happens to be?" He finds a straw and sticks it in his mouth.

"No, that ain't it, Dan'l."

"That'll be Syndic Boone to you, Marco," Boone tells Godfrey.

"Yes. But. No. We fit over what century it is . . ."

"I keep tellin' this ignorant rapscallion that this ain't the new century," Alexander Phillips interrupts. "This is 1800. Next century don't begin till 1801."

"A damned falsehood." Marco Godfrey starts for Phillips, but the constable steps between the two. Godfrey tries to leap over the constable, yelling, "It ain't seventeen-nothin' no more. So this gots to be a new century."

"Sit down," Boone orders.

Immediately, they obey.

"You broke up a sermon — good one, from what I hear — and scared a lot of womenfolk — Missus Anderson fell in the mud — over an argument as to if this new year that started seven months ago is the beginnin' of the nineteenth century or not."

"That proves it, Syndic Boone," Phillips says. "Nineteen. Not eighteen. You don't start counting at zero."

Before another ruction can commence, Boone finds his rifle, butts the stock against his thigh, and touches the trigger. He's careful not to hit any part of the elm.

The men, even the Frenchman, look at their feet.

"The more I listen to you two, the more I gets to feelin' like I'm just some ol' struldbrug." He pulls himself to his feet, and takes the whip that hangs over one of the elm's branches. "Put down what day it is right now and the year, Will — and don't mention no century — and write this down:

" 'This day come before me, syndic for the District of the Femme Osage, two Yahoos, one bein' Marco Godfrey and the other bein' Alexander Phillips, both said to have disturbed the peace at the church services held on the banks of the Missouri River. There, said defendants admitted that they come to blows, knocked one ol' widow woman on her hindquarters, and done considerable damages to property and decency.' " He lets the end of the whip fall to the ground.

"You can take this case on up to St. Charles, boys, or you can be whipped and cleared. Which'll it be?"

"Whip," Godfrey says.

"Whip," Phillips says.

"All right. Two stripes for you, Phillips. One for you, Marco, as you seem to have gotten the worser in the fracas."

"No, sir!" Marco Godfrey takes a few steps toward Boone, and puts his hands on his hips. "I ain't spendin' this century or next listenin' to that rapscallion braggin' that Dan'l Boone give him two lashes and me only one."

III

"Can I talk to you, Pa, for a minute?"

Boone has his copy of *Gulliver's Travels* in one hand, his dinner in another, and the long rifle tucked underneath one shoulder as he walks toward the door.

His daughter, Susannah — Will Hays's wife — wrings her hands.

"Not right now, Daughter," Boone says. "I got to do my syndic-in' at The Judgment Tree."

She nods, respectfully, even opens the door for him, and Boone walks out. A hound rises out of the shade and follows him.

He has come to enjoy this part of the job. When he isn't busy, he can sit under the elm and read Jonathan Swift. Or whittle. Or scratch whatever dog or dogs decide to follow him to The Judgment Tree.

Nathan Boone is there this morning, acting as the court . . . whatever you call these notetakers who send their findings to St. Louis. Sadly, *Captain* Will Hays has gotten so a body just can't trust him. Spends more of his time in the taverns than at home. Which, probably, is what Susannah wants to talk about.

This case proves a mite more difficult. Nathan's good, but he speaks neither Spanish nor French, and the two men appear to be arguing over a jug of whiskey. Nathan has found the jug, shaken it, and reported to his father that it appears to be about half full.

Between them, the Spaniard and the Frenchman know maybe ten words of English, most of which are blasphemy.

Finally, through a mix of sign language, gestures, and vile oaths, Boone understands.

"So . . . you both claim this jug of whiskey.

That's what this all comes down to, ain't it?"

The Frenchman and the Spaniard nod. Boone's head shakes.

I probably could have said, "You're both ugly as sin and your parents was Tories," and they would have nodded to that, too.

"Nathan, run down home and fetch me an axe."

He sets the jug between the two men. They seem to think he plans on chopping off their heads.

"One of the first stories Ma ever preached to me," Boone explains. "The Book of Kings. If it worked for Solomon . . ." After he sets the blade of the axe on the cork, Boone tilts his head toward the Frenchman. "You get this side." Then nods at the Spaniard. "You get this side." He raises the axe over his head. "Now, this bein' stoneware, it's likely to shatter in pieces, but it'll be split."

Unlike the mothers in that Bible story, neither begs to give the jug to the other, to save at least the whiskey, so the axe shatters the jug, soaking the field with corn liquor and sending bits of stoneware onto the two men's pants.

"Divvy up your jug, boys," Boone says.

"You take half. You take the rest. Case be cleared."

As Boone and Nathan watch the men head to the footpath through the woods, their hands filled with bits of stoneware, Nathan says, "Pa, you rule with equity."

Smiling, Boone sits beneath The Judgment Tree and opens *Gulliver's Travels*.

IV

Hounds are smart critters. Outside, in the darkness, they wail in the night . . . like they already know what has happened.

The curtain draws back, and the old woman with the crooked nose and the rheumy eyes steps into the room. She nods at Boone, as the women surrounding him begin to cry.

You can't find a doctor, good, bad, or in between, in the Femme Osage. All they gots here is this old hag. Some have used her as a midwife. I figure she's a witch.

He walks into the room to find Susannah, her pretty hair hanging off the end of the table, most of her body covered with a blanket.

"You may kiss her goodbye," the witch says.

Ain't right, ain't fair. Man my age, any age, ought not have to see his children pass first.

Even if I don't count young Willie, called to Glory practically after he got birthed, how many have I done loss? James tortured and butchered by them Shawnees. And Israel? Balls and arrows is whistling by us, and that boy, game as a bantam, saying, "Father, I will not leave you." Always thought that losing Israel would be the hardest. Till now.

He wants to remember Susannah alive, laughing, but all he can think about is:

"Can I talk to you, Pa, for a minute?" . . . *"Not right now, Daughter. I got to do my syndic-in' at The Judgment Tree."*

He sighs. When had that been? Six weeks. Longer.

"She is at peace," the witch says.

Boone fingers his daughter's hair, so soft. He stares at the face, moves his hand to one swollen lip, then at the bruise underneath her left eye. He sees the markings on her throat, too.

"Peace?" Boone gives the witch a hard stare.

"Bilious fever killed her," says the witch, whose eyes burn with such a ferocity, even Boone looks away. "The bruises did not."

V

"Write this down in the book, Nathan," Boone says, out of breath. " 'Leviticus

Bryant, hog thief. Whipped and cleared. December thirteenth, eighteen-aught-four.' " The frigid air burns his throat. Hanging the whip over the limb, sinking into the folding seat his other sons, Daniel Morgan and Jesse Bryan, have given him, he realizes that 1805 is almost here. For roughly four-and-a-half years, he has been coming to The Judgment Tree.

This should be the only case to come before the syndic today. It's too cold to do any judging, certainly any more whipping, so Boone figures he might as well read again about Gulliver and the Lilliputians. Till he can find enough strength to walk his old self home.

As Leviticus Bryant is helped toward the creek that runs beyond the field, Boone spies a bunch of men coming from the settlement. Spilling out of the woods, they shout and shove a tall young man forward. Sighing, Boone lets Jonathan Swift settle back into the leather bag.

"Judge Boone . . ."

He can just make out the shouts. Another word causes him to stiffen as he and Nathan exchange glances.

"Murder!"

Boone uses his long rifle to push himself back on his feet. He stares at the treeless branches above him. The clouds are gray, threatening to snow. He wets his lips.

"He has taken the life of the capt'n!" another man shouts, and shoves the tall man again. "Capt'n Hays! Will Hays has been murdered!"

Nathan whispers. Boone keeps himself steady by leaning against the rifle, driving the butt as deep as he can get it in the frozen earth.

He almost slips when he recognizes the tall man. James Davis. Will Hays's son-in-law. Davis had married Susannah's daughter, Jemima — named after one of Susannah's sisters.

This here Missouri. So beautiful . . . so vast . . . so wild . . . So Old Testament.

"Shot him dead, Judge Boone!" Marco Godfrey yells. "Just as he come out of Jarman's Inn. When the capt'n come out, the boy shot him down like a dog!"

Why does everybody get shot down like dogs? Never shot no dog myself except them that got the hydrophoby.

"You saw it?" Boone asks.

"You're damned right he saw it, Boone!" That comes from a face Boone doesn't want to see here. Enoch Hays . . . Will's brother.

106

"I saw it, too. We need to hang this murderer!"

The crowd takes up the cheer. Boone pulls his rifle up, cradling it in his arm. Off to his side, he sees Nathan reaching for the pistol he keeps tucked behind his back in a scarlet sash.

"Leave it be," Boone whispers. "For now."

He studies the young man who married his granddaughter. They have roughed the boy up a mite. Boy? Boone blinks. James Davis has to be pushing thirty years old.

The cold does nothing good for Boone's rheumatism. He doesn't know how much longer he can stand in this weather. Yet, he makes himself ask Godfrey, "You didn't answer, Marco. Did you see it?"

The man fidgets, kicks some frozen dirt clods around, snorts, spits, and finally shakes his head. "No . . . don't reckon I saw nothin' . . . but I heard it." His head bobs rapidly. "We opened the door, and I seen the capt'n writhin' on the ground. And the boy holdin' his rifle."

"Where was Enoch when you heard the shot?"

"Boone, you callin' me —" Boone's rifle, now braced against his shoulder with a finger against the trigger, silences Will Hays's brother.

"I'm asking you, Marco. Where was Enoch?"

"Well, iffen I remembers right, Enoch was at the bar fetchin' us a jug."

No witnesses then.

"You sure Will's dead?"

"Well, he weren't movin'," Godfrey says.

The crowd has grown silent, uncertain. Boone thinks he might be able to get out of this conundrum with one quick question.

"Boy," he asks James Davis, "you want to tell me what happened?"

The lad doesn't look at Boone, doesn't even raise his head, but he speaks in a defiant voice:

"I shot the son-of-a-bitch. And if he isn't dead, take me back to the inn and I'll finish the job."

This time, Boone has to fire his rifle over the heads of the mob. He's glad to see Nathan standing, leveling the pistol at the men.

Minutes go on for eternity. Finally, Boone says, "This ain't a job for no syndic, no homespun judge like me. You all know that. We'll hold young Davis at my house. I'll fetch him to St. Charles in the morn. Trial, I warrant, will take place later, after some real law can figure things out. Remember, we's under American rule now, boys."

Which has been the case since these young United States bought the territory.

"You boys got that?"

The answer is unintelligible.

"All of you?" He stares hard at Enoch Hays.

"Now, please get off my land."

VI

Reckon I can follow the Missouri to St. Charles. But that'll leave me boxed in. I be too old to swim a river that wide. Cold as it is, I'll freeze to death before they can fill me, and young Davis, full of holes. Now, I can take a canoe, but that'll mean paddling upstream. Nah. That's no good at all. Enoch and them boys will just pick us both off from afar. Me and that boy'll wind up feeding catfish.

"You ready, James?" Boone asks.

The young man nods.

Once he opens the door, Boone feels the bite of winter. He looks at his sons. "Don't follow me, boys. I mean that. I'll be back directly."

Twenty miles. Roughly. I've walked that in no time. Back in Kentucky, folks most likely be riding horses these days. That's what civilization does to a country. But try to find a road in this Missouri.

He's sweating. Thirty degrees, and he's sweating underneath his hunting shirt. The rifle weighs a ton, and he doesn't know what his daughters gave him to eat, but it feels like cannon balls in his pack. The rheumatism practically kills him.

"James . . ." Just speaking that hurts. "You look tuckered out. Let's rest a mite."

"Sounds good, Mister Boone."

After sinking to the ground, Boone finds a tree that can support him, grabs the canteen, and drinks thirstily.

Can't sit here all day. Stand up. You ain't old. Seventy ain't old. Well, it ain't ancient.

"You rested enough, James?"

"Yes, sir."

"Good." He groans. "Let's get movin'."

They move two more miles . . . at least, it feels like two miles . . . before he rests again. This time, he sleeps.

"Mister Boone?"

His eyes open. It's dark, but he can see. He can see because the boy has a fire going. He smells tea boiling in a kettle, and corn pone heating up in a skillet. He feels warm, and touches the blanket that covers him.

"You been busy, boy," Boone says. "But your fire's too big. And get that skillet off it. Smells travel a far piece. In case we's bein' followed."

"We aren't," Davis says. "I checked while you rested."

Boone frowns. *That should've been my job.*

"Are we lost?" Davis asks.

Boone swallows. "Never been lost. Been confused. But never lost."

He sips tea, then sleeps.

He wakes at dawn, tries to move, and sees the man who killed Will Hays stoking the coals, getting the fire going again.

"We best be movin', boy," Boone tells him.

"Yes, sir," the kid answers, and Boone falls back asleep.

"Used to like winter," Boone tells Davis. "Townfolks think winter be like bein' dead, but that ain't it at all. It ain't death. It's the beginnin' of rebirth. But now . . . you feel different. Cold feels colder. You get to be seventy, boy, and you'll know what I mean."

"Likely," Davis says, "they'll prevent that from happening in St. Charles."

"How long we been here?" Boone sips tea from a copper cup. The warmth in his fingers pleases him. The tea tastes fine. He feels like he might be able to eat a bite of jerky. Better yet, some bear meat . . . if he could find him a bear to kill.

"Three days," James Davis replies.

"God a'mighty."

The lad shrugs.

"You could've run off," Boone says.

"Daniel Boone wouldn't have." Davis refills Boone's cup with tea.

"Don't you bet on that. I run many a time. That's why I'm . . ." He sighs, and sips more tea. "Don't get old, boy," he says.

"Like Jemima's mother?" The kid's eyes harden. They lock on Boone's cold blues, but Boone is strong enough, now, to stare the boy down.

"You want to know why I killed Captain Hays?" the kid asks.

Boone sets the cup on a rock. "I know why, boy. I should've done it myself."

VII

Some courthouse. A tavern ain't the same as The Judgment Tree. This time of year, back along the Femme Osage, you smell the fields. They be thawing out. Winter's passing, and spring's coming. You see the sky, clear as my eyes. And rain? Nothing smells better than rain. But here? These chambers stink of yesterday's supper, of pipe smoke, spilled ale, and dishwasher's soap. Me? I prefer The Judgment Tree.

"Tell him what happened, boy," Boone says.

James Davis nods, then looks at the American judge who's new to this new territory of the United States.

Boone thinks:

Not long ago, I left America, but now America's caught up with me. Reckon Missouri'll be crowded like Kentucky in no time.

"Captain Hays," Davis says, "wasn't a bad man. But the spirits got to him. Left him bad tempered. His drinking only got worse after his wife, my wife's mother, died, be five years come October, not long after we got here. Well . . . well . . . well, he rode up to our place, in his cups, and Jemima — that's my wife — she took him to task. He slapped her hard. I walked up from the hogs about then, and I see him standing over her, raising his hand, saying that no . . . I can't use the word he used, sir . . . daughter of his would speak to him that way.

"We got into a tussle. I hit him. He hit me. Jemima gets up and screamed at him to go. Just go. Well, he left, but he said if he ever saw me, he'd kill me. Then he'd come back to teach Jemima about being respectful to her pa."

James Davis pauses. He stares at his feet.

"I didn't know Captain Hays was in the

tavern. Wasn't even going there. I was stopping to order some feed. That's when Captain Hays stepped out of the tavern. He carried his long gun with him. Like most men who come from Kentucky, he didn't go anywhere without his rifle. He shoots, but the pan doesn't flash, so he starts with his powder horn, laughing, saying I'll be shouting at Lucifer in a minute. I yell at him to stop. He won't listen. I run to the mercantile, where I left my rifle. He comes at me. Aims his gun, pulls back the . . ." He sighs. "I don't remember shooting. But I shot him."

The judge clears his throat. He looks no older than James Davis.

"It has been sworn here in this court that you told several men, including Mister Boone, that you shot him, or words to that effect, and that if Captain Hays were not dead, that they could return you to the settlement and you would . . . I believe the exact words were . . . 'finish the job.' "

"I said it, Your Honor." He's looking the judge right in the eye. "I meant it. I'm away from the house, in the fields, hunting up some supper, or tending to the pigs. He'd come back to Jemima, Your Honor. He'd beat her. Just as he beat his dead wife."

114

■ ■ ■ ■

Boone settles on the whiskey keg, empty, that serves as the witness stand.

"Mister Boone," the judge says, "you have requested a chance to testify to the character of the defendant. You must like the young man, as I see that you posted his three-thousand-dollar bond this past December. You may say your piece, sir."

Boone clears his throat.

"This fellow, well, I can't say I know him. He married the daughter of one of my daughters, and he came with us from Kentucky. But . . . well . . . first of all, when I was bringin' the boy here, from the Femme Osage last December, well, I got a trifle sick. He stayed with me. Could've lit out for anywhere he wanted. Left me to die. He didn't. That says a lot about a fellow."

Enoch Hays leaps from a chair. His fist slams against a table. "He's still a foul-hearted, cold-blooded murderin', lyin' little bastard!"

The judge pounds a gavel on the bar. "Silence."

Enoch Hays isn't finished. "And my brother never laid no hand on no woman."

"Silence! One more outburst, sir, and you

will feel the lash against your back for contempt of court."

Boone waits for the din to subside.

"I don't know about what happened at the settlement, Judge. Weren't there. Didn't know Hays had been shot till the boys brung him, young Davis, to The Judgment Tree. But . . ."

His head shakes. "Hays always made Susannah — my girl, Hays's late wife — dress, just covered with clothes, even in the hottest day of summer. Even made her wear gloves. I'd hear him tell her, 'Cover your entire body, my dear, for you don't dare catch cold.' Judge, I reckon I know about Indians. I know about some things. Tracking. Hunting. Following a trail. And, though I've got a wife and had me a fine mother and a slew of daughters, I don't know nothin' 'bout women much. Didn't think nothin' of it, till that day . . ." He clears his throat. "That day when my Susannah was called away. I saw the bruises on her cheek, her throat. If I'd turned her over — if I thought I could've stood it — I knowed I would've seen the stripes on her back. Young James Davis killed Will Hays. But we all know it wasn't murder. It was self-defense. He's a good man. Good for Missouri. Good for our United States. Yes, sir. Self-defense.

Had I done it, which I should've, it would've been revenge. Pure and simple."

VIII

The flatboat lets him off on the western banks of the Missouri. He pays the helmsman, grabs his pack, his long rifle, and starts for home. A few steps from the river, a slave hands him a slip of paper.

"Squire Boone," the old Negro says, "Mister Hays come to me and says to give this to you."

Boone unfolds the note.

Ill B waytn 2 setel our akounts at tH juggment Tre

— E hayS

It riles Boone to see Enoch Hays, on this land, leaning against Boone's elm tree.

Hays stands, and brings his rifle up. Boone walks till only fifty feet separate them.

"You're a lyin' son-of-a-bitch," Hays says. "You know my brother never done nothin'. You got that murderin' skunk off. So I'll send you to hell. Then I'll be visitin' Davis. You're both to blame. You both killed my brother."

Boone feels seventy years old.

"That all you got to say?"

117

Hays nods.

Boone lets his rifle fall to the ground.

"Then go ahead, Enoch, and get your revenge. You're sitting under The Judgment Tree. You be the judge. If it makes you feel better, go ahead and kill me. I ain't got many years left."

He waits for the rifle to rise. It doesn't.

"Come on, you damned coward. I'm the one who deserves to die. Not young Davis. I should've killed your sorry brother. Had I done that, I might still have Susannah with me."

Now the rifle rises. Boone spreads out his arms, fills his lungs with cold spring air. He waits to see the puff from the pan and then the barrel. Waits to feel the ball enter his chest. He won't close his eyes. No one will ever say Daniel Boone is a coward.

He waits.

The rifle lowers. Enoch Hays's head drops. Boone releases the air from his lungs, as his son-in-law's brother walks away from the elm, and stops beside Boone. Tears fill his eyes.

"Will didn't kill her, Dan'l. You gots to know that." Hays's gaze falls to the muddy ground. "And that boy, Jemima's husband, he didn't kill Will, neither." His head nods, convincing himself of his truth. "It was the rum. The rum done it. It was the bloody rum."

Slowly, Enoch Hays walks to the footpath that cuts through the woods.

IX

He leans against the elm. Sighs. Looks up at the branches. Leaves are just beginning to show, and larger ones flutter in the wind. A cloud, white as snow, rolls past the sun.

I'll just sit. No Gulliver's Travels *today. No dogs. Hounds don't even know I'm back. Till this place gets organized, I'm still syndic, or judge, whatever the Americans want to call me. But nobody's comin' today. And one day, fairly soon, it'll be me standin' here, waitin' to hear my judgment.*

His eyes close. His head tilts back. He smells the mud, the tilled soil.

He remembers hard, trying to picture what she looked like. How her voice sounded. Underneath his eyelids, he can feel his tears.

And if He comes to judge me today, that'll be all right.

Because right now, he sees her face. Not bruised. Not pale. Not dead. He sees her all those years ago, back in North Carolina. She's screaming with ear-splitting excitement, running across the floor, leaping to his arms, knocking him into his chair, saying that it's her birthday — sixth, it sounds like — and she's so happy he's home. And he feels so contented, because for this moment, he's not off hunting, not fighting Indians, not doing his syndic-ing, not leaving his wife and family and friends to explore some new country. He's inside the cabin he built, with the family he made, bouncing a six-year-old girl on his knee and hearing her say how much she has missed him, how glad she is that he has come home — the best gift anybody has ever gotten on any birthday. She says how much she loves him, and he says, "And your pa sure loves you, chil'. And he always will."

Above him, the wind blows through the limbs of The Judgment Tree.

■ ■ ■ ■

Johnny D. Boggs has won a record-tying seven Spur Awards from Western Writers of America. A native of South Carolina, he lives in Santa Fe, New Mexico, with his wife and son. His website is JohnnyDBoggs.com.

■ ■ ■ ■

WREN'S PERCH
BY VONN MCKEE

■ ■ ■ ■

From my father's sawmill on the edge of town, from the far end of the last pew in church, from across the throng of a hundred Saturday socials . . . I had watched Lydia. I was a handful of years older than she, just a sturdy built fellow with sawdust in my boots and hardness in my hands. Not tall or handsome enough to attract her interest nor homely enough to garner her sympathy.

Lydia reminded me of the willows by the creek: slim and graceful, with a quiet rooted strength. I could recognize her deep auburn hair and slender form from all angles and from a great distance. If I were lucky enough, I would catch sight of her walking past the mill to take her piano lesson at Theo Weimer's house at the end of the street. When I was manning the saw, I didn't dare steal more than a glance. Sometimes, fortune intervened and I would be levering a log from the pile, which allowed me to fiddle long enough to see her all the way to the Weimers' front door. I confess that I pictured myself offering my arm as she walked onto the stoop.

"Albert!" my father would shout. *"Zu arbeiten, Junge!"* To work, boy!

He ran a wood yard in the southeastern corner of Iowa and, with new homesteads sprouting up on the surrounding prairies, we worked long days to keep up with lumber orders. I told him once he ought to have had more than one son and not so many daughters.

Of course, we never worked on Sundays, which made me thankful for many reasons. I looked forward to being clean, at least for a day. Also, my head would be cleared for a while of the jarring *poota-poota* of the steam engine and the high-pitched scream of the saw as it bit into logs two and a half feet in breadth.

We would all go to church and, since I was now considered to be a young man, I was not expected to be seated with my family. Hence, I began sitting in the last row, beside my friend Simon. This afforded a good vantage point for seeing Lydia enter through the wide door at the rear and make her way to a pew three rows ahead of me. I was content with a view of the back of her head, hair caught into a bow, but I was especially thrilled whenever she turned to the side, revealing the curves of her face.

On one of these Sundays, I was in my usual place and peered past Simon to see Lydia walking up the aisle, her hand on the arm of Nelson Parks. I'm sure my face must have gone white, for I felt suddenly cold and faint. Sure enough, Nelson led Lydia to an open pew and proceeded to sit beside her, their arms nearly touching.

I remember nothing else of the service that day. The sermon and songs were distant, hollow dronings in my ears. My hopes for any future with Lydia were dashed and I condemned myself for my lack of boldness. Of course, she would find a suitor! I hadn't so much as approached her. Afterward, I was intent on getting home as quickly as I could, but Simon caught up with me before I left the churchyard.

"Going quail hunting late afternoon tomorrow if you'd like to tag along. We could meet at the creek after work."

"Depends on how far along we get at the mill. I'll take my shotgun with me just in case."

I could not help watching Lydia stepping up into Nelson's buggy, with his assistance, of course.

"What do you know?" said Simon. "I had heard that Nelson was courting Lydia Hancock. Well, he could have done worse for himself, eh, Albert?"

It took all my will to smile and nod yes.

The wedding was in early autumn and, ours being a small town, all were invited to attend. Lydia looked more ladylike than I'd ever seen her. She wore a blue dress and a hat with late-blooming roses tucked into the band. It was plain to me that Nelson was a good choice. He was tall and straight, a towering white pine to her slender willow, and was well-liked for his wit and work ethic. Nelson farmed his own homestead north of town and whatever he set his hand to seemed to flourish.

Fewer orders came in at the sawmill with the approach of winter. We sold the wood scraps not used for the engine's boiler for firewood. My father enjoyed the ritual of closing down the mill for the season: hauling off the sawdust for fill, nailing down loose shingles on the shed roof, greasing the moving parts of the carriage and saw.

Father also enjoyed a taste of beer now and then. We were walking home on an October afternoon and decided to stop at the tavern.

"*Danke Gott,* it's been a good year," he said, raising his drink to mine.

I could only force a smile in response. My heart still ached when I thought of Lydia, although I tried to comfort myself by considering her happiness. We listened for a while to the other patrons' news accounts from around the county, as men can be bigger gossips than women. Finally, my father started for the door, waving off those who badgered him for going home to his wife so early.

He was reaching for the doorknob, me right behind him, when the door burst open and Orrie Johnson came barreling in, all out of breath.

"Just came . . . from the Parks place. Nelson . . ." Orrie steadied himself at the back of a chair and dropped his head to take deeper breaths.

"Slow down, Orrie," my father said. "Here, sit down. Breathe deep and tell us what's wrong."

"Nelson . . . he was patching up the pen where he keeps his bull . . . nailing a board when . . . when the beast broke through the fence trying to . . . get at the cows. He . . . gored Nelson. Badly, I'm afraid. I rode in and fetched the doc, but I don't see how . . ."

Orrie shook his head, as if denying what he had seen. Someone set a beer in front of him.

"We ought to go see what can be done. Doc will need help, no matter what."

I was not sure who spoke but a couple of the men hurried out. I heard the slap of reins and clattering of a buckboard when they took off. I suppose I was too shocked to volunteer to go with them. *Lydia! How distraught she must be!*

I hardly slept that night for seeing visions of poor Nelson. A farmer's life could roll along with nothing of excitement happening for years on end. Then, something tragic came out of nowhere . . . a lantern exploding, a frightened horse, a fall from a hayloft . . .

The next morning, the news was confirmed. Nelson Parks was dead. Left behind was Lydia, his wife of only five weeks.

I'd taken up whittling and simple carpentry as a boy. Often, I picked up chunks of pine or basswood at the mill and took them home. Sitting on the porch and carving with a pocket knife brought me calm, especially when my sisters were at each other. As I got older, I acquired a few tools and built a workbench in a small unused granary on our property. The little workshop was my sanctuary, and I spent all the spare time there I could manage.

I was nearly finished with a wren house, the most ornate piece I'd ever attempted. The bric-a-brac trim and scalloped shingles took weeks to shape with my hand-cranked scroll saw. At the last minute, I decided to add flat pieces at the front to resemble columns and a pediment. A proper entrance for Mr. and Mrs. Wren, I thought.

The idea for the wren house came after my mother mentioned in passing that she had seen Lydia's aunt at the mercantile. Nelson's farm had been sold to his brother and Lydia moved back to the Hancocks' home. According to this aunt, Lydia's parents had decided to shorten her period of mourning — owing to her young age and the circumstances of her brief marriage — from the usual two and a half years to one year.

"Sounds as though Mr. Hancock is ready to shove her right back out of the nest," my mother said.

She had no way of knowing how that morsel of information set the wheels and cogs turning in my head. *In a year and day after her husband's death, Lydia would be allowed to accept callers. Might she show particular favor to a caller who arrived with a gift in hand?*

Knocking lightly on the Hancocks' front door was the boldest act of all my twenty-two years. I reached for the knocker three times before finding the courage to lift it, and was relieved when it was Mrs. Hancock who answered.

"Albert? Good afternoon . . ." It was more a question than a greeting, perhaps because of the bulky paper and twine-wrapped bundle tucked under my arm.

"Yes, good afternoon, Mrs. Hancock. I mentioned to your husband at church that I might be stopping by today."

I had recited these words a dozen times on the walk from my house. Still, they sounded like a schoolboy's nervous class-room speech. *Was I being too forward? I had waited a year and two weeks . . .*

"Oh, yes, yes. It is Friday, isn't it? I'm sorry, come right in."

She ushered me into the parlor and pointed to a chair. I put my parcel on the floor beside it and settled carefully onto the green silk cushioning. I traced the pattern carved on the wooden chair arms with my fingers . . . three long grooves that ended in the shape of curved animal claws.

"Well, I take it you are not here to visit me," said Mrs. Hancock, straightening a lace runner on the mantel. She was not making it easy for me.

"Oh, well . . . I'm happy to visit with you, ma'am. I thought that I might . . . have a word with . . . Lydia, if I could."

I realized at that moment how few times I'd spoken Lydia's name aloud, and saying it now felt both pleasant and terrifying. Mrs. Hancock tilted her head as if sizing me up, then walked over and sat in a chair matching mine. With only a smoking cabinet between us, I could see that her hair was the same color as Lydia's, but streaked with white. She folded her hands in her lap.

"Albert . . . as you are aware, Lydia suffered a great shock last year."

"Yes, ma'am. It was a shock to us all, Nelson's death. I can only imagine Lydia's grief."

"She is much, much better. Of course, she is a different girl than before, understandably."

I had observed this myself, on the few occasions I had seen Lydia in public. The ordeal had left a droop at her shoulders, and her face — even thinner now — bore the strain of it.

"I'm glad you decided to come," she

133

continued. "We . . . Lydia, as well . . . think that she's ready to move on with her life. My husband and I did not want her to spend too much time dwelling on her sorrow. After all, the marriage was very brief, and we hope . . ."

Mrs. Hancock's eyes dropped to her lap.

"We hope that there is happiness ahead — or some degree of it — for our daughter."

My hands closed tightly over the carved animal claws. I had not rehearsed any conversation beyond my introduction at the front door. I willed the words to come.

"I have always admired your daughter . . ." I could not believe I was confessing my devotion to Lydia's own mother. "While I am most respectful of her . . . need for healing after this tragedy, I am here to offer her my friendship. Perhaps even . . ."

I bit my lip, unable to voice my secret hopes. Mrs. Hancock studied my face. After a moment, she surprised me by leaning forward and placing her hand over mine.

"You are a good soul, Albert. Please . . . be patient with her. She is . . . fragile, at times."

Before I could respond, she stood quickly and smoothed her skirts.

"I'll fetch Lydia now. There is still half an hour before her piano lesson begins. She's decided to take up her studies again."

Lydia stepped quietly into the parlor and took the same seat her mother had just left. There she sat, looking right at me, asking me about my day! For the first time, I was close enough to see that her eyes were the color of moss, and that she had light freckles sprinkled across her nose. So much to make note of!

And so, I spent thirty glorious minutes with Lydia. She was quiet but kind, listening to my inane sawmill stories and complaints about growing up in a houseful of sisters. My nerves made me unusually talkative, I guess. When I handed her the package, she opened it carefully and with a restrained curiosity. She held up the wren house, which I had painted white, and examined it intently. Suddenly, I had never seen such a crude and artless piece of carpentry. *What had I been thinking? Why would Lydia want something so absurd as a wren house?*

An image of the handsome and capable Nelson Parks popped into my mind, alongside one of myself. I pictured him as a sleek thoroughbred, outpacing a dull, plodding ox named Albert.

Lydia touched the shingles and trim at the eaves, then ran her finger along the smoothly sanded perch below the entrance hole.

"Why, Albert," she said. "It's beautiful. I can't wait until spring when I can put it up in the yard. Thank you . . . so very much."

I was unprepared for the effect her smile and direct eye contact had on me. I left the Hancock house with a light heart, and feeling at least a couple of inches taller. Over the next several months, I devised all manner of ways to spend time with Lydia. Aside from visiting in her parents' parlor, I borrowed a sleigh for a ride through new-fallen December snow, invited her to a Christmas social at the church, and even endured a spring spelling bee at the schoolhouse.

Lydia seemed accepting of my company, but I had to grow accustomed to those times when her eyes seemed no longer to see me. For a couple of minutes — sometimes longer — she went somewhere far away and I had no choice but to wait patiently, as Mrs. Hancock had suggested, for her return.

By late May, I had two proposals in mind. I had lost Lydia once to another and was determined not to let it happen again without making my best effort to win her hand. The second, and most difficult, was to my father. If, by chance, Lydia agreed to marry me, I decided we would do well to make a new start in another town, far from old places and painful memories.

I pulled up a chair as my father was scribbling numbers with the stub of a pencil. A vacant lot next to the mill had become available for purchase and he was considering expanding operations. Given that, I knew he would not be pleased to lose his only employee.

"What do you think?" I asked. "Will it pay off?"

He shrugged. "Maybe. The town is growing, for sure. The railroad has helped, and there's talk of building a courthouse. It could be worth a try."

"Yes . . . well, I have an idea about that. As you say, the railroads are changing everything. There are towns popping up like corn rows all along the new lines. Most of the lumber to build them is coming out of Minnesota and Canada, as you know. We have a piece of that business now, but we could get more."

"Easy to say. Not so easy to do."

I swallowed hard. I had, of course, rehearsed this speech. "If we opened a lumberyard further west . . . in one of these growing towns, the mill here could supply the material, shipped by rail."

I watched his thick eyebrows working up and down as he pondered the idea, and could almost read his sequence of thoughts. He laid down the pencil and looked at me.

"And who is going to manage this lumberyard? Your sisters?"

"I . . . I would like to try it myself. Simon is looking for work and would take over for me at the mill, I think. He asked me recently if you needed extra help."

My father rubbed his chin.

"Why couldn't Simon run the second yard, in the other town?"

"Well," I answered. "Simon is a hard worker, all right, but not much good with numbers. Also, I was thinking . . . with all the new construction going on, I might go into the building business as well. Besides . . . I'm considering asking Lydia to marry . . . and it might be best to settle elsewhere, given her circumstances."

Considering asking Lydia to marry! I'd thought of nothing else for the last year. I braced myself for his harsh answer. He picked up the stubby pencil again and squeezed it hard a couple of times in his fist. After stewing for half a minute, he slapped the pencil down in front of me and shoved the paper with his scribbled columns across the table.

"Show me," he said, turning the paper over to the blank side, "how you think it can work."

The numbers and sketches flowed through the little pencil like water. I drew him a map of rail connections, spurs and timetables, and sketched a proposed warehouse location. I added and subtracted figures, demonstrating how I would leverage a modest bank loan, and how long it would take to operate in the clear.

"Once I get going, I believe the new property and lumber warehouse would be paid off with the sale of the first house I build. That could be the first or second year, depending on the weather."

My father paced around the room, hands in his pockets, listening to my scheme. After I said all I could think of to convince him, I sat in silence . . . and more than a little dread. He walked to the cuckoo clock, brought from the old country, that had hung on the same wall for all my life. He pulled the chains attached to the wood pinecone-shaped weights, ratcheting them up until the weights touched the clock, winding it for the week.

"I remember . . ." he said, still facing the clock on the wall. "I remember having this same talk with my own father a long time ago. The girl, the business, the sailing west . . . all of it."

I had seldom heard my father speak of his Bavarian home. Usually, he mentioned it in winter, laughing over Iowa's "mild weather."

"I promised him," he continued, "that I would go back and visit him, when things got going. That was . . . not to be."

My mind had been so filled with plans, I had not stopped to realize that I would be leaving my home and family behind. I had also failed to appreciate the sacrifices my father had made for us.

"But that was an ocean, Father. We will only be a day's travel away by train. I would not want to separate Lydia from her parents for long at a time, or me from my family. Besides, you and I will remain business partners."

Finally, my father came back to the table. He folded the paper covered with my business plans into a little square and stuck it in his shirt pocket. Then he shook my hand firmly, and said, *"Mein sohn . . ."*

Before he turned away, I thought I saw tears shining at the corners of his eyes.

I stopped the buggy at the crest of a gentle hill, with an eastern view of the treetops along the Des Moines River. The town of Fort Dodge lay beyond. I turned to Lydia. It had been almost a year since we had married in the Hancocks' parlor, with only our family members and Simon present. The rough sketches I'd made at Father's table had transformed into reality. A lumber warehouse in a new town further west, and hard work from dawn to dark.

"A nice spot, don't you think? Now that the lumberyard is up and running and I'm finished with the Lowell house, I can start work on our place. You must be tired of living in a hotel."

Honestly, I didn't know whether Lydia was tired of the hotel or not. She never expressed an opinion — in favor of or against — much of anything. In public and in our private moments, she kept herself in a quiet place of acquiescence, always a slight smile on her pretty face. I sometimes wondered what her green eyes were seeing. We did talk from time to time about things, like news from our families and comments on the landscape and wildlife we passed during our Sunday buggy rides.

Lydia pointed to a scrubby crabapple tree twenty yards away from us, where a tiny wren perched on the end of a branch. The bird burst out in chirruping song, bringing delight to Lydia's face.

"There," she said breathlessly. "Build the house there."

I resolved just then to build her the prettiest house in all of Webster County.

By summer's end, I had finished — with the help of two youths from a neighboring farm — a two-story, four-bedroom house with sweeping eaves edged in hand-carved trim and a porch on two sides. At Lydia's suggestion, I added a three-story square tower at the corner, covered in scalloped white shingles, so she could see the river from the small room at the top. We christened the gleaming white house Wren's Perch. I thought it resembled a wedding cake atop the hill.

On the day we moved in, I nailed the little wren house — my first gift to Lydia — to a fence post in the front yard.

I stayed busy with work right up until the first frost. This time of year was always difficult for Lydia. Two Octobers ago, she had lost Nelson, and she'd been keeping to herself even more than usual. She was still sleeping when I'd left the house. By the time I rode home at day's end, the sky was darkening.

I saw her silhouetted in the top window of

the tower when I was halfway up the road. A lamp glowed behind her but I noticed the rest of the house was dark and there was no smoke at the chimney. Worried, I pulled the buggy right up to the gate and left it there, sprinted to the porch, then cleared the steps in one jump.

As I opened the front door, I could hear Lydia's footsteps coming quickly down the tower staircase. She appeared in the doorway to the entrance hall, a shawl wrapped around her and her hair slipping down from its pins. The look on her face was the same as when she'd seen the little wren . . . pure, girlish delight. I thought she was about to run into my arms.

I took off my hat, wondering what had made her so happy. Suddenly, the broad smile melted from her face, replaced by complete confusion . . . then disappointment. All within a few seconds.

"Oh," she said. "I thought you . . ."

She looked at me again and, just as quickly, regained her usual pleasant composure — the little half-smile on her lips.

"I thought you would have been home earlier," she said. "It's nearly dark."

"The days grow shorter and shorter, don't they? It's chilly in here. I'll build a fire," I said.

"Yes. Well, if you don't mind . . . I think I'll lie down for a few minutes. My head aches. Thank you . . ."

Lydia disappeared down the hall into the bedroom. I hauled in wood and got the fire blazing. An hour later, I stared into the flames, thinking about what had just happened. There was a gnawing in the pit of my belly and I did not want to admit what I knew to be true.

She'd thought . . . I was Nelson.

A burning log settled, spraying golden sparks. I sat for a while, considering my lot in life. I had to accept that, in spite of my devotion and hard work and carefully laid plans, my future was inescapably entwined with Lydia's past.

Lydia had once admired a mahogany sewing chest with mother-of-pearl inlays at the general store, so I bought it to give to her for Christmas. Two sisters named Ada and Essie owned the store and went on and on about what a thoughtful gift I'd chosen.

Essie offered to wrap the chest while Ada tallied my order, including some penny candy and apples.

"You know, Ada," Essie said, cutting a length of red paper, "I think that Albert and Lydia make such a nice pair. So devoted to each other. Do you know what I saw on my way back from visiting our cousins in Carroll County?"

"No, Essie, what?"

The sisters discussed me as if I weren't standing across the counter from them.

"I passed Albert's house and saw that pretty Lydia standing in the window of the tower, watching for him to come home! Is that not the sweetest thing you've ever heard of?"

Ada saw my discomfort and gave me a wink.

"Now, Essie, you're embarrassing Albert here."

I paid for my purchases and slipped out the door. I climbed onto the buggy seat and sat there, slumped over, until the knot in my stomach eased. When I could sit up straight, I picked up the reins and urged the horse toward home.

I decided that we'd take the train and spend Christmas with our families back home. There was much news. Two of my sisters had married since I'd moved away and one was expecting a little one soon. Mother had talked my father into buying new rugs and a settee. I knew he could well afford it, since our venture had been even more profitable than I'd hoped. Simon dropped by on Christmas Eve and surprised us all by announcing his engagement to my youngest sister.

"We'll be brothers at last, Albert!" he said.

I couldn't have been more pleased. I had a notion that my parents were pleased, as well, to have their one remaining daughter married off.

We lodged at the Hancocks' home, since they had more room, and ate Christmas dinner with them. I could tell that Mrs. Hancock wanted to question me about how things were going with Lydia, but I was careful to not find myself alone with her, thus avoiding the interrogation.

At the train station, both families saw us off and promised to visit Wren's Perch to see the tower Lydia told them so much about. We settled on an Easter gathering, before the lumber business got into full swing.

But, as my father once said, that was not to be.

We made it through the winter. We'd had little snow, following a year of little rain. Spring came early, and although the farmers were able to plow ahead of schedule, they fretted over planting in such dusty soil.

My gut continued to give me fits, especially when I sensed that Lydia was having one of her faraway spells. One Monday morning, I felt too ill to go into town to work. I put a few drops of peppermint oil on my tongue, which sometimes helped. I walked out onto the south-facing porch and sank into a chair. The fresh air soothed my nausea.

I must have dozed off. I was awakened by a dead sycamore leaf blown onto my face by a gust of wind. When I shook myself into awareness, I saw a bank of dark clouds rolling in from the southwest, flickering with lightning. I hurried to the barn in back to secure the doors in case there was a real storm in store.

"Lydia?" I called out when I walked in the back door of the house. I did not find her in the kitchen or sitting room. She did not normally take a nap this early in the day, but I checked the bedroom anyway, with no luck.

Pain stabbed at my middle as I ran up the stairs to the tower lookout room. I tried to remember the last time I'd gone up there. It must have been just after I'd finished building the house. When I reached the top landing, the door to the room was closed.

"Lydia! There's a storm on the way. You

should come downstairs."

I opened the door and paused at the threshold. All the windows were raised and the curtains whipped and twisted in the strong breeze. Dry leaves swirled across the room. The only piece of furniture was an overstuffed chair facing away from me and toward one of the front windows. I found Lydia there, wrapped in her shawl, with her knees pulled up to her chin. She stared outside, seemingly unaware of the approaching storm.

"Lydia, listen to me! We have to get downstairs . . . now!"

I began slamming the windows shut. When I got to the south side, I saw the clouds — much closer now — tumbling over themselves in greenish gray billows. I turned back to Lydia, but she was still curled up in the chair. A broken branch flew against a windowpane, cracking it.

I had no choice but to carry her. When I reached under the shawl to put my hands around her waist, I realized she was holding something close . . . a heavy garment of some kind. I tried to take it from her, but she wrapped her arms more tightly around it. It was now as dark as twilight outside, though I knew it was well before noon. Lightning shattered the sky all around us and the house trembled with shocks of thunder. I scooped Lydia up from the chair, my arms under her shoulders and knees, and made a run for the stairs. I turned sideways to carry her down the narrow stairwell. Doors slammed throughout the house and I heard glass breaking.

Just as we reached the landing at the foot of the stairs, we were surrounded by a fierce churning sound followed by a horrendous groan from above. With one great *whooof,* the roof and top floor separated from the house and I looked up to see ragged shards of the stairwell walls twisting over our heads. I laid Lydia on the square of floor we'd been standing on and covered her body as best I could with mine.

The storm was not through with us yet. I heard outside walls blowing apart and, when the stair treads began peeling off and flying upward like a deck of cards in the wind, I knew we were likely doomed. I felt myself being lifted up, up from the floor and, instinctively, I pulled Lydia's limp form close to me. Wherever I was going, I was not going to leave her here alone.

"Albert?"

I was aware of light rain pelting my face, and something else. Something damp that tickled my cheek and neck. It seemed like a long time before I could open my eyes. I lay on my back looking up at a silvery sky.

I had my arm around something . . . or someone. I cut my eyes to the right and saw Lydia's face, inches away, as she knelt over me. A red scrape covered her cheek, and her hair was down, the wet tendrils touching my neck. That's what I felt tickling me. *She was alive. I was alive. Or was I?*

"Albert . . . can you move? Can you speak?"

Those were very good questions. I wasn't sure how much of me there was to move. I also couldn't think of anything worth saying at just that moment. I willed my lips to form words.

"We . . ."

"Yes, Albert?"

"We . . . surely . . . needed the rain."

Lydia drew a sharp breath, then began to giggle. The giggle opened up into a full laugh. She lay her head on my chest, shaking with mirth. But then, the laughing turned to choked sobs, then to crying.

I did find the wherewithal to sit up and pull her close. Her body racked with deep, guttural sobs. Lydia melted against me and finally began wailing with abandon. Next to us, on the ground, was the garment she'd been holding in the tower. I recognized it as a woolen coat, but a very ragged one.

With my free hand, I dragged it closer. The coat wasn't ragged from wear. It was ripped in several places, and darkly stained.

Bloodstains! Not recent but . . . there was no mistake. It had to be Nelson's. The one he was wearing when he was killed. She'd kept it all this time!

Lydia, her sorrow down to a mild weeping, raised her face and saw me staring at the coat. She snatched it from my hand and held it out at arm's length. Her lower lip trembled as she looked at the mangled wool. Then, she turned her eyes to me and fresh tears spilled onto her cheeks.

"Albert, Albert . . . I'm so sorry. You are so good . . ."

"Oh, no. That isn't true, dear. *You* are good . . . you are the best and most beautiful thing I've ever known . . ."

"I'm not, I'm not . . . oh, I . . ." Lydia shook her head pitifully. Without looking at it again, she turned and flung Nelson's coat behind her, into the yard and out of our sight. Then, she lightly caressed my forearm, which I noticed was bleeding in a few places.

"Albert, you've only ever wanted to . . . take care of me . . . and I haven't allowed it. You have every reason to hate me . . ."

151

Without thinking, I kissed her forehead. She surprised me by throwing her arms around my neck and kissing me full on the mouth. I couldn't meet her gaze for long. I didn't somehow feel deserving of it. She lay her head against my shoulder and I looked over her at the splintered remnants of our home. The front gate and fence were gone . . . but there was a lone surviving fence post.

Now it was my turn to laugh. Lydia looked up to see what had come over me, then in the direction I was pointing. We had one fence post left, all right. And on it, steady as a rock, sat the little white wren house.

■ ■ ■ ■

Vonn McKee, Louisiana-born and descended from "horse traders and southern belles," has worked as everything from country singer to riverboat waitress to construction project manager. Now based in Nashville, she turns her experiences and love of history into stories of the West.

■ ■ ■ ■

RIDER FROM BORDEAUX
BY JOHN D. NESBITT

■ ■ ■ ■

Race Campbell rode past Larkspur Canyon as he followed the trail to the way station. In the open area of the canyon, the grass had turned to the pale green and tan hues of late summer. The larkspur blossoms, which had hung dark blue, almost purple, earlier in the season and were poisonous to horses and cattle, were dead now. Along the edges of the canyon and in the crevices, the chokecherry leaves were turning red, as were the tips of the wild plum bushes. Sporadic yellow leaves appeared on box elder trees, and a few had fallen and been carried by the wind, so that here and there a yellow leaf of autumn lay in the sun on the dry, curly grass.

Campbell watched the ground flow beneath his horse's feet as the palomino moved at a fast walk. The horse's cream-colored mane undulated with the motion, and the animal's breathing added to the peaceful sounds of thudding footfalls and creaking saddle leather.

Campbell raised his head and scanned the area around him. Outside the way station, four or five horses were tied at the hitching rails. Now that Campbell thought of it, he did not often see more than one or two other riders at the station, and it was common to find no travelers, just the owner and the two people who worked for him.

As Campbell rode up to the station, he counted the horses — two at the near rail, three at the other. He wouldn't have minded seeing none. At moments during his ride, he had wondered how others would see him today in his tall-crowned, light-colored hat, tawny sheepskin vest, white bandana, and red shirt. He thought he cut a nice figure, with brown leather chaps and an ivory-handled Colt .45 as well, but he hadn't dressed for an audience. His main interest had been to look good to Rachel, and now he had five other fellows in the way.

Campbell drew rein at the hitching rail that had only two horses. The palomino let out a sigh as Campbell swung down from the saddle and stood still. No sounds came from within the way station. Campbell loosened the cinch and looped the reins around the rail. He stood for a few seconds and listened again for voices. He heard none.

Still curious, Campbell glanced at the window on the left side of the doorway, but his vision was blocked by what looked like a gray blanket covering the entire window area from the inside. Campbell saw a reflection of himself in the pane, a duller version than he had pictured earlier when he imagined how he would look to Rachel. With the prospect of seeing her foremost in his mind, he opened the door and walked into the station.

At a glance, he counted five men — two seated at a near table, and three at a table across the room. He recognized the two on his left as cowpunchers, but the other three eluded him.

Of the three, the man in the center seemed to be the leader. He sat up straight, chin raised, with a column of cigarette smoke rising in front of him. His very posture emanated authority. He wore a dusty black hat with a creased crown, a deep blue wool shirt, a shiny black vest, and brownish-black trousers. A pistol with dark grips came into sight as he pushed back from the table, hiked one leg over the other, and took a drag on his cigarette.

"Well," he said, "Who do we have here?"

Campbell hooked his thumbs on his belt to keep his hands in plain view. "My name's Race Campbell. I work for the Randolph outfit over by Bordeaux."

"That's what I thought. Seen you in Chugwater."

"Could be. I've been there."

Campbell glanced at the other two men. The one on his left, also pushed back from the table, was a full-chested man who sat taller than average. He was dressed in shades of brown from his hat to his boots. The third man, leaning with his elbows on the table and holding a cigarette to his mouth, had a dark hat, a bad complexion, pale blue eyes, a dirty blue bandana, a gray shirt, and a sickly yellow vest.

Campbell said, "I think I might have seen you gentlemen around, but you'll have to refresh my memory."

The man in the center took another drag on his cigarette. "Names don't matter much. We don't intend to be here very long."

"My name seemed to matter when you asked me."

"I just wanted to be sure. I thought you were the stool pigeon who got Jarvis and Meyer sent up, and I was right."

Campbell drew his brows together. "I

think I know you now. You're Al Endicott, and these others are Nick Wheeler and Jackie Fulton."

Endicott said, "Well, you're smart, aren't you?"

For the first time since he walked in, Campbell laid eyes on Frank Delfino, the proprietor, where he stood in front of the counter. "Good afternoon, Frank."

" 'Lo, Race."

"Is there something I don't know yet?"

"I'll let them tell you."

Campbell shot a quick glance at the other two punchers, caught no response, and directed his attention again at Al Endicott. "Is there something going on?"

"Not much. We were just waiting for a third rider to come in so we could all get a change of horses. I don't think much of the landlord's."

Wheeler, the tall and sturdy man in brown, stood up, crossed the room, and opened the door. Daylight showed on his face as he said, "Nice fat palomino. Looks like he rode 'im easy, didn't break a sweat."

Endicott took a last drag, dropped the butt on the floor, and stepped on it. His boot had a two-inch heel, and the spur jingled. He said, "Good. Maybe I'll ride that one."

Wheeler closed the door. "Well, that's three. We can get started."

"Not until we eat." Endicott raised his chin and settled his eyes on Frank Delfino. "What's takin' the girl so long?"

"I'll go see."

"Wait here. Jackie, go take a look."

The man with the bad complexion and yellow vest pushed himself up from the table and headed for the kitchen.

Campbell gave another look at the two punchers who sat together. Their names came to him now: Harry Wainwright and Ed Merwin. "Afternoon, boys," he said.

" 'Ullo," they said together.

Endicott's voice rose on the air. "Nick, take our visitor's gun and put it in a safe place."

Campbell peered at Endicott and found himself staring at the barrel of the man's Colt. He glanced at Wheeler and registered the man's looming shape. He gave in to common sense and let Wheeler reach across him and take his pistol.

Movement at the kitchen door caught Campbell's eye. Two people came into view — Rachel jabbing her elbow, and Fulton of the yellow vest hanging onto her upper arm.

Ed Merwin half-rose from his chair until Endicott's voice cut the air. "Sit down, puncher." Then, "Let her go, Jackie."

Rachel shook herself and stood up straight. Campbell thought she looked fine in her tan dress and white apron. Her dark hair flowed in back of her shoulders, and her bronze face had a sheen from working in the kitchen.

"What do you want?" she asked. She relaxed her facial features, but her dark eyes were shining with defiance.

"What's takin' so long with the grub?" Endicott gave her an up-and-down appraisal.

"It has to cook. Bacon and potatoes aren't any good raw." She tossed a glance toward Campbell. "Hello, Race."

"Afternoon, Rachel."

Endicott let his six-gun rattle as he set it on the table. "We're a cozy bunch here, aren't we? Everyone knows everyone."

"I don't know your names," said Rachel.

"Just call us Little Jimmy Jackson and the Jigger-Y Waddies."

"Like Little Tommy Tucker. Do you sing for your supper?"

"We don't have to. And don't get too smart, sister. I haven't decided all the details yet. What's the old man doing?"

"He just finished peeling the last of the potatoes. He's watching the skillets."

"Send him out here. We don't need more than one of you in the kitchen from now on. Jackie, go with her."

As Rachel and Fulton turned to leave, Endicott said, "Sit down, Campbell. Sit at that table by yourself, and don't get in my way. I want to be able to see your two pals."

Campbell sat at the table nearest him, in the middle of the room. As he did, he realized he had not seen where Wheeler had put his pistol. Wheeler himself was standing back from the table where he and the other two had been sitting.

The kitchen door opened, and an old man came shuffling out ahead of Fulton. Campbell recognized him as Ode, the swamper and stable keeper of the way station.

"Sit down at the table with Pretty Boy," said Endicott. He had picked up his six-gun and now waved it at Campbell's table.

Ode sat across the corner on Campbell's left and gave an apologetic smile. With his washed-out blue eyes, flushed face, broken skin, and sunken cheeks, he looked harmless. He opened his mouth, showing his pink tongue and toothless gums, and said, "Got the desperadoes here today."

Campbell blinked but did not venture a nod. Within, he was rebuking himself for not keeping track of his pistol.

Endicott spoke in the direction of the proprietor. "I don't suppose you have any beer."

"No, I don't."

"Whiskey?"

"I have some of that."

"Let's have a bottle."

Wheeler pulled up his belt where his belly weighed on it. He squared his shoulders and drew himself up to his full height. "Let's not get too settled in here," he said.

"No hurry," said Endicott. "The grub's not ready yet, and for all we know, someone might ride in with a fourth horse for us."

"What do we need another horse for?"

"Like I said, I haven't decided all the details yet. But we might want to take the girl."

Merwin shifted in his chair and tapped the table with his fingers.

Endicott said, "I think I know what ails you, puncher. You'd be better to let it rest."

Merwin had dislike written all over his face, but he said nothing.

Frank Delfino crossed Campbell's field of vision, carrying a whiskey bottle and a glass. He set the two items on the table in front of Endicott. After a nod, he moved back half a step and waited with his hands folded in front of his white apron.

Endicott still held his six-gun and rested it on the back of his free hand. He said, "Pour me about half a glassful. And don't block my view."

The proprietor poured the whiskey, set the bottle down, and returned to his place by the counter. Once there, he raised both hands and ran his fingers through his dark hair.

Ode began to move in a strange, gyrating matter, rocking his shoulders and moving his chin forward and back.

Endicott said, "What's eatin' on you, old man?"

"I'd like to have a drink of that whiskey."

"You don't need any."

"I get nervous. You've got us here like rats in a cage, and you keep a gun pointed at me."

"Get used to it. If no one acts up, no one gets hurt."

Wheeler stood with his hand on his hip as he kept an eye on the five hostages. "Let's not drag things out," he said.

Endicott set down his glass after taking a sip. "We're waiting for grub. If you want to do something, go to the kitchen and make sure Jackie's not up to anything. We don't need him tryin' to get his finger in the pie."

Wheeler pivoted and left the room.

Campbell made a quarter turn and saw the smoky glare that Merwin was giving Endicott. With Wheeler and Fulton both out of the room, Campbell thought there might be a way to rush Endicott, if only he, Campbell, could communicate with Merwin.

The moment passed as Endicott kept his pistol pointed at Merwin and said, "The kitchen girl asked if we sing. Well, I don't. How about you?"

Merwin shrugged.

The front door swung open without any sign of caution, and a blond young man walked in. He wore his hat with the brim turned up in front, and he had a blue bandana knotted and hanging from his neck. He was slender and wore a loose-fitting gray work shirt with no collar. His vest was unbuttoned, and his pistol butt swayed as he walked forward in an easy motion.

"What's the party?" he called out. "I never seen this many fellas here all at one time."

"Hold it right there," said Endicott as he brandished his pistol.

The young man's face fell. "What's going on?"

"Shut up and sit down. But first, take your gun out careful-like and set it on the table here in front of me."

The young man laid his gun on the table.

"Where'd you come from?"

"Dutch Flats."

"That's good. Now you sit down with those other two, and do what I say."

The young man gave a sulky look and sat down next to Wainwright, across from Merwin.

Wheeler came out of the kitchen at a jaunty gait with his hand on the butt of his pistol. "Got another one, huh?" He reached for the young man's handgun on the table.

Campbell watched as Wheeler set the pistol in a brown valise sitting on the floor next to Endicott's chair.

Wheeler straightened up. "I sent Jackie out to look over the horses."

Endicott said, "We need to change saddles, you know."

The blond young man said, "What kind of a holdup is this, anyway?"

"You'll find out," said Endicott. "Just stay put."

Wheeler remained standing with his hand resting on his pistol.

Campbell sensed again that the moment for revolt had passed. He would have to be ready for the next possibility, and he assumed the outlaws would be ready as well.

Wheeler said, "Grub should be out in a few minutes."

"Good." Endicott set the bottle farther aside and took a sip from his glass.

No one spoke for a couple of minutes. Faint, dull sounds came from the kitchen. Campbell imagined Rachel moving cast-iron skillets on a cast-iron stovetop.

The front door opened, and Fulton walked in. His yellow vest caught the daylight, while his rough-complexioned face lay in shadow. He stood in the middle of the room. "This latest horse ain't much," he said.

Campbell gazed at Fulton. The man's head swayed, almost in a swagger, as if he enjoyed the chance to be superior. Time slowed for a few seconds, and then things broke loose.

The blond young man moved quick as a cat, throwing his left arm around Fulton's throat and grabbing with his right hand at Fulton's pistol. The gun did not slide out at first, so the young man gave another yank. Meanwhile, Wheeler stepped to one side and fired two shots. Fulton sagged out of the young man's grasp, and Endicott fired a shot that hit the young man in the chest. The hat with the upturned brim slid away, and the blond man showed a wide, surprised look as he opened his mouth and fell backward.

Campbell, the old man, and the other two punchers had all scrambled out of the way of the gunfire and now crouched in their separate places as they kept their eyes on the center of the room.

Fulton was crawling on all fours.

Endicott's spurs jingled as he rose from his chair. He said, "Are you hit, Jackie?"

"I think so."

Wheeler spoke in a steady voice. "I'm sorry, Jackie. But I had to shoot this bird before he got all of us." Wheeler held his gun at his side. "Where are you hit?"

"In the ribs, I think."

"Is it bad?"

"I don't know. It hurts like hell."

Endicott spoke in a commanding tone as he waved his pistol. "The rest of you fellas, get back into your seats. Where's the owner?"

Frank Delfino raised his head from behind the counter. "I'm over here."

"Well, get out where I can see you. Jackie, are you going to be able to ride?"

Fulton said, "I think so. I hope so."

"Good. Get over here and sit where you were before."

Fulton, still on all fours, tried to rise but

fell back onto his hands. He said, "I'd like someone to look at me and tell me how bad it is. I can't tell, but it might be worse than I thought. It hurts like a son of a bitch."

"All right." Endicott hesitated, then spoke to Wheeler. "Nick, take Jackie's gun so no one lays a hand on it." As Wheeler moved, Endicott waved his gun again and said, "Now, you, landlord, and you in the red shirt, Campbell, the two of you help Jackie get up. Lay him out on the counter, open his shirt, and see what it looks like."

Campbell stood up and waited for Frank Delfino, whose hands were shaking. They stood on either side of Jackie Fulton and lifted him by his upper arms. They helped him stagger to the counter, and once there, they boosted him up and turned him so that he could lie stretched out.

The yellow vest was stained with blood, as was the gray shirt. Campbell unbuttoned the vest and set the two halves aside. The shirt had only two buttons at the top, so he could not open the shirt but rather had to pull it up. As he did, the wound came into view.

He shuddered at the sight of the pulpy red hole with blood oozing out and an irregular bloodshot area spreading away on all sides in blue and purple splotches.

Campbell went around the counter to the other side, where he would not have to reach across the man's abdomen. Standing close to Fulton's hip, he reached forward in slow motion and touched the man's ribs. From there, he moved his hand and pressed with his fingers. Whatever lay inside the rib cage, a third of the way to the navel, had the path of a bullet torn through it.

"What's it look like?" said Fulton. His hat was gone, and his pale forehead contrasted with the rest of his face, which was weathered and also dotted with rough red spots.

"Not very good," said Campbell. "It did more than graze you. It went through here. Can you feel this? I'm not sure what's there, as far as your insides, but there's damage. I would guess that it's bleeding inside as well as out. But I'm no doctor."

Fulton nodded his head, closed his eyes, and let out a long, heavy breath.

Campbell caught a direct look from Frank Delfino but didn't know what to make of it. Then his attention was distracted by Endicott's voice as he spoke to Wheeler.

"Let's take a look at this one and make sure he's done for."

Campbell felt something in the boss's tone. Endicott was keeping Fulton at a distance and changing the focus of his attention. Campbell sensed, with certainty, that Endicott was steeling himself to leave Fulton behind if he had to.

As Endicott and Wheeler went to stand over the body of the dead blond man, Campbell met Frank Delfino's eyes. The innkeeper made a slight frown and directed his gaze downward. After Delfino made the gesture a couple of times, Campbell followed its direction by standing back and stealing a glance beneath the counter. A gray towel covered an object about the size of a moccasin or slipper.

Campbell stepped forward and let his eyes rove over Fulton's wound and his rising and falling midsection. At the same time, he felt with his hands. He found the towel, worked his hand under it, and felt the cool metal surface of a six-gun.

He raised his eyes to meet Delfino's, and an understanding passed between them. The landlord was telling Campbell where the gun was, and he was expecting him to use it. Delfino had gone as far as he was going to go, and the rest was up to Campbell.

Endicott's spurs sounded as he and Wheeler turned away from the body on the floor. In a voice that was a little too loud and had an artificial tone of encouragement, Endicott said, "How are you doing, Jackie?"

Fulton opened his eyes, and without moving, he said, "I don't like the way I feel. I'm thirsty, and everything seems dizzy."

"That's normal," said Endicott. "You've lost a little blood. We'll get you some water." Turning to Ode, he said, "Gramps, get a glass of water for this man."

The old swamper stood up, unsteady on his feet. He rested one hand on his chair, and the other was shaking. "Can I go to the kitchen?"

"Of course you can. And tell whatsername to bring that grub out here." Turning to Campbell and Delfino, he said, "You two can sit down."

Campbell said, "I'll help him with his water when it gets here, if you want."

Endicott directed his gaze at Delfino. "Landlord, sit at the table where the old man and this fellow have been sitting."

Campbell stood idle, trying to look as dumb as possible. At the same time, he was tormented with the idea that a pistol lay within reach, but a false move could make things twice as bad as they already were.

Endicott moved toward his own table, made a slow turn, and sat down. Wheeler remained standing, then stepped around the table to the chair where Fulton had sat earlier. After taking a full view of the room, he patted his pistol in its holster and took a seat.

The kitchen door opened, and Rachel came out carrying two platters of fried food. As she walked past, Campbell recognized the reddish-brown strips of bacon and the golden-brown slices of fried potato. The aroma drifted in their wake.

Rachel set the two dishes on the table and turned to leave.

"Stay here, sister," said the boss as he reached across the corner of the table and took her by the arm. "We might want something else."

Rachel pulled away, and once free, she swallowed hard. "You don't seem bothered much by just having killed a man. Enjoy your meal."

"He brought it on himself," said Endicott. "I'm not goin' to sit here and let someone shoot me. Neither is Nick."

Rachel turned to leave, and Endicott's voice barked.

"Stay here."

"I have work in the kitchen."

"You're done in there for right now. Sit down." Endicott pointed at the table where Frank Delfino had taken a seat.

"I don't want to sit down."

Endicott raised his chin. "Don't make me

put you in your seat."

Merwin stood up and said, "Don't touch her, mister."

Endicott made a slow turn, his hand hovering over his pistol. "Everyone wants to be a hero." He motioned with his head toward the body on the floor. "That could be you. And for your information, I already touched her. I'll do it again if she doesn't do as I say."

Rachel took a chair next to her boss, where she faced Endicott and Wheeler. Ed Merwin sat down.

Campbell kept still, hoping to remain inconspicuous. As his eyes wandered over the scene, he realized that Rachel was wearing a red ribbon in her hair. She hadn't been wearing it earlier. He wished he was in freer circumstances to appreciate it and to think about how to act in response.

Half a minute passed by, and Ode came hobbling out from the kitchen. Instead of a glass of drinking water, he held a long-handled pot with both hands. Steam rose from the pot. The old man headed toward the outlaws' table.

"What's that?" said Endicott. "I told you to bring him some water to drink."

"You'll need this to clean the wound." Ode stood with the pot trembling in his hands, and his eyes shifted.

Campbell had a strong hunch that the old man had come with the idea of flinging the hot water on Endicott, and now he had lost nerve.

Endicott spoke with full authority. "Set that pot on the table, and go get a glass of water like I told you."

The old man did as he was told, lowering the pot to the table in front of Endicott. He backed away a step and turned. After a second's delay, in what seemed to be an act of frustration, he kicked at a chair next to the table where Rachel and Delfino sat. They both flinched, but Endicott showed repose by lifting a strip of bacon and putting it in his mouth.

For no apparent reason, Frank Delfino fell out of his chair and slumped on the floor.

This is it, Campbell said to himself. Delfino was providing the distraction. Campbell pushed his hands under the counter, flipped away the towel, got a grip on the pistol, and brought it out. Time seemed to slow down as Campbell saw the nickel-plated .45 for the first time and raised it to find his aim. He had to keep his eye on two men.

Nick Wheeler rose from his chair, drew his sidearm, and turned toward Campbell.

At the same time, Al Endicott pushed himself back from the table, drew his pistol, and fired two shots in the direction of the other two punchers. Merwin, half-risen from his chair, spilled over backwards.

Campbell settled on Wheeler. The big man made a clear target fifteen feet away as he faced Campbell and pointed his six-gun. Campbell drew back the hammer on the unfamiliar pistol, held steady with both hands, and pulled the trigger. As the gun roared and Wheeler fell back, Endicott stood up and turned. He raised his pistol with one hand, pointing it as if he was pointing his finger, and fired. The gun jerked, however, and his shot went wide. In one smooth motion, Campbell lined up again with both hands, cocked the hammer, settled the front sight into the notch, and squeezed the trigger. The blast filled the room.

Endicott's black hat tumbled away, and his pistol clattered on the floor. His hand turned crimson as he pressed his abdomen. Time stretched out again for a long few seconds until his knees buckled and he fell. His spurs gave a faint jingle and went still.

Campbell surveyed the room. He was the only one standing. Rachel and her boss were crouched beneath their table. Harry Wainwright lay flat on his stomach with his head lifted as he watched the scene. Jackie Fulton had rolled off the counter and landed on the floor. The old man, Ode, had disappeared.

Campbell helped Rachel to her feet as Frank Delfino crawled out and stood up.

Harry Wainwright pushed himself up straight and walked to the center of the room to join them. "Ed's done for," he said.

Campbell frowned. "Why did Endicott shoot him, anyway?"

"He was just standing up."

"That's too bad," said Frank Delfino. "There was nothing wrong with Ed." He raised his eyes to meet Campbell's. "I'm glad you did what you did, Race."

Campbell realized he still had the landlord's pistol in his hand. He turned it around and held it out, butt forward. "There was no other way, I guess, once things went that far. But none of this had to happen." He looked down at the body of Al Endicott. "Poison," he said. "I don't know if they're born with it or they turn that way, but that's what it is."

■ ■ ■ ■

John D. Nesbitt lives in the plains country of Wyoming, where he writes western, contemporary, mystery, and retro/noir fiction as well as nonfiction and poetry. His recent books include *Dark Prairie, Death in Cantera,* and *Destiny at Dry Camp,* frontier mysteries with Five Star.

■ ■ ■ ■

An Hour Before the Hangman by Michael R. Ritt

■ ■ ■ ■

EASTERN COLORADO, 1885

"I was fourteen when I killed my first man."

Toby Lang sat up in bed and swung his legs over the edge. He pulled his boots on over his stocking feet and looked at me sideways to see if his confession had shocked me at all. I glanced at him through the steel bars of the cell that had housed him for the past twenty-nine days. Jotting down a few notes in my notebook, I looked up at him and asked, "Who did you kill?"

"My pa."

He must have seen the shocked expression in my eyes when he said that because he smiled.

"You killed your own father?"

"Yep." He lay back down on his bunk and placed his hands behind his head. He waited for the question that he knew I was going to ask.

"Why did you kill your father? What were

the circumstances?"

"The circumstances were that he was a mean bastard. The only thing that he liked more than beating on my ma and me was drinking, and drinking made him even meaner."

"This was back in Chicago?"

"Yeah, we moved there from Ohio in '72, when I was nine years old. My pa worked as a laborer rebuilding parts of the city that were destroyed a year earlier in the big fire."

I made another notation in my notebook while Lang continued.

"After a year or so, he went to work in the stockyards. One night he came home, staggering through the front door. I was in my bedroom, but I could hear him and my ma in the kitchen. He started yelling at her about dinner being cold, and he started slapping her around. I heard her crying out as she was being knocked around; dishes were breaking; Pa was yelling; I couldn't take it anymore. I knew that sooner or later he was going to kill her, and when he was done beating her, he would come after me. That was his pattern."

He stopped talking and laid there on his bunk, staring up at the corner of the ceiling. I thought at first that he was being introspective, only to realize that he had been distracted by a cockroach that had crawled out of a crack in the plaster and was making its way across the ceiling of the ten-by-eight cell.

"What did you do?" I asked, bringing him back to his story.

"I made my way into the kitchen, grabbed a knife from the table, snuck up behind him, and buried the blade to the hilt in his back," he said nonchalantly.

He sat back up again and got to his feet. He walked over to the front of his cell and stared at me as I sat in the chair in the hallway on the other side of the bars that separated us.

"Are you going to put that in your story?"

I removed my derby hat and took a handkerchief from my coat pocket. The eastern plains of Colorado were hot this time of year, and I used the handkerchief to wipe the sweat from my brow and from the inside of my hat's brim.

"I'll put it in, but it's up to my editor to decide what to print," I said. I knew that my editor would leave it in. This was the sort of sensational stuff that sold newspapers, and the folks in town would want to know all about the convicted killer that was sitting in their jail waiting to be hung.

Not that they didn't already know about

him. Toby Lang's trial had been front page news for the past week, and the details of his brutal killing of twenty-five-year-old Lester Rhodes were well known to everyone in the small community. But my editor had sent me here to get the "story behind the story," as he called it. So here I was on this hot August day, sweltering in this jail, interviewing a killer, when, if I had had my way, I'd of been sitting under a cottonwood along the banks of the South Platte with a cane pole in my hands.

Lang shook his finger in my direction and said, "You make sure that he keeps that part in. That's an important detail."

He walked back to his bunk and sat down. He leaned forward, resting his elbows on his knees, and waited for my next question.

"What happened after you killed your father?"

"My ma was in shock at first, lying on the kitchen floor with a bloody nose and a swollen eye from where he hit her. She grabbed me and pulled me close. The two of us sat there on the kitchen floor, holding onto each other and crying. Ma was really scared for me because of what I done. She brushed away her tears and said, 'You've got to leave.' Searching through my pa's pockets, she found fourteen dollars and sixty-three cents. She shoved the money into my hands and told me to get as far away as I could."

He hung his head and sighed. Without looking up, he said, "I left Chicago that night and never went back. I ain't seen my ma since."

"How long ago was that?" I asked.

He looked in my direction only a moment before turning away and hanging his head. We sat in silence for a few moments. Afterwards, I heard him quietly mutter, "It's been eight years."

"Did you never try to write to her; let her know where you were or what you were doing?"

"What was I supposed to write to her about?" he said. "Should I have told her all about how I had become a thief and a killer? No," he shook his head from side to side, "it's best that she never finds out what's become of me."

Toby jumped to his feet as a thought occurred to him. He walked over and stood in front of me. Placing his hands on the bars of his cell, lines of worry creased his brow. "If this story goes into your paper, is there a chance that she can read about it back in Chicago?" He had only considered his local notoriety. The thought that his story might have national appeal never crossed his mind.

I knew that there was a chance that the Associated Press would pick up the story. Eastern newspapers were always eager to print accounts from the "wild and untamed" western states. My own thinking was that it offered them a distraction from reporting on the stories of political corruption and industrial greed that filled the pages of their own papers.

"There's always a chance," I told him, "but she would have to pick up the right paper on the right day, so the chance is probably pretty slim."

My answer seemed to satisfy him, so he resumed his seat on the edge of his bunk. He continued his narrative without waiting for me to ask another question.

"After I left home, I made my way to the rail yard and stole aboard a train that was pointed toward the setting sun."

"That must have been frightening for you, being on your own at such a young age."

Lang cocked his head to one side and looked at me. His blue eyes were rather startling when you looked at him. They were bright and piercing; intelligent eyes that could have belonged to a teacher or a minister. He had light brown, wavy hair, and although he hadn't shaved in at least a month, there was barely any facial hair on his boyish face. "Not really," he replied. "I mean it was and it wasn't. I'd never been away from home before. That was scary. But I was excited to be on my own. It was an adventure."

"Where did you wind up?"

"I had a little food and water that I had left home with. It lasted me two days, and I stayed on that train the whole time. Once I ran out of food, I jumped off at the first stop that it made. I had no idea where I was. I found out later that I had landed in some little God-forsaken place in Dawson County, Nebraska, along the Platte."

The point of the pencil stub that I had been using had worn down to the wood, so I removed a small penknife from my pocket and proceeded to sharpen a new one. I wiped away some shavings and blew gently along the length of the new tip and continued with my interview.

"What did you do when you got to Nebraska?"

Lang smiled and laughed. "Have you ever *been* to Nebraska?"

I laughed at his joke. I thought it was unusual for a man who was about to be hanged to be cracking wise, and I decided to try to work it into my story if I could. "I don't imagine that fourteen dollars lasted very long. What did you do to survive?"

"There was an elderly Mennonite couple named Stauffer that owned a store. They took me in. They let me sleep in a room in the back of the store and Mrs. Stauffer fed me good. She was a real good cook, although some of that German food was a little strange. Old man Stauffer let me work in the store, sweeping floors and stocking the shelves. It was a pretty good setup. They were good people."

I saw the corners of his mouth turn downward, and he had a sad, faraway look in his eyes. I asked him, "How long were you with the Stauffers?"

He gave a weak smile and said, "Two years."

"What was it like living with them?"

Lang stretched out on his bunk again. He bunched up his pillow under his head and lay on his back with his hands folded on his chest. When I looked up from writing in my notebook and saw him like that, for a second or two I saw him stretched out in a cheap, pine box that the county would buy. I saw the lid nailed down and the coffin lowered into a cold, dark, unmarked grave in the cemetery outside of town.

When Lang did start to answer my question, it startled me, and I think I actually jumped a little to hear him speak.

"Those two years were probably the happiest time of my life. The Stauffers were kind to me. I was well fed, I had a job, and I had a place to stay. I even started to go to the Mennonite meeting house. Mr. Stauffer was an elder in the church, and I used to like to listen to him when he stood up in front of everyone and read from the Bible. He had a deep, thundering voice when he read the scriptures. If I closed my eyes, I could believe I was hearing Moses standing on the shore of the Red Sea, commanding the waters to part."

Lang went silent at that point, lost, I could imagine, in a vision of rushing chariots of Egyptians chasing the Hebrew children into the parted waters of the Red Sea; watching as the wall of water on either side came crashing down on the pursuing army as the Hebrews climbed safely out on the opposite shore.

I stared at Lang as he lay there, lost in his thoughts. I took a good, long look at him. My God, I thought, he's only a boy. Not much older than my own son. How is it possible that a young man could throw away his life before it had barely begun?

I thought about my own son, who was in his second year of college studying engineering at the Colorado School of Mines. He got good grades; he was popular and well mannered. He had his whole future ahead of him.

I began to think about what happens when someone dies. Not the details of death, but the impact of a man's death — especially a young man. Toby Lang could have had a productive life. He could have been a farmer or a tradesman of some kind. He might have met a girl and fallen in love. He could have gotten married and had children and grandchildren. And who knows what any of them might have done with their lives; doctors, teachers, maybe even a President. He could have been the seed of something great. Instead, in less than an hour he would die at the end of a rope and all of what could have been will die along with him.

But was it really his fault, or was he the victim of circumstances? After all, he was brought up in poverty with an abusive father. That's a rough way for anyone to have to start out. Maybe if he had been brought up in a healthy environment, with loving and supportive parents, he would have turned out differently.

Then I remembered John Wesley Hardin, who was in Huntsville Prison down in Texas. He killed his first man when he was fifteen years old; almost the same age as Lang. He had a loving mother and his father was a Methodist preacher.

I felt sorry for Lang, but I also felt strangely angry at him. He should have made better choices with his life. He chose to stab his father. He chose to shoot Lester Rhodes to death. Only Lang knew how many others he had killed. He had no one to blame for his predicament but himself.

"What are you gonna call your story?" Lang's question brought me back from my contemplation. I looked over at him. He had rolled over onto his side, with his elbow on his pillow, and was resting his head in his hand.

"What's that?"

"The story you're writing about me . . . what are you gonna call it?"

"I haven't really thought about a name yet."

Lang jumped off of his bunk and walked over to stand in front of me. "I think you should call it, 'The Daring Exploits of Toby Lang,' " he said excitedly. "Or," he said, snapping his fingers and grinning, "you could call it, 'Toby Lang, Devil of the West.' " He hitched his thumbs in his collar and puffed out his chest. "Yeah, I like that one." He strutted over to the far side of the cell, obviously pleased with his suggestion.

"I usually don't name the story until after I've written it," I informed him, "But I'll take those suggestions into consideration."

"I think that last one that I gave you is pretty catchy. You should use that one."

Smiling, I nodded and asked, "You were telling me about your time in Nebraska. If you liked it there so much, why did you leave?"

A scowl formed on his face and his eyes narrowed. "That's all because of Bob Harper."

"Who's Bob Harper?" I wrote the name down in my notebook.

"There were four of us boys that use to hang around together. Bob was the oldest. He was nineteen and he was also the biggest. I guess you could say that he was our leader. There wasn't a whole lot to do in town, so he would get a bottle of whiskey and we would all go down to the river and get drunk. Bob always seemed to have some money on him, but none of us knew what he did to earn it. He didn't have a regular job of any kind.

"I guess I started neglecting my sweeping and other duties at the store so I could hang out more with the boys. One time we got so liquored up that we stole some horses from the livery and raced them through town. Another time, we stole some dynamite from the railroad and blew up an outhouse." Lang had a good laugh over that recollection. "There was nobody hurt, but they found pieces of the seat in Mrs. Nelson's flower garden a quarter of a mile away."

"It sounds like this Bob Harper wasn't a very good influence on you."

"Me and the rest of the boys thought he was dandy. We looked up to him. But one day I drank too much and couldn't make it back home. I passed out right in the middle of the road in front of the store. Mr. Stauffer came out and picked me up and carried me inside and put me to bed. I guess that he got pretty mad. He stormed out of the store and down the street to the saloon where Bob was."

"Did he confront Bob?"

Lang had taken a seat on the floor and had his back up against his bunk. He was seated at a right angle to me. His knees were up in the air and he had his arms wrapped around them. When he talked, he rocked slightly back and forth. I could tell that this particular memory was a difficult one for him to talk about.

"I only heard about what happened afterwards. Remember, I was passed out in my room in back of the store. I heard that old man Stauffer did the last thing that anyone would have expected a Mennonite elder to do. He marched into the saloon and walked right up behind Bob. He spun him around, grabbed him by the collar, and lifted him right off of the floor.

"They told me that Bob's eyes were big as saucers. No one had ever stood up to him before, and Stauffer was a big man.

"Mr. Stauffer told him that if he ever came near me again that he would drag him down to the river and hold his head under so that he was properly baptized to meet his maker. He threw him down on the floor like a rag doll and turned and walked out of the saloon.

"Bob, who was still on the floor, where Mr. Stauffer had deposited him, got up, grabbed a bottle from the bar, and stormed out with the sound of laughter from the bar's patrons ringing in his ears."

Lang was rocking back and forth more quickly now, staring at the floor in front of him.

I waited, but Lang had stopped talking, so I asked, "What happened next?"

"Later that evening, the Stauffers were getting ready to close up the store, when Bob came in and shot them both dead."

Lang continued to stare at the floor in front of him. He didn't look in my direction, but he made no effort to hide the tears that were in his eyes. He wiped them away with the back of his hand and took his time getting to his feet. I gave him a few seconds to compose himself before I asked, "What happened next?"

"After Bob shot them, he and one of the other guys we hung out with — Danny Motson — took the money out of the cash drawer and left town. I was so stinking drunk that I slept through the whole thing."

Lang walked over to the front of his cell and stood there facing me. His eyes were wide and when he spoke, it was with an earnestness that belied his usual haughty demeanor. "I tell you the gospel truth. I have done a lot of bad things since that day, and I'll own up to every one of them. But I swear I haven't touched a single drop of liquor in the six years since."

Putting his hands into his pockets, Lang turned slowly and walked to the opposite end of the cell. Pivoting on his heels, he turned around and walked back. He did this several times before he returned to his bunk. "The church buried the Stauffers a few days later. I had some money saved up, so I bought a horse and gun and I took off up the Platte, cuz that's the direction that Bob and Danny had gone when they left town. I told myself right then and there that I wouldn't rest until I had caught up with Bob and made him pay for what he had done. Consequences be damned, he was gonna get his."

I had been writing everything down that Lang had been saying. I knew that this was front page material. It was precisely the kind of a story that my editor was looking for. I flipped over another page in my notebook and asked, "Did you ever catch up with them?"

"I didn't know anything about tracking at the time. I had a general direction to go, but I had no idea where they had gone or if I would ever see them again. Almost three years went by before I ran into one of them, and that was Danny."

I had been sitting for too long and my legs were starting to go numb. I stood to my feet to start the blood circulating again. I rolled myself a cigarette and asked Lang if he wanted one too. He walked over to the bars and took one from me. We stood there leaning against the bars, he on one side, me on the other, while we smoked.

I picked up my pad and pencil, which I had left on my chair. "What did you do in those three years leading up to your encounter with Danny?"

Lang took a draw on his cigarette, letting the smoke escape from between his lips. It drifted upward until it reached the plastered ceiling, which had been stained a yellowish-brown from previous years of accumulated cigarette smoke. "I did what I had to. I learned to steal, I learned to gamble, and I learned how to ride and how to shoot. I also grew a couple of inches and put on a few pounds."

"Did you kill anyone else during that time?" I looked him square in the eyes. He met my gaze and answered back without blinking.

"I shot a few people who didn't rob easy. I suspect some of them died."

He dropped the cigarette stub onto the floor and rubbed it out with the tip of his boot. Walking back over to his bunk, he took the pillow and fluffed it up, resting it against the wall. He sat down on his bed with his back against the pillow and crossed his legs Indian fashion. Reaching down with his left hand, he produced a deck of cards that had been stashed under the mattress and proceeded to deal out a solitaire hand.

I finished my cigarette and sat back down. Turning to a new page in my notebook, I asked, "So, where did you run into Danny and what happened when you did?"

Lang sat there, flipping over cards as he continued with his story. "It happened over in Julesburg about three years ago. I had been in town less than a day and was out walking around to see what it had to offer. Who do you think steps around a corner right in front of me? That's right, Danny Motson, standing no further away from me than you are right now. We both stood there, frozen, staring at each other. Before I could say anything, he went for his gun. I was faster and my bullet caught him right in the center of his chest.

"My shot had spun him around a little and pushed him back into the corner of the building. He slumped down onto the board-walk and sat there with his hand on his chest. I remember seeing the blood pump-ing out of his wound through his fingers. 'What'd you draw on me for, Danny?' I asked. He had a hard time breathing, so he couldn't talk too well.

" 'I figured you were after me and Bob,' he struggled to get the words out.

"I got down on my knees and helped him to lie down on his back on the boardwalk. People were gathering around us to see what had happened. I said to him, 'You didn't have no part in killing the Stauffers. It's Bob that I'm after. Where is he?'

"Danny's breathing was shallow and his lips were turning purple. There was frothy blood trickling out of the corners of his mouth and out of the hole in his chest. He mumbled something that I couldn't make out and he died before I could find out where Bob Harper was."

Lang stopped talking so I looked up from my writing. There was genuine sadness when I looked into his eyes. "How did you feel about shooting Danny?"

Lang frowned and slowly shook his head. "I've killed people and never given it a second thought, but I regret killing Danny. He was my friend."

From outside of the jail, we heard a creaking noise followed by a thud. Lang got up and walked over to the one tiny window that his cell provided. He had to grasp the bars and stand on his tiptoes to see out into the yard that butted up against the side of the building. We could barely make out a couple of men's voices.

"That ought to do the trick," said the first man.

"What are you trying to accomplish?" asked the second man. "Are you aiming for a clean break, or are we going to get to watch him dance around for a bit?" The second man laughed at his own joke.

"I get paid to perform a humane hanging," said the first man in a more subdued tone, "and that's what we're gonna have."

"Well, you're the hangman," said the second man. "Your way may be more humane, but it certainly isn't very entertaining."

We heard the trapdoor on the scaffold creak as it dropped open, followed by a thud as the sandbag dropped through the opening, drawing the rope taut with a snap.

Lang backed away from the window. He bumped against his bunk and sat down heavily, scattering the cards that he had laid out on the bed. His eyes were wide and his face was ashen. His mouth hung open and he muttered something that I couldn't make out. He looked at me with eyes like those of a scared child. "Have you ever seen a man get hanged before?" he asked.

I told him that I had.

"I heard that when a man gets hanged, he shits himself. Is that true?"

I uncrossed my legs and leaned forward in my chair with my elbows on my knees. I was uncomfortable talking to him about it, but I figured that this is where his life had brought him; this was the culmination of a life's worth of decisions for him. He might as well know the truth. "It's a common thing when someone dies, whether it's from hanging or being shot or dying of old age — it doesn't matter. The muscles that constrict the bowels and the bladder relax and the dying person empties himself. It's natural."

I could see his Adam's apple moving up and down as he tried to swallow, but his mouth seemed too dry for the effort. He sat silently on his bed for several minutes. He seemed pretty shook up, and I was afraid that he wouldn't be able to continue with the interview. "Are you okay to go on?" I asked.

Lang looked at me and nodded.

"All right, do you want to tell me what happened after you shot Danny?"

When he spoke, his voice was weak and shaky. He cleared his throat and hesitated a moment before continuing. "Julesburg was a rough town. Not like it was in its earlier days, but there were still plenty of rough characters around. They were used to fights and people shooting at each other. They had a town marshal, but witnesses testified that Danny tried to draw down on me first. As it turned out, the marshal was impressed by my ability to handle a gun. He was short-handed, so he offered me a job as deputy."

I stopped writing and looked up from my notebook. "Are you telling me that you were a deputy town marshal over in Julesburg?"

Lang walked over to the bars and leaned casually against them. He laughed at my incredulity. "Is that really so hard to believe? You'd be surprised how many men walked a fine line between lawman and outlaw — men like Ben Thompson, King Fisher, Luke Gains; even Billy the Kid wore a badge when he rode with the Regulators."

Of course, Lang was right. The distinction between lawman and outlaw was often a blurry one, and a lot of men would jump from one side to the other when it suited them.

"How did you like working as a deputy?"

Lang gave a shrug. "Parts of the job were okay. It made me a big man in town and I liked that. Here I was, only nineteen years old, and I was rounding up drunks and troublemakers, throwing them in jail. I got into a couple of gunfights, so my reputation started to spread."

He asked me for another cigarette, so I got one out and handed it to him. "What didn't you like about the job?" I asked as I struck a match and stuck it through the steel bars of the cell.

Lang took a long draw of the cigarette; closing his eyes, he exhaled slowly, savoring the taste of the tobacco, or maybe it was the aroma of the smoke that he was enjoying. He opened his eyes and smiled. "You know, my ma caught me smoking once when I was ten years old. She blistered my hide so bad I couldn't sit down for a week."

I smiled and told him that the same thing had happened to me when I was twelve.

He walked over to where the barred window was located and sat down on the floor beneath it with his back against the wall. There were still some muffled sounds coming from outside, but they apparently had finished testing the gallows so the sounds had subsided considerably.

As he sat there, I watched the smoke from his cigarette being drawn upward where it escaped between the bars and out the window into the sunshine of the Colorado grasslands. I wondered to myself if Toby Lang had ever considered trying to escape from jail during his past month of incarceration. I made a notation in my notebook to remind me to ask him about it before I finished with the interview.

"What didn't I like about the job?" Lang repeated. He finished the cigarette, flicking the stub into a corner. "I guess the worse part was the pay. Being a civil servant didn't pay worth beans. Being a deputy was only my second regular job, but it wasn't like working for the Stauffers. I had to pay all of my own expenses; rent, food, clothes, and whatnot."

"How did you manage?"

"There was one other deputy besides me. He was the one that came up with the idea of him and me starting an 'insurance' company."

I wasn't sure what to make of his statement, so I said, "Something tells me that your insurance company wasn't strictly on the up-and-up."

Lang laughed as he got to his feet and walked over to stand in front of me. "There was a time when the marshal had to go to Denver for a couple of weeks, so he left me and Jake in charge — Jake was the other deputy. He was a tall, thin fellow who was almost twice my age. He had the reputation of a bully, but him and I got along all right. I think he always figured that he should have been the town marshal, so when Marshal Cooper left for Denver, Jake's head swelled up with his new authority.

"Anyways, we figured that it was our job to keep the peace, and if the town council wasn't going to compensate us sufficiently, we would have to make other arrangements. So we started charging some of the businesses in town a fee for our insurance services. We would allow them to run their businesses as they saw fit — without any interference from the law — and they would pay a small percentage of their daily take. We didn't bother with any of the small businesses in town. Mostly it was the saloons, the gaming houses, and the bordellos."

"And they went along with that?" I said in disbelief.

"Well, the first saloon we approached didn't buy into it. They said they could get along without our insurance. Unfortunately," he said with a wink, "that night someone broke into the place and busted it all to hell. After that we didn't have any trouble with any of the others."

I made some notes in my notebook, underlining the word "extortion" for my story. "You do realize the difference between legitimate insurance and what you were doing, don't you?"

Shrugging, Lang went back to his bunk and lay down. "Insurance might not be the right word, but it was a business arrangement that worked out nicely for everyone involved. For a few dollars a day, Jake and I would look the other way at some activities that Marshal Cooper wouldn't allow. The saloons wound up taking in more than they otherwise would have been able to do, and Jake and I made more money in those two weeks than we could have made in two years on a deputy's pay."

"So what happened when Marshal Cooper got back from Denver? What did he think of your 'insurance' company?"

"There's no one more by the book than Cooper. When he got back to town and found out what was going on, he came looking for Jake and me. I had already figured to make as much money as I could in those two weeks and hightail it out of town. I didn't want any trouble with Cooper. I was pretty good with a gun, but Cooper was the real deal.

"Jake, on the other hand, figured that he had a good thing going and had no intention of giving it up. He figured he could kill Cooper and bully the town council into keeping him on as the marshal."

"I take it that's not the way that it played out."

Lang grinned as he replied, "If anyone could have used insurance that day, it was Jake. He tried to draw on Cooper but didn't even clear leather before the marshal shot him dead. I got out of town in a hurry, and for whatever reason he had, Cooper never saw fit to come after me."

I flipped the page in my notebook and continued to write. We were getting closer to the part of Lang's story that I was already familiar with, but there were still a few more details that I wanted to document. "What happened after you left Julesburg? Where did you go from there?"

Lang swung his feet over the side of his bunk and sat there for a moment before getting up. He started pacing nervously, to the extent that his tiny cell would let him. We could both see the sun through the cell window, and knew that it was getting close to that time when the sheriff would be coming for him. He stopped pacing and leaned against the wall and said, "I had a good stake of money that lasted me quite a while, so I drifted around for the next couple of years; Cheyenne, Denver, Colorado Springs. I did a lot of gambling and had quite a run of good luck. Eventually, however, my luck ran out and I wound up taking a job on a ranch near Fort Morgan.

"I had been working as a cowhand for nearly six months, and I was a pretty fair hand too. I liked the work and I liked being outside. Most people, other than the Stauffers, have been a big disappointment to me, so I enjoyed the opportunity to stay to myself. I got along fine with the other hands, but I didn't go out of my way to make any friends. All the while that I was there something kept eating at me."

"What was it?"

"All of that time alone, riding fence and chasing strays, gives a man plenty of time to ponder. I found myself thinking a lot about home."

"You mean Chicago?"

Toby grinned and shook his head. "No, I mean Nebraska and the Stauffers." He walked over and stood in front of me with his hands in his pockets. He was biting his lower lip, like he had something on his mind, but couldn't quite find the words to express himself. "What's that word for when you have an all-of-a-sudden idea?"

I thought for a moment. "You mean an 'epiphany'?"

"Yeah," he said, "that's the word. I had an epiphany."

I stopped writing in my notebook and leaned forward, eager to hear what he had to say. "What was it?" I asked.

Toby had walked back to his place below the window and resumed his position, leaning against the wall. When he answered, he spoke slowly and deliberately, choosing his words carefully. "I had spent years looking for Bob, wanting to make him pay for what he did. What I come to realize was that Bob didn't act alone. He had an accomplice."

I stared at Toby wide-eyed. "Who was it? Was it Danny Motson? I thought you said he had nothing to do with the killings?"

Toby shook his head. The tears that ran down his face glistened in the sunlight that was pouring through the lone window. "It wasn't Danny. It was me. I killed them as sure as if I'd pulled the trigger myself. If I hadn't been drunk; if I hadn't gotten in with the wrong crowd; if I hadn't of been passed out in the back room, Mr. Stauffer wouldn't have gone after Bob and Bob wouldn't have shot him and Mrs. Stauffer. Bob might have pulled the trigger, but I put the gun in his hand." He sniffed his nose and wiped his sleeve across his eyes. "The fact is, the Stauffers were dead the day I stepped off of that train and into their lives."

Neither one of us said anything for a long while. Lang's was a tragic waste of a life. Bad choices had led him here to this jail cell, and in a few more minutes, his choices would lead him to the end of a rope. He could have been like other men whose executions I had witnessed; men who were defiant to the end; men who went out kicking and cussing and cursing everyone and everything for not giving them a fair shake; men who never took responsibility for their own actions, but always blamed their situation on others. Lang wasn't like that.

I had been staring at the floor in front of me, not wanting to look up, not wanting to break the reverence of the moment. When I did look up, Lang was standing beneath the window, his eyes closed and his faced lifted heavenward, bathed in the rays of the August sun. It was noon.

I could hear a stirring in the outer office and I knew that the time had come, but I still had one more question that I needed answered. "Why?" I asked. "Why did you kill Lester Rhodes? Witnesses testified that you killed him in cold blood. They said that you walked into his barbershop, drew your gun, and shot him dead. You never gave any defense for the shooting during your trial. Why did you kill him?"

Lang turned to look at me. He had a smile on his face, which was still awash in the glow of the sun that was pouring in through the window. The sun's rays produced a soft aura around Lang that made him look almost at peace.

"What does it matter," he said. "I killed a lot of people. Shouldn't I have to pay for that? What difference does it make which one I'm hung for?"

The door to the outer office opened and the sheriff and two deputies walked through. I stood up and moved my chair to the side as the sheriff slipped the key to the cell door into its lock and gave it a twist. The lock clicked and the steel door swung open with a squeak that was amplified in the small cell.

"It's time," said the sheriff, as the two deputies stepped into the cell and up to Lang. One of the deputies put a pair of shackles on Lang's wrists while the other placed a similar pair of shackles on his ankles.

Lang didn't offer any resistance to the deputies, but he did start to shake as the color drained from his face until he was as pale as a bed sheet. He started to sob, and the shaking became so severe that the deputies grabbed him, one on each arm, and led him to the edge of the bed where he could sit and compose himself.

No one spoke for three or four uncomfortable minutes, while Lang sat on the edge of his bed sobbing. The only other sounds were coming from outside where people had started to gather to witness the hanging. I couldn't help but notice the difference between the atmosphere in the cell, which was solemn and heavy, and the sounds coming from outside, which were almost festive.

After a bit, Lang wiped his eyes on his sleeve and said, "Let's get this over with."

The two deputies helped him to his feet. He was still a little shaky, but he had pulled himself together pretty well, considering.

The sheriff took the lead, followed by the two deputies on either side of Lang, as we walked out of the jail and around the back to the jail yard where the scaffold had been built. The county prided itself in fast, efficient, and humane executions, and the scaffold was solidly built and held a place of honor in the center of the yard. All around, people had gathered to watch the proceedings. A few laughed or shouted out curses to Lang as we walked toward the steps leading up to the platform. But most everyone became reverently quiet the closer that we got.

As we approached the first step, Lang nodded in my direction and asked the sheriff, "Is it all right if he comes up on the platform with me?"

The sheriff looked at me. "Are you up for it?" I nodded my consent. Turning back to Lang, he answered him, "If that's what you want."

When we reached the top of the platform,

the deputies positioned Lang above the trapdoor. Lang stepped gingerly into place, as though he was testing the trapdoor to make sure it would hold his weight. Once Lang was in the right spot, one of the deputies slipped the rope over his neck and pulled the knot securely in place.

A thought occurred to me and I called out, "Toby."

He turned to look in my direction.

"I've decided what title I'm going to give my story. I'm going to call it, 'An Hour Before the Hangman.' "

He grinned and nodded his head. "I like that. That's a good one."

The hangman stood with his hand on the lever that would trip the lock on the trapdoor, and a hush fell over the crowd as the sheriff read through the declaration that contained Lang's charges as well as the verdict and the sentence of the court.

The sheriff looked at Lang and asked, "Is there anything you would like to say before the sentence is carried out?"

"I do have something that I want to say," Lang answered, "but only to him." He nodded his head in my direction.

The sheriff gave his consent, so I stepped over and stood in front of Lang. He bent slightly forward so he could whisper in my ear. "I wanted to give you an answer to your question about why I killed Lester Rhodes. I killed him because his real name was Bob Harper."

My mouth hung open in shock as I looked into the eyes of Toby Lang.

"I got the son of a bitch," he said to me with a smile. "Now we will both pay in hell for what we did."

I stepped back to my place on the platform and stood there dazed as the sheriff gave a nod to the hangman. In less than a moment it was over, and when they cut Lang loose and lowered his body to the ground, he still had that same smile on his face.

■ ■ ■ ■

Michael R. Ritt lives in a small cabin in the mountains of western Montana with his wife, Tami, their Australian shepherd, Lucky, and their nameless cat. He enjoys studying history, theology, and natural science, and has published several short stories and poems in anthologies and magazines.

■ ■ ■ ■

THE PRAIRIE FIRE
BY LARRY D.
SWEAZY

■ ■ ■ ■

The Wapihanne ran so slow it looked like it was standing still. Rain had been sparse of late, but the river's current continued to push underneath the surface, invisible and deceptive at first glance, but it could drown a weak swimmer even though it looked harmless. Naxke held a secret fear of water, of the power it held over her. She never told anyone of her fear, and she only stood on the edge of the Wapihanne when she had to. Even when it was calm and peaceful, the water could take a life. She had seen it happen more than once when the river raged, after the spring rains.

At the right angle, and in the right light, the water looked like a white cloth cutting through the flat, grassy lands of the koteewi. The air wasn't cold enough to freeze the river, the leaves still pulsed green. Naxke knew that what she saw was the river bottom reflecting upward.

A blue jay chattered, and a chickadee fluttered inside a berry bush searching for insects on the leaves, not the fruit. It was a perfect day, at least on the outside. The sun poured down on her stiff shoulders, though there was nothing the bright orb could do to encourage or warm her. Kitha was late. That was something that had never happened before, not in all of their life together. Kitha was as reliable as the moon and the stars, and now he wasn't where he was supposed to be.

"You look ill." It was the voice of her sister, Seke.

Naxke was the younger of the two, her hair the color of a blazing maple. She had hated her hair and fairer skin when she was young. It made her different, made her stand out from the others, but as she had grown in to a woman, she had become accustomed to the trusses, to the differences. Oddity was the curse of her family. She longed to look like Seke, to look like the rest of the tribe, though her sister had her own otherness to deal with, too.

"I am only worried," Naxke said. "Kitha has me in fits. The sun falls again and the ground underneath my feet grows cold."

"I warned you."

"You warn me about something every day.

How do I know which of your words to hold on to? You are sitting on the edge of a storm, meddling under the thunderclouds for something to gossip about."

Seke cast Naxke a childish glare and turned her back to her. Seke's black hair glistened in the soft light of the setting sun. There were whispers that she flew with the crows at night, listened to the dead speak in the wind, but it was only because Seke could read shadows and was a teller of sad tales. The others treated her as if she had a stink on her, and she did nothing to discourage that way of thinking. Seke liked walking alone. That was her *difference.* The stink made Naxke glad of her fire hair on better days.

"I worry, too, that's all," Seke said.

"What do you know?" Naxke stared downriver, her eyes suddenly hopeful at the promise of movement, but it was only a drifting log, not a pair of canoes. Her heart sank quickly back into its thick pocket of despair.

"I only know what I told you. He should not have gone. You should have stopped him. I know nothing more than that or I would have told you. There are men not to be trusted beyond our village. The world is changing faster than any of us know."

"The whites?"

"Perhaps."

Naxke sighed, nodding. "You know there is nothing I could have done to stop him. You know him as well as I do."

Seke turned back to her sister. "I do. You are right about that. I know Kitha's will is as strong and pure as the current underneath the river."

The scream for help came at the first sight of a blinking star in the sky. Naxke didn't stir, didn't run to find out what was wrong. She knew what she would find, knew her fears were about to come true. Seke had been right. It was a far more dangerous world than it used to be.

Naxke pulled a blanket over her head and could hear her own heart beating loudly. She wondered if it were possible to suffocate herself, drown in her own breath, so she didn't have to face what was to come next. There was no water nearby to dive into; she had only air and the emptiness and silence of her empty bed.

Stamping feet rumbled the ground underneath her, the rush of the tribe. Naxke roused and pulled herself from under the blanket. She could hear words and murmurs beyond the wigwam, through the woven reed walls, down the open smoke hole. The fire had long since gone out; it smoldered in ribbons, then wafted away, out into the world. From the outside, her life looked normal.

"He's dead." It was a whisper and truth that she had felt in her heart when she was talking with Seke. Kitha no longer walked in this world. She had felt him leave two moons ago. She had told no one. Not even her sister.

Naxke stepped out of her wigwam and her eyes met the gray mist of evening. Light had drained from the sky, but had not completely disappeared. The one star had now become two. Darkness supped on what light remained. She could barely breathe. Everyone was running toward the river. She walked slowly, forcing one heavy foot in front of the other.

Seke joined Naxke at the bank. As they walked to the canoe, the people parted, lowered their heads, and said nothing. An owl hooted in the distance. The hoot quickly faded into silence, dread, and the uncertainty of what had happened, of what had led them all to the edge of the river.

Tu-Co-Han, the chief's son, stood at the front of the canoe, his arms crossed and his head lowered. Beyond him, a white man, a familiar fur-trader, sat at the bow with his head lowered, too, his arms pulled captive behind him. The other canoe was empty, full of deerskin blankets. Sadness hung in the air like a stray rain cloud.

"Where is he?" Naxke said.

Tu-Co-Han raised his head and met her gaze. "There, covered up. He is dead, fire woman. I could not save him from Galligan's greed."

So it was the fur trader, Galligan, the white man with shifty gray eyes. He looked up when Tu-Co-Han said his name, then looked away from Naxke's glare, from her teary eyes. *He's dead.* She had heard those words already, but she didn't want to believe it, wouldn't believe it until she saw Kitha's face, even though she had felt his death in her bones, in her heart. Seke had confidence in black wings and uncertain things, not her.

Tu-Co-Han reached out to comfort her, but Naxke pulled away. She could offer nothing in return other than a sob. Her cries immediately erupted into an uncontrollable, guttural scream.

The owl lit out of a nearby cottonwood, startled, its own voice caught in its throat as it disappeared into the night, silently, with the quick flap of a wing as if it had something urgent to tell the others.

■ ■ ■ ■

The council house was ablaze in light. Naxke stood outside, her back against the north wall, braced, keeping her from falling to the ground and collapsing into a useless heap.

"They will kill him," Seke said. "Or banish him after punishment. Either way, he will be gone."

"It is the way," Naxke answered.

"Unless he is innocent."

"Why would you say such a thing?"

Seke pulled back and hissed at her sister. "The way is not always the bearer of truth."

"He killed Kitha," Naxke said.

"We have not heard his story."

"He has not said a word."

"He is afraid for his life."

"He should be."

The men of the village rose to their feet as Naxke and Seke entered the council house. The same reeds as her wigwam were used to build the house, but it was five times the size and the roof was covered with pulled skins. A fire burned in the center of the house, warming it beyond comfort. Naxke broke into a sweat at the sight of Galligan.

His face was swollen, his eyes black and blue. She wondered when he had been beaten. She hadn't noticed any bruising at the riverbank.

The sisters sat at the front of the room on an empty wood bench. Tu-Co-Han sat opposite Galligan. Kitha's brother, sister, and mother sat directly in front of the chief, Matheundan. No one spoke a word, only the fire had a voice, and it only offered short snaps and pops from green wood.

Finally, after everyone was settled, Matheundan stood up and spoke, "We have come here tonight to face a tragedy brought upon us by a man we once called friend." The chief looked weary, his face worn with time, age, and worry. This was not the first time they had lost one of their own by the hand of a white man. "Tell us, Tu-Co-Han, how this came to be. How did we lose our brother, Kitha?"

Tu-Co-Han stayed sitting for a long, deep breath, then rose up and stood stiff, his shoulders squared, almost as if he was a proud warrior ready to go off to battle. "We came across Galligan at the forks. He told us of many new beaver lodges he'd found beyond a swampland. It was a lie."

Naxke shivered, said nothing, stood up, and walked out of the council house. She heard whispers of disapproval follow her, but she didn't care. There was nothing for her to hear. There was no use in reliving Kitha's death. She didn't need to know how he had suffered, whether it was for one minute or one hour. It didn't matter. He was dead.

The air had cooled and night had completely fallen. The sky was full of silver beads on the black cloth of forever. Most everyone was back in their wigwams. All except the men, they were seeing to Galligan's fate. No good would come of it. He would die, too. It was the way: a death for a death. Only then would the wrong be settled, be even. Oddly, Naxke felt sorry for the fur trader. He looked afraid, as sure of what was to come as Matheundan, Tu-Co-Han, and the rest of the men. She could do nothing to save him. She wouldn't, even if she could.

Tears streamed down her face as she walked. Naxke did not slow her pace when she heard footsteps coming after her. She expected it to be Seke, but she was wrong. A strong hand reached out to stop her, then spun her to face him.

"You must hear what I have to say," Tu-Co-Han said.

"Let go of me," Naxke said. "I do not have

to hear anything."

"You must know the truth. You must accept it or no one else will."

In that moment, a bitter taste spread at the back of Naxke's throat and a tremble of recognition rocked her feet. She didn't know what she thought, but something was wrong. Tu-Co-Han's eyes had never been so hollow.

There was little time to mourn. Kitha would be buried inside tree bark in a deep grave. The burial would occur the next morning as the sun ate away at the darkness. It was The Between Time: when the sun, the moon, and the stars shared the sky with their wonder and knowledge. Naxke's people believed it was an opening, a spirit path to travel safely.

Naxke could hardly think of Kitha being gone but still so close to her. She longed to see him one last time. Death was like Seke's differences. It had a smell that stuck to you, threatened to take you, too, if you got too close to it. Touching a dead person was taboo.

A soft tap came from the outside and Seke eased into the wigwam, her head lowered, the shadows following her like they were beloved companions. "I am still worried about you, sister."

The last word stung, called Naxke away from imagining Kitha in his grave, then on his way into the sky. "Why do you say such a thing? Call me sister now?"

"There's no need to be angry. I offer comfort, that is all."

"What do you want?"

Seke had stopped inside the door. She hesitated, "I think you should speak to Galligan."

"I have nothing to say to him."

"You know he is to die under the next moon."

"I know what they will do." Naxke frowned and looked away from Seke.

"His hole is dug, too. He waits for death to rescue him from his troubles."

"I can't save him."

"You are the only one who can."

No wind spoke and a thick blanket of clouds covered the stars. A thin fog hovered over the tops of the drying grass. The koteewi thirsted for moisture. Fog was not enough to save the land, to turn it green again. That season was over, even though fire still danced in the sky, distantly, above the clouds, threatening to jab the earth and set it ablaze. Grass snapped under each step.

The whole world felt fragile, about to break or burn at any second.

It was the middle of the night. All of the tamed flames in the village had fallen to embers, guarded from spreading by fear and watchful eyes. The air smelled of wood smoke and slumber. Nothing stirred. Not animal or man. Only the Creator watched and Naxke hoped He was looking away as she slipped out of the wigwam.

Her heart raced as she padded quietly to the edge of the village. Her eyes welcomed the darkness. She was glad she knew the way, but it wouldn't have mattered, her heart would have pulled her to her destination. Seke had been right. She had to know Galligan's side of the story.

Naxke had to know of Kitha's last moments, that he had not suffered, that his death was quick. She hoped she remembered enough of the language to understand what the fur trader had to say.

Galligan's place was in the bottom of the hole. The ground was so dry the walls threatened to crumble and cave in. A strong grid of oak branches barred the top of the hole. There was no escape for the white man.

Tu-Co-Han's best friend, Lo-te-Kay, guarded the hole. The sloppy man slept deeply, his snores rising into the night air like Naxke had been counting on. An owl answered the man's nasal grovels in the distance.

She stared at Galligan's hole, but avoided the other one at the edge of the hickory grove. That hole was empty for now. It existed for Kitha's body, nothing more.

Naxke crawled to the edge of Galligan's prison, hugging the ground, hiding from the sleeping guard, hoping that she was nothing more than a shadow. "Galligan, do you hear me?" she whispered.

Something stirred behind her and Naxke froze. She feared being caught speaking with Galligan more than anything else. Lo-te-Kay had not moved. It must have been a night creature that had roused.

"I am here," Galligan said. "Go away. My presence has caused you enough pain."

"Tell me of his death. Tell me that Kitha was brave and faced the darkness without fear."

"He was already dead when I found him, attacked from behind with a rock or a tomahawk, I cannot be sure. I saw no weapon lying about."

"Did you stand for yourself?" Naxke said.

"Who would believe me? There were many ready to speak out against me even though they were not there. My fate was sealed before I arrived back in the village."

Naxke buried her face in the earth. She wanted to scream, to lash out, but she knew that would do no good. The dirt was freshly turned; dry as a maple leaf in winter. It tasted of secrets. Finally, she said, "Tell me, did Tu-Co-Han kill my beloved? Did he? Is that what you say?"

"I cannot know. I saw nothing to say so. He was my captor, but perhaps only because he wandered upon me when I found Kitha. I had blood on my hands. I was trying to save him by stopping the bleeding, but it was too late."

"Why should I believe you?"

"Why would I tell you a lie?"

Naxke slid into Seke's wigwam, still hoping the shadows would protect her from the Creator's eyes. "What do you know?" she demanded. Dirt was smeared across Naxke's face, striped in crumbles under her eyes, like war paint.

Seke stood beyond the fire; her eyes shone like polished black agates. "I know many things, but nothing of which you ask."

"Did he kill Kitha?" Naxke said.

"Galligan?"

"No. His brother? Did Tu-Co-Han kill

Kitha for his place next to his father? He will be chief now."

"It is an old tale."

"That doesn't matter."

"It does. One man will do anything to have what is not his, while the other man who has it does not want it, and does everything to lose it. Kitha had no interest in being chief, you of all people know that to be true. Yet, he would not step aside. How could he? He loved his father and our people too much. There was no trade, no bargain between the two brothers. Their resentment had grown from day to day until the years mounted a campaign of hate. You know this is how we all saw Tu-Co-Han."

Naxke twisted her lip as a tear slipped down her cheek. "You knew Kitha's fears."

"You knew his heart."

"Are you no different than Tu-Co-Han?"

"We share no blood."

The twist of Naxke's lips turned to gritted teeth. "I did not choose to be here. Our parents did not leave me to the beasts when they found me. You know that. I was alone, orphaned by the cruelty of others and weather. I would have died if I had not been rescued and brought here."

"We share their love, sister. I meant no harm. It is true, I loved Kitha, but not in the way you do, or did. He would have been a wise chief, regardless. He found discomfort in my presence, but he came to me for counsel like his father came to our mother."

"It is the way," Naxke said, relaxing, putting her own stories of resentment to the side. "What do you know?"

Seke walked across the wigwam and embraced her sister, kissed her forehead, then pulled away. "My heart tells me to believe Galligan."

"That only means that he did not kill Kitha. We don't know what happened to him. We don't know that Tu-Co-Han is guilty of anything. Is that true?"

"That is true. However, we must find out. We have little time. They will begin to fill in Galligan's hole as soon as the first light cracks the sky. He will know true darkness once the moon rises. They will make sure he suffers until he takes his last breath."

Both women knew there was only one person that they could go to for the truth: Tu-Co-Han himself. It was better to seek him out together, not alone. There was a risk to their plan, making an enemy of the chief's only remaining son, but they agreed that there was no choice. Naxke had to know if Galligan was lying or telling the truth.

"Why are you here?" Tu-Co-Han said.

"I seek answers," Naxke said. Seke stood behind her, nearly out of sight, almost hidden by the darkness.

"You should not have run out of the council house. I had my say then." Tu-Co-Han turned away, intending to go back to his bed of furs and blankets.

"Galligan claims innocence."

Tu-Co-Han stopped and stomped his foot. "You are forbidden to use your language."

"I am not forbidden from searching for the truth."

Tu-Co-Han growled. "Come in. We must put an end to this."

Naxke hesitated. She had never been inside Tu-Co-Han's wigwam.

Tu-Co-Han was tall, like Kitha. As the younger of the two, he'd had more time to play and to hunt, to develop muscles and endurance. Kitha had been softer in body and spirit. Tu-Co-Han's face looked as hard as the stone at the bottom of the Wapi-hanne, but not white, dark, bronzed by the sun and a beating heart. There was nothing gentle about his ways. Even his wigwam was sparse and cold.

"Sit," he commanded. There was no one else inside the wigwam. Tu-Co-Han had not taken a wife, had not fancied one woman enough to share a blanket with her.

Both women obeyed.

"Did you see Galligan kill Kitha, Tu-Co-Han? Did you see him strike out in rage or greed?" Seke said. Naxke had fallen pale, her eyes teary and suddenly afraid. She realized what she had done. Spoke the white man's words and accused the chief's son of something no man should ever consider.

"I did not see the kill," Tu-Co-Han said. "But Galligan was there, next to Kitha. He wore my brother's blood on his hands."

"That much we know," Seke said. "Galligan said as much. The wind and owls have other stories to tell."

"Do not threaten me with your false magic, Dark Sister. I do not believe in your skills any more than my father does."

"Kitha came to me. He feared you. Did you know that?"

Tu-Co-Han circled the two women like a bobcat on the prowl. His face was void of any feeling. He was stalking nothing that Naxke could see, unless he couldn't find the words to say.

Tu-Co-Han stopped near the center of the wigwam. A little fire struggled to give light and warmth to the wigwam, but there, Tu-Co-Han's face was visible. He was angry. "Kitha chased many ideas, dark, and light. He had nothing to fear from me."

"Many of us believed otherwise," Seke said. "Your father's time here grows short. If a change was going to take place, it would serve you best if it happened before the chief meets the Creator."

"What are you accusing me of, woman?" Tu-Co-Han demanded.

Anyone else would have recoiled, shivered at the tone, but Seke didn't waver. "It will do me no good to accuse you of anything. I know my place. I am telling you that there are stains you carry. Killing Galligan will not remove them. If you both claim innocence, then it is possible that Kitha stumbled, fell, and hit his head. Did you consider that, Tu-Co-Han? Or did you need to prove yourself so badly, that you are willing to let a man die?"

"A white man," Tu-Co-Han sneered.

"A life is a life. Only the Creator has the power to take that away."

Tu-Co-Han maintained the sneer, the anger, but there seemed to be a consideration of Seke's words. His voice dropped, was quieter when he spoke. "There are things you do not know, Seke. Change is coming. Kitha's death foretells of a darker time for our people."

"Now who is dabbling in shadows?" Seke smiled when she spoke.

"I speak the truth. Naxke knows of which I speak. News of a treaty with the white man has reached our place in the world. It will move us from this land. Kitha was heartbroken and begged to go on the journey with us so he could heal his anger at our father for not fighting. I am not the one with war in my heart," Tu-Co-Han said. "It was Kitha who longed to fight, to rise up."

Seke looked to Naxke, confused. "Is this true, sister?"

"Yes," Naxke whispered. "Yes, it is true. We must all leave here. We are ceding our lands and dreams. No fight will stop it."

"And you didn't tell me?" Seke said to Naxke.

"It was not my place. It was Matheundan's place to tell his people of their future. That time has not yet come," Naxke said. "The sun will rise soon and everyone will know of the destiny that awaits us all."

"This changes everything," Seke said.

"It does," Tu-Co-Han answered. "It does."

Naxke drew in a deep breath and said, "Swear to me, brother, that you brought no harm to Kitha. That you speak the truth."

"I speak the truth."

"Then I will believe you."

The horizon shimmered with a thin, gray line. It was a thin peek of light, enough for the proceedings against Galligan to begin. The men of the village had begun to gather at the hole, waiting at a respectable distance. Naxke and Seke stood next to one of the towering oak trees, lost in the shadows, though everyone knew they were there. There was no need for them to hide.

Once all of the men assembled, and dawn engaged the night, Matheundan and Tu-Co-Han made their way to the crowd.

Matheundan walked cautiously with a stick, stooped over with age, in the dim light. Tu-Co-Han followed close behind, his head lowered, the emotion on his face impossible for Naxke to read. She held her breath and tongue. Seke did the same. They had done everything they could do. There was nothing left to do but wait and see what would become of Galligan's fate.

The chief stopped short of the fur trader's hole and Tu-Co-Han eased to his side. They exchanged whispers and nods, then turned to face the men of the village.

Matheundan cleared his throat and spoke as confidently as he could. A crack in his voice echoed across the dry grass. "On this solemn day, we send my son on his final journey and decide the future of the man accused of killing him. It is a day a father never wants to see come."

Tu-Co-Han stiffened and looked over his shoulder. Even in the darkness, Naxke knew his intent to search her out. She stepped out of the shadow of the tall oak and showed herself to the village. It was her right to be there. No one would deny her that. Seke stayed back.

"Come closer, sister, so that you may hear what I have to say," Tu-Co-Han said to Naxke. Matheundan nodded with a gentle urge.

Naxke made her way to the two men slowly, aware that every waking eye was on her. She stopped behind the chief and his son.

Tu-Co-Han turned and faced all of the men of the village. "I am the accuser of this man, Galligan, and have called into question his intentions. I do not deny anger at all white men. Our lands are lost to us. Our lives have changed for the worse by their presence. When I saw my brother, Kitha, lying in stillness, blood on his head and blood on Galligan's hands, I allowed rage to blind me. I believed he had killed my brother out of greed, that he wanted all of the pelts for himself, that he was no different from other men who kill. I did not listen to Galligan's protests, but now that time has passed, I have to reconsider what I saw and why I saw it the way I did. This is no easy thing for me to say, brothers, but I now think Galligan should be free. I believe Kitha died by accident and not by the hand of a white man. Putting Galligan to death will not bring my brother back to this earth or return our lands to us. This Treaty of St. Mary's has been signed, and our time here is short. Another death will not heal our pain."

Murmurs of disapproval rippled through the crowd of men. Naxke watched them all closely. Tu-Co-Han's words were not what they had expected to hear. Setting Galligan free was the last thing anyone — even her — expected to come from the man's mouth. The bigger blow was the confirmation of the fear they all had: the treaty was real. There was no turning back. A new unknown land awaited them all, not only Kitha.

No one outwardly protested, but voices were raising higher at each breath.

Matheundan raised his hand and every voice went silent. "My son has shown great wisdom in sparing the life of our friend,

Galligan, but he alone cannot set the man free. Naxke's voice must be heard."

Another eruption of grumbles broke out. Naxke knew why. It was not only because of the color of her hair, the color of her skin — the same as Galligan's — but she was a woman casting a vote in a matter she held no power in. She knew better than to utter a word. Naxke walked forward and stopped in front of Matheundan, then nodded.

Galligan would go free, but Naxke wondered what damage Tu-Co-Han had done to himself. Had he shown wisdom or fear? Only time would tell how the people would see the outcome, and ultimately, how they would see Tu-Co-Han. Was he a true leader, or a shadow of what Kitha might have been? Naxke saw the path open, and knew she had to walk on the side of wisdom instead of fear. That was the way Kitha would have wanted it.

The day of Kitha's burial and Galligan's release, Matheundan put out the word that they would move before the winter winds set in permanently. There was much sadness in the village. Many of the people had never known any other home. Naxke had joined the people as a scared child and Seke had been born to them. Neither of them wanted to leave, but there was no choice. The land was no longer theirs to live and die on.

Later in the evening, as the sun set on the day, Galligan called on Naxke in her wigwam. He was on his way out of the village. "You can come with me," he said.

"That is kind, but this is my home," Naxke said.

"But it is not. You don't know what awaits you on your journey."

"What awaits me with you? I know nothing of your ways, of the ways I am expected to behave and talk, and be with people I do not know."

"You can learn. I will help you. It's the least I can do. It was you who saved my life."

Naxke studied Galligan's earnest face, cleaned of his prison dirt. His eyes were sincere. She was certain that he believed what he said, that he would care for her in the white world. She had considered leaving once upon a time, thought of running away, of finding people of her own blood. The others had made life hard when she first arrived, even Seke had been difficult, but Kitha had shown her a love like no other, and once he had done that, so, too, did everyone else. In the end, Naxke had spoken when she'd had no right to. This was her home. She knew her place. Her heart would remain buried under an oak tree.

"The people are my home, Galligan. Wherever they go, I will go. It is the way."

The fur trader sighed in agreement, acknowledging that Naxke was right and there was nothing he could do to convince her otherwise. He left the wigwam, never to be seen or heard from again.

The clouds were angry on the day of the leaving. Lightning danced across the sky, but no rain fell. People walked along the Wapihanne, and others eased their canoes into the water, drifting with the slow current. There was no turning back; there was no place to seek shelter. They had no home, only the way ahead of them to some unknown place.

Naxke and Seke walked shoulder to shoulder behind the chief and his son. They did not speak, did not cry.

The thunder clapped so loud that the earth shook. They both heard the lightning strike the ground, heard the sizzle of dry grass erupt into a fire. They smelled smoke, but they did not quicken their step or look back. Everything would burn, the wigwams and the memories of life left behind. The earth would erase their presence, and before long, no one would remember that they had been there at all.

■ ■ ■ ■

Larry D. Sweazy (www.larrydsweazy
.com) is a multiple award-winning author
of thirteen novels. He lives in Indiana with
his wife, Rose, two dogs, and a cat, and is
hard at work on his next novel.

■ ■ ■ ■

OLD GUN WOLF
BY FRANK LESLIE

■ ■ ■ ■

Wilbur Calhoun wasn't always sure he could trust his senses.

One, he was old.

Two, he'd been known to imbibe a wee bit more than his fair share and had watched a whole bevy of Cheyenne girls, naked as the day they were born but a whole lot better filled out, dance Spanish tangos in front of his fieldstone hearth one New Year's Eve in a lonely hideout shack along some owl-hoot trail on the Mogollon Rim.

But the old ex-gunslinger/ex-outlaw was now the sole resident of a small "shotgun" ranch in the foothills of the San Juan Mountains of southern Colorado, still a relatively unsettled place at the turn of the century. And he was pretty damn sure that the shadowy figure just now dipping its snout into the hindquarters of a dead calf on the hill beyond was the same old, charcoal gray wolf he'd seen countless times over the past six weeks, hunting these winter-white, pine-stippled hills for the slowest moving of Calhoun's livestock.

Lying in the snow at the crest of one such hill, Wilbur dug his ancient spyglass out of the pocket of his quilted elk-hide mackinaw. He telescoped the brass-cased piece, his one possession of any value that had made it through the War of Northern Aggression as well as the Indian Wars, and held it up to one grizzled brow and rheumy blue eye.

"Ah, hell, you old bastard," the old rancher said through a long sigh. "It *is* you, ain't it? Well, *damn* your worthless hide!"

Wilbur closed the telescope and returned it to his pocket. He grabbed his old Spencer repeater from where he'd leaned it against a gnarled piñon to his right, and worked the trigger-guard cocking mechanism, levering a .56-caliber cartridge into the chamber.

He raised his left gloved hand to brush snow from his brow and then pressed his leathery cheek up against the Spencer's rear stock. He pulled the heavy hammer back to full cock. The grinding metallic clicks sounded inordinately loud in the still wintery silence, causing a crow to light from another pine several yards away.

Caw! Caw! Caw! the black bird complained, winging out over a snow-socked valley to the west.

"Shut your fool mouth, winged whore," Wilbur rasped at the crow.

To Wilbur Calhoun, all annoying women of his own species and those creatures he assumed to be females merely *because* they annoyed him, he addressed as whores even if they did not actually practice the calling. He cast his gaze at the wolf. Either it hadn't heard the crow — maybe hard of hearing? — or it had come to a point in its old life when food was more important than crows, which were known to grow hysterical over very little.

Wilbur lined up the Spencer's sights on the side of the shaggy gray beast — a loner probably banished from the pack because the others saw no reason to share food with one so old and worn out. Wilbur slid the sights around before settling on the area just above and behind the stock-thieving beast's left front leg, aiming for the heart.

The wolf lay on its belly, its long snout shoved up the ass of the calf it had killed, and it shook itself as it tore at the likely still-warm organ meat — probably the liver and gall bladder, closest to the anus, which was the easiest, most practical way into the beast's inner sanctum.

Even with the wolf moving and driving

itself deeper into the calf's carcass with its hind legs, it was an easy shot. Even from a hundred and twenty yards away. Even for a sixty-three-year-old, stove-up ex-outlaw, and "whiskey-swilling servant of the devil," as one of Wilbur's ex-wives had once called him.

That had been before he'd kicked her out of their shanty in the Poudre Canyon, south of Laramie, to go find some mucky-muck who owned a buggy with high, red wheels or one of them new, loud, and smelly motorcars, which was all the old whore had seemed to want out of life, given her cater-wauling on the subject.

As the wolf rose to all fours and hauled a thick, heavy-looking chunk of organ meat out of the calf's hindquarters, Wilbur tightened his right index finger on the Spencer's trigger. A second later, that same finger went slack.

Wilbur lifted his head away from the gun to scowl down at it, as though the carbine were to blame for his sudden inaction when he'd had the stock-killing wolf dead-to-rights.

"What in tarnation?" he muttered.

And then, in the upper periphery of his vision, he saw the wolf scramble away from the calf. It ran up the snowy hill, lunging through the crusted snowdrifts, and over the hill's windswept crest and out of sight down the opposite side.

Wilbur looked around, cautious, and his wiry gray brows drew down over his eyes.

What had spooked the old wolf was a rider just now cresting another hill to the east of the calf and on the other side of a draw between the next hill and the calf's hill. The stranger rode a sleek sorrel, and he was loping at a slant down the hill toward Wilbur, who heaved his tired old self to his feet with a weary sigh, and absently brushed snow from his patched denim breeches as he watched the rider approach.

The man wore a black, high-crowned Stetson with a chin thong bouncing against his chest. He also wore a buckskin mackinaw with a wool collar and a cartridge belt strapped around the outside of the buttoned coat. Two holsters flapped against his sides; they were filled with long-barreled revolvers.

The man dropped from sight in the crease between the hills, but Wilbur's keen old ears still picked up the thuds of the sorrel's hooves. The thuds grew steadily louder and then the man reappeared, cresting the slope that Wilbur was on. He loped over to within twenty feet of the old rancher, checked his mount down, and curveted the fine, white-hocked gelding.

The horse tossed its head and chomped its bit as the rider drew back on its reins.

The stranger studied Wilbur closely — a young man with long, wavy brown hair, thick mustache and sideburns, his cold blue eyes nearly as wild as the hard-ridden horse's. A handsome lad he was, twenty-five or so, with the look of the dandy about him. "Why'd you let him go?"

"Why'd I let who go?"

"The wolf, you old coot!"

"Oh, him," Wilbur said, meeting the young stranger's hard, vaguely sneering gaze with a mild one of his own. "He's just doin' what wolves do, I reckon. I got enough beef for both of us."

The young man chuckled at that. "You must be a rich son of a bitch."

"Just an old one with only himself and his dog to feed."

The young man got his horse, who probably didn't like the wolf scent on the wind overmuch, settled down. Then he rested his forearms on his saddle horn and stretched his lips away from his teeth — a full set, as far as Wilbur could tally. A full set of choppers was right odd for these parts. He'd likely been city-bred.

"Why, you're a damn fool," the kid said, dimpling his cheeks.

Wilbur nodded. "I reckon if it takes a fool."

The kid studied Wilbur closely and laughed. He'd likely been born either grinning or laughing, Wilbur absently opined. God help him go out that way. "You don't know who I am, do you?"

"Hell, boy, I can't remember if I took a shit this mornin' or last night," Wilbur said, "but since I don't feel a heavy one comin' on, it must have been this mornin'."

"I'm your son, you old mossyhorn."

It took a lot to rock a man of Wilbur's years and experience back on his heels, but the possibility that this well-setup, well-dressed, wild-eyed kid on such a fine sorrel gelding could be his son managed to do just that.

Wilbur narrowed one eye and turned his head askance. "Pshaw."

"Sure as hell I am!"

A heavy darkness pressed against Wilbur's heart and drew his shoulders down. It was a feeling he knew well — one whose lifting he always celebrated while dreading its return. He heard a woman's scream in his head but blinked it away as well as the following, muffled report of an old Confederate pistol, and said, "Devlin?"

"That's right, *Pa.*" The kid sneered at that last. He plucked one of his fine Smith & Wesson .44's from its holster, and rested it across the saddle horn, aimed at Wilbur's heart. He rocked the hammer back with his thumb. "And I'm here to take you back on that tiresome old murder charge, *Pa!*"

Wilbur looked from the gun to the kid holding it. Regret was like an anvil on him now; it was a shadow over the sun. "By god, I loved that woman."

"Then why'd you kill her?"

"That was a hell of a time, boy. Hell, you were two years old."

"No, but I learned about it later. And ever since I was able to understand it — how you shot my ma in a jealous rage — I vowed I'd one day hunt you down and kill you."

The stranger named Devlin reached up and jerked the top of his coat open, revealing a deputy United States marshal's moon-and-star badge pinned to his wool vest. "And I'd do it legal!"

Wilbur whistled at the shiny, penny's worth of nickeled steel. "Well, if that don't beat a hen a-flyin'."

"Unbuckle that gun rig," the young lawman ordered. "And hand over that rifle."

Wilbur sighed, glancing at the cocked

Smith & Wesson aimed at his chest. He handed the Spencer up to the kid and then unbuckled his cartridge belt and old Colt Navy jutting from his cross-draw holster. He handed those up, too.

"You got a horse out here?" the kid asked.

Wilbur scanned the low, gray clouds from which a fine snow was falling. "Too late to head back to Denver tonight, son. How 'bout we lay over the night at my cabin, get a fresh start in the mornin'?"

"Don't call me 'son.' "

"Well, now I'm confused . . ."

"You're my pa in blood only. What you are first and foremost is an old outlaw who killed my mother back twenty-five years ago. And you're gonna hang for it."

Wilbur fingered the frost-rimed gray beard hanging off his chin, and studied the lad closely.

"We can get to the Wolf Creek Stage Station," Devlin said, hanging Wilbur's cartridge belt from his saddle horn. "That's far enough today. There'll be a stage along tomorrow. We'll catch the train at Pueblo."

"Wolf Creek's a good half-day's ride," Wilbur said. "My horse is fresh. He'd make it. That sorrel won't make it another hundred yards."

The young lawman looked at his horse,

giving a half-grimace when he saw that the beast was blowing hard and shifting wearily on its tired feet.

Wilbur said, "Besides, we're about to get several inches o' snow. I know 'cause both my elbows and the big toe on my right foot itches. Froze the toe one winter up in Dakoty . . . durin' the war with Red Cloud."

"Ah, shut up, you old stump-jumper. I'm not one bit interested in your stories about Red Cloud." Devlin blinked up at the gauzy sky. Several granular flakes caught on his long, brown eyelashes. "But I reckon we'd best head for your cabin. It is a cabin, isn't it, and not some Injun tipi? I heard how you took up with a squaw for a time."

"Took up with two," Wilbur said. "They were sisters. Talked a lot, both of 'em. I outlived them, too." He began walking down the hill in his bandy-legged fashion, beckoning to the lad behind him. "Come on then, if you've a mind. I need whiskey an' a fire!"

"How many men have you killed, Calhoun?" asked Wilbur's long-lost badge-toting son as they were riding along the edge of a shallow, brushy ravine toward Wilbur's cabin.

"You'll have to count the notches on that old Colt hangin' from your saddle horn. I fergit." Wilbur turned to the young man riding to his right. "Let me ask you somethin' — how'd you find me?"

"I been lookin' for you most of my life. When I was passin' through Taos the other day with a couple of other marshals — we were headin' back to Denver after wrappin' up an assignment in New Mexico — I heard the name Calhoun bandied about a woodstove by several old loafers in a general store."

Devlin glanced at his father. "Been awhile since you went by your real name. Of course, I didn't know if it was really you and not some other man with the same handle. Just decided to take the chance. Glad I did. I knew when I glassed you from atop that hill yonder that you're the old killer I been lookin' for."

The younker thrust his gloved hand into his coat pocket and withdrew what appeared to be two scraps of heavy paper. "I have the picture you had made when you joined the First East Tennessee Mountain Volunteers. That's you and Cousin Tapp and Uncle Earl. Remember them? And that second one there is after you killed my mother, ran off, and got 'galvanized' in the war against the Indians by General Sherman."

Wilbur merely glanced at the pictures and then turned away, fingering frost from his drooping mustache. A man who'd been running from his past as long as Wilbur had, had little interest in old pictures. He wished he could look away from his memories, but those were lodged in his brain.

Devlin leaned back to reach into one of his saddlebag pouches.

"And this here," he said, pulling out a rolled, age-yellowed paper, "is the most recent wanted circular I have with your ugly mug on it. You weren't so old in this likeness but getting up there, maybe forty or so. I stumbled onto this one four years ago, hangin' in a post office in Amarillo. It was old even then, had been up there for years. You were goin' by the name of Henry Wallace and ridin' with the Jimmy "Dead-Eye" Johnson bunch of train robbers. But that's you, all right. You of about twenty years ago. Wanna see it?"

"No, thanks."

"What the hell is that?"

"What's wha— ?"

Devlin drew one of his six-shooters, clicked the hammer back, and aimed into the ravine on his right.

"Hold on!" Wilbur said, jerking his reins and ramming his coyote dun, Goliath, into the young lawman's sleek sorrel.

Devlin's Smith & Wesson popped, blowing a snow-dusted branch off a leafless chokecherry shrub tangled against the side of the ravine. Devlin cursed. At the same time, a yip rose from the brush nearby, and a shaggy, black and white collie dog lifted its head, ears pricked, eyes wary.

"That's my dog, you cork-headed younker!"

"Dog?" Devlin lowered his smoking revolver and stared at the collie mutt staring back at him from about twenty yards downslope, only its white-streaked black head visible above the winter-barren brush. "I thought it was a wolf. Hate dogs, too. Can't stand the sight of 'em."

Wilbur thought he'd heard everything. He preferred all breed of animal except skunks and rattlesnakes to people — dogs most of all. "How in the hell could a son of mine not like dogs?"

"I was raised by good people," Wilbur said. "Dogs are vermin."

"Well, not that one. You take another shot at Shep, I'll take that pistol away from you and shove it up your ass so far it'll tickle your tonsils." Wilbur glanced at his dog whose tongue was now hanging, eyes brightening. "Come on, Shep. Let's git on home before our peckers freeze to our legs!"

Wilbur spurred Goliath into a lope. Shep

dashed up the side of the ravine, glanced warily at the young lawman, then took off running after his master.

Later that night, in his cabin warmed by a dancing fire in the fieldstone hearth, Wilbur said, "Here ya go, Shep!" He plucked the steak bone off his tin plate and tossed it to the collie, who had been waiting patiently — one ear erect, the other curled forward — while Wilbur and his lawman son ate at the crude pine table.

Shep snapped the bone out of the air and hunkered down with it, growling as he tore at the remaining meat.

Devlin grimaced at the dog lying on a braided hemp rug in front of the fire, and shook his head. "Dogs are outdoor creatures."

"Not that one. Fact, he makes a good pillow."

"You must be *joking*! He sleeps in your *bed*?"

Wilbur chuckled, rose from his chair, his old knees popping with the effort, and turned to the Z-frame front door. Devlin grabbed the pistol he'd kept handy beside his own plate, and loudly cocked it. "Where you think you're goin', old man?"

Wilbur scowled at the kid. "I'm gonna yellow the snow off my stoop. That all right with you, Wyatt Earp?"

Devlin narrowed one eye in warning. "You better not have a gun out there."

"If I did, it's buried by now," Wilbur said with a grunt, and went out.

When he'd stepped to the edge of his narrow porch and was unbuttoning his fly, feeling the cold snow pellets dancing against his face, he heard the kid yell from inside, "You try to run off, I'll hunt you down and shoot you . . . and then I'll kill this filthy dog of yours!"

"You talk more than both my Injun wives put together!" Wilbur said as he got an erratic stream going, and chuckled.

He ambled back inside, stoked the fire in the hearth as well as the one in the small, iron range — an old man could never get warm enough — and then refilled Devlin's coffee cup as well as his own. He hauled a bottle down from a shelf.

"Whiskey?"

Devlin smiled shrewdly as he swiped a stove match across the table, lighting it, and then touched the flame to the long, black cigar he'd stuck between his teeth.

Puffing smoke, he said, "Don't think you're gonna get me drunk and shoot me. A man like you — on the run as long as you've been, as many banks and trains as you've robbed, men you've killed — you'd do anything to keep from stretching hemp."

"Damn, boy," Wilbur said, chuckling, pouring the forty-rod into his own smoking cup, "you make me sound like somethin' conjured by the imagination of ol' Dead-Eye Dick!"

"Just smart. I hear I take after my mother that way."

"How would you know what your mother was really like?" Wilbur sat down, making his knees as well as his hide-bottom chair creek. "You never knew her."

"No, thanks to you."

"You sure about that?"

Devlin stared at him with those frosty blue eyes through the weblike smoke cloud drifting over the table toward the lantern hanging over it from a rafter. "How dare you disparage her to me. Have you not even one iota of common decency? Why, I don't even know why I'm wasting time with you. I should have shot you by now. Who would know?"

"Oh, but you'd know, dear Devlin. And you're an upstanding citizen. A do-right lawman."

"That's right I am, and you'd best be grateful and don't push me."

"Oh, hell, I'm too old to push anymore, Devlin." Wilbur sipped his coffee, enjoying the burn of the liquor. He sniffed and rubbed a grimy sleeve across his goat beard and mustache, and sagged back in his chair.

He studied the kid, who was studying him while he smoked, his cold eyes narrow. Devlin had removed his hat. His thick, wavy, dark-brown hair was parted on one side. It hung down over his ears. A right pretty lad, thought Wilbur. And a snappy dresser — all in tweed complete with a gold watch chain and a gold ring on his right little finger. Those cold, blue eyes belonged to his mother, though they hadn't looked as cold on her.

"You gonna tell me about her?" the kid said at last.

"You wanna hear about her? About what happened?"

"I do indeed," Devlin said, dipping his chin, his voice steady, serious. "As long as it's not all big windies."

"No windies. Just the simple truth." Wilbur took another sip of his coffee. "June and I married just before the war got burnin' good after Sumter. Then I went away for three long years. When I came back home to our little farm outside Maryville — a couple patches of corn and cotton south of my folks' place — I learned we had a child. You. All was well for a while. I got to farming again and raising chickens, sold the eggs in town.

"Got back from sellin' eggs one day a little earlier than usual and caught your mother with the town banker's son — Virgil Allen Boatwright. That little mucky-muck's old man had enough money to buy Virgil a substitute soldier, a free ticket out of the war that the rest of us *had* to fight."

Wilbur drew a deep breath and wrapped both hands around his coffee cup, staring down into the muddy, steaming blackness. "Somethin' snapped in me. You don't know how much I'd missed that woman when I was off fightin', watchin' my friends . . . my kin . . . get their guts strewn across battlefields from Gettysburg to Chickamauga. When I realized what had been goin' on while I was away fightin' for the Confederacy, I got out my old Leech & Rigdon pistol — the one I'd used for killin' Yankees — and I drilled that son of a bitch's son of a bitch of a Boatwright through his pea-pickin' heart!"

The coffee cup shook between Wilbur's hands. "At least, I thought I got him through his heart. Must have just clipped it. He had enough life left in him to grab his own

LeMat off the dresser and snap off a shot. Your mother had just scrambled up off the bed, screaming, and that bastard shot her in the back."

Devlin canted his head slightly and blew smoke at the table from which it wafted up against Wilbur's face. "So you say."

"So I say."

"But it really changes very little, doesn't it? Whether he killed her by accident or you killed her in a fit of rage — killed them both — they're both still dead. My mother is dead . . . because of you."

"It makes a hell of a lot of difference to me." Wilbur held the young man with a hard, grave stare, his nostrils flaring. "By god, I loved that woman. Loved her since I first met her in the lane in front of her daddy's place. We were both twelve years old. Only woman I ever loved in all my rotten years. Not the only one I had by a long shot, but the only one I loved. But that son of a bitch —"

"Easy, there, Calhoun — his family raised me after I left your mountain people when I was ten."

Wilbur blinked at that, then shook his head. "Why?"

"The war ruined your clan. The Boatwrights took me in. Adopted me. Gave me

269

a full set of clothes and an education." Devlin wrinkled his upper lip in disgust and shook his head. "Your people — poor, dirty mountain people. They just got poorer and dirtier. Hardly any of 'em left by now, I'd think."

Wilbur gave a sour laugh. "I reckon you were shittin' in high cotton with them yella-bellied Boatwrights. They fell in with the carpetbaggers after the war they were too skeered to fight! Sold their own folks down the road!"

"They did what they had to do. Look at you. You ran off when the smoke was still curling from your gun, after killin' my mother and the man she *really* loved. Headed west to kill Indians. Became a common bank and train robber. Now look at you — ghostin' around out here alone, too sap-headed to shoot a wolf eatin' your stock . . . waitin' to die in this old, drafty cabin with that mangy, flea-bit cur. You've outlived your time, Calhoun. This ain't the Old West no more. Your holin'-up days are over. They'll be throwing a necktie party in your honor back in Maryville. Gonna hang you in front of all us Boatwrights you hate so much!"

Devlin threw his head back, had a hardy laugh at that.

Wilbur's entire stooped, stringy body shook with fury. His heart thudded in his temples. He stared at the slick Steve sitting across from him until he finally slid his chair back, heaved himself to his feet, and grabbed his bottle.

"Come on, Shep," he said, glaring at the kid still laughing hysterically inside the cloud of billowing cigar smoke. "I've done wearied of tonight's company. I believe we'll retire."

The dog buried its bone under the rug, glanced over its shoulder at the laughing stranger, gave a snarl, and then followed Wilbur through a curtained doorway.

Sleep did not come easy for Wilbur Calhoun.

He lay awake for several hours, listening to the wind blow the snow against the cabin. Over and over, the wind became June's scream as she rose up on the bed and faced an enraged Wilbur. Her blue eyes were large as saucers as she sobbed, "Wilbur, honey, you was away *a long time!*"

Boom!

The bullet tore into her back and exited under her left arm, spitting blood against the mirror it shattered. It threw June forward off the bed. She hadn't hit the earthen floor before Wilbur screamed, *"No!"* and emptied his old Confederate popper into the fish-belly white chest of Virgil Boatwright.

Boatwright slumped against the wall, his pale pecker drooping between his long, thin legs.

Wilbur didn't remember much after that. He vaguely remembered cradling June's naked body in his arms for a time, rocking her, calling her name. But then he saw Virgil leaning back in a corner with a silly smile on his dead face and realized that if he stayed there on the farm he'd likely hang in a matter of hours from the big mossy oak in the courthouse square.

The Boatwrights were a wealthy clan. They wielded a formidable power around Maryville.

Wilbur ran.

And now he was here in the foothills of the San Juan Mountains, sitting straight up in his narrow cot, a cold sweat streaming off his body despite his room's icehouse chill.

"June," he said, sobbing into his hands as he lay his head back down against his pillow. "Ah, *June . . . June . . .* !"

Shep rose from his bed in the corner and rested his chin on Wilbur's quivering arm.

And then it was suddenly morning and Wilbur got up and let Shep out to yellow the snow and sniff around for mice and cottontails. It was a bright morning, the sun reflecting off the newly fallen powder like diamonds. Tracks leading off to the barn told Wilbur that Devlin Boatwright had gone out to saddle the horses.

Wilbur built a fire in the range and boiled coffee. He let Shep back in and the dog promptly shook snow all over the wooden floor fronting the door. Wilbur rewarded him with an ear scratch and a steak bone.

He was sitting at the table, near the warm, ticking range, smoking a tightly rolled cigarette and sipping his coffee spiced with a liberal portion of forty-rod, when he heard the slow clomps and crunches of horses in the snow.

The clomps and crunching grew louder, as did the faint chinging of spurs.

Through the frost-crusted window left of the door, Wilbur watched Devlin lead his sorrel and Goliath toward the cabin from the barn, breath frosting in the crisp, golden air around his handsome head. When Devlin had tied the horses to the hitchrack, he mounted the stoop and opened the door. He stood in the doorway with his big Smith & Wesson drawn.

He smiled a little sheepishly at Wilbur, who was leaning back in his chair, casually smoking. "Thought you might try to pull somethin'," the kid said.

"Like what?"

"Maybe beef me with a gun you had hid. You once had a reputation for bein' a pretty wily gun wolf, you know."

"That was a long time ago, kid. That man's long done passed over the divide."

"Yeah, well, it's time for this one to pass over it, too."

With a mewling yip, Shep bolted up from the rug in front of the fire and barked threateningly at Devlin, lurching forward, tail and hackles raised. The dog snapped his jaws and showed his fangs.

The young lawman glared at the dog. "All right, I had enough of that cur. He ain't goin' with us, and he'll likely just starve here, so it's the best thing, Calhoun. I'm gonna put him down." He gave a cold grin, dimpling his cheeks. "Can't say as I'm sorry to do it, either."

Devlin raised the revolver and narrowed an eye as he aimed down the barrel at the snarling, barking collie.

Ka-boooommmm!

The sawed-off shotgun that Wilbur detonated from the strap iron brace beneath the table hammered Devlin with two pumpkin-sized clumps of double-aught buckshot. They punched through his belly, lifted him two feet in the air, and hurled him straight back out the door, across the stoop, and into the new-fallen snow beside the nickering horses.

Leaving the shotgun in its hideout cage, Wilbur slid his chair back, rose, took a deep puff from his quirley, and walked to the door. Shep had run out before him and was sniffing the fallen Devlin, who lay in the snow, limbs akimbo, blood and guts oozing from his middle. His pistol lay several yards away, nearly buried.

The young lawman had a stunned, almost bland look. He blinked rapidly. Blood slithered down his mouth corners, beneath his carefully trimmed mustache.

Wilbur walked out to the edge of the stoop and stared down at the fast-dying younker.

"Why . . . you old . . . gun . . . dog!" the kid wheezed.

"Once one, always one, I reckon." Wilbur took another puff from his quirley. "You sure ain't the fruit of *my* loins. Why, you're that yellow-livered Virgil Boatwright's boy!"

Devlin scowled bewilderedly up at him, his life fast fading as the snow around him grew quickly crimson.

"Know what tipped me?" Wilbur asked, his eyes growing sharp with cunning. "You're too damn purty, and you don't like dogs."

When the kid had stopped breathing but left his eyes open, Wilbur donned his hat, shrugged into his coat, and tied a rope around the dead lawman's shoulders. The old outlaw swung up onto Goliath's back, dallied the rope around his saddle horn, and reined the horse away from the hitchrack.

Shep sat on the stoop, eyeing Wilbur curiously, one ear cocked, the other curled forward, head tipped to one side.

"Come on, Shep," Wilbur called as he began dragging the Boatwright trash from his yard. "Let's go feed the wolf!"

Shep gave a bark and went running.

■ ■ ■ ■

Peter Brandvold has published over a hundred fast-action westerns under his real name and his penname, Frank Leslie. Recent books have been published by Five Star. All are available at Amazon and elsewhere, and many are now available in audio editions from Graphic Audio.

■ ■ ■ ■

DIRTY OLD TOWN
BY GREG HUNT

■ ■ ■ ■

Ridge Parkman halted his horse to gaze at the wall of dark storm clouds racing across the rolling Kansas prairie. He judged the squall to be at least ten miles away. But it was coming on fast and would be on top of him soon enough.

A swirl of clouds dipped down into a slender column that writhed and danced along the ground like a dangling length of rope. Although there wasn't much for it to tear up and haul skyward out on the plains, Parkman had seen what tornadoes could do in other places. But this twister was short-lived, and soon got fatter and lighter in color, then dissolved away like chimney smoke.

Parkman turned to gaze southeast and studied a far-off line of trees that banded the Neosho River. He could barely make out a cluster of buildings in one spot, tiny and insignificant at such a distance.

If he got good directions back in Emporia and made the right choices where the winding, dusty roads branched on the ride down, that should be his destination, Abolition, Kansas. The storm was traveling a lot faster than him, and he was in for a soaking before he got there. But at least he would sleep indoors tonight, maybe even in a bed.

By the time he reached the outskirts of Abolition an hour later, the storm had blasted through, done its work, and moved on. Parkman was soaked despite the oilskin draped over his head and body during the worst of the deluge. Remarkably, the storm had taken an unexpected swing north before it hit Abolition, and the town was still powder dry.

It was hard to imagine anything as serious as a range war going on in a drab, backwater ink spot like this one. But that's what the telegram said. And the fact that the call for support had come from Major Lionel Casey himself gave the request all the gravity needed to dispatch a U.S. marshal to Abolition. If Casey asked for help, the problem was serious.

Abolition seemed to have grown up haphazardly on the west bank of the slow-flowing Neosho River. Businesses and homes were scattered randomly, some facing the main road, and others set back and positioned however their builder decided. Quite a few of the businesses were closed down, and a good number of the houses uninhabited. Some had boards nailed across the windows and doors, and others had signs out front pronouncing their fate. A few had only that sad, empty look.

The storm that missed Abolition left the whole town still blanketed in prairie dust. It was an odd thing, Parkman thought, being soaked to his drawers from a downpour, and riding down a street where dust puffed up with every fall of his horse's hooves.

Parkman spotted a saloon, The Sodbuster, but two planks were nailed across the front door in a clumsy X. He hated to see that because he had been looking forward to a beer, cold if he was lucky. Other businesses were similarly deserted, including a saddlery, a dry goods store, a café, and even a pretentious boardinghouse named the Pride of Kansas Hotel. The streets were empty in the heat of the summer afternoon, adding to the ghost-town look of Abolition.

He steered his horse, General Grant, toward one place that remained in business. A middle-aged woman sat in a rocking chair on the front porch of Eldrich's General Mercantile, knitting something that looked like it might someday be a sweater. Her faded bonnet shaded her eyes, but from the slight lifting of her head he assumed that she was looking at him.

Parkman peeled off his damp hat and gave her a smile, which she didn't return. "Good day, ma'am," he said.

"Looks like you got caught out in it," the woman said, like it was his own fault. "Just the luck of this old town. A storm like that blows by when we need all the rain we can get, but leaves us without even a drizzle."

"Never can tell about those summer storms," Parkman said. "But at least it carried the twisters away with it."

"Might be the best thing if one of them cyclones wiped the whole town off the map. Like shooting an old dog that's got no use to its life anymore."

There wasn't much use sucking on this sour lemon anymore, so Parkman got down to business. "I'm looking for the town marshal," he said. "I've got business with Lionel Casey."

With a nod, the woman indicated the way Parkman had already come. "The jail's back up Liberty Street. You rode past it. Last building on the left, under that big mulberry tree."

"I must have missed the sign."

"Nope, you didn't. Casey took it down."

Parkman wondered why, but didn't ask. "I thank you, ma'am," he said, donning his hat. "Name's Ridge Parkman. Nice meeting you." She mumbled something as he turned to ride away, but he didn't wait to find out what. Probably nothing good.

The mulberry's spreading branches provided welcome shade for the two horses tied to its lower branches. Both animals were smaller than General Grant, lean, agile cow ponies. The simple plank building the woman had pointed him to sat close by. Parkman looped his reins over a mulberry branch and walked over. On the ground, leaning against the wall, was a sign that read "City of Abolition, Marshal's Office." The door was partly open, so Parkman mounted the log steps and went in.

Instead of the town marshal, he was surprised to find two young men lazing inside, one leaning back in a chair with his feet up on a desk, and the other dozing across the room.

The office was simple and austere, less than he expected for the office of a man like Major Casey. Only one old single-shot shotgun populated the gun rack, and the curtains over the two small windows on either side of the building were threadbare, stirring lazily in a hint of a breeze. A scorched pot sat on a cast-iron woodstove, and beside it a heap of empty tin cans buzzed and churned with flies. A bucket of water with a metal dipper sat on the floor.

The fellow at the desk eyed Parkman with a sneer. A shiny new Colt lay on the desk beside his crossed legs, just out of reach unless he sat up. Parkman wondered if he saw something like a challenge in the young man's eyes. The other one across the room meandered over to the desk. He was trying to look tough, but was too young to pull it off.

"I'm looking for the town marshal, Lionel Casey," Parkman said. This setup rang a note of warning to him, but it didn't seem like anything he couldn't handle.

The pair glanced at each other in amusement. "He's around here someplace," the one at the desk said.

"Where?"

"Asleep in back. Sound asleep, I'd say." He cocked his head toward a wooden door in back. It had a grill of metal bars that served as a window, and a hasp and padlock above the latch. The fellow looked to be in his early twenties, too dandied up to be a working cowboy. The boy standing nearby was sixteen or so, wearing faded work clothes and scuffed boots. But the hand gun strapped to his side made him man enough to be wary of.

"Who are you fellows?" Parkman asked. "Not deputies, I'm guessing."

"Who's askin'?"

Parkman's patience was dwindling. He took a step forward, and noticed a splotch of blood on the front sight of the revolver on the desk. "I'll try one last time. Who the hell are you, boy, and why are you making yourself comfortable in Marshal Casey's chair?"

"Name's Kid Tulsa. Maybe you've heard of me from down Oklahoma way. And this here's Tim Garnett. His daddy owns the biggest ranch in this part of the state, and pretty much owns Abolition, too. I was just seeing what it felt like to sit in an honest-to-goodness legend's chair."

"Kid Tulsa?" Parkman said. "A real terror, I reckon. Lightning draw and all that."

"You want to find out?"

Parkman shook his head in annoyance, deciding it was too late to turn this thing around. Like so many of his kind, this fellow was probably fast with a gun, and not afraid to put a bullet in just about anybody. That gave his type a reckless bravado, but not necessarily the good sense to think every fight through before it started. It hadn't occurred to this one yet that Parkman's last step had put him closer to that gun on the desk than he was. Clearly Kid Tulsa had more sass ready, but Parkman wanted to get this over with. He swept the revolver off the table with his right hand, then drew it back and swung a hard punch at the boy named Tim standing by the desk. Tim had already started fumbling for his own holstered revolver, and as he stumbled back and slammed into the wall, it went off.

As the sound of the shot echoed in their ears and the gun smoke fogged around them, they all paused for an instant to take stock. Parkman realized he wasn't shot, and re-holstered his own revolver, which had leaped into his hand almost of its own choice.

"Damn you, Tim! Here I am trying to teach you a thing or two, and look at what you done to me!"

Both young men were on the floor. Tim Garnett was down from the punch Parkman delivered, looking half-witted, and Kid Tulsa, terror of Oklahoma, had managed to fall out of his chair. Parkman decided it was time to display his status in society. He took out his U.S. Marshal's badge and pinned it on. Then he leaned over the desk and looked down at Kid Tulsa.

"You're bleeding, Kid," Parkman said.

"I know, dammit. I know!" Kid Tulsa was twisting around to look at his wounded leg. "That ignorant sum bitch shot me."

"Better him than me," Parkman said. "With honest-to-goodness gunslingers like yourself, I generally aim just above a man's nose. There, or the second shirt button down from the top."

"You can go to hell! I need help!"

Across the room Tim was starting to get his wits back, and was realizing his own nose was streaming blood. Lionel Casey wasn't likely to be pleased about so much blood decorating his office.

"You, other kid. Tim," Parkman said. "Come here and help your buddy."

"I can't," Tim said, near hysteria. "I'm hurt my own self." He had two fingers stuck up his gushing nostrils.

"You shot him, so unless you want him to bleed out, you get your ignorant tail over here and do something about it. I'll tell you what to do, but I'm not about to get blood all over my last clean shirt helping this weasel."

Tim crawled reluctantly over to them, and under Parkman's supervision, he ripped Kid Tulsa's shirt to shreds and turned it into a clumsy bandage around the bullet hole in his thigh.

"You'll need to get him to your town doctor," Parkman said, "So he can sew that hole closed. Maybe he can set your nose, too. Looks a little lopsided."

"Abolition don't have a doctor," Tim said. "Last one we had went off with the army and never come back. Used to be a woman who did some doctoring. But I think she died. Or maybe got married."

"Well, take him someplace," Parkman said with growing irritation. "I've got an idea there's another hurt man in back that I need to see to, and his life's worth ten of yours on his worst day." Tim helped Kid Tulsa to his feet, and as the pain settled in, he began to squall and cuss. They left two trails of blood as they shuffled out the door.

"The next time I see you boys, you'd best show some respect," Parkman called out after them. "It would've been easier just to shoot you both and have done with it."

Their spunk didn't start coming back until they had mounted their horses. "My daddy will be around to settle up for this," Tim Garnett called back.

"I hope he's a better shot than you, boy," Parkman said, "else nobody in town will be safe when we have at it."

Parkman went to the door in back and opened it. The back room was dim and stagnant, but he got a general idea of the layout. Three low bunks were built against the far wall. A man laid in one bunk with his back to the door, snorting and gargling restlessly.

"Major Casey? Marshal?" Parkman said quietly. The man didn't respond to his name, and when Parkman went over and shook him, he only moaned and grumbled. There was a long, deep gash on his temple, caked with drying blood, and a split on his lip.

Parkman went out to his horse to get a roll of cheesecloth and a small bottle of whiskey that he carried for times like this, and took a bucket of water into the back with him. Lionel Casey came around while Parkman was working on him, yelling and swinging a feeble fist as Parkman washed his wounds. He raised hell again when Parkman poured a splash of whiskey over the heavy bandage he had tied around the man's head. Parkman knew it burned, but the rotgut would stop the wound from festering.

"Got any of that stuff left?" Casey said at last.

"The whiskey?" Parkman asked.

"No, the water. My mouth's dry as ashes." The marshal drank three dippers full, then Parkman helped him into the front room, where he settled into his chair with a grunt.

"Lawdamercy, look at all this blood," Casey noted. "Hope none of it's yours."

"Most of it's from a wannabe gunhand that calls himself Kid Tulsa. He hails from Oklahoma, and thought highly of himself. The rest is from some local boy, Tim something."

"Tim Garnett. They're the ones that's worked me over. Much obliged, mister . . ."

"Ridge Parkman. I'm a U.S. marshal down from Kansas City. You sent for me, and it seems I got here right on time. What was this about?"

"Abe Garnett sent 'em. He owns the Circle Cross down south of here, and he sent them to tell me he wouldn't tolerate any interference when they did what they had to do."

"What do they have to do?"

"Shoot up Chet Morgan and his JM crew, I figure."

"Is that part of the range war you mentioned in your telegram?"

"Something like that."

Parkman didn't know Lionel Casey, but had heard plenty about him. His reputation started during the war as a major in the Union Army, charged with taking the northwest quarter of Missouri back from the rampaging bushwhackers who supported the southern cause, despite the fact that their home state had never seceded. It was a no rules, no battle lines, no quarter fight right to the end of the war and after.

Casey was commonly credited as the man who ordered the head of Bloody Bill Anderson cut off and left to rot on a fence post as revenge for the horrors he had inflicted on the town of Centralia. Shortly after the war's end, Casey and his unit tracked Bill Quantrill, the renegade leader, across three states, cornered him in Kentucky, and kept him in custody until he died of the wounds he received during his capture.

Soon after, Major Casey resigned his commission and headed west. Over the next few years he worked as a town-tamer in Colorado and Utah. But he hardly looked like a legend now. Everybody got old if they didn't die first.

"I'll give it to you straight-on, Parkman," Casey said. "I'm not no town marshal anymore, nor much of anything else, I suppose. Half the people who lived here have moved on, including most of the town council. They stopped paying my salary some time back, and I only stay here now 'cause I've got no place else to go."

"Well, sir, I'm truly sorry to see that things have taken such a bitter turn for you," Parkman said. "The last I heard some time back, you were the law in some little boom town out in the Rockies. I forgot the name."

"That would be Winchester. But I had to give it up," Casey said. "I got so I could hardly breathe up in the high country. I'd get so dizzy out of nowhere that I'd stagger around and fall down like a drunk. An' this here rheumatism was coming over me somethin' awful. Hands, knees, ass, and elbows. Pretty much all over." He pointed to a long staff leaning in a corner and said, "Yonder's my best friend nowadays."

"My grandpa had that, and it's no picnic."

"Four years ago, me and my deputy was hot after some scalawags north of Winchester. When we caught up to them, he got shot all to hell 'cause I wasn't fast enough to do my share." Casey's gaze drifted away out the window, as if looking back at that time and place. "When I did get my Colt out, I was too dizzy to shoot straight, and a fine young man named Jonathan Newton died because of it. Because of me. That's when I knew it was time to come down to the flatlands. I didn't have anybody left back home in Illinois, and no home place to return to. So I found this little town here on the prairie, and used my big-shot reputation to hire on as the local law. I been here three years, and most of the first two was pretty good. But look at me now. And I just turned sixty-two."

"Men in our business don't expect to live so long," Parkman said. "Too bad it wasn't you that got it that day instead of your deputy." On the surface, it seemed a harsh thing to say, but Casey understood.

"Amen to that, Parkman. Sooner or later, the wheels fall off even the best wagon."

"Well, are you the town marshal or aren't you?"

"Somewhere in the middle. They stopped paying my salary, so for spite I took off the badge and pulled down the sign. I keep my gun up there," he said, pointing to a rolled-up holster and sidearm on the shelf near the stove. "Gourd Eldrich down at the general mercantile is the onliest council member left. He's sort of the mayor now. But that greedy old hag he's married to ain't about to let him pay me out of his own pocket."

"I met her on the way in," Parkman said. "She's a real charmer."

"Anyhow, Gourd and I worked out a side

bargain," Casey said. "I got no place else to go and no money to get there, so I stay here and sleep in back. If any little ruckus happens I pin on the badge and strap on the iron, and I handle it. But only the easy things, like a drunk cowboy or a chicken thief. I ain't much with a gun no more 'cause of the rheumatism . . ." He showed Parkman his swollen, knotty fingers. ". . . but I still got some bluff left."

"Then what about the telegram you sent to the marshal's office in Kansas City about a range war? Captain Randolph said to get down here in a hurry. He said if Major Casey wired for help, things must be bad." His frustration was beginning to rise, wondering if he had ridden all that way to stop a range war in a ghost town.

"Like I said, I still pin on the badge once in a while, but mostly for small stuff," Casey explained.

"So, tell me about the range war, Major. They're generally fights over grazing land, but it seems like there's plenty of open land hereabouts, and not many cows."

"It's an old feud between two outfits that's been going on for years, but after the hard times last year and this, things finally came to a rolling boil."

"Hard times? I thought things were never

better for the cattle business."

"Just about everyplace but here," Casey said. "First it was the grasshoppers that blew through last summer like some kind of Old Testament plague. They ate the prairie grasses down to nubs, and after they moved on, there wasn't much left for the cattle. The ranchers had to sell their herds cheap, and the smaller outfits folded. Times were tough here in town, too, but most people stuck it out 'cause they figured things would get better in the spring."

"But they didn't, I'm guessing," Parkman said.

"Hoof and mouth," Casey said simply. "Most of the breed stock the ranchers held onto came down with it, along with the calves that dropped over the winter."

"So they couldn't sell what was left."

"Nope. One feller, Greene Norris, got so desperate that he drove a small herd southwest into Oklahoma, then turned back north toward Wichita and tried to pass them off as Texas beef. But it didn't work. They shot his whole herd, and when Greene got stirred up about it, they shot him, too. The rest of the ranchers just killed their herds off. After that only two big outfits were left, the Circle Cross and the JM."

"So we're back to my first question," Parkman said. "Isn't it foolish to start a range war over range that's got no cows on it?"

"Not if you know what came before," Casey said. "It's not really about cows. Abe Garnett came to Kansas in the fifties with that lunatic John Brown to make sure Kansas came into the Union as a free state. After Old Brown went back east and got hisself hung for insurrection, Abe started up the Circle Cross spread and the town of Abolition.

"Jim Morgan didn't come here and start up the JM brand until after the war. He'd been a farmer in western Missouri, but the border raids by the Kansas Red Legs had wiped him out by the end of the war, carrying off his slaves, burning his crops, and such. So he moved to Abolition 'cause the land was cheap and the cattle market was booming."

"I can see how those two outfits wouldn't mix," Parkman said.

"They kept a lid on things for a few years because the money was there for both of them. There was a few killings, now and again, but there always is. Now, with the cattle gone and the town dying, the old squabbles are starting up again. A few weeks back, somebody shot Jim Morgan dead. Walked right up on his porch and shot him through the window. Morgan's two boys blamed Garnett's bunch, and commenced to having at Garnett's men when they could. Then Garnett's men started doing the same. It might not be a range war, but it's more than I can handle."

"It's more than any one man can handle. Does this county have a sheriff?"

"He's clear across the county and not much interested in our problems. Not hardly any votes left in Abolition," Casey said. "The marshals was my last resort."

"Makes sense," Parkman said. "If they've started bringing in outside talent like this Kid Tulsa to fight this fight, there's probably not much good sense left anywhere around. Maybe tomorrow I should ride out to both spreads and parley. You reckon they'd shoot me if I just rode right up?"

"Maybe not, if you shouted out from away far off that you were the law, and kept that badge on where they could see it. Maybe not then."

Not very reassuring, Parkman thought.

Major Casey gave Parkman directions to the abandoned livery barn. The livery man had loaded up everything his wagon would hold and headed toward Emporia. But there was no way he could haul away the hay in the loft, and there was still enough to feed the General. Parkman wiped him down with his saddle blanket, kicked a four-foot pile of hay out the loft door, pumped the water trough full, and set him loose in the corral.

There were two other animals in the corral, a brace of sturdy mules that he figured belonged to the owners of the covered wagon nearby. Nobody stirred around the wagon so he let them be. With the hotel boarded up, Parkman resolved to spend the night in the barn.

It was dusk by the time he got everything done, and he decided to wash off the trail grime. As he walked through the scattering of cottonwoods and willows on the way to the nearby Neosho, he heard a woman coming up from the river through the trees, humming softly.

Parkman spoke out from a distance. "Evening, ma'am. How's the water?"

He expected to see caution on her face, but instead she gave him a bold smile. "Wonderful," she said. "Not cold, but just cool enough." She had long black hair, still damp and frizzy. The light tan hue of her skin and the almond shape of her dark eyes hinted of some foreign blood, Mexican maybe, or some even more exotic mix. She was pretty, but it wasn't the kind of soft, captivating beauty that had men picking flowers. It was more of a tough, challenging beauty, the kind that men fought over. She raised one hand and pinched the bodice of her damp blouse closed in a gesture of faux modesty.

"I'm glad I didn't get here in time to embarrass you," Parkman said.

She gave him that teasing smile again. "Must be I found myself a gentleman. Your type is scarce in these parts. My name is Isadora."

"I'm Ridge Parkman." The hand she offered him was surprisingly strong and her grip was firm.

"I'm not a shy girl, Ridge."

"I can tell, ma'am."

"And I'm not a ma'am. I'm just Isadora, Isadora Faust."

"Suits me, Isadora."

They talked a moment longer, and Parkman felt relaxed in her company. The wagon and mules were hers and her father's. They traveled all over, she explained, although she was vague about their journeys. Peddlers, Parkman supposed.

"I should go," Isadora said at last. "I have to fix my papa's supper. He's not feeling well."

After his bath, Parkman returned to the barn and ate a meager supper of jerky and stale cornbread, not wanting to make the effort to fix anything tastier.

It was dark inside the barn, but the full moon slid blades of light between the plank walls to help him lay out his blankets. Following an old habit, he laid his Colt within easy reach beside him. He was asleep in minutes, and dreamed of a pretty girl with black hair who laughed and smiled and promised that if he stole a kiss, she wouldn't tell her daddy.

Parkman's eyes opened immediately when he heard his horse huff and snort in the corral out back of the barn. He glanced toward the loft opening and saw the gray-rose hints of early dawn. The hinge on one of the barn doors squeaked. "Hello? Ridge Parkman, are you in here?" It was Isadora.

"Up in the loft," he said. "Give me a minute to pull my boots on."

Isadora Faust looked fresh as a spring rose this morning. She wore a colorful skirt and a loose cotton blouse, and her hair was brushed and shiny, spilling down her back like a cape. She smiled, and her eyes danced. This one could twist a man into knots before he even knew it happened.

"Will you come over to the wagon for breakfast?" she offered. "I have biscuits baking on the coals. And I have eggs, real chicken eggs."

"Sounds too good to pass up," Parkman said. "I can add some bacon to the menu. I have a pretty good chunk that hasn't gone rancid yet."

"That's perfect. Papa loves bacon, if he feels well enough to eat anything this morning."

Isadora's father sat in a wooden chair in their simple camp. The old man's shoulders sagged forward, and he stared at the small cooking fire as if the flames had mesmerized him. His clothes hung loose on his frail frame, and the flesh of his face and hands had turned to wrinkled old leather. He looked up as they got near, and Isadora introduced him to Ridge as Geraldo Faust.

"Pleased to meet you, sir," Parkman said, reaching out for a handshake that never happened. Geraldo Faust awarded him with only a slight nod and a sour glance of disapproval, then raised a small brown bottle to his lips and took a gulp. Parkman glimpsed the word "elixir" on the paper label.

Isadora laughed when she saw Ridge watching. "He likes that stuff better than coffee in the morning."

"What's it good for?"

"Not much except to make your head spin

if you drink too much. But we sell a lot of it when we're in some town big enough to get a crowd together. Professor Faust's Miracle Elixir. Grain alcohol, molasses, hot pepper sauce, a splash of turpentine, a dash of salt, a dash of alum, and some herbs."

Isadora moved to the fire to tend her cooking, and Ridge went over to watch since her father seemed to be dozing off. "So is that what you do for a living? Sell elixir?" he asked. "You and your papa?"

"We sell other things, too, lotions and potions for almost anything that ails you. But the elixir is our best seller, especially to the old biddies with aches and pains. They'd never put a drop of whiskey in their mouth, but they drink that stuff like buttermilk. And we have a little show we put on if the town is big enough. We pitch a tent and I dance out front while Papa plays his fiddle. Then I go in the tent, and any grown man with ten cents to spare can come in to see what happens next." She looked up from laying the thick slices of bacon into a sizzling iron skillet and gave Parkman a smile loaded with meaning. "I've been performing the Dance of Desire since I was fourteen."

Isadora had only two eggs, which she scrambled with an onion and a sliced potato. Then she served up metal plates for Parkman and her papa with scrambled eggs, crispy slices of bacon, and a couple of buttered biscuits still too hot to pick up with your fingers. "Fit for a king," Parkman said as he dived in.

"That's good, because Papa is a king, or was at least, back when we traveled with the caravan."

"What's a caravan? Is it like a wagon train?"

"Oh, no, the caravan of our people. We traveled all the time, like nomads in the desert, and still do, but always alone now. That's the only home I've ever had," she said, pointing to the wagon.

"Interesting life," Parkman said. He would have liked to ask a lot more questions, but something held him back.

"When we came to this town I could tell that there was no use trying to set up and sell our wares, but Papa was getting sicker, and I didn't want to leave until he felt better. But we might have to go soon because I'm running out of money. In the store, they charge anything they want because they can."

Isadora was kneeling by her papa, delivering small bites of food to his mouth. With his eyes barely open, he accepted some and turned away others. At last, he raised one hand and gently pushed her arm away, then lifted the elixir bottle and took a nip.

"Papa, you're drinking up all our inventory," she said, looking down at him with a tender smile. She stood and began eating what was left on his plate.

Later, Parkman rode down to the jail. He found Casey sitting on a chair with an old military bayonet in one hand, bracing a tin can between his legs with the other. Parkman knocked on the doorframe and went on in.

"Mornin', Marshal Parkman," Casey said. "You eat yet?" The bayonet descended with fortunate precision and punctured the can, then the old man began to twist and shove the blade until he had it somewhat open. "Gourd gives me the can goods he can't sell 'cause they're too dented or the paper label's come off. Sometimes I don't know what I'll be having 'til the can's open. One time, peaches, another time butter beans. It makes eating a real adventure. But I don't know what I'd do without them. Grab yourself a can. Get a dented one with a label if you're particular."

"Some traveling folks down by the river shared with me," Parkman said.

"Hot diggety," Casey said, laying the

bayonet aside on the stove. "Yams in sugar syrup." He began fishing out chunks of sweet potatoes with his fingers and popping them in his mouth.

"You must have ate with the gypsies," Casey said. "I need to go have a talk with them, maybe run them on out of town. But it's too long a walk, and I hadn't felt up to it. I do hate them damned gypsies with a burning vengeance."

"They seemed like nice enough folks," Parkman said. "Just a pretty, flirty girl and her old daddy, who seems on his last legs."

"Wal, they shared somebody's food with you, but it prob'ly wasn't theirs. Two women in town have come by and told me things was disappearing from their gardens, a little bit of this and that, but enough to notice. And Widow Willaby, who's got a little place half a mile down the road, stopped in this morning to gab. She said she hadn't found a single egg in her chicken coop for two days. She thought they'd stopped laying 'til she heard there was gypsies about. I expect the chickens will start disappearing, too."

"Well, how about I handle that for you?"

"Fine with me," Casey said gruffly. "I despise them people. I mixed it up with them more than once out west. And the women, I swear they're the worst of the lot.

Best be careful, son, or you'll wake one morning with empty pockets."

Parkman stopped by the general store on his way out of town. The surly woman he had spoken with yesterday was not in sight. Instead, a balding man wearing a linen apron over his street clothes was tending the place. Parkman introduced himself as United States Marshal Ridge Parkman right off so there would be no misunderstandings.

"And you must be Mayor Gourd Eldrich," Parkman said.

"Councilman . . . mayor . . . I'm not sure which," Eldrich admitted. "One's as good as the other, at least until we have another town election. And you must be the lawman that Lionel sent for to help with the feud going on here. You're a welcome sight, Marshal."

"Glad to hear it, Mayor," Parkman said. "I'm riding out now to see if I can do anything to cool this squabble down. But that's not why I stopped by your store."

"Needing supplies? I should have anything you need, even cartridges for that Colt. I just got back from Topeka with two loaded wagons, so I'm fully stocked now. No teamsters around to drive the wagons, so I go myself, me and a Mex."

"I only want to open an account for now," Parkman said, laying a ten-dollar gold piece on the wooden counter. "There's a girl and her father staying in a wagon down by the livery barn, and I've hired her for my cook while I'm here. Anything she buys, take it out of that."

"Oh, them," Eldrich said, making a face like he'd just got a whiff of the outhouse. "Hortense told me that woman was in here, and said she might of stole some things when Hortense had to go in back for a minute."

Parkman ignored that, realizing that possibly it was the truth. "But keep this in mind, Mr. Eldrich. She'll be spending my money, and I know what things cost," he said.

"Yes, sir, Marshal. Yes, sir. But tell that girl that nothing better fall into her basket by accident. We've got laws."

"I'll tell her."

Parkman thought about dropping by the livery stable to tell Isadora about her newly established credit at the store, but then didn't. He had a lot of riding ahead today, and he needed to get started. Following Casey's instructions, he rode south out of town on Liberty Street, which soon became an ordinary wagon road that followed the rises and contours of the Kansas landscape. The sky was vivid blue without a wisp of clouds, and the still air promised a hot ride later. The prairie grass was thick and lush all around, but the browning tips signaled a growing need for rain. Several miles south of town, he found a weathered sign pointing down a side road to the "JM Ranch."

From time to time he saw the handiwork of the deadly disease that had stricken the local herds. The rotting carcasses of cattle had been left where they were killed, sometimes one or two together, and other times in tragic clusters. It would take years to recover from this loss, and like Casey said, many of the ranches could not survive this kind of devastation. No wonder people in these parts were in such a sour mood.

Eventually, he spotted a distant cluster of buildings that must be the ranch headquarters. Soon he himself was noticed, and four riders mounted up and headed his way.

Topping a rise, he saw that the welcoming committee was no more than a few hundred yards away. They weren't riding fast and hard, but there seemed to be resolve in the gait they set their horses to. He halted General Grant, looped the reins loosely over the saddle horn, and stepped to the ground. Glancing at his two rifles, he chose the

Winchester over the Sharps, and drew it from the scabbard, cradling it in the crook of his arm. If they drew up close and trouble started, he could drop the rifle and rely on his revolver, but if they had at him from farther out, the rifle was the thing.

As they neared, Parkman sensed the likelihood of danger diminishing. "United States Marshal," he said loudly. "I came to talk."

The riders stopped twenty feet from Parkman. They didn't fan out like men ready for a scrap. They sat casually in their saddles, hands not hovering near their sidearms. One rider let his horse wander ahead of the others, which identified him as the boss.

"Name's Chet Morgan," the man said. He glanced at the badge on Parkman's chest, then at the rifle, then at the Colt, and then back at his face.

"I'm Ridge Parkman, down from Kansas City."

"I have to say, Marshal, you'll set my mind at ease if you stow that rifle."

"Glad to oblige," Parkman said, returning the Winchester to its scabbard.

"The ugly, lanky one back there on the bay is my kid brother, Horace," Morgan said. Horace, a young man of about twenty, tall and stout, shook his head as if the tease was an old one. "And the other two are my

hands, Willie Johnson and Red Canfield."
Willie was the oldest, pushing fifty, and Red
was maybe half that. "Willie makes the
worst coffee in Kansas. Come on along and
find that out for yourself."

"I'm game," Parkman said.

During the ride to the ranch house, Chet
Morgan rehashed the hard-times tale that
Major Casey had described the afternoon
before. Morgan's version was much the
same, but a lot more personal because it
was his cattle whose carcasses lay rotting
along the trail. "I've been a cattle rancher
half my life, Marshal," he said, "but I
haven't sunk my teeth into a steak since I
don't know when. A man can only eat so
much jackrabbit stew without going batshit
crazy. 'Specially the way Willie cooks it."

"You want your pay back, boss?" Willie
grumbled from nearby. "Naw, I guess that
won't work . . . 'cause you haven't made
payroll in three months."

"You know I'm good for it, old man,"
Morgan said. "And didn't I promise we'd
go to town and get drunk soon as Gourd
Eldrich gets back with some liquor? That's
all you spend your money on, anyway. That
and whores."

"If they was any whores," Willie said.
"Which they ain't."

"Eldrich is back, if that's what you've been waiting for," Parkman said. "I talked to him this morning."

"You hear that, Red?" Willie asked. "Gourd's back and we're as good as drunk already."

The JR headquarters was typical for a working ranch. The main house was a one-story building, and another long, narrow structure served as the bunkhouse. Midway between them was the cookhouse, with a variety of sheds and a fenced-in garden behind. The barn was large, with several corrals, mostly empty. There were a few horses there, and surprisingly, perhaps two dozen head of cattle. Those must be the fortunate few that had so far escaped the deadly blight of hoof and mouth.

"Come in, Marshal," Morgan said, dismounting. "Horace, you and Red take the horses out to the corral. Willie, coffee."

Parkman handed his reins to Red and turned to the house. It was a simple plank affair, sitting on a fieldstone foundation with stone chimneys at either end. One front window was boarded over, which must be where Jim Morgan's assassin had stood.

Chet led him into the front room on the right, which was a den of sorts. The furniture was humble, mostly homemade, and the windows were covered over with folds of coarse linen nailed to the walls. Dust coated everything, and in one spot on the floor was a blackish brown stain where the family patriarch must have died.

"There's no women here, so we're not much on cleaning," Morgan said. Then, noticing Parkman looking at the dried bloodstains on the floor, he added, "That's where Daddy died. Some bastard shot him through that window over there. We ain't settled up for that yet, but we will."

"Casey told me about that," Parkman said. "If you know who did it, I'll arrest him. We can have a trial in Abolition and hang him."

"I don't know who pulled the trigger, but I know who sent him." Morgan's voice hardened. "When I get close enough, we won't need no trial."

Parkman decided it was as good a time as any to say his piece. "This is why Marshal Casey brought me here to Abolition, Mr. Morgan. He told me there's bad blood between your outfit and Abe Garnett's. But the war's been over for near ten years now, and it's time to put a stop to all this hating and killing."

"Nothing ain't over for us, Marshal. Daddy came here in sixty-six to make a new start, and he did a good job of it. But Garnett never let up on him for all those years, same as during the war when his kind never stopped raiding over into Missouri to do all kinds of murder and mischief."

"The Missourians did the same, and gave back killing for killing," Parkman said. "I had family in the middle of that, and I can tell you one thing. Both sides thought they were doing what was right, what they had to do, sometimes even what they thought God told them to do. But from all I saw, God didn't have a hand in none of it."

Willie came in with a steaming coffee pot and two metal cups, which he unceremoniously set on a table. "No milk, no sugar, and this is the second time I boiled them grounds," he grumbled. "If I boil them one more time, they'll hardly stain the water."

"We'll stock up on all the basics when we go into town tomorrow," Morgan said irritably.

"And get drunk," Willie remind him.

"Drunk as Cooter Brown's dog, old man. Now scat so we can talk."

Parkman poured himself a cup of coffee and took a sip. It lived up to Morgan's dire predictions.

"Two years ago," Morgan said, "the JM was one of the best ranches in this part of

Kansas. We were running twenty-eight-hundred head, and our crew was so big we built onto the bunkhouse. The other outfits around here were doing just as well. Abolition had three saloons, a fancy house, a bank, and a Baptist and a Methodist church on either end of town. And then the plagues of Egypt started. I s'pose the frogs are next."

"Well, you've got to look ahead, Morgan," Parkman said. "You've still got the land, and the start of a new herd out there in the corrals. I grew up on a farm in Virginia, and I know there ain't no certainty in that line of work. It's the same for ranching. I'd bet you've got more now than your daddy had when he first came here, and you're still a young man. You can build your spread back up."

Chet Morgan took a drink of the coffee and made a disgusted face. Looking at him, Parkman understood that none of his logic was going to drag this man up from the dour mood he had settled into. And who could blame him? Nearly broke, a whole cattle herd dead and rotting out on the plains, and a murdered father in his grave. Who could fault him for the way he felt?

Within an hour, with two cups of Willie's coffee still churning in his guts, Parkman was back on his horse riding east. When he asked Morgan for directions to Abe Garnett's Circle Cross spread, you'd have thought he was asking if he could knock the man's front teeth out with a shovel. But he finally gave them. The blazing sun that was now past its apex showed no hint of mercy for any living thing. They needed more trees hereabouts, Parkman thought. If he lived here, he'd be planting trees every chance he got.

The marker for the turnoff to the Circle Cross pointed only toward more broad expanses of Kansas prairie. The Circle Cross spread was larger than the JM, but the decorations were much the same — dead cows scattered all over, rotting and stinking in the relentless summer sun.

The shot came from somewhere ahead and to the left, a rifle from the sound of it, maybe fifty yards or more away. General Grant squealed and reared, and though Parkman could have stayed in the saddle, he chose to pull his boots from the stirrups, drop the reins, and slide back across the horse's rump to the ground. For a moment, he lay flat and still in the powdery dirt, only moving one arm enough to ensure that his revolver was still strapped in its holster. The front of his shirt was smeared with streaks of blood, odd in their configuration, but he didn't feel shot anywhere. It was his horse's blood, picked up during the slide off.

General Grant was a short distance away, huffing and dancing nervously, turning his head back and trying to see the source of the pain he was feeling. Blood was running down his hindquarters, but Parkman couldn't tell yet how bad he was hit. That had to wait.

Right now, there was somebody out there with a rifle that he needed to deal with.

It seemed like a bad fix to Parkman. He didn't know if his horse was rideable, and couldn't risk getting up to find out. But there didn't seem to be anyplace close by to use for cover, not even a ditch alongside the road. There was nothing he could do but lay out in the open like a dead man and hope his chance came.

He rolled over slowly onto his belly and splayed his legs out awkwardly, like a dead man's might end up. Then he laid his hat beside him, drew his Colt, and slid it under the hat.

Parkman heard his attacker coming before he saw him. The man seemed to be cussing his mount as it struggled up out of the creek cut where he had been hiding, coming on with the full confidence that he had taken out his prey with the first shot. Watching with squinted eyes, Parkman didn't move a muscle, even holding his breath as his assassin rode up close.

"Lookie yonder, Sadie. By gawd, I finally got myself a decent horse," the man said. From his hillbilly twang, Parkman figured he must be from someplace in the Deep South, maybe Arkansas or Mississippi. "Now you can go back to pullin' a plow, which is all you're good for." He still had the rifle pointed down at Parkman, but his eyes were all over General Grant.

As the man drew one leg out of the stirrup to climb down out of the saddle, his mount turned irritably to the side as if he might be considering bucking off his load. For an instant, the man's back was to Parkman and the rifle muzzle went skyward. Parkman raised his revolver and took his shot. The rifle went off as it flew from the man's hand, the startled horse skittered sideways, and the man toppled backward to the ground, yipping and cussing as he landed hard on his rear end.

"You ain't dead," the man squalled out. "Damn you! You shot me in the hind end."

"Right where I was aiming," Parkman said.

"Why's that? I never heard of shootin' a man in the heinie before. It hurts like the dickens."

"I wanted you to get a taste of what my horse is feeling about now," Parkman said. He was on his feet by then, holstering his revolver and putting his hat back on as he walked toward his attacker. The danger was past. The rifle lay a few feet away from the wounded man, and he wore no sidearm.

"You work for Garnett?" Parkman asked. He picked up the rifle, jacked the cartridges out, and hammered it against the ground until the stock broke off. Then he took it by the barrel and threw it far out into the sage grass.

"I do," the man said. "And he'll be none too happy when he sees what you done to the rifle he loaned me." He was lying on his side now, reaching around with both hands to try and determine how bad his wound was. The back of his pants was caked with gooey red mud, but Parkman figured he wasn't hurt too bad or he'd be complaining more.

"It might turn out to be a lesson learned," Parkman said. "If he's going to loan a weapon out, he should put it in the hands of a man that can shoot straight."

"By gawd, I can shoot! I grew up down in Ozark with a gun in my hands from a young age. I just ran out of cartridges for my own rifle, and I didn't have time to sight this one in before he sent me out here on watch. Seems like it leads a little to the right."

"Right and low, I'd say. But that don't matter anymore," Parkman told the man. "Take your shirt off. I need something to clean my horse up with." He called General Grant over, poured water from his canteen onto the deep furrow on his rump, and blotted the blood away with the man's shirt. Then he laid the damp shirt across the wound.

As he mounted up, he looked down at the man, still lying in the dust, and said, "This wouldn't have gone well for you if you'd done worse harm to this fine animal."

"Didn't go well as it is," the man grumbled. "Where you goin'?"

"To have a little talk with your boss."

"I don't know if I can get my hands on ol' Sadie now, nor if I can sit the saddle if I do. You just gonna leave me here like this?"

"Hell, yeah," Parkman said, and flicked the General's reins lightly.

He rode ten more minutes before the Garnett place came into view. He stopped on a rise, still a safe distance away, to take stock of what he was getting into. The two-story house and outbuildings were located beside a shallow stretch of the Neosho. At first glance, it appeared to be a larger operation than the JM spread. He was spotted as before, which was his intention, and eventually two riders came out to take his measure. They stopped well short of where he was, but within shouting distance.

"State your business," one of them called out. The men wore sidearms, but didn't have rifles out, so Parkman didn't bother to dismount or haul out the Winchester this time.

"I'm down from the U.S. marshal's office in Kansas City. Name's Parkman, and my business is with Abe Garnett. Is that either one of you?"

"Nope, but he's expecting you. Come on in." The two riders didn't wait for him, but turned and rode away as Parkman got General Grant started. They had reached the barn and disappeared inside by the time Parkman rode up to the main house. He noticed that there was a man with a rifle at the door of the barn loft, and another one sitting in a chair on the roof of the bunkhouse. A gray-whiskered mutt growled at him from under the front porch, but didn't venture out.

Garnett made him wait a while before he came out. The sun was blazing hot now, so Parkman ground-reined his horse under a tree in the yard and mounted three steps up to the covered front porch. He had his back to the door, looking around, when the screen door squeaked open behind him.

"I knew you'd make it out here sooner or later," Garnett said, signaling that Parkman was not a welcome guest by not offering his hand. He wore no sidearm, but carried a shotgun casually in both hands. Parkman saw that the hammer was back and his finger was dangerously close to the trigger guard.

Garnett was older than Parkman expected, near sixty at least, but still stood tall, lean, and unrelenting. He sported one of the longest beards Parkman had ever seen, bringing to mind the impressive whiskers of Old Brown himself.

"You can sit if you're of a mind to," Garnett said, pointing to the chairs around a small table on the porch. They both took seats, and the rancher laid the shotgun down, the muzzle a few inches from Parkman's chest. Parkman had a mind to take the damned thing and throw it out in the yard, but reached out and shoved it aside instead, giving Garnett an *I don't scare that easy* glare.

"We heard shooting a while ago," Garnett said, "and since you're all in one piece, I guess you must have killed another one of my hired hands."

"He's not dead, not even close. If he's caught his horse by now, he's prob'ly riding kind of lopsided. And if he's got good sense, he'll be riding straight away from here. But what do you mean by *another*?"

"That young fellow I sent to town yesterday, John Hardesty, is laid out in the barn, waiting for Daniels to finish his coffin."

"The one that called himself Kid something-or-other? All he had was a leg wound."

"He bled out on the way back from town."

"Well, the world ain't lost much there," Parkman said, "but I'm not the one that shot him. Is that what your son told you?"

Abe Garnett just sat staring at Parkman, his dark eyes revealing little about what was going on in that old gray head of his. Finally, he turned to the side and called out, "Charlotte, send the boy out. Now!"

"I don't know what you sent them two into town to do," Parkman said. "But they pistol-whipped Major Casey, and him a war hero and a hobbled-up old man. They locked him in his own jail, and then just stayed around for devilment. That Hardesty fellow all but called me out, and it could have been me that shot him if things had gone a little different, but . . ."

Garnett stood as his son Tim came out the screen door, head down, moving slowly as if to delay whatever was coming. His nose was crooked, as Parkman predicted, but it was hard to guess how he would look later. Both eyes were puffed up crimson and purple, barely open enough for him to see, and his nose was twice the size it had been before.

"Yessir?" Tim said. His father towered over him by several inches.

"Is this the man you said shot young Hardesty?"

"Yessir." His eyes went over to Parkman briefly, then shifted down to his feet.

"He says he didn't do it."

"Just the same as," Tim stammered. "When the fight started, I reached for my gun to back the Kid up, but then this fellow hit me and my shot went wild. It wasn't my fault. If he hadn't . . ."

That was all the explaining Abe Garnett could abide. He backhanded his son with a powerful sweep of his arm, knocking the boy off the porch and several feet into the yard. Tim ended up in a crumpled heap in the dust, and had the good sense to stay there. His nose started bleeding again, but this time he was too afraid of his father to pay much attention to it.

"I send you into town to see how a man like Hardesty handles a problem," Garnett roared, "and you end up killing him."

"The Kid might not of died if there was somebody in Abolition who knew what to do," Tim started up. But then he recognized the futility of it and stopped. Garnett stomped down the porch steps and moved toward the boy, who was crabbing desperately away from him.

"That's enough, Garnett," Parkman said. The rancher looked at him, then glanced toward the shotgun on the table, which was too far away to do him any good. "I didn't ride all the way out here in this heat to watch you bloody up your son."

A hunched old woman dressed in a drab cotton dress and a limp cloth bonnet had come to the screen door to watch. That was probably Garnett's wife, but she was not about to get mixed up in this. Ranch hands began to drift in their direction to see what the commotion was about.

"So why did you come?"

"First off there's this. I'm lookin' for the coward who murdered Jim Morgan. I don't s'pose you'll turn him over to me, but if I find out who he is, I'll make sure he's tried and hanged for it."

"None of us know nothing about that," Garnett said, "but I sure don't mind that Morgan's dead. I'll guarantee you he's not sitting at Jesus' feet about now. He was an evil man, a soulless slaver of the blackest sort, and the sooner those sons of his join him in hell, the better I'll feel."

"That's the second thing," Parkman said. A half-dozen men had gathered in the yard, some armed and some not, giving him hard looks. He let his arm drop to his side, planning in the back of his mind which ones he'd take down first if they cut loose on him. "Major Casey got me here by claiming that he had a range war on his hands, but it's not hard to see that something a lot different is going on. You and that crew over at the JM have a lot of hate stored up, mostly for things that happened ten or fifteen years ago. It ain't against the law to hate somebody, Garnett, but it sure as hell is against the law to murder them. I won't tolerate it."

He could tell by the look on Garnett's face that he might as well be making this speech to a stump. But it needed saying.

"And as for you men over there," Parkman said, turning toward the crew in the yard. "Do you really want to get dragged into the middle of this old man's craziness? There's plenty of work other places where you won't have to put your life on the line for somebody else's feud. Out west of here in Colorado, and on south in Texas and Oklahoma, the cattle are doing just fine. You like staying alive, don't you?"

"Gettin' in the middle of this could be the worst mistake you ever made, Parkman," Garnett said, his voice ferocious. "It's the same message I sent those boys into town to deliver to Lionel Casey yesterday. This business ain't done, and you need to stay clear of it."

The first thing Ridge Parkman did when he reached his horse was pull the Winchester out and hold it at the ready as he mounted up, but Abe Garnett and his crew let him leave without challenge. It was small consolation, though, because all he had accomplished was to add his name to their enemy list.

At the first creek he came to, Parkman again cleaned the deep bullet furrow on General Grant's wound, splashing some whiskey on it and nearly earning himself a kick in the head. He rinsed the bushwhacker's shirt in the creek, and tied it back over the wound with a loop of rope. He thought he might be able to get some kind of healing potion from Isadora later.

It was pitch dark by the time he reached

the abandoned livery barn. He was staggering tired, but he hadn't eaten since morning and hunger was gnawing at his insides. He unsaddled his horse and got him settled in for the night. As he was finishing those chores, he saw Isadora sashaying up from her wagon, carrying a lantern in one hand and a basket in the other.

"I was worried about you, Ridge," the young woman admitted as she hung the lantern on a metal hook and spread a small blanket by its light. "I saved some supper for you."

"I'm much obliged," Parkman said, settling on the blanket and pulling off his boots. "Where I've been today, nobody's offered me much but lead." The food she brought was simple, a sliced tomato and a handful of radishes, leftover biscuits, and three small potatoes roasted in the coals. He ate with an enthusiasm that pleased his young companion.

"Nobody in this town speaks to me," Isadora said, "but I heard two women talking in the store about the trouble that's coming."

"Yeah, it could get rough. Maybe you and your daddy should hitch up and get on out of here before it starts."

"He couldn't travel, Ridge. He's getting

worse and worse, not eating anything and lying on a blanket in the shade all day. He talks to the devils inside him more than he talks to me."

"I'm sorry to hear that," Parkman said. "Do you have any notion of what's wrong with him?"

"Nothing that can be cured. Nothing that the elixir can help with." She paused a moment and her eyes met Parkman's. "It's the great sadness of life itself. All he wants is to die, but not quite yet."

"I've known some miserable people, Isadora, but none so low that it kills them straight out. First they have to suffer."

"Papa thinks God has turned His back on him, and sometimes I wonder if that's true." Parkman saw tears glistening in the girl's eyes, but she distracted herself by searching around in her basket until she found a final treat. She pulled out an oatmeal cookie and handed it to Parkman proudly.

"Man oh man!" Parkman said, taking a bite.

"I bought it for you in the store." Isadora hesitated for a moment, then said, "The man there told me what a kind thing you did for us."

"Did he charge you fair for the things you bought? I told him he'd better."

"Near enough," Isadora said. "But why did you do it? The people in the places we travel are never so nice to us."

Parkman gave her a wry grin. "Seems like they might have good reason. I hear there's been some nighttime foraging from the gardens and chicken coops around town. Marshal Casey said he might have to look into it if it didn't stop."

Isadora nodded knowingly, but seemed to show no shame at being caught. "It is the way of our people," she said. "In bad times, we find ways to get what we need and feel no shame. But we never take from people who can't spare it."

"Stealin' is stealin' in my book," Parkman said. "But now at least that poor old man up at the jailhouse won't have to hobble the quarter mile down here an' try to run you out of town."

"It might be better if he did. At least it would be all over with."

"How so?"

"We know this man from what he did to us years ago, and that's why we came to this town," Isadora said. "Papa blames Lionel Casey for his downfall, and cannot rest until he's taken his life."

"What's that about? I've always heard Casey was a fine man."

The young woman hesitated, then seemed to decide that she could trust him. It happened years before in a Colorado town called Steepleton. The town was riding high on a crest of recent gold strikes, and the gypsy caravan of eight wagons that Isadora and her family traveled with saw many opportunities for profit. At the time, Geraldo Faust was "king" of the band, a respected leader.

No one was ever quite sure how Lionel Casey, the town marshal, managed to catch the fancy of Geraldo's wife, Theodora, or what made her decide to take her scant belongings from their wagon and move in with Casey in his hotel room.

"All our lives changed forever when my mother left the people," Isadora said. The cuckold husband, Geraldo Faust, had only one clear option. Honor demanded that he kill both his unfaithful wife and the man who had stolen her. One night he set out to take his vengeance, but was met by a vigilante mob on its way to the gypsy encampment at the edge of town, intent on forcing them to leave or suffer the consequences. Lionel Casey was their inspiration, their leader. With women and children at risk, the gypsy band packed up and was on the move before dawn.

In the months that followed, Geraldo Faust sank into a well of anger and bitterness. Eventually, because of his failure to avenge his dishonor, the elders removed him from his station and sent him and his daughter away to the solitary, nomad life they now led. When they returned to Steepleton, Casey had already moved on, nobody was quite sure where. It was much the same for Isadora's mother. Some said she was killed in a knife fight in a whorehouse, and others said she had gone north with a party of miners chasing the next big strike.

"For years, everywhere we went Papa asked about Lionel Casey," Isadora said, "but after a while it was like he had simply disappeared. I tried to convince Papa that he was probably dead, but Papa wouldn't believe it.

"Then one day we heard he was in Kansas. We spent months traveling from town to town, asking about him, until at last we ended up here."

"That's a heck of a story," Parkman said. "I don't think I ever heard one like it."

"But what's so strange," Isadora said, "is that we're here now, and the man we've been looking for so long is right down the street. But Papa is too sick and weak to finally finish this thing."

"And Lionel Casey don't even know what you came to do."

"Will you tell him?"

"I'll have to think on that for a while," Parkman said. "If this is all true the way you said, then the marshal did a shameful thing, and deserves to be called to account. But if your father kills him, then he's likely to die for it, from my hand or some other. And what happens to you then?"

"I'll worry about my own future another day."

Parkman and Isadora were quiet as she gathered things up and prepared to go. She took the lantern off the hook and started toward the door, then stopped and looked back.

"You've been so kind to us, Ridge Parkman, I must repay you," she said. "I'm going to settle Papa in for the night, and then I'll be back."

"It don't work that way, Isadora," Parkman told her quietly. "You don't have to do nothin' of the sort."

"I need to come back. I want to know just once how it feels to sleep with a good man's arms around me."

Parkman was alone when he woke the next morning. The sun was already well up in the sky, and he couldn't remember how long it had been since he slept so well.

Later that morning he and Isadora tended to General Grant's wound, applying some exotic, foul-smelling herbal mixture that she mixed up. He was pleased that the bullet furrow was starting to dry up and heal.

Later Parkman gave the nasty, fly-ridden jail a good cleaning. In the time he spent with Casey, the subject of the gypsies never came up, and Parkman still debated what his part in this drama should be. Maybe, he thought with a measure of guilt, the old gypsy would go ahead and die, and then the matter would be settled for good.

In early afternoon, the two men made their way to the General Mercantile, Parkman matching his steps to Lionel Casey's slow hobbling pace. After the closing of the last restaurant in town, the Eldrichs had taken to cooking up a big pot of one thing or another in a clearing out back of their store. Today it was smoked ham hocks and beans. Casey ate with relish, refilling his bowl twice from the iron cauldron, and stuffing palm-sized squares of cornbread in his shirt when Hortense Eldrich wasn't looking. It was like watching an old bear trying to fatten up for the winter.

"They sell whiskey and beer out back here

of an evening," Casey told Parkman. "Closest thing we got to a saloon now, but better than nothing if you can abide the mosquitoes. Gourd buys the cheap stuff and charges two prices for it, but it gets the job done."

"We should wander over this evening for a snort," Parkman said.

After eating, the two lawmen returned to the jail, and Casey went in back for a nap. Parkman walked down to the river and relaxed on the bank to watch the fish rise and to think. Soon he dozed off.

A gunshot somewhere in town woke him from a deep sleep. There was only that one shot, and it wasn't close by, so he didn't feel like it was any cause for alarm. In a place like this, people might fire a gun for any number of reasons besides trouble. The sun had dipped down into the trees to the west, and the heat was beginning to diminish as Parkman returned to the jail.

Casey was still asleep in the oven of his back room, but Parkman woke him. While he was waiting for the marshal to put on his shirt, britches, and boots, another shot rang out. It seemed like the right direction and distance to be coming from Eldrich's store down the street. While he was away, he supposed, the last café in town had become the last saloon.

Night had settled in by the time they reached Eldrich's. The owner had strung lanterns along a rope, and smudge pots sat on the long, rough-cut lumber table to discourage mosquitoes. Eldrich's wife had set a full whiskey bottle down on the table in front of Chet Morgan's crew and was carrying away an empty. She glanced at Parkman and Casey like they were skunks that had wandered into her yard, then climbed the two wooden steps and went in the back door of the store.

The first bottle of whiskey had already gone to work on Morgan and his companions. Even Chet's lanky young brother, Horace, had a cup in front of him. The whole bunch welcomed the newcomers, obviously glad to be around someone besides each other for a change.

"And here's that You Ass Marshal, just in time to buy the next round," the old ranch hand Willie Johnson said with a besotted grin. He raised his revolver and fired a random shot in celebration. Red, the other ranch hand, laughed out loud and raised his tin cup to Parkman in a salute.

Parkman took no offense, understanding that the old man was just letting off steam. "I bet a man could go broke trying to pay for whiskey as fast as you could swill it down," he said. He and Casey sat down across the table from the JM crew.

"Only one way to find out," Willie slurred. He watched as his boss poured three fingers into his tin drinking cup.

Hortense Eldrich returned carrying another bottle and two more cups, which she sat in front of Parkman and Casey. "I wouldn't mind a beer chaser if it's anything close to cold," Parkman told her.

"No beer, cold, hot, or any other way," the woman said. "Gourd didn't have room for the barrels on his last supply run. It's this or nothing."

Casey was already pouring whiskey into their cups.

"You pay up front," Mrs. Eldrich said sternly.

Parkman fished two silver dollars from his money pouch and laid them on the table, but with an impatient gesture of her fingers the woman indicated that she expected more. He put another dollar down, and she picked the money up.

"Highway robbery," Chet Morgan grumbled. "You're the law, Parkman. Can't you do nothin' about it?"

"I don't guess so. Not if I want a swallow of whiskey," Parkman said. Lionel Casey's cup was already half empty. Parkman wondered if he would be able to afford this old man's bad habits.

They sat for a while, enjoying each other's mismatched company as best they could, talking about things that had nothing to do with grasshopper plagues, cattle diseases, failing ranches, or the trouble that was in the air in these parts. About all that was left to discuss was the heat and the mosquitoes, until finally Casey began spinning yarns. It turned out that after a couple of drinks, the old veteran soldier and lawman could tell a pretty good tale. The one about the pursuit, capture, and death of Bill Quantrill was hands down the best.

When the story ended, Willie stood up and announced to the world that he was going to take a piss. Soon after he staggered into the darkness behind the store, they heard a heavy thump back there somewhere, followed by a low moan. Nobody went to investigate.

Chet Morgan reached across to pour Major Casey another drink, but the city marshal waved him off. "Much more of that and I'll end up like Willie out there," he said. "I can't tolerate the stuff no more."

Sitting across from Morgan, Parkman was surprised when a hard frown suddenly washed over the rancher's features. Was it such an insult that Casey had turned down a drink? Then he realized that Morgan was looking past Casey, not at him.

"This is about what I'd expect of Jim Morgan's heathen seed," a stern voice said from several feet back. Parkman turned and saw three dim forms standing just within the light cast by the lanterns. Old Abe Garnett held a shotgun in the crook of his arm as if it grew there, and two of his men were resting their hands on holstered sidearms. "I bet your daddy's lookin' up from hell right now, just a'wishin' he could join in this debauchery."

"This ain't the time or place, Garnett," Parkman said. "These men are just having a little fun and doing you no harm."

"One time's good as another," Garnett said.

"If you start anything, I'll be glad to haul you down the street and lock you up in Marshal Casey's jail." Despite his brave talk, Parkman wasn't quite sure how he might manage that. He saw Casey thumb back the hammer of the shotgun he'd brought and start to bring it around.

"Don't you be takin' sides in this, Lionel Casey," Garnett warned. "Besides being an old man who can't walk to the outhouse without his stick, you're not the law in my town anymore."

"Maybe not," Casey said. "But I still know right from wrong."

A shot sounded unexpectedly from out in the darkness where Willie had gone, and the old ranch hand cut loose with an honest-to-goodness rebel yell, something Parkman hadn't heard in years. The man on Garnett's left grabbed at his side and bellowed out. That set everything else off like a lit fuse.

Chet Morgan gave the table in front of him a heave, toppling it over into the faces of Parkman and Casey. Casey's shotgun went off, and then Garnett's, followed by a fusillade of gunshots on all sides. Parkman was on the ground, with the heavy table pinning his legs. He grabbed for his Colt, but the holster was empty. He found it on the ground beside him, picked it up, and thumbed the hammer back. But then he realized that he didn't know where to point it or who to shoot. The air around him was thick with acrid smoke, and for a moment it seemed like everybody there was firing but him.

The whole thing was over in just a few seconds, which sometimes happened at close range like this. He heard a low, anguished moan somewhere nearby.

"No, no! You killed her!"

Footsteps tromped down the wooden steps at the back of the store, and through the smoky haze, Parkman saw Gourd Eldrich. The shopkeeper moved closer, his face aflame with pain and rage, carrying a rifle in his shaking hands. "You worthless old cripple. You shot my wife, my precious Hortense!" he cried out. The rifle was pointed down at Lionel Casey.

"It was an accident, Gourd! By God, I'm so sorry! Morgan threw the table up, and the shotgun just went off . . ."

"Don't shoot him, Eldrich," Parkman said. "Stop and think . . ." But his warning was pointless. Eldrich raised the rifle resolutely to his shoulder and tilted his head to peer down the sights. When his finger slipped into the trigger guard, Parkman shot him in the chest. Eldrich's body crumpled across Casey.

"Damn it," Parkman said. "I just shot the only man here that didn't have a dog in this fight. Damn it all to hell!"

"And I kilt his wife. We're sure a pair, ain't we, Parkman?" Casey shoved away the body of his dead friend. "You should of let him shoot me."

On all sides, the living were sorting themselves out from the dead. Across the table,

Chet Morgan lay on his back gazing up at the stars with sightless eyes. The bloody wound in his chest was peppered with splinters, carried there by Abe Garnett's buckshot as it tore through the table. The dead man's brother knelt beside him, shaking his arm as if to wake him. At last, he looked over at Parkman and Casey, his face streaked with tears and dumb with shock.

"You can't bring him to, boy," Casey said softly. "He's gone on now."

Parkman rose and looked around. Hortense Eldrich was sprawled out on the back porch of the now-ownerless store, her midsection a bloody mess from Casey's shotgun blast. Taking a few steps in the direction Abe Garnett had come from, he saw the old rancher and one of his hands lying side by side on the ground, both shot all to hell. Beside his boss, the other ranch hand sat in the dirt, a bloody hand covering his stomach wound. It was a bad place to get shot, Parkman thought, and even though the pain hadn't hit hard yet, plenty was on its way. The man looked at Parkman with scared, desperate eyes, pleading wordlessly for help.

"I warned you boys yesterday," Parkman reminded him.

A tall figure moved up beside Parkman. It

was Red, the other JM hand who had been getting happily drunk with his boss and the others minutes before. He looked sober enough now as he stared down at the corpse of Abe Garnett. "First man I ever kilt," Red said. "Him, and the other one, too, I reckon. I didn't think about nothin' when it happened. I just kept pulling the trigger."

"Well, you've got two notches now."

"I don't never want to do something like that again," Red said. "I feel plain awful."

"Good for you. That's the way a man should feel after something like this. Now, go find your pardner out there in the weeds, and try to get him sobered up. Things need taking care of here."

"Yessir," Red said. "When we're done, I think I might head back to Tupelo and make myself a preacher like daddy. I don't want no notches."

It was a long night. A few townspeople showed up, and with the help of Willie and Red, they carried the dead inside the store and lined their bodies up on the floor so the wild animals couldn't get to them. Lionel Casey stayed around until he was about to collapse from fatigue, then trudged back to the jail. Parkman stayed with the gutshot ranch hand for hours, keeping him warm and pouring whiskey into him, until he finally died. Toward the end, the man fell unconscious, which was a blessing to him, and gave him an escape from his agony.

Parkman looked across the room at the bloody corpses of Abe Garnett and Chet Morgan, now side by side as peaceful as you please. The Abolition, Kansas, range war was over now, with no winner on either side, and plenty of shame and regrets to go around. Eldrich lay beside them, his eyes wide open, and Parkman imagined he could still see the anguish on the dead man's face. He figured he'd leave tomorrow, after he helped dig the graves. There probably wouldn't be any real funerals, unless Red wanted to try out his new calling sooner than expected.

He fell asleep on the floor amidst the dead, and his dreams were troubled. He knew Gourd Eldrich, and maybe even some of the others there, would be back to visit him from time to time over the years, partnering up with so many other souls who returned to haunt his rest. It came with the badge.

A flurry of several gunshots woke Parkman, and at first, he thought it was his own confused mind rehashing last night's gunfight. But as he opened his eyes and recognized the glow of dawn outside, one last shot disturbed the morning quiet.

As he stepped out the front door of the store, Colt in hand, Parkman realized where the shots had come from and what had happened. The gypsy wagon was stopped down the street in front of the Abolition jailhouse. He took off at a run in that direction. A thin haze of gun smoke drifted out the open front door. Parkman approached cautiously, not even calling out to announce his presence. He had an idea what he would find inside.

Isadora Faust sat beside her fallen father, cradling his head in her lap, whispering softly to him as her tears fell on his face. He was unconscious, but not gone yet. Two bloody splotches stained the front of his red and gold silk shirt, probably his best, worn for this occasion. His chest rose slightly as he drew his last breaths, gurgling with each exhale. Isadora looked up at Parkman but said nothing, her eyes a sea of pain. A revolver lay on the floor beside her.

Across the room Major Casey was slumped in his chair behind the desk, staring across the room as if in deep contemplation. There was a small bullet hole high on his left shoulder, just below the collarbone. Blood pulsed freely from the wound with each pump of his heart. Parkman went over and knelt beside the old legend, but made no attempt to stop the flow of blood. Casey would be dead in a minute.

"I hardly even remembered the woman," Casey rasped. "The shine wore off in a few days, and she packed up and left me the same way she did him. Nobody could have told him, but he was better off without her."

"He lost face over it," Parkman said.

Casey nodded his understanding. His eyes sagged shut and Parkman thought he passed out, which would have been a mercy, but after a few seconds they opened again.

"That old man can't shoot worth shit," Casey said. "He fired at me four times, and nary a one hit me before I got my gun up and squeezed off a couple of rounds myself." Parkman glanced at the wall behind the marshal and saw shafts of morning sunlight stabbing in through four random holes. "Then that gal come in, and she did a better job of it. I'm obliged to her for that."

When it was over for Casey, Parkman went back over to Isadora and saw that her father had gone on, too.

"Leave the gun on the floor beside your papa," Parkman said. He hooked a hand under her arm and pulled to her feet. "You need to get out of this sorry town before the folks here show up and see this. They wouldn't understand what happened here, and might take it out on you."

"I can't leave Papa here like this," Isadora said.

"It'll be okay," Parkman told her. "We've got graves to dig today, and I'll make sure his name is over one. But you've got to get along."

Isadora allowed him to lead her out to the wagon and help her up onto the seat. She took one sorrowful look back at the jail, where her father lay in view on the floor. "I told Papa he did it . . . he finally killed Lionel Casey," she said. "My last words to him were a lie."

"It don't matter even a little bit. Where are you headed from here?"

"We talked about going north after, toward Emporia," Isadora said.

"I'm headed the same direction soon as I finish up here. Maybe I'll see you on the road." Parkman decided he'd make a point of catching up with Isadora Faust. She was alone now, and would need consoling of one kind or another.

■ ■ ■ ■

Greg Hunt is a seasoned western and frontier fiction writer, with over twenty novels in print. This is his first frontier short story.

■ ■ ■ ■

A Small Thing
by Matthew P.
Mayo

■ ■ ■ ■

I ladled more venison stew into Uncle Drift's bowl. It was peppery and the smell tickled my nose. He nudged his spoon with a big knuckle but did not tuck in. No matter how hungry he is, he waits for me. Drift Macallam ain't one to forget his manners. He also ain't one to use the word *ain't*. But I am.

Thomas Dettweiler, he's the first one I heard use that word, right after Bible class, then he got clouted on the left ear by his mama. Times like those I am satisfied with my lot. No surly mother to clout me, only Uncle Drift to keep me in line. And as long as I don't shirk my tasks, as he puts it, I have little to complain about. I still complain, but that's the way it is with me.

I sat down and picked up my spoon. I should have got a mouthful in, but I made the mistake of peeking over at Uncle Drift. And he was peeking right back at me. Well, not peeking so much as looking at me. Uncle Drift, he doesn't peek. He looks. Those big, twitchy-bird eyebrows of his twitched and he didn't have to say a thing.

I set down my spoon and put my hands together. "Thank you, Lord, for this food."

Uncle Drift sat with his head bowed, didn't put his hands together, though. He never does. Finally, he reached for his spoon. "That was brief."

"Yep," I said. Because it was. I thought he'd like it, seeing as how he doesn't talk much himself.

"You spend enough time with the Dettweilers, I thought you'd stretch it out some." He tasted the stew, nodded his fondness for it as he pulled in air to cool his mouthful.

"They are a prayerful bunch," I said, knowing he would nod without looking at me.

I always make certain to serve supper hot as I can make it. Uncle Drift likes it that way. Me, I don't much care. I eat mostly to get it over with. I am forever behaving like that, rushing through a thing to get to the next thing, or else back to a book. I am fond of reading, can't seem to help it. Like picking at a scab on your knee, you just have to.

Last week Uncle Drift borrowed a hefty

book for me from his boss, Mister Lins-more. It's called *Constantine Xavier's History of the Known World.* Seems big-headed to put your name in the title. Mostly the book confuses me, but I will give it a good going-through, then give it another, in case I missed something important on the first pass.

Sometimes Uncle Drift will say, "Having you around is like having a squirrel loose in the house." But he smiles when he says it. Every so often he will also say, "Watching you makes me tired." Which isn't the truth. Uncle Drift is always tired because he works a lot. Mostly for Mister Linsmore. The man with the books. He's the biggest rancher around. Uncle Drift's been at Linsmore's Lazy R my whole life. Or at least as long as I have been here, which is as far back as I can recall. That'd be twelve years.

I know this because today is my birthday. Well, as close as I will ever get to knowing what day I came to be in the world. Most folks are born, no choice, they just pop into a family and that's where they're stuck. But Uncle Drift, he says I am special because no one can prove I was born. Then he winks.

He says we discovered each other. That's why today is my birthday, it is the anniversary of the day he found me. But I am getting ahead of myself.

Once a month, when he is paid, Uncle Drift will come home later than usual. His cheeks are bright above his bushy, woolly-worm mustaches, and I know what he's been up to. Mostly because I got worried one time and looked all over town for him, then I found him at Ace's Bar and Livery. He was in the bar part, not the livery.

That said, Uncle Drift isn't much of a drinking man. He'll have a glass or two of beer on those days when he is paid, but the most it does is redden his cheeks and make him chatty. Well, chatty for Uncle Drift. He'll say four or five words instead of two or three.

Might be that's why I like visiting with the Dettweilers. There are about a dozen of them running around their place, all fleshy — they are a well-fed bunch — and loud and hoorahing and funny all at once. Their house is big and falling apart and smells like boiled shoes or, depending on the day of the week, spicy apple cake. And spending time with them is about what I imagine a circus is like and I love every minute I am there. At the end of it, I am exhausted and can't wait to get back home.

Me and Uncle Drift, we don't have what most folks consider much. We have a tidy little home with a front room that used to be a settin' porch but now it's closed in. That's where Uncle Drift sleeps. There is a little bedroom in the back, that's where I sleep. It's off the kitchen and stays warm in winter. Out back we have a woodshed, and beside that, the outhouse, far enough away from the house proper that in summer when it gets to smelling sweet, we are spared the worst of it.

As I said, today is my birthday. It is also the first time I know of that Uncle Drift's payday is on the same day as my birthday. It doesn't much matter, but I prepared that nice venison stew I know he likes.

I was over to the Dettweilers earlier and Mrs. Dettweiler asked me why I was so smiley — I have been accused of being gloomy, but I am not, as a rule, a gloomy person. I might look it, but I am often in deep thought. I get a notion in my head and there's no end to the thinking I get up to — what would the world be like with no trees? How come a cow's hair will reach a certain length and then stop growing, but a person's hair will keep on getting longer and longer? And how long will that be? Has anyone ever found out?

Such thoughts keep me awake long into the night. I tell Uncle Drift about them over breakfast, and he nods and his eyebrows hunch together. I know he is listening, but he never says much. Just, "Uh-huh," or "Hmm." And once he said, "That's something, that is." That sort-of smile is always there on his face, but I know he's not funning me, never would. He says he takes me very seriously.

Anyway, I told Mrs. Dettweiler it was my birthday and she squealed — which, if you have met her, wouldn't be a sound you'd find unusual coming from her. That was petty of me, especially considering what she did. She ran from the room, sort of ran, anyway. And came back with a very pretty little snatch of calico, brown with tiny orange and yellow flowers set on it.

She put it in my hand and said, "This is for you."

Now, I don't sew all that well, enough to repair tears in Uncle Drift's clothes, though he is more of a hand at mending than I am. Every button I sew on ends up lost lord-knows-where. Poor Uncle Drift, his sleeve cuffs flap loose half the time, but he doesn't say much about it. Just shakes his head and gives me money for buttons and then shows me one more time how to sew them on.

I felt something inside the calico. Mrs. Dettweiler nodded at me. By then half the kids were hugging her skirts like fuzzy chicks around a mama hen, all watching me. I unwrapped that cloth and rolled up in there was the prettiest length of blue hair ribbon.

"It's French silk, dear. I bought it for you some time ago."

"For me?"

She nodded. "I've been waiting for your special day, as I couldn't for the life of me recall which day was yours. Now it has come and so there you have it."

"You bought this for me?" I can be thick at times. I also was in danger of choking up a little.

She nodded again. "Yes, I saw it and I just knew it would look so pretty in your hair. Now turn around and let me help you with it. There should be enough for a nice bow."

You see, I have long hair, it's mostly not black, but reddish brown, and my eyes are grayish blue. That's how Uncle Drift says he knew I was no Indian child when he found me. He said that true-blood Indians can't have blue eyes. I do not know why and neither does he, though I asked him a pile of times.

After the third or fourth time, he nearly smiled, then plopped on his hat, tugged up one side of his braces, and walked out back to split rounds for the stove. That was on my birthday, too, about five years ago. I was just a child then.

Every birthday he tells me the story of how he found me. Discovered me, is how he put it once — that's the word I tell him to use if he slips back into saying he found me.

Tonight, he begins the story the same way he does every year: "Now, what's important to remember is I am not really your uncle. I am not any sort of relation to you. What I am is the man who ended up with you. And I am a lucky man for it."

"And I ended up with you," I say. "And I am powerful lucky, too." I nod, but don't say anything more. Getting Uncle Drift talking can be a task, so I daren't slow the wheels. I sit on the floor and he's usually sitting in the rocker that was his mama's and he says one day will be mine. I do not like to dwell on when that day will be.

"We'll, I'll tell you, Katharine. When I come upon you that night, near dark, I was confused. Didn't seem as though what I was seeing could be possible. Why, I thought I'd come upon a little dog, lost and near starved out there on the trail. Then I leaned down out of the saddle and saw it was a child." His eyes grew wide then, as though he were right back there at that moment a dozen years before.

I don't mind admitting that I trembled as he said it. Like I do every year. To think we were both there that cold, dark night so long ago. Us and no one else.

"I figured you'd been lost, left behind by a raving gold-seeker like in one of those stories I read in the newspaper. People are forever acting foolish where money is concerned. They get fevered up and discard everything they should hold dear. Lose a child on the trail and they're so worked up about the sniff of silver or gold they don't notice until it's too late! My word . . ."

He rubbed his big hand along his chin, it made a soft, scratchy sound. That was the first I noticed he'd not shaved this morning.

"So, I stopped, made a fire, and heated up some grub. I didn't have any trouble coaxing you over. You were friendly enough . . . for a lost doggie."

That always got me to roll my eyes. I did it again, too.

"Now, I hadn't been hungry for a long while. And a good thing, too — for a little mite, you ate like a boar-grizz!"

"Did I say anything?" I knew the answer, knew it as certain as I know my name.

"Naw," he shook his head. "You grunted

plenty, though."

He grinned full-on then, something Uncle Drift doesn't do often. I like seeing that. "My word, but you were such a small thing."

Then he did something he never did before on my birthday. He stopped right in the middle of the story. He leaned forward in his rocker and put his elbows on his bony knees. Looked like a bird folding himself up. His big-knuckled fingers curled around themselves, all callous and sharp bends. They worked over each other while he decided on how to say what he was going to say next.

"Katharine," he said, looking at me.

I got a little scared, not because he said my name. He always calls me that, or "squirrel," but because it felt like something was going to change. I didn't want anything to change, I like it just fine the way things are. I stood up. "I expect you could use some coffee. I'll fetch —"

"Katharine. Sit down. I aim to tell you something."

I never disobey Uncle Drift. Leastwise not to his face. Sometimes I will skip praying before I go to sleep. Who's going to know besides me and God? And I figure God's so busy I can double my efforts tomorrow night. I reckon I owe the Lord a couple-dozen nights by now.

I sat down.

"But the story . . ." I said.

"Katharine, you've heard it enough so you can tell it better than me, I expect. I have something more to say to you. You see, that night when I found you out there on the trail, I was on my way somewhere."

This didn't strike me as anything worth saying. Aren't we all on our way somewhere? "Are you feeling okay, Uncle Drift?"

"Course I am, just let me get down to it, will you? Like a chatty jay all the time." He tried to smile but his eyes couldn't do it.

"I was . . . oh, I don't know what I was, but I had no plan, no good thing to do." He sighed. "I have told you about my wife, Karina."

I nodded. He'd talked a little about her before. And once, when he was gone to work, I rooted around in the little trunk he keeps in the corner. I dug down through all manner of things piled atop, as if what is in there has to be covered up, pushed down, hidden away.

The key has always stuck out of the front of it, though, like a little brass nose. I turned it, opened the lid, and found a passel of letters, most of them written in a woman's looping hand, all addressed to "My Dearest Dover."

Took me a long time to figure out that Dover was Uncle Drift's name. I'd also like to say I didn't read those letters, but I'd be lying. I read two of them, then I saw a photograph of a handsome young man in a suit, no mustaches or big eyebrows — took me a few minutes to work out it was Uncle Drift. He stood behind a woman seated in a chair.

She was pretty, dark eyes and dark hair tucked in a bun. She wore a dress that came up around her neck, all fancy lace at the top, marked at the throat with a small brooch. Uncle Drift held a hat, a bowler, of all things, before his chest, the other hand resting on the woman's shoulder. One of her hands rested on her lap, holding a hanky, I think, the other held his hand on her shoulder.

Neither of them were smiling, but it looked to me as if they were fit to burst, as if the moment that photograph was taken they ran on out of that studio and had a whangdoodle of a time. I am learning of such things as what new-married folk get up to, but I choose to think Uncle Drift and his bride went somewhere and had themselves a fine feed. Not every day you get yourself married, after all. Nothing better than a good meal to mark an occasion.

Uncle Drift squeezed the arm of the rocker. "Katharine, I've thought a lot about this, but I reckon I didn't really need to. Truth is, that night I found you, you saved my life. I was headed for something, likely I was aiming to ride and ride until me or the horse give out."

He looked at me, eyes filling. I have never seen Uncle Drift tear up. I followed right along and did the same.

"She died before we could ever have a baby. A sickness brought on by a traveling family, lugged it with them. Cholera, likely."

His voice was higher than normal. That man had never looked old to me before, but with his silvery whiskers and those tears, he did right then.

"She was helping them, no thought to herself, and do you know? It worked. A couple of weeks, then they moved on, healthy enough to get to wherever was so important to them. Wasn't a day later Karina came down with the chills and stiff joints. She suffered so." He shook his head, tears slipped down his face. "She didn't last but a week. My word, we'd been married shy a year."

He was scaring me, but I didn't know

what to say. Neither of us did. We sat quiet for long minutes. Then, of course, I spoke first.

"What happened next, Uncle Drift?"

He sort of smiled. "Oh, you mean when I discovered you?"

That isn't really what I'd meant, but no matter. He slipped back into the story we knew so well.

"Why, it took three days, but I drug that little squallerin' beast back here — that'd be you, by the way." He said it in a low, rumbly sort of way, like it was a secret. "I set up that room at the back for you."

"Wasn't that your old room?" I asked again, as I do each year.

He always says yes. Tonight, he only nodded. "I'd not intended to come back to this town, truth be told. But with you, seemed like the thing to do. Was night when we made it back. I laid you down in that bed, covered you with that old patchwork quilt. I slept in this here rocker." He patted the arm with a big hand.

"Come morning, you were curled up on me like a squirrel, all tucked into a ball, your little head under my chin. I never . . ." He gave me that half-smile again. "And for more mornings after that than I could count, same thing. Like a little squirrel you

366

were." Then his smile slipped away again.

Tonight, of all nights, my special birthday night, something was different. I put my hand on his knee. "Uncle Drift, what's wrong?" I whispered it.

He peeked at me. I know what I said about him not being a peeker, but he did it just the same. Then he looked down again, like the Clumpett twins when they got called to the front of the schoolroom for sassing Miss Binder. Not looking up any more than they had to. It broke my heart to see him looking at me like that. I asked him again what was wrong.

He held my hand. Every so often I am reminded how big his hands are. Looking at mine between his scared me.

"I have done you a terrible wrong, Katharine."

I shook my head. "Uncle Drift, you've never done anything wrong."

He snorted. "Now that is a windy if ever I heard one."

The last of that quick smile slipped away. "You see, Katharine, I never put effort into tracking down your family."

I didn't say anything. I don't care one whit about people who would leave their child to die in the wilderness. Uncle Drift is all the family I ever needed. I was about to say as much when he commenced talking again.

"One day came and went, then another and another." He shrugged as if I'd asked him a question he didn't know the answer to. "Before long you were jabbering like a jay, and then going to school . . ." His eyes got all squinty. "And now look at you, nearly grown."

"I am not," I said, but in truth I liked to hear it. In case you haven't met me, I am not a tall person, nor very large in any way. I guess you'd say I am small. Not long ago, I asked Uncle Drift if I would grow much more. He said I would be as big as I needed to be. That was no help.

Oh, but the evening had become confusing. Everything is changing and I want it to do that more than anything. I also want everything to stay the same forever. None of it is fair.

He had been watching me, one side of his mouth tugged up. "I gave you your name, Katharine, because it reminded me enough of Karina so I wouldn't go all sad every time I said it. But it's a good name. A big, strong name."

"But I ain't big nor so very strong, Uncle Drift. I am just me."

"Katharine, you're about the strongest person I know. As to size, well, I know a whole lot of big folks who are a lot smaller than you, girl."

I resolved to think on that later. I expect there is something wise in it.

"Other than my last name, one that you are welcome to keep for as long as you see fit, I don't have much else to offer. What's mine is yours, always will be. But it would please me if you'd take this." He reached long fingers into the breast pocket of his flannel shirt, pulled out something that stayed hidden in his hand. He held it out, palm down, and nodded toward it. "Put out your hand, Katharine."

I did, and felt his fingers let go of something. He pulled his hand away and there in my palm was a pretty little pin I'd seen somewhere before, though at that moment I could not recollect where.

"That belonged to Karina."

And then I knew where I'd seen it. It was the brooch she'd been wearing in their wedding photograph. I tried to thank him, but I am afraid I cried a little. Any words I meant to say never made it up out of my throat.

"She didn't want me to . . . send it with her, begged me to save it. Said I would have a use for it one day. And now I have. My word, but she was a smart one. I like to think if we'd had a child she would have been just like you. Yes, I believe Karina would have been a good mama to you, Katharine."

"But if she was . . . still here, you never would have discovered me." I snuffled and admired the pin.

"That is a fact, Katharine. Always two sides to the coin for you, isn't there?" He stretched out his long legs, rested his hands on his lean belly. "Now, tell me about that pretty ribbon in your hair."

My eyes widened. I'd forgotten all about it, what with supper and then our story. "Mrs. Dettweiler gave it to me. Said she'd been saving it just for me."

"Well now," said Uncle Drift. "Isn't that something? They're good people, that family. The whole lot of them. They are prayerful, and I don't guess that's a bad thing. I am not much of a hand at it, haven't been in a long time." He sipped his coffee, which I am sure had gone stone cold. "I see how you and Thomas are chums."

I looked at him. I thought that was an odd thing to say, especially as I'd known Thomas my whole life. "Uncle Drift, what are you dancing around?"

He smiled, leaned back. "I swear if you don't remind me of Karina. Never could talk around a thing with her, either. She always cut right to the core of the apple."

I blushed. I like being compared with her, someone I think of as my long-dead mother. Someone who I know is watching over me, even though I never met her.

Uncle Drift cleared his throat. "Katharine, much as I like the Dettweilers and their boy, Thomas — and I do like them . . ."

I nodded. He said as much not a minute before.

"I think you should have what I heard are called options."

"Options," I said, not certain at all what an option was.

"That's right," he nodded, looking as uncertain as I felt. "They're sort of like different meals laid out before you. Like having your choice of stew or a beefsteak or, oh, I don't know . . ."

"Pie?" I said. I have always been partial to pie. I can't bake a pie to save my skin, but I like it just the same.

"Sure, pie. Anyway, what I have been trying to tell you is," he sighed, then continued. "I have been saving money for some time now, Katharine. Truth be told, you were here about a week when I started."

That long ago? "Why?" I said.

"That was when I knew for certain you were my little squirrel. Figured it would take a heap of money to raise you right. Course, it hasn't cost all that much, other than all that food you take in." He waited for me to look shocked, which I did, then he winked. "I have been saving it instead of spending it on foofaraw. Now it's time I told you why."

I didn't know what to say to that, so I kept my mouth shut, which is a trial for me.

"You see, Karina didn't come from Colorado. She traveled out here from back east as a young woman. She was sent by her church to do the Lord's work. But what she really wanted was to teach school. She was an educated woman. I met her at a social affair right here in town. I'd been living at the ranch, but whenever there was a social, why, me and the boys would draw straws to see who got to go." He winked at me. "I got lucky."

He sipped his cold coffee again. "All that come back to me when I brought you here as a little squirrel. I determined you would have as fine an education as Karina got, if I could afford to give it to you. Mister Linsmore, he was kind enough to keep me on at the ranch, especially after he met you. Thought you were the cutest nubbin. Still does."

"He is a nice man," I said, and not just because he likes me and lets Uncle Drift bring home books for me to read.

"As I said, I've been thinking on this for too long. But what I come to is this." He held up a big hand to stop me from talking, and it's true, I was about to speak. He knows me better than I expect I do.

"Those folks Karina helped, they were headed west, for some other life. Must have thought it was better than whatever it was they were leaving behind. But they robbed me, at least that's the way I looked at it for the longest time. I spent the better part of two years drinking and living in this little house, cursing God and doing my best to do what I thought I should be doing, but what I really wanted to do was die. I wanted so badly to die. I couldn't imagine life without my dear Karina. So, I climbed up on that poor old horse, only thing I could afford to ride. I took a little food, and the rest of my saddlebag was filled with bottles of rye whiskey. No plan, figured I'd reach some sort of end and that would be that. I didn't care." He sat in silence.

"Then you discovered me," I said.

"Yep." He nodded. "But when I did, I cursed God again. I wanted to hate you, so help me I did. Wanted to leave you be, in your filthy little rag of a dress, the child of travelers just like those who took my Karina from me. But you . . . you crawled on over to me like I was something worth crawling up to."

He shook his head as if he'd been told a windy. "It was as if the folks who took everything from me gave me a gift right back. I don't expect that to make much sense. Heck, I didn't parse this out as such for a few weeks myself, but somehow it all felt right, you see? So, we come back here and I toed the mark, built up a new life. Not a life I ever imagined, I tell you that now, but different is all. Not better or worse, just different. I am pleased with it."

That was the most I'd ever heard him speak all at once. "Why did you tell me now, Uncle Drift? This year, after all this time?"

He shrugged again, but I knew his thoughts were serious. "Been gnawing me from the inside. Most days I keep it tamped down, but seeing you today, wearing that pretty ribbon, growing into a woman all by yourself. I don't know that I have any right to be proud, but I tell you now, Katharine Macallam, I am proud of you, girl. Figured I owed you the whole story. That way you know your ol' Uncle Drift is no better than anyone else. Not the fellow you think he is."

We sat quiet for a long moment. The small room had grown dark. For the first time in a long time, I felt like his little squirrel again. I crawled up in his lap, my head tucked under his big chin.

I fell asleep holding that pretty little brooch tight to my chest, not wanting anything to change, but knowing now it would. Everything would change.

So help me, I felt a little excited about it, too.

■ ■ ■ ■

Matthew P. Mayo is a Spur Award–winning author. He and his wife, videographer Jennifer Smith-Mayo, rove North America in search of hot coffee, tasty whiskey, and high adventure. Visit him at: www.Matthew Mayo.com.

■ ■ ■ ■

LITTLE CHEYENNE
BY ETHAN J. WOLFE

■ ■ ■ ■

CHEYENNE, 1930

The old man was asleep in a rocking chair on the front porch of a boarding house when the dark sedan arrived and parked curbside. He was in his eighties and not many knew who he was or even his name. He was quiet and kept to himself and most didn't even know he existed.

Three men got out. One was Jack Stills, a powerful Hollywood movie producer. The second was Bill Atkins, a movie director. The third was John Wentz, a location scout for Stills Productions.

Stills took the steps to the porch and gently placed a hand on the old man's shoulder.

The old man slowly opened his eyes.

"Excuse me, sir, but are you the man people in town told me about?" Stills asked. "The man who knows the location of an old ghost town north of here."

The old man blinked a few times and then said, "I am."

"My name is Jack Stills. I'm a Hollywood film producer," Stills said. "My company is producing a new western centered on early Cheyenne and the railroad. Is it true that you know the location of an old ghost town not far from here?"

"It's true," the old man said.

"Can you take us there? We'd like to look the place over for possible location sites," Stills said.

"It's a piece," the old man said. "Forty miles or more."

"In my car that's hardly more than an hour," Stills said. "Would you be willing to take us there? I'll pay you for your time."

"Pay me?" the old man said.

"Time is money, sir," Stills said.

"As long as we're back in time for my radio shows," the old man said. "I do love my radio shows."

"No problem, sir," Stills said.

The old man rode in front with Wentz, who drove the powerful V-8 sedan with expert precision.

"We have a wrangler for the film that was born in Wyoming," Stills told the old man as the old man guided them out of Cheyenne and north onto a dirt road.

"A wrangler?" the old man said.

"He's an expert with horses," Stills said. "He'll instruct the actors on how to ride a horse and look the part of a cowboy."

"Look the part?" the old man said.

"It's acting, sir," Stills said. "They look the part and the camera does the rest."

"Excuse me, but we've run out of road," Wentz said.

"It will be nothing but an overgrown patch of weeds by now," the old man said. "Stick to it for another thirty miles or so."

Wentz said to Stills, "Jack, we can't make good time on this road."

"We're in no hurry," Stills said.

"Would any of you fellows happen to have a store-bought cigarette?" the old man asked.

"Sure," Wentz said and handed the old man his pack and lighter.

The old man smoked the cigarette and watched out his window as the scenery changed and he spoke very little the rest of the way.

After what seemed like a very long time, Wentz said, "Jack, I see something up ahead there."

"Yeah, I see it too," Stills said. "Maybe a quarter of a mile. Is that it, old man?"

"I reckon so," the old man said.

Wentz stopped the car about a hundred feet from the remnants of what once were twelve or thirteen buildings constructed in a horseshoe shape.

Stills, Wentz, and Atkins got out of the sedan and looked at the old buildings.

"Old man, do you want to come out for a look?" Stills asked.

"I seen it before," the old man said. "I'd be obliged for another of those cigarettes, though."

"Help yourself, the pack is on the dashboard," Wentz said.

"Come on, let's have a look around," Stills said.

CHEYENNE, 1879

I

Sanchez, a Mexican vaquero, put a five-dollar piece on the bar at the Dead Dog Saloon and carried it to his table. At the table were Ryan, Quincy, brothers Dave and Tom Kitchen (a rather odd last name Sanchez always thought), and Dan Carr.

Carr was the leader of the bunch. As ruthless a man as ever drew breath, Carr was quick to shoot but also smart enough to know when not to shoot. A week ago, they robbed a stagecoach in Nebraska that was carrying a buyer for the Army beef contracts. The man had ten thousand dollars in new cash money on him.

Carr wanted no shooting if possible. A posse was sure to follow and was probably on their trail even as they sat and drank Dead Dog whiskey. He didn't want to stir the pot by adding murder to it, but the Kitchen brothers couldn't help themselves. They were a bloodthirsty pair, those two.

They shot the driver, his shotgun rider, and the Army buyer in cold blood for the fun of watching them bleed out.

"How long we sticking around here?" Sanchez asked.

"I been studying on that," Carr said. "I figure we'll ride north across the Platte and head west into the Big Horns and hole up there for the winter. Come spring nobody will be looking for us no more and we can separate or stay together."

"The Big Horns are a good place to hide out in," Sanchez said. "They got this place no one knows about except outlaws."

"You been there?" Carr asked.

"I been there," Sanchez replied.

"Finish your drinks, boys," Carr said. "We'll pick up supplies and ride out of here as easy as you please."

"Me and Tom was kind of hoping for a sporting woman," Dave Kitchen said.

"Then you boys can stay behind while the posse catches up to you," Carr said.

After buying a week's worth of supplies at the general store, Carr led his bunch north out of Cheyenne. They rode fifteen miles before making camp. The following day they road twenty. The day after that, after about five miles in the saddle, they stopped and dismounted.

"There ain't no town between Cheyenne and Casper," Carr said.

"Maybe so, but we're looking at one," Quincy said.

"Let's go have us a look, boys," Carr said. "At the town that ain't supposed to be here."

II

The town of Little Cheyenne was commissioned out of necessity a few years earlier when ranchers and farmers grew tired of a week's ride to either Cheyenne or Casper for supplies.

They got together and suggested building a small way station where they could get supplies in a day's ride for most, two days for those furthest away. They paid for the building supplies and labor and overnight Little Cheyenne was born.

Thirteen buildings in all.

Thirteen because one of the ranchers said that in order to claim township there had to be more than twelve erected buildings. Once they were complete, a contract was made with the Cheyenne Freight Company to deliver goods every ten days from Cheyenne and Casper.

The arrangement worked well. Ranchers and farmers shaved a week's traveling time to resupply. Little Cheyenne also had a saloon where local cowhands could come on a Saturday night to let off steam from the week's work.

Besides the small saloon, there was a hardware store, general store, livery stable, clothing store, a freight office and warehouse, a small hotel for the freighters to stay overnight in, and a restaurant run by the hotel. There were three two-story homes where those that didn't have living quarters in back of their stores resided in.

The final building of the thirteen was a tiny jailhouse that had yet to be used for anything other than extra storage space.

Baxter was sweeping off the wood sidewalk in front of his general store when he looked up and spotted six riders a quarter mile to the east and riding in quickly.

Baxter paused for a moment, studying the six riders. He put the broom aside and entered his store and went to the storeroom where his son was stocking shelves.

"Lonny, listen to me now," Baxter said.

"Yes, Pa," Lonny said.

"I need you to pay close attention and remember what I tell you," Baxter said.

Lonny, at nineteen, was slow of mind but fleet of foot.

"I want you to slip out the back door and run all the way to the preacher's place and tell him six strangers are riding into town," Baxter said. "Tell him to come quick. Can you remember all that, son?"

"Yes, Pa."

"How long do you figure it will take you to run to the preacher's place?" Baxter asked.

"I reckon about twenty minutes."

"All right. Go."

While Lonny slipped out the back, Baxter returned to the sidewalk and continued with his sweeping. A few others were about as well. James Hicks at the Cheyenne Freight warehouse who also served as the blacksmith and livery manager was at the furnace making shoes. Across the street at the hotel, Mr. Potter was taking coffee on the porch. The widow Abigail and her daughter, Trudy, were sweeping the wood sidewalk outside the restaurant that they ran.

The six riders were less than a hundred yards away when Potter noticed them and stood up to look. He must have decided real quick that he didn't like what he saw because he hightailed it into the hotel lobby.

Hicks stayed at his furnace, hammering away at shoes.

The widow Abigail took Trudy by the arm and led her into the restaurant.

Baxter stayed where he was until the six riders entered town and rode right to his general store.

"Howdy," Baxter said.

"Howdy," Carr said. "How comes there's no sign of this town on the map or trail?"

"Well, we're more of a way station than a town," Baxter said.

"Way station?" Carr said.

"For the ranchers and farmers," Baxter said. "So they don't have to spend a week traveling with a wagon to and from Cheyenne to get supplies. It was them that built this place, you see."

"You don't say," Carr said.

"You fellows just passing through?" Baxter asked.

"You might say that," Carr said. "Is that a hotel?"

Baxter nodded. "The freighters need a place to stay overnight when they deliver."

"Any objections if we stay the night and get a fresh start in the morning?" Carr asked.

"None from me," Baxter said.

Carr turned to his men. "Boys, bring the horses over to that livery there. Sanchez, you come with me."

"Hey mister, you got a sporting woman in town?" Dave Kitchen said.

"A sporting woman?" Baxter said. "No. That's one thing we don't got."

"Knock that off and see to the horses," Carr said. "Sanchez, let's go."

Carr and Sanchez walked across the street to the hotel and entered the small lobby. Potter was behind the front desk. He swallowed hard when Carr and Sanchez approached him.

"How many rooms you got?" Carr asked.

"Six," Potter said.

"Any in use?" Carr asked.

"No," Potter said. "Freighters won't be back for another five days."

"Give me three rooms on the second floor," Carr said.

Potter took a deep breath. "That's two dollar a night for each room."

Carr placed six dollars in silver coins on the counter.

"Is the food at that little restaurant any

good?" Carr asked.

"We all eat there three times a day," Potter said.

Carr nodded. "Let's go, Sanchez."

"How come you ain't got no sporting woman?" Tom Kitchen asked Hicks as Hicks led the horses into the livery barn.

"No need a' one," Hicks said.

"No need of a sporting woman?" Dave Kitchen said. "Who ever heard of such a town with no sporting woman?"

"Well, we ain't got one," Hicks said.

"That's enough of that," Carr said as he approached the livery. "They got hot grub at that little restaurant there and I'm fixing to get a meal."

Abigail watched through the window as the six men approached the restaurant. She turned to Trudy.

"Get in the kitchen and stay there," Abigail said.

"Why, Ma?" Trudy asked.

"Do as I say, girl, and don't you come out for any reason," Abigail said.

"Yes, Ma."

Trudy went into the kitchen. Abigail went behind the counter. Trudy, at seventeen, had the body of a grown woman but was naïve and inexperienced. She was also quite lovely and those men were going to want a woman, Abigail was sure of that much.

They entered and approached the counter.

"We're looking for a hot meal," Carr said.

"Take a table," Abigail said. "I'll bring you a pot of coffee."

Carr and his men took a table for six by the window. Napkins and coffee cups were already in place.

Abigail entered the kitchen and returned with a pot of coffee. She turned over each cup and filled it.

"So, what can I get you boys?" she said.

Baxter watched out his store window. The men left the hotel and entered Abigail's restaurant.

That they went to the hotel meant they planned to stay the night.

He didn't see anything good coming of this.

Hicks left the livery and walked to Baxter's store and entered.

"Those men, they asked about a sporting woman," Hicks said.

"I know it," Baxter said.

"We ain't got a gun in the whole damn town," Hicks said.

"We ain't had a need for one," Baxter said.

"I have the feeling we need one now," Hicks said.

"Best get back to the livery," Baxter said.

Carr and his men ate plates of fried eggs with bacon and potatoes, biscuits with honey, and coffee.

"Right fine grub, ma'am," Carr said. "Where can we get a drink in town?"

Abigail went to the window. "See that little building connected to the general store? That's the town saloon. Ask Mr. Baxter to open it for you," she said.

"What do we owe you for the grub?" Carr asked.

"A dollar a plate," Abigail said.

Carr entered the general store while his men waited in the street.

"Me and the boys would like to have us a drink," Carr said.

"I usually don't open the doors until after six unless some cowhands come to town," Baxter said.

"We're cowhands," Carr said. "And we come to town."

Baxter sighed. "I'll open up," he said.

"Thank you, kindly," Carr grinned.

Lonny ran the three and one-half miles in twenty-five minutes and nearly collapsed from the effort. The last twenty yards to the preacher's front door was more of a walk than a run and he arrived gasping for air.

When he regained some strength, Lonny yelled, "Preacher, Preacher, come quick."

When there was no response, Lonny went up and opened the unlocked screen door.

"Preacher," he yelled.

He wasn't in the house. Lonny went to the large barn behind the house and the preacher's rig wasn't there. The preacher had nearly two hundred acres of farmland and he was probably checking things out.

He didn't know what else to do, so Lonny returned to the house and sat on the porch to wait.

At a glance, the preacher appeared to be a tall drink of water of a man. At closer inspection, especially when he had his shirt off and was working, it became clear that the preacher was solid muscle from head to toe. Years of hard work had burned all the fat off the man and what was left was two hundred pounds of grit spread out over a six-foot-three-inch frame.

As he did three times a week for the past

several years, the preacher rode out to the border of his land and hacked away at the massive tree stump that prevented him from planting the final ten acres.

Felling the tree was no problem. Some of the wood built the barn and corral. It was the massive stump that was the problem. Ten feet in circumference at the base, the roots were thick and well dug into the earth.

After several hours of hacking away at the stump, Preacher tossed water from his canteen over his head, put on his shirt, and rode over to check his horses. Preacher raised several dozen horses a year and sold them to the freight company in Casper and Cheyenne. Sometimes the Army purchased what the freight companies did not.

He joined the Union Army at the age of sixteen after Rebel sympathizers from Kentucky rode north and burned the family farm in southern Indiana. After the war, he went west and settled in Arizona and then Wyoming because there was nothing or nobody to hold him back.

He came close to marriage a few years ago to a woman from Casper, but at the last minute she decided she didn't want to live in the middle of nowhere with so few people around.

The "in between" years were hard living

and full of danger and Preacher never dwelled upon them.

After checking the horses, Preacher rode back to the house to find the Baxter boy sitting on the porch steps.

The boy jumped up and ran to the rig.

"Preacher, Preacher, Pa says to come quick," Lonny said.

Preached stepped down from the rig. "Take it easy, Lonny, and tell me what it is your pa wants," he said.

"Six men rode into town," Lonny said. "Pa said to come quick."

"Six men? Did you see them?"

"No, but Pa did."

"Let me switch out my horse for a fresh one and I'll ride you back to town," Preacher said.

Carr and his men took a table for six by the swinging doors so they could watch the street.

Baxter brought a fresh bottle of Tennessee whiskey and six shot glasses to the table. "Do you want the bottle?" he asked Carr.

"Leave it," Carr said.

"That will be five dollars," Baxter said.

Carr put a five-dollar piece on the table.

Baxter picked up the coin. "I'll be in the store if you require anything else."

■ ■ ■ ■

After changing out his horse, Preacher and Lonny started back to town.

"Are you going to wear your badge, Preacher?" Lonny asked.

"Tell you the truth, Lonny, I forget where I put it," Preacher said.

"What about Tig?" Lonny asked.

"He'll follow us along," Preacher said.

Sure enough, Tig, Preacher's mutt dog, came running out of the bar and ran behind the wagon.

"He hasn't got the legs anymore," Preacher said. "He'll jump on after a while."

After about a mile, Tig tired and Preacher slowed the wagon to allow the small dog to hop into the buckboard.

"What the hell are we doing in this shithole of a town?" Sanchez said. "We ought to be making tracks for the mountains."

"I was sort of wondering that myself," Quincy said.

"At least, if they had a sporting woman, we'd have something to do besides looking at Sanchez's ugly mug," Tom Kitchen said.

"A town ought to have at least one sporting woman a man can wet his bean with."

Dave Kitchen echoed his brother.

"Boys, we're going to finish this here bottle of fine sipping whiskey," Carr said. "Later, come suppertime we'll have a nice meal in that café across the street. Then maybe we'll have us another bottle to pass the time. Tonight, we'll sleep in soft hotel beds. Come morning, after a nice breakfast, we'll load up on supplies and strip every nickel from this town like it was a bank giving away money."

Sanchez grinned, tossed back his shot glass, and said, "I see through the window someone is coming in a wagon."

Preacher stopped the wagon in front of the general store. He and Lonny stepped down to the wood sidewalk and entered the store. Tig hopped down and followed.

"I brung the Preacher, Pa," Lonny said to Baxter.

"You did good, Lonny," Baxter said. "Go on back to your stocking."

"Yes, Pa," Lonny said.

After Lonny went to the storeroom, Preacher said, "What's this about six men come to town?"

"Rode in a couple of hours ago," Baxter said. "They're next door in the saloon."

"They bother anybody?"

"Not so you could arrest them for, but they will once they're liquored up enough," Baxter said. "They asked about a sporting woman."

"They did, huh? Did they see Trudy?"

"I don't know. Maybe."

Preacher sighed. "Guess I better have a talk with these fellows."

"Maybe you should wear your badge," Baxter said.

"Tell you the truth, I forgot where I put it," Preacher said.

"You left it here," Baxter said. "I put it in the register."

Baxter opened the register and removed the brass sheriff's badge and gave it to Preacher.

Preacher pinned it to his shirt pocket.

"Guess I'll go see those fellows," he said. "Do me a favor and hold Tig in the store for me."

"Someone is coming," Sanchez said as he hung onto the swinging doors.

"Who?" Carr asked.

"That man from the wagon."

"Come sit down," Carr said.

Sanchez returned to the table and sat.

Preacher pushed open the swinging doors and entered the saloon. He paused and looked at the six men at the table.

"Howdy, boys," Preacher said.

Carr looked at the badge pinned to Preacher's shirt.

"How do, Sheriff," Carr said. "Care to join us for a friendly drink?"

"It's a bit early in the day for whiskey for me, but I believe I will have something from the bar," Preacher said.

He went to the bar, reached behind it, and came up with a bottle of soda pop. He pulled the cork and took a sip from the brown bottle.

Walking to the table, Preacher said, "So, you fellows passing through or you aim to stick around?"

"What's it to you?" Tom Kitchen said.

"Why, Tom, there's no reason to be inhospitable to the sheriff, is there?" Carr said.

"Oh, I'm not elected or anything like that," Preacher said. "The folks in town sort of gave me this badge as kind of a part-time job, you see. It comes with no pay. I have a small farm and ranch a bit north of here. It's what I do mostly, farm and raise some horses."

"That's a heap of information, Sheriff," Carr said.

"I try to be friendly," Preacher said.

"Kiss my ass," Tom Kitchen said.

"Tom, I ain't going to tell you again," Carr said. "You'll have to excuse young Tom Kitchen there, he wasn't raised properly."

"Kitchen. That's a right peculiar name, young fellow," Preacher said. "That fellow on your left there wouldn't happen to be your twin brother?"

"Our ma was a fifty-cent whore in El Paso," Tom Kitchen said. "She gave birth to us on the kitchen floor of the whorehouse and died shortly thereafter. Folks didn't know what to call us so they took to calling us the Kitchen boys. How about that, huh? The Kitchen boys."

"That's a right entertaining story," Preacher said.

"What do folks call you, Sheriff?" Carr asked.

"I'll tell you, a couple of years back folks around here took to calling me Preacher on account of I read from the good book on Sunday," Preacher said. "We use the hotel lobby as a meeting place, you see. Course, it doesn't come with pay just like this badge doesn't."

"Well, Preacher, to answer your question, me and the boys are headed west and figured to stay the night and get a fresh start in the morning," Carr said. "Is that okay with you?"

"That's fine," Preacher said. "Maybe I'll see you for supper later."

"Planning to stay in town tonight?" Carr asked.

"We'll see how it goes," Preacher said.

"Hey, Preacher, do you always go unheeled?" Tom Kitchen said.

"Why, do I need to be?" Preacher said.

"No need of that kind of talk, Tom," Carr said. "Sheriff, we'd be happy to see you for supper later."

Preacher nodded and walked out to the street still holding the bottle of soda pop. He turned and entered the general store.

"Best stay inside tonight, Baxter," Preacher said. "Those boys are getting liquored up and there will be trouble. My guess is, come morning, they plan to clean out the town and maybe do some shooting in the process."

"We're helpless, sitting ducks against men with guns," Baxter said.

"Best take it easy, Baxter," Preacher said. "Keep Lonny in back and stay off the street. I'll be back in a while."

"Is that true about your name?" Sanchez asked the Kitchen brothers.

"Course it's true," Dave Kitchen said. "Who'd make up a shit story like that?"

"It could've been worse," Tom Kitchen said. "We could've been born in the out-house."

Sanchez and the others laughed at the joke.

"Boys, grab a fresh bottle and let's head over to the hotel," Carr said.

"What for?" Dave Kitchen asked.

"So I can have me a bath and you can watch the street," Carr said. "A man can see better from a higher vantage point."

"Those boys are fixing to cause some trouble," Hicks said.

"There's a good chance of that," Preacher said. "I want you to close up shop early today, Jim. Stay out of sight."

"I ain't no coward," Hicks said. "Besides, I'm making shoes for the Double R. One hundred of them. The Foxx kid should be here around four to pick them up."

"Foxx? Which one of his boys?" Preacher said.

"Jepson most likely," Hicks said. "You know he's sweet on Trudy and uses every chance he gets to come visit."

"That's a two-day ride," Preacher asked.

"At least."

Preacher sighed. "All right, but stay out of sight until the boy arrives," he said.

"I ain't no coward," Hicks said.

"I know that, Jim," Preacher said. "But bare fists are never a match for guns. You think on that and I'll be back directly."

"I feel the need for a hot bath," Carr told Potter. "I assume you got a tub room?"

"We do," Potter said. "Second floor. We got two tubs."

"How long to get one ready?" Carr asked.

"Half hour," Potter said.

"I'll be in my room," Carr said. "Knock when it's ready."

"What are we supposed to do while you're taking a bath?" Dave Kitchen said.

"Sit on the porch and drink that bottle," Carr said. "We'll have supper around six if you're sober enough."

Preacher looked out the window of the restaurant. He held a cup of coffee in his right hand and took a few sips.

Abigail stood beside him.

"Abigail, there's going to be trouble," Preacher said. "Those boys are getting liquored up pretty good there at the hotel. They're going to want a woman. I need you to keep Trudy out of sight."

"Oh, God," Abigail said.

"You have no back door so we can't sneak

her out that way, but maybe if they go into the hotel we can get her out the front door and into the alley," Preacher said. "She can walk to my place and stay the night."

"It will be dark soon," Abigail said. "We can try when it's dark."

"Soon as those boys enter the hotel, we'll try, dark or not," Preacher said. "Go tell her to get ready."

"Who's the better with a gun between you two Kitchens?" Sanchez asked.

The second bottle of whiskey was close to empty and Tom Kitchen swilled the last drop, tossed it in the air, drew his Colt sidearm, and blasted it to pieces with one shot.

"I can beat that," Dave Kitchen said.

"We ain't got another bottle," Tom Kitchen said.

The window on the second floor opened and Carr stuck his head out. "What are you boys doing?"

"Nothing. Practice," Tom Kitchen said.

"Knock it off and get up here," Carr said.

"They've gone up," Preacher said. "Go tell Trudy to get ready."

"Look," Abigail said.

Preacher looked out the window and saw

a wagon roll up to the livery across the street. It was driven by the Foxx boy, Jepson.

"I best get out there," Preacher said.

Preacher walked out to the street and met Jepson as the boy walked to the restaurant.

"Hi, Preacher," Jepson said. "Didn't expect to see you in town."

"I want you to listen to me carefully, Jep," Preacher said. "Some men have come to town. I make them for outlaws. They're well armed and pretty liquored up. There's going to be trouble. Get your shoes and ride out and don't look back. If they find out about Trudy . . . well, they're going to want a woman. Do you understand me, Jep?"

"Trudy?" Jepson said, loudly.

"Be quiet, son. Those men are . . ."

"Did something happen to Trudy?" Jepson yelled.

Preacher slapped Jepson across the face, knocking the boy to the street.

"Are you trying to get her killed?" Preacher said.

Jepson looked up at Preacher.

"Get up. Go to your wagon and go home," Preacher said.

Preacher heard a window open across the street. He looked at the hotel and saw Carr hanging out the window.

"I said, get up," Preacher said.

Jepson got to his feet and Preacher walked with him to the wagon.

"I need my shoes," Jepson said.

"Forget the shoes and go home," Preacher said.

"Hold on a second there," Carr said as he crossed the street.

Preacher and Jepson turned around.

Car and his men were crossing the street.

"What's the rush, boy?" Carr said to Jepson.

Jepson looked at Carr.

"I asked you a question, boy," Carr said.

"My paw is waiting on me," Jepson said.

"Well, you must have come to town for something," Carr said.

"Horseshoes," Jepson said.

Carr looked into the wagon.

"Son, there's no horseshoes in there," Carr said.

"I best get them," Jepson said.

"Boy, I think you're holding out on me," Carr said.

"That will be enough. Jep, go get your shoes," Preacher said.

"Preacher, I don't recall asking you a damn thing," Carr said.

"We heard you yell 'Trudy,' "Tom Kitchen said.

"I did not," Jepson said.

"You're a liar," Tom Kitchen said.

"You hold on there, mister," Preacher said.

Dave Kitchen drew his Colt sidearm and stuck it in Preacher's belly.

"Back off, Preach," Dave Kitchen said. "This is a private matter."

"I ain't no liar," Jepson said.

"I think you are," Tom Kitchen said. "What do you think of that?"

"I ain't no liar," Jepson said.

"Prove it," Tom Kitchen said.

"Give them some room, boys," Carr said.

"This ain't necessary," Preacher said.

"If the preacher tries to interfere, kill him," Carr said.

"I got no gun," Jepson said.

Tom Kitchen removed his gun belt and gave it to Carr.

"Now, I got no gun, either," Tom Kitchen said.

"Give them room, boys," Carr said.

Jepson stared at Tom Kitchen.

"Best put your hands up," Tom Kitchen said.

Jepson put his hands up and Tom Kitchen punched him in the face, knocking the skinny boy to the street.

"Get up, boy," Tom Kitchen said.

Jepson rolled over and slowly got to his

feet. He was bleeding from the nose and mouth. Tom Kitchen punched him in the stomach and as Jepson folded over, he punched him in the jaw, knocking Jepson to the ground again.

"Maybe this will convince the boy to quit telling lies," Tom Kitchen said and started to kick Jepson in the face and stomach.

"That's enough," Preacher said and stepped between Tom Kitchen and Jepson.

"Told you not to interfere, Preacher," Carr said.

Preacher looked at Tom Kitchen. "How are you when the man fighting back is a little bigger?" he said.

"You?" Tom Kitchen said.

"Want any?" Preacher said.

Tom Kitchen moved forward and Preacher proved to be an excellent boxer. He jabbed Tom Kitchen three times in the face and then dropped him with a solid left hook.

"Get up, Tom," Carr said.

"You sum bitch," Tom Kitchen said and jumped to his feet.

And promptly got knocked down again.

"Get him, Tom," Dave Kitchen yelled.

Tom Kitchen got to his feet, but it was apparent that he was no match for the skill and size of Preacher. As Tom Kitchen hit the ground again, Dave Kitchen jumped in and quickly was beaten to the ground by Preacher.

"You're handy with them dukes of yours," Carr said.

Carr drew his Colt sidearm and smacked Preacher across the jaw with it and Preacher went down on his hands and knees.

"There. I softened him up a bit for you," Carr said.

Tom and Dave Kitchen got to their feet and for the next several minutes beat Preacher senseless with their boots.

It ended when Baxter yelled, "For the love of God, stop."

Tig came running across the street and attacked Tom Kitchen.

Dave Kitchen drew his gun and shot Tig, killing the dog instantly.

Baxter and Hicks rushed to Preacher's side.

"Why?" Baxter said to Carr.

"I don't like being lied to," Carr said. "Boys, let's go have a look at what they're hiding from us."

As Carr and his men walked to the restaurant, Baxter waved to Hicks at the livery. "Give me a hand getting them inside," Baxter yelled.

Abigail stood in front of Trudy in the

kitchen. Abigail held a long kitchen knife at arm's length that she waved back and forth.

Carr laughed at the sight.

"Mother, you best step away and show me what you're hiding," he said.

Abigail waved the knife at Carr.

"I'll cut you," she said.

"Little mother, I'll put a bullet in your gut and at this range it will pass right through you and hit whatever it is you're hiding," Carr said. "Boys."

Five handguns were suddenly drawn at Abigail.

"One way or another," Carr said.

Abigail lowered the knife and it fell to the floor.

"Step away," Carr said.

Abigail didn't move.

"Step . . . aside," Carr said.

Slowly, tears streaming down her face, Abigail moved away from Trudy.

"Well, now," Carr said. "Ask and ye shall receive. Boys, take the girl over to the hotel. I'll take mother. I like me a seasoned woman."

IV

Hicks watched from the window of the general store as they took Abigail and Trudy across the street to the hotel.

"By God, we have to do something," Hicks said.

"Getting shot in the street like Preacher's dog doesn't seem like the right something to me," Baxter said.

"Are we going to sit here like a pair of old women?" Hicks said.

"Maybe if the others didn't take a holiday to Casper and we had us four more men we might stand a chance, but just us against six armed men is suicide," Baxter said. "And that don't help Abigail and Trudy none."

"Pa, Jep's awake," Lonny said as he came from the hallway that led to the living quarters.

"The preacher?" Baxter asked.

"He's still out, Pa."

"Go back with Jep," Baxter said. "I'll be along directly."

"Yes, Pa."

"It's getting dark," Hicks said.

Lights came on in the windows of the hotel.

"By God, we have to do something," Hicks said.

"You go over there and interrupt their doings and they'll shoot you as easy as they shot Tig," Baxter said. "Keep your eyes open and stay put. I'm going to check on Jep and make us a pot of coffee."

■ ■ ■ ■

Baxter returned with two cups of coffee and gave one to Hicks.

"Trudy has stopped screaming," Hicks said.

"She either passed out or they gagged her," Baxter said.

"Abigail hasn't made a sound I could hear," Hicks said.

"She wouldn't," Baxter said. "She survived an Apache attack when Trudy was nothing but a baby. That's where her husband was killed. She carried Trudy for eight days alone in bad country until she stumbled on a patrol of Texas Rangers. No, I wouldn't expect Abigail to make a sound."

"How can men be such animals?" Hicks asked.

"We are animals, all of us," Baxter said. "We have to be taught right from wrong. Some of us never learn the difference."

"Come sunup, those men are going to strip us to the bone," Hicks said. "Supplies we can spare, but they will take every nickel and valuable we have."

"What are you suggesting?" Baxter said.

"Surrending our valuables to them doesn't seem right thing to do," Hicks said.

411

"None of this is right," Baxter said. "But if they don't get our valuables come morning, they will probably kill Abigail and Trudy out of spite."

"I wish to God we weren't four days from Cheyenne," Hicks said.

"Wishing won't make it closer," Baxter said.

"How is the preacher?" Hicks asked.

"Might be out until morning," Baxter said. "That hit to the head from the handgun probably gave him a concussion."

"What's that?" Hicks said.

"The short of it is a cracked skull."

"So he could die?"

"Many have from a concussion."

"What can we do?"

"Wait."

V

Carr sipped the last bit of whiskey as he looked out the hotel window at the brightening sky.

He set the empty bottle on the dresser and turned and looked at Abigail in the bed.

"It wasn't so bad, was it, little mother?" Carr said.

Covered in the sheet, Abigail stared at Carr.

"Me and the boys will be riding on in a

412

bit, but first I want you to get dressed and go down and fix us breakfast," Carr said.

Abigail continued to stare at Carr.

"Well, little mother, up to now your sweet daughter ain't been hurt," Carr said. "But that could change in an instant if you catch my meaning."

Without making a sound, Abigail flung the sheet off and then stood up.

"I'm partial to fried eggs and bacon in the morning," Carr said.

Baxter and Hicks stood at the window of the general store and watched the street. To their amazement, Abigail came out of the hotel and walked toward the restaurant.

Hicks moved toward the door.

"Wait," Baxter said. "She's going to make them breakfast."

"What?" Hicks said.

"They're holding Trudy," Baxter said. "She's got no choice."

Carr looked at Potter, the housekeeper, and Potter's assistant and laughed. All three were roped and tied to chairs in the lobby. They had gags in their mouths and had passed out during the night.

"Boys, our breakfast should be about ready," Carr said to his men. "Head over and I'll join you directly."

"What are you going to do?" Tom Kitchen asked.

"Believe I'll have me a turn with the girl first," Carr said.

The girl wasn't unconscious when Carr entered the room on the second floor. Her eyes were open but she stared straight ahead with a blank look in them.

Her wrists were tied with rope to the bedposts. She was naked but acted like she didn't know or care.

Well, neither did Carr.

"Little sister," Carr said as he removed his shirt. "It will all be over in a moment."

Abigail stood with her back against the wall and watched as the five men ate their breakfast.

"Way I see it is after we leave, these folks are going for the law," Tom Kitchen said. "Probably to Cheyenne for the federal marshal."

"So what?" Sanchez said. "By the time they reach Cheyenne and get back we're almost a week gone."

"Federal marshals don't quit," Tom Kitchen said. "Even if we hole up in the Big Horns, come spring, they will still be looking for us."

"Tom's right," Dave Kitchen said.

"You are anxious to pull the trigger, eh," Sanchez said.

"It ain't about anxious," Tom Kitchen said. "It's about having a federal posse on our ass the rest of our days."

"I believe Tom is right," Quincy said.

"And what does Carr say?" Sanchez said.

"We ride with Carr," Dave Kitchen said. "That don't mean we got to hang with a rope around our necks with him too."

Sanchez grinned. "We will see," he said.

Carr rolled off of Trudy and went to the window to look out.

"It's a nice morning," he said. "I can smell the bacon from here."

Preacher stumbled from the living quarters to the store where Hicks and Baxter were at the window.

"Preacher," Baxter said.

"Abigail and Trudy?" Preacher said.

"Abigail's at the restaurant," Baxter said. "Trudy is still in the hotel with the leader of the pack. They had their way with them all night."

Preacher sighed heavily.

"The others are having breakfast," Hicks said.

"Having breakfast?" Preacher said.

"How's your head?" Baxter said.

"Stay inside," Preacher said.

"Where are you . . . ?" Baxter said.

"Just . . . stay inside," Preacher said. "All of you."

Preacher left and stood on the wood sidewalk for a moment while his eyes adjusted to the bright sunlight.

Once his eyes were adjusted, Preacher crossed the street and entered the tiny sheriff's office. It was dim inside and he lit the oil lamp on the desk. There was barely room to move, so much freight was stacked against the walls.

Preacher sat at the desk. He unbuttoned his shirt pocket and dug out the key that unlocked the bottom desk drawer. Once it was unlocked, he slid open the drawer and removed two items.

One was a pint bottle of bourbon whiskey. The other was a black leather holster that held a Colt revolver. The revolver was solid black, even the handle, and on the handle was a raised gold crucifix.

Preacher removed the Colt and checked to see that all six chambers were loaded. There were eighteen slots on the belt and each slot held a .45-caliber round.

He set the holster aside and picked up the pint bottle of whiskey. He sighed, took a sip, sighed, and took a second sip.

Then Preacher set the bottle on the desk and stood up and reached for the holster.

Fully dressed, Carr returned to the window. He was shocked to see Preacher walking across the street toward the restaurant. The man didn't so much walk as glide. Even from a distance, Carr could see the gold crucifix on the Colt in his holster.

Only one man, Carr knew, ever wore a gold crucifix on his Colt, but that man was dead at least three years.

Yet there he was, walking there in the street.

Carr felt a panic rise up in his throat.

He bolted from the room and ran down to the lobby and out the back door of the hotel.

As he stepped up to the wood sidewalk in front of the restaurant, Preacher removed the Colt from the holster and cocked it.

He drew a shallow breath and held it for a moment. Time seemed to stop. He released the air in his lungs and moved to the door.

Preacher saw five men eating breakfast at

a table. Carr wasn't one of them. Abigail stood with her back against the far wall.

She saw him before they did, but she didn't move.

Preacher opened the door and stepped inside. The one called Quincy saw him first and started to stand up and Preacher shot him in the throat.

What happened next took mere seconds, but to Abigail seemed to draw out like a blade.

The remaining four men jumped up and reached for their sidearms.

Preacher shot Sanchez in the left lung.

The one called Ryan froze in place and Preacher put a bullet in the man's heart.

Dave Kitchen drew his Colt and fired a shot wide of Preacher and Preacher shot him dead on the spot.

Tom Kitchen had his Colt out but it was by his side. He looked at Preacher.

"Don't kill me," Tom Kitchen said. "We ain't kilt nobody. You can't kill a man that ain't kilt nobody."

Preacher looked at Tom Kitchen and said, "Sure I can," and shot Tom Kitchen through the heart.

The one called Sanchez was still alive on the floor. He was wheezing badly from the lung shot and looked at Preacher.

"Don't waste a shot," Sanchez said. "I am already dead."

Preacher nodded at Tom Kitchen. "That's dead," he said.

"You go to hell," Sanchez said.

"I plan to," Preacher said. "Save me a seat," he said and shot Sanchez in the head.

Immediately Preacher opened the loading gate on the Colt and calmly removed the spent shells. He looked at Abigail and she simply stared at him without moving or speaking.

Once his Colt was reloaded, Preacher walked out of the restaurant and Baxter and Hicks were running toward him.

"The one they call Carr, he ran to the livery," Baxter said.

Preacher entered the livery. One horse was gone. Preacher looked through the rear doors and spotted Carr's horse several hundred yards away.

"Take my horse," Hicks said. "He's the fastest between here and the Kentucky Derby."

By the time Hicks saddled his horse, Carr had increased his lead by another hundred yards.

Preacher mounted the saddle and yanked hard on the reins and the horse raced out of the livery.

Hicks spoke the truth, the horse could fly.

Carr had a sizeable lead, but the distance between them was growing shorter. After a minute or so, the gap had closed considerably. Although Carr was still well out of range, Preacher drew his Colt and fired a shot to let Carr know he was being pursued.

Carr glanced back and then used the reins to whip his horse's neck.

Another minute passed. Carr's horse tired badly. Preacher's horse raced on and closed the gap considerably.

Carr's horse began to wobble and Carr did a very odd thing, Preacher thought. Carr stopped the horse and dismounted.

Preacher rode to within twenty feet of Carr and stopped his horse.

"I read in the newspaper that you was kilt in Abilene three years ago," Carr said.

"Obviously, as you can see, that story was wrong," Preacher said as he dismounted. "The good people of Abilene decided to give me a fresh start and wrote that I was killed. Then you come along and force me to return to my old ways."

Carr removed his gun belt and it dropped to the ground. "I didn't kill nobody," he said.

"No, but you did the devil's work," Preacher said.

"I'm unarmed," Carr said. "You can't kill an unarmed man."

"Pick up your gun then," Preacher said. "Or use that derringer you got hidden in your right hand."

Carr stared at Preacher.

"Go on, use it," Preacher said.

Carr cocked the two-shot derringer in his right hand, but never got the chance to fire it. Preacher drew and fired his Colt and shot Carr in the chest so quickly that if Carr wasn't bleeding from a hole in his lung, he would be in awe of Preacher's ability with a gun.

The derringer slipped from Carr's hand as he slumped to his knees and then fell onto his back.

Preacher holstered the Colt and stood over Carr.

Carr spit up blood. "Finish me, you bastard," he said.

"No, sir," Preacher said. "You'll die when you've a mind to. That will give you time to reflect on your sins and prepare for what the man upstairs has in store for you."

"And you," Carr said.

"No denying that," Preacher said.

Preacher mounted his horse and slowly rode back to town.

"Finish me, you son of a bitch," Carr yelled.

Preacher rode about a hundred yards before he heard the lone shot behind him.

LITTLE CHEYENNE, 1930

As they walked through the remnants of Little Cheyenne, Jack Stills said, "What do you think, Bill?"

"I think this place is perfect for the scene where the cowboy and the woman hide from the outlaws in a ghost town," Atkins said.

"John?" Stills said.

"With some dressing up, some tumbleweed and such, it works nicely for that scene, Jack," Wentz said.

"What's that?" Stills said and pointed to a spot behind the old livery about a hundred yards away.

"Let's have a look," Wentz said.

They walked to what was an old cemetery.

"They had their own boot hill," Stills said. "We can use this, can't we, Bill?"

"A perfect place for the woman to hide in at night," Atkins said.

The headstones were made of wood with the information burned into them.

"Six unmarked graves dated 1879," Wentz said.

"That one over there reads Preacher

422

1879," Atkins said.

"What's that little one over there?" Stills asked.

"Says Tig 1879."

"Tig?" Stills said.

"Guess 1879 wasn't a good year in these parts," Atkins said.

"Maybe they have a library or historical society we can do some research on this place," Wentz said.

They returned to the car and found the old man asleep. He awoke when they entered and Wentz started the engine.

"Old man, do they have a library or museum we can do research on this place back in Cheyenne?" Still said.

"They got a history of the railroad museum and another on the old west," the old man said.

"Let's go," Stills said. "Maybe they'll know who Tig was."

"Tig," the old man said. "Tig was my dog."

■ ■ ■ ■

Ethan J. Wolfe is originally from New York City and has traveled the west in search of realism and authenticity for his western novels. He is the author of ten western novels to date, including his popular Regulator series, and is always hard at work, researching and writing a new one.

■ ■ ■ ■

MY BROTHER'S KEEPER
BY BILL BROOKS

■ ■ ■ ■

Ten years in prison breaks a man.

It broke him.

Youthful indiscretions had landed him with the wrong bunch.

Now he was a free man again — had a new wife and three kids. Had found the Lord and Jesus and preached off a stump for a full year, winter, summer, wind, rain, and snow. Folks started coming 'round listening to him preach. Fire and brimstone, the wages of sin, Glory Hallelujah.

She was a good woman, Anne Pryce. Her kids were good too. Treated them like his own and he loved them greatly.

The community got together and built him a small church. Put up the frame in one day. Started on a Wednesday and the whole thing was up and ready for a full-out sermon by that Sunday.

He could smell the fresh pinesap warmed by the sun. Looked out at the faces upturned and thought: What'd I do to deserve all this?

He worked hard trying to raise enough vegetables to feed them all — a hog to be butchered in the early winter. Between these and scant donations they got by. Preaching wasn't fast money, it wasn't even slow money. You didn't have to take money from people — whatever came, they readily gave. And if they didn't give money, sometimes they gave a chicken or vegetables and once a shoat hog. It was a different life than the one he'd led and he liked it better this way than the old way. Getting by on little and having around you those who loved you, those you could trust, was a sight better than having a lot and not being able to trust anybody, worried about getting shot in the back by a man who called himself "friend."

That's all he needed, was to stand it, figuring it would sooner or later come to better times financially if he could just hang on long enough, get through enough winters. Anne took in laundry, the kids helped best they could. Three years as a free man came and went. He thought sure he'd die old in his bed now he'd got beyond the early years of wildness and settled down. Thought maybe he'd die in the rocking chair reading the good book, Anne there by his side, the kids singing him to his heavenly home with sweet hymns.

He thanked God for his good fortune of finding her and them, for finding the path of the straight and narrow life. This new life helped him forget about those long lonely days looking through iron bars at freedom.

But it was always there, in the back of his mind, how they'd broke him good.

Then the third winter came and brought sickness with it. The littlest girl was the first taken. Little Alice they all called her; little and sweet she was too. He led the prayer over her grave, felt soul's grief sliding down his cheeks. Her little face like a doll's wearing a tatted bonnet. In less than a month the same sickness took the two boys, Ike and Jack, and it seemed like to him he'd suddenly and somehow been handed the life of Job.

"Please, no more," he prayed aloud, down on his knees in that small church they'd built him. Folks stopped coming around, afraid the sickness was still there in the walls, the floor, and all around. Feared God had for some reason saw fit to curse the place, the man, his family, even though they couldn't name a reason why their maker should. He couldn't blame them for not coming, for being afraid. They were folks who believed in unseen powers, and left all reasoning to God. He was having trouble holding on to his own belief, for what God would bring down such hardship? He told himself and her, they'd be no different if the shoe was on the other foot.

"You're wrong," she said.

It came down to just him and her, and still she believed in him, but he knew she was all wrung out with sorrow. Every day he had to look into those sad, hollow eyes and try and lift up her spirits when he could barely lift up his own.

"I ain't as strong as you might think," he said to God.

She got so she wouldn't eat and went about calling the names of her dead children as she stalked the night, the empty rooms. Word got around she'd lost her mind and it scared folks even more. They stopped coming to the house, as well as the church. They stopped bringing by pies and chickens and a little something from the garden. Superstition is a powerful thing that spreads like its own sort of disease and sickness and infects everyone.

"All those years I was locked up," he said to the God he could neither see, nor who spoke back to him. "It's as if prison wasn't enough punishment for the wrong things I done? Why this? Why them kids, those innocents? And why her, now, after all she's already suffered? Better me than them. Kill me, crush me, break me upon your wheel and let her be. Have them put me back in prison. Anything but doing it this a way."

But the God he sought remained silent in the silent heavens. The winter bore on long and harsh as he'd ever seen a winter. Its weight of snow was like a white mountain. Its sharp winds were like knives. Its cold was like iron you couldn't break.

He found her on just such a brittle cold morning. She had tied the bucket rope they used to lower into the well around her neck. She must have tied it sitting on the rock wall's edge, then slid off into the black hole. He went out looking for her and the taut rope drew his eye. And then the pair of small button shoes empty in the snow beside the well.

Prison had broken him but this broke him worse than prison ever could.

He did not know if he could survive after finding her like he did. He hauled her small, frail body up from the well. He carried her into the house blinded by his own tears. He no longer had any purpose he could see. And, as if all that weren't enough, someone came in the night and burned the church to the ground after word got out Anne had gone mad and killed herself in that terrible way. He figured rightly enough that those who had built it felt it their rightful duty to destroy it, and thereby destroy whatever curse had befallen the place and the man who stood in its pulpit — the man who had now lost his entire family through unexplainable tragedy. Surely there must be some reason behind all the terribleness!

He'd awakened in the night to a dream of flames that seemed like hell had surrounded him, saw the fiery yellow tongues licking at the black demon night. He heard the window glass shatter, heard the crack of timber, its sap popping. He saw first the roof cave in, then frame walls collapse in on themselves as the church came tumbling down. He did not bother to get out of bed.

In the morning, he walked among the charred and blackened wreck poking through a fresh snow. Strangely enough he found his Bible, the pages curled and brittle so that when he picked it up the words of God sifted through his fingers like tiny dead black birds.

"That's it," he said to no one. "It's finished." And immediately felt crucified but not redeemed.

He took a trip to town and bought all the

whiskey he could afford and drove back again to the small clapboard house, wondering if they'd take it in their head to burn it down too, maybe with him in it. The cold wind reddened his face and chafed his hands while the whiskey fortified his innards and stole his senses. He wandered drunkenly among the unmarked graves of his wife and children, the sunken places sagging with snow, and sat cross-legged and talked to them.

He figured just to lie there next to them and drink himself to death. He had heard that death by freezing wasn't such a bad way to go. Heard it was just like going to sleep.

U.S. Marshal Tolvert found him before he had a chance to expire and put him into the back of his spring wagon, then wrapped heavy wool blankets around him and took him into town thinking he could well have hauled in a corpse by the time he got there. He had hauled in plenty of other corpses and this would just be one more.

The town's physician did not believe in such things as spirits or vengeful gods or curses, but believed in science and medicine and, with these, revived Wesley Bell to working order by means of hot compresses, rubbing his limbs with pure wood alcohol and submerging him in a copper tub of brutal hot water and Epsom salts.

"It's a wonder you didn't lose your parts," the marshal said afterward. "I've seen men with their fingers and toes froze off. Even saw one feller had his nose froze off and another with both ears turned black."

"You've wasted your time saving me," he said. "I don't appreciate your interference."

"Duly noted," the marshal said. "But you wouldn't be the first I hauled in half dead, nor the first I hauled in fully so. As an official of the law it is my duty to save those I can and kill those that need killing."

The next day the marshal came again, dressed in his big bear coat and sugarloaf hat and said, "Well, since you ain't going to die this time around, how'd you like to do a decent deed and make some money doing it?"

"I don't give a damn about money or doing any more decent deeds," he said.

The marshal winced at such talk. "I thought you was a preacher."

"I was a lot of things I ain't no more."

The marshal had eyes as colorless as creek water that danced under shaggy red brows that matched his shaggy red mustache. "From what I understand you are a man who has fallen on hard times. Now tell me this, what does a man who has fallen on such hard times and without a pot to piss in or a window to throw it out of plan on doing next?"

"I'll tell you what such a man plans: he plans to join his wife and children."

"Well, sooner or later you will get your wish, that is a natural fact. But for now, maybe you'd be interested in a little job I'm offering."

"You must spend all your time in opium dens, Marshal." This brought a chuckle from the lawman.

"I'm an excellent reader of a man's character," he said. "I've had to deal with woebegone folks and fools and killers all my professional life. I'd judge you to be somewhere in the middle of that bunch. I don't believe you want to die while still an able-bodied man with plenty of good years ahead of you yet. Why, you can't be more than forty. Look here, I'm proposing to offer you a fresh start. Who can say what awaits us, or why God intends us to be here on this earth or what our purpose is?"

"Believe what you want, lawman. But me, personal, I'm done believing. I'm quitting the game." The marshal slipped a fine Colt Peacemaker with stag-horn grips from his holster and handed it over butt first.

"She's fully loaded with .45-caliber hulls," he said. "If you aim to finish yourself, might as well do it right this time. But, before you pull the trigger, let me stand back out of the way because I'd not feature having your blood and brains splattered all over this nice coat of mine."

And the marshal stood away from the sickbed there in the physician's fine old house with its gingerbread scrollwork and tall windows and fancy shake roof and flocked wallpaper.

Wes took the revolver and remembered in an instant when such a thing in his hand was as familiar to him as breathing. But it wasn't nothing he wanted to be reminded of now, nothing he wanted to take up again.

He thumbed back the hammer.

"Just one more thing before you pull that trigger," the marshal said. "I understand your people rest in unmarked graves?"

Such talk pinched Wes's nerves.

"Wind and time will rub out any trace of your wife and children. Is that what you want, for them to be forgotten, yourself along with them?"

He turned the cocked gun instead at the man who had offered it to him.

"It don't matter about me," he said.

"Shooting me won't solve any of your

problems," the marshal said. "It'll just make them worse, something you'll learn when they slip a noose over your neck. Let me tell you, hanging is about the worst way a man can die. Bullet's much easier and quicker and a lot more honorable, case you place any stock in honor."

Wes lowered the hammer on the pistol and set it on the bed.

"I'd pay you good money," the marshal said. "Enough to buy your family some nice headstones, maybe a little wrought-iron fence around the graves. There is a fellow in St. Louis, an Italian who carves the best headstones you ever laid eyes on. Carves them out of marble, puts angels on them if you want. The marble comes all the way from Italy. He gets a handsome price, but you could easily afford it on what I'd pay you. Think how nice that'd be, them headstones for your wife and children. Why a hundred years from now people would be able to see who they were and where they rest, maybe put flowers on their graves out of sheer kindness 'cause that's the way some people are. They aren't all like you and me, Wes."

"You've got a hell of a gift of gab," Wes said.

"Don't I, though?"

"How much money?"

"Let's say two hundred dollars, cash."

"What do I have to do for this cash money?"

"Kill a no-good son of a bitch who needs killing."

"What makes you think . . . ?"

The marshal lit a cigar he'd taken from the pocket of his waistcoat, blew a stream of blue smoke toward the plaster ceiling, and noted the fine wood furniture that adorned the room. French, he thought.

"I know all about you, Wes Bell. I know more about you than your ma."

"You don't know nothing about me."

"No, sir, you're wrong about that. It's my job to know about people, and what I don't know, I find out, and I found out everything about you. I know before you took up preaching you was in Leavenworth prison. I know how bad you was. And that is why I've come now, to ask you this thing, because I know you're the right man for the job."

"Killing for money ain't part of me, never was. I did bad things, but I never killed for money."

"I'll take your word on that, but you've killed plenty for free before the law caught you and put you in the jug. Now tell me if

I'm wrong."

"That was a long time ago and I never killed nobody who didn't deserve it or wasn't trying to kill me first."

"Well, that sort of makes us even, then. But you haven't forgot how to pull a trigger on a man, have you? It's like riding a bicycle. You just never forget."

"No, I haven't forgot how."

"Let me just go ahead and tell you about this fellow," the marshal said, retaking his seat by the bed and taking up his hogleg again and putting it back in his holster. "He's a scourge, worse'n the plague. Everywhere he goes he leaves a bloody trail behind: dead folks, raped folks, hurt folks. He ain't never done a good thing in his life. At least you seen the light, Wes. You got broke down and turned your life around 'cause that's what a normal human will do at some point when he saw the errors of his ways. But not this fellow. This fellow is as bad a seed as ever was planted in the devil's garden and he needs weeding out."

"It makes no sense you asking me to do it. You're the law, why don't you do it, if he's so bad?"

"Oh, believe me, I'd do it in a heartbeat, wouldn't think twice about it. Hell, I'd hang him and then shoot him and then burn his body just to make sure no man, woman, or child ever had to cross his path again. But I can't do it, Wes."

"Why can't you?"

" 'Cause I'm a dead man myself. Got cancer of the ass. Eating me up bad and there's no way of knowing how much longer I got, but probably I'd not find him before the grim reaper finds me."

The marshal smoked casual as though waiting for his steak to arrive from a kitchen in some café.

"There is one other thing about this fellow, Wes, one more reason I come to find you and no other for this job."

He waited to hear what the marshal's reason was.

"He's your brother, Wes. This no-good son of a bitch is your kid brother, James, and if there's anybody knows his ways and where he'd go to ground when he's being chased, it would be you, Wes."

"James?"

"None other."

James was only ten years old when Wes left home and later got sent to the pen. And while behind those bars, his ma took James to somewhere in New Mexico, he'd heard, and married a miner and all contact between them was lost.

440

"I haven't seen him since he was a kid," he said to the marshal.

"Yes, that's probably true, but kin is kin and blood is blood and I do believe of all the men in this world you are the one who could find this little murderer and put him down. Do you want to know what all crimes he's committed? Should I tell you about the raping of women and young girls, how he slashed their throats afterward? Should I tell you about how he murdered an old man and his grandson who weren't doing anything but fishing and he shot them in the back of their heads merely for what was in their lunch pails? Shall I tell you how he burned down a house with a man and his family still in it because they were colored? Shall I tell you such tales, Wes, or will the money be enough?"

"Oh, you give a long and windy speech, Marshal . . ."

"Yes, I do, Wes. Yes, I, by God, do."

"Even if I agreed to do it I wouldn't know where to begin and would not know if and when the time came I could do it, kill my own flesh and blood. Could you do that, Marshal?"

"Yes, by God, I could and I would."

"Still . . ."

"I know all about blood being thicker than

441

water — but it's blood he's spilling more than water and the blood stains you as it does all your people who ever carried or will carry the Bell name and only blood kin can make it right in the eyes of the innocent. Only you can set things right with James, Wes Bell."

The marshal blew a ring of smoke toward the ceiling and watched as it became shapeless before dissolving altogether. Then he leveled his gaze at Wes.

"You see, I have studied you like a schoolboy studies his books and I know everything about you and everything about that little killing son of a bitch brother of yours. Ironic, ain't it, in a way, you're preaching the gospel and him named James, which was Jesus' brother's name. You ain't Jesus, are you, Wes? You ain't the second coming, are you?"

"To hell with you."

"To hell with us all if that boy keeps up his killing and rampaging. To hell with every last man, woman, and child he comes across in this old world unless you stop him."

Then the marshal reached into the side pocket of his bear coat and pulled out a triple-framed tintype of a woman holding an infant and two other children, a boy in each of the attached frames. Anne and her youngsters — and pressed it into Wes's hand.

"Your precious dead, Wes. And to hell with them too," he said, "for the sickness that took them is no less than the sickness that sets in that wild boy's mind, Wes. No different. Dead is dead no matter how you come to be that way. But what is different is whether or not you just drew a bad hand in life's game or some no-good bastard come along and took life without the right to do so. How'd you feel if it was James killed your wife and those kids instead of them dying of sickness?"

Then the marshal stood and adjusted the weight of his heavy coat and settled the sugarloaf on his head.

"I'll come 'round tomorrow for your answer, Wes. And the two-hundred dollars if you so decide."

"Five-hundred," Wes said. "Gold double-eagles, no script, and the name and address of that stone carver in St. Louis."

"Well now, Wes, you sure you wouldn't like to make it thirty pieces of silver . . ."

And, so it was that the very next morning the marshal came again and stacked two gold double-eagles on the bedside table and a piece of paper with the St. Louis stone carver's name and address written on it.

"Down payment," the marshal said. "The rest is waiting for you at the bank upon your return and proof the deed is done. Now raise your right hand so I can swear you in official with Doc Kinney here as eyewitness."

Doc Kinney looked on at the abbreviated ceremony.

Then the marshal placed a small badge stamped out of brass next to the double eagles and said, "Get her done, son. Sooner rather than later. I'd like to still be breathing when I read the good news."

"What makes you think I won't just take the money and run?"

"Well, you could do that," the marshal said, with an air of confidence. "You know what the inside of that state prison looks like and I venture to guess it ain't worth no two-hundred dollars to go back. I hired you and I can hire others to track you down and for a lot less money. Sweet dreams, bucko."

Fifteen days had passed since he struck his bargain with the marshal.

He began the trail where the marshal said the last crime had been committed — a place called Pilgrim's Crossing, a small Mormon community in the high country of Utah. Saw the woman's grave and asked her husband to describe the man who had raped and killed her. The man described him as having a mark on his cheek like a red star. James had been born with it; the one single thing he could recall about the kid before they hauled him off to prison: the red star birthmark.

The man had pointed to some distant mountains when asked which way the killer went.

"I just come in from working in the silver mines when I saw a man on a paint horse riding fast away toward them mountains, then found Lottie tore up and dead, fella was dressed in dark clothing, looked like a crow taking flight."

"What lays that way?" he asked the man.

"Just a shanty town called Brother, is all I know," the man said.

"How come you didn't follow?"

The man gave a slight shrug. "I have other wives to care for," the man said. There were four small houses on the land, each with a bonneted woman staring from the door-ways.

"Well then, I suppose you are one lucky son of a bitch you got spare wives to concern yourself with. Most men just have one and some don't have any." He felt disgust and turned his horse toward the north road.

Another day's ride and he met a man pulling a handcart.

"How far to Los Brother?" he asked.

The man was large as an ox and needed to be. The cart was burdened with a full load of watermelons.

"Five or ten miles, maybe," the man said, thumbing back over his shoulder.

"You come from there?" he asked. A blue scarf kept his straw hat tied down against the cold air.

"No, nobody is from there."

"Any chance you come across a man with a red star on the side of his face?"

The man shook his head.

The man took up his load again and the rider rode on, each man seeing to his duty.

Two more days of riding brought him to the top of a rocky backbone of a ridge where he looked down upon a shambles of a town. In the long distance, a line of snow-covered saw-toothed mountains shimmered under a cold dying sun. A song of wind sang along the ridge and fluttered through his clothes and ruffled the mane of his horse. It chilled his blood, or something did.

He glassed the town below him with a pair of brass Army field glasses. Then he swept them along the brown slash of road that ran uneven west and east. He saw nary a solitary thing moving along the road.

Nothing moved in the town, either, but it was still some distance off and maybe too far to see human activity. He was sure from the campfire he'd found that morning, he had closed the gap between him and the kid brother; embers still sighed in the ashes.

"We'll wait," he said to the horse. There was nothing for the horse to graze on among the rocks. "When the sun is down good and proper, we'll ride down there and find James."

He squatted on his heels and waited for the sun to sink below the mountains, thinking of his lost family as he did, the real reason he was doing this thing, and when the sky turned dark as gunmetal and night came on like a cautious wolf, he tightened the saddle cinch and mounted the horse and began his descent into the town he figured had to be Brother.

With darkness, he saw a few of the town's lights wink on. A hunter's moon rose off to the east, casting the landscape in a vaporous light. He and the horse traversed the slope and came to the very edge of the town's first buildings.

He went on.

The street was empty but he could see shadows moving behind the lighted windows. And farther up the street he heard the sound of a piano being played roughly. He followed the sound to its source, a solitary saloon, false-fronted, in the center of town.

He tied off and stepped cautiously through the doors.

Rough-looking men were bellied up to the long oak bar, the soles of their worn boots resting on the tarnished brass rail. They drank and laughed and swore. A cloud of blue smoke hung over their sweat-stained Stetsons, the smoke so thick it turned the men into ghostly figures of men.

The interior of the saloon was long and narrow like the inside of a cave — and there was a feeling about the place that did not set well with him: a feeling of trouble and danger and worse.

The saloon girls were dressed in dark crimson gowns and looked like wilted roses lost in their seeking of the sun as they moved wraithlike among the men.

Along the wall opposite the long bar, men played cards at tables, their backs to him, their faces shaded by the brims of their hats.

He shut the door, keeping out the cold wind. Nobody bothered to look up. His right hand rested inside his mackinaw on the butt of his revolver. He'd had plenty of time to think about what it would be like to shoot his own brother. Told himself he wouldn't feel anything because he never knew the boy that well, and if he was as snake mean as the marshal had claimed, well, then it was simply an act that if he didn't do, someone else would. Blood and kin had nothing to do with it, he told himself. Justice had nothing to do with it. Italian marble headstones is what it had to do with.

His gaze took in the men along the bar and he did not see anyone with a red star birthmark on his face. Even without the red star birthmark, he figured he would know James in spite of the long passage of time. Like a mother cow knows its calf, a brother knows his brother.

Then his gaze shifted to the card players and not one of them looked familiar to him, either.

He moved farther into the saloon, pushing his way through the crowd, fingers curled around the gun butt riding his left hip. He wanted to see who was there in the back. A sloe-eyed woman with wild looks, neither young nor pretty, pressed suddenly against him. She had the cloying scent of dead flowers, and awful teeth when she opened her mouth. He tried not to look at her directly for fear of what he might see.

"How's about buying a gal a drink, cowboy?" she said, and before he could stop her, her hand snaked between his legs. "A drink will get a free toss with me."

He looked down then, but her own eyes were averted to where her hand now rested. "Well, how about it?" she said through the din.

He'd consorted with many such women in his younger days and taken pleasure from them. He had drank with them and fornicated with them. He was as wild and woolly and reckless as a Texas cowboy. This woman's presence reminded him of every such woman he had sinned with and he didn't have any want for her, or any other woman since Anne.

He took two bits and set it on the wood and said, "There's your drink, Miss, but the rest don't interest me." He pushed on through the crowd toward the back where he saw a wheel of chance and a faro table with men bucking the tiger. But none of them at either station had a red star birthmark on his face.

There was a low flat stage against the back wall and to the left of it a set of stairs leading up to the upper level where several private boxes ran the length of the saloon.

These were the places the saloon gals took men and fleeced them of their money and their pride and still left them wanting more. He knew from his preaching that desire was a thing too easily had and just as easily lost.

His every sense told him James was in this place, in one of those boxes, for he'd watched some men and the bar girls going up there and some others coming down.

He took the stairs and looked down upon the crowd below, the miasma of writhing human desperation like a scene straight out of Revelations it seemed to him, and he was just as glad to have left it down there. To see them from this vantage point caused his belly to clench, his flesh to sweat, his muscles to knot. He could not imagine himself like those below ever again.

An odd thing happened just then as he was looking down: a face of one of the men at the bar looked up, and it could have been his twin. Then the man looked away again, down at his drink there on the hardwood. Wes was sure it was all his imagination.

He pulled his revolver and eased down the narrow hall to the first private box and drew back the curtain enough to peer inside. A pudgy man stood with his trousers down around his ankles, facing a woman sitting on the side of a narrow cot doing what such women do in such positions.

Wes let the curtain fall back and he moved on to the next box. This time he saw a young soldier sitting, talking to his gal, both of them facing away, just sitting there on the small bed holding hands the way lonely people do.

He moved to the next box and the next, finding three in a row empty.

Then there was just one curtain left to draw and he moved to it, the pistol in hand, cocked and ready. Oddly, he felt calm. His heart rhythm was slow and steady as an old Regulator wall clock. He nearly always felt the same way as a young buck when trouble presented itself. He didn't know what it was or why the calm had descended on him, it just had. And, when he eased the curtain back with the barrel of his pistol, he saw the man he'd been looking for, his brother James, the red star birthmark sitting in the bed, his eyes shut. A slattern with black hair lay against his chest, his hand stroking her head as one might a cat.

It would be easy enough just to push his way into the room and empty every round and be done with it. But he'd have to kill the woman to do it. He didn't ride all this way to kill a woman.

Looking upon that rosette marked face,

he saw a single scene from their past, when James was just a small kid running around in a hardscrabble yard chasing chickens, flinging rocks at them. Even then the boy had a cruel streak in him. The old man whipped James with his strap, trying to beat the meanness out of him, but it could be he'd just beaten more meanness into the boy than out. And maybe the old man knew the family secret, that James wasn't of his own seed, but the seed of another man and that's why he beat him so terrible.

There on the bed's post hung a gun rig within easy reach. A holster with a fine ivory-handled Colt. It was the sort of gun a man used to gunfighting might own. Not your typical twelve-dollar single action bought in some hardware store to let rust on your hip.

And in spite of everything, he suddenly felt a strange connection to the boy, but not one that could be described exactly as brotherly love, more a simple indebtedness of same bloodlines.

James suddenly shifted his weight and the woman fell away from him, exposing the stain of blood on a hairless white chest. Wes could see now the gaping wound of her exposed neck.

He drew back the curtain fully now and

stepped quickly into the room, aiming the revolver right where the woman's head had rested. James's eyes fluttered open.

"Wes," he said as casually as if they'd just seen each other yesterday, that there'd never been any separation between them. "I figured you'd be along some day, and now here you are."

"And now I'm here," he said.

"They sent you, didn't they? Them who want me dead?" James looked at the still form of the woman beside him. "Her name is Chloe," he said. "She was real nice to me for a time. Then she got like the others, like Ma used to get. You don't remember none of that, I bet. You was up in the prison doing your time whilst I was at home doing mine with Ma once the old man passed, and she went in search of another. A gambling man he was, and a pimp to boot. Made sure we earned our keep, Ma and me." A smile drew the boy's lips up at the edges. "He was the first son of a bitch I ever killed."

So there it was, some of the reason at least, if James could be believed, and maybe he could, or more likely not.

"Call me sinner, Wes, call you the saint. Heard you went to preaching and married yourself a fine woman. How's that working out for you, big brother?"

"Never said I was nothing but what I am, but I never killed a woman or anyone else that was innocent."

"Innocent! Ha, ain't none of us innocent, Wes. You think she was? You think any son of a bitch in this place is?"

"I only came just for you, James."

"Then you're a fool, Wes."

"Maybe so. I guess time will tell."

"I guess maybe it will."

"I'll give you a chance to defend yourself," Wes said. "I reckon we're still kin of some sort according to the heavens, otherwise I'd already have shot you."

"Jesus Christ, Wes, but that's awfully white of you."

"You can defend yourself or not, either way, I'm going to pull this trigger."

"Hell, you're wasting your sweet time, boy. We're already dead, men like you and me, been dead since we first drew breath. Same God that made you, made me. Go on and pull your trigger, Wes. I'm ready to go. Question is, are you?"

"I wouldn't be here if I wasn't," Wes said.

James was snake quick just like Wes thought he would be.

Both men fired at once. Witnesses said later it sound like a single gunshot, but they were wrong.

At last he felt a great peace, for the first time since he'd fallen in love with Anne and his days of winter became days of summer. He saw James buck on the bed, then his hand open, empty of the smoking gun, and close his eyes as if falling asleep, a bright ribbon of blood flowing from his heart.

Goodbye, James.

Suddenly Wes found himself ankle deep in new snow playing with Anne and the children, throwing snowballs, laughing madly. Anne's smiling face bringing him a great happiness. It was a dream, there behind his eyelids. And then it was gone.

He opened his eyes and found himself standing on a rocky windswept ridge glassing the town below and the road that cut through it and saw not a solitary thing moving. Somewhere down there in that place they named Brother was the man he was looking for, one of his own.

He waited until dark, then rode his horse down the slope in the moonlight and entered the town from the east and went on up the street to the only establishment open — a saloon with the words LAST STOP painted on a hanging sign out front that the wind blew back and forth on two creaking chains that needed oiling.

He tied off his mount and went in and

worked his way through the smoky crowd until he saw the stairs, the private boxes on the upper level. A woman in a blood red dress cut him off and asked if he wanted to buy her a drink. He swept her aside with a hard look and went up the wood steps leading to the upper boxes.

He tried each chamber until he came to the last and found James marked by the red star cheek and a dead woman. And, for a moment, it was uncertain as to what he would do and what James would do, but now that they had faced the storm, there was nothing to be done. James's pistol was in his hand just that quick, a wicked grin like the devil's own followed in a split second by a resounding blast of gunfire.

And in the white storm that followed, he opened his eyes and found himself again standing on the same windswept spine of rock overlooking the ramshackle town below, the shimmering mountains beyond, the dying sun in a glazed sky off to the west.

He had a deep and abiding sense he had been here before, that he had ridden in the moonlight down the slope of loose rock and entered the town and found James, but how was that even possible? He thought he heard Anne's voice calling him and looked around but no one was there. And when he looked back down toward the town again, he saw a lone man riding a white horse ascending the ridge.

The rider came on steady, the hooves of his mount clattering on the loose shale until at last the rider and his horse topped the ridge and rode along it to where Wes stood. The rider dismounted. He had a red star cheek.

"You might as well give in to it, Wes," James said.

"Give in to what?"

"To the fact you're dead."

"Like hell I am."

"Yes, you are dead and so am I. We killed each other that night in the Last Stop, don't you remember?"

"No, I don't remember nothing except I put a bullet in you."

"You sure enough did, and I shot you," James said, rolling himself a shuck and lighting it with a flame from his thumbnail, then letting the wind snuffle it out and carry away the first exhalation of smoke.

"I was goddamn fast, but you weren't too slow, big brother."

He saw it then, James, quick as a snake strike, jerking his pistol free of the hanging holster, felt faintly the bullet's punch even as James bucked back on the bed, eyes rolling up white in his head.

"It ain't as bad as you'd a thought," James said. "Is it?"

Wes turned 'round and 'round looking in all directions, the world spread out, the sky, the mountains, the town. He felt like if he'd had wings, he could fly.

"We're still down there," James said pointing to Brother. "We're down there with all the others who died there in those glory years when the mines were still giving up their silver. We're still down there with the whores and the gamblers, the merchants and the pimps who came for the easy money. Some were lucky and left when the silver ran out, but you and me and some of the others weren't so lucky, Wes. We came and never left."

The wind sang over the ridge like angel voices.

"Come on, Wes, let's go back down — they, they're waiting for us, Chloe, the one you found me with that night, and that whore who wanted you to buy her a drink and you wouldn't; she killed herself that same night, Wes. When a whore can't sell herself for the price of a drink, she's got nothing left.

"Me, it was my time to go. Sooner or later, some law dog or bounty hunter would have run me to ground if you hadn't. In that way, I'm glad it was you and not some stranger. I'm sorry I killed you. You were always the better of us two. You didn't give me no choice. I guess it was meant to be like everything is, like brother slaying brother, Cain and Abel. It's in us to kill when we feel we have to. We're a lonesome bunch to be sure . . ."

"No," Wes said. "I was hoping you would. I let you do it because I didn't have nothing more to go home to. I just wanted to go home to them is all."

"There's nothing for any of us to go home to, Wes. Yonder is your home. Down there in Brother. No heaven and no hell, just the place we died in where our corpses rot and our bones turn to dust again, and our spirits are once more free. That's what going home is, Wes."

And then he could see along the road something raised up the dust.

"What is that?" Wes said.

"Something they call automobiles, Wes. It's how they get around these days. Horses are merely for looking at and pleasure riding. Those folks down there are curiosity seekers, historians, tourists. They want to see how we once lived, to see a town that is as dead as us. A ghost town. What better place than where we got ghosts aplenty? They come because they read about the gunfight, about how two brothers killed each other in a whorehouse over a woman or over gold; the story keeps changing with time and every telling. They tell how one was a good Christian man and the other was an outlaw. And they like to believe we're still there, in the town, raising a little hell, scaring the kids, the hucksters selling us like boiled peanuts and ice cream, putting our photographs on picture postcards.

"They even stage the gunfight with actors, men with bellies hanging over their belts, only they do it out in the street and not inside in that little whore box where it happened. They bring folks in on buses just to see you and me kill each other three times a day except Christmas, of course. They must have written a hundred stories about that night and that town. And we'll be here as long as the sun rises and sets over the mountains. We'll be here as long as it rains and the snows fall and the oceans curl against the shore. We are legend, Wes. They'll never let us die or rest in peace. We'll live forever as punishment for our sin, you and me. Come on down, brother. Ride with me for a little while."

■ ■ ■ ■

Bill Brooks has written more than forty historical novels and is a full-time writer these days. He lives in Florida.

■ ■ ■ ■

To Ride a
Tall Horse
by L. J. Martin

■ ■ ■ ■

"It is not necessary, Juanito," his old grand-uncle, his *tío,* told him. "I have seen the grain bin empty many times in my years."

"I am old enough, Tío Jorge. I have fourteen years. It is not so long a journey."

"Ah, Juanito, you have thirteen years . . . Remember, I was nearby, sipping *aguardiente* with your father when the midwife slapped your behind." His uncle smiled, showing rosy gums where his teeth had been, then his old face furrowed again. "It can be a journey onto the tangs of diablo's pitchfork. I made it one time in the summer months many years ago, in search of Yokuts who had stolen the horses of Don Alfonso Valadez. We had three days without *agua.* We lost three horses and almost our own lives." The old man scratched his bony ribs through the jerga shirt. Then again focused watery eyes on his nephew. "It is three days of hard walking through the hills to the San

Joaquin, then another three days south to the San Emigdio . . . and if it is dry in the valley? You cannot carry enough water in the goat skin even to make it across the *lomarias,* the low hills, on foot. It would be better to wait for winter when, God willing, the water holes are full."

"I will be fourteen soon . . . And there is said to be work there now, *tío.* To wait for winter would be to wait for us all to starve."

His uncle stared off into the dry hills beyond the little pueblo of Paso Robles. "If only we had a horse," he muttered. But he had no answer to his nephew's dilemma.

For the first time in his few years, over the last two months Juan Ochoa had watched the bins in his mother's *cocina* sink to the point you could see their board bottoms, the few handfuls of kernels left there scraped up against one side — the first time he had seen his brothers and sisters cry with not enough to eat. Beans, corn, wheat, and wild fava; each bin was almost empty and his mother was rationing. For the first time since Juan could remember, they had gathered and ground acorns, but even those were scarce. There had been no rain since the celebration of Corpus Christi. Since they had journeyed the eight-mile walk north to Mission San Miguel, and listened to the old priest who still occupied the rectory there. Who still held mass even though his vestments were torn and tattered, as run down and almost as vacant — for the old priest was skin and bones — as was the ramshackle old mission itself.

It was a bad time for the proud old Californios who occupied the few adobes at Paso Robles. Since the gold was discovered in the north, and the gringos came, things had not been as they were — as his Tío Jorge told him they had been in the years before he was born. When the ranchos were great and prosperous — before the land reforms, as the gringos called the time, or the great theft, as Tío Jorge called it. Before the meat hunters had come and killed off the elk and antelope and most of the deer and bear. Before the ranchers had driven their cattle to the north to be consumed by the thousands and thousands of gringos who worked the gold fields.

And it had not helped that his father had died last year — it had been the great family catastrophe of Juan's young life. The gringos, for a time, worked a mine back in the hills of Nacimiento. They mined cinnabar, a red rock they heated in order to obtain mercury. And his father had worked for them in the mines, then later in what

467

they called the retort, which was a great iron tower where they cooked the cinnabar ore over oak charcoal fires to boil out its mercury and gather it in vents. The longer his father worked there, the sicker he became, until his vision began to fail and he had to come home and not work at all, because he was blind. Then he coughed blood until he died. It had been a hard time for all the family — Mama, Juan's four younger brothers and sisters. And even old Tío Jorge who now only tended the garden or gathered the wild fava beans from along the creek beds, or trapped wild pigeons and quail and rabbits as he had learned to do as a boy. The garden failed because of the drought, and the fava beans and mustard did got grow along the creek sides as there was no water in the creeks. And the pigeons, quail, and rabbits were few. Even the horse his father had owned had come up lame not long after its master's death, and it too had become jerky for the pot. But now, even that was gone.

So Juan decided it was time he took work away from home — he was a man, and large for his age, even if he did not have his full height yet. He could send a little money back to help. He had heard of work in the great valley to the west from passing vaqueros, the San Joaquin Valley. Work at one of

468

the great ranchos, the San Emigdio, said to be two days' south of the new gringo town of Baker's Field.

And it would mean that he would learn to become a vaquero.

He would ride a tall horse.

One of many that would make up his remuda of horses.

His mind was made up. He would leave at first light.

Tío Jorge centered his walking stick at the side of his chair so he could rise, and teetered up to his feet. "I will go to check the traps now. Maybe there is a fat rabbit."

"No, Tío. I will go. It will be the last time I can help you for a long time." Juan would go, but he knew he would find nothing in the rabbit snares or the bird traps. They had found nothing for over a month.

Even the wildlife had abandoned this parched land.

"You are a good boy, Juan." Tío Jorge collapsed back into the chair.

"No, a man, Tío. I am a man now."

"As you say, Juanito."

"Juan, not Juanito. Juan Ochoa, the vaquero."

Juan hurried away as his uncle stared after him. Then the old man's eyes misted over and his throat burned. "A man," he muttered to himself. "Hardly a man," and a vaquero? Not a vaquero for many years, until many skills were acquired. He could ride, but that was far from being a vaquero, a caballero. If only he finds a compassionate *segundo,* or foreman, at the San Emigdio; a man who remembers a time when he was young. For to get that far and not find a job would be a terrible thing — Jorge could think of nothing worse for his nephew. Except not making it to the San Emigdio because of the drought.

He hung his head, refused to think of his grand-nephew dying on a parched trail, and began to doze.

He didn't remember his niece, Juanito's mother, Angelina, helping him to bed.

Jorge lay awake on his frame leather-laced cot before sunup and listened as Juan rose from his sleeping mat and pulled on his jerga pants and shirt. The younger children now slept in the smaller of the two rooms of the small adobe, with their mother, and he and Juan slept in the large room that served as bedroom, dining room, and kitchen.

Jorge did not look forward to explaining to Angelina where her oldest son had gone, for he had agreed not to tell her that Juan was leaving — it had been an agreement, just between the men.

Juan made his way to his mother's single cupboard and pulled aside the cloth covering and removed four tortillas and placed them in a small cloth sack he would take with him. Then he moved to a bin and dipped out a handful of beans and they joined the tortillas in the sack. He padded quietly back across the room and looked down into Jorge's eyes, to see if he was sleeping.

"I am awake, Juanito." Jorge whispered. "Show those valley vaqueros how tall an Ochoa can stand, how tall he sits the saddle . . . And take my sombrero. It would not do for a vaquero not to have . . ."

"Yes, Uncle." Juan reached down and squeezed the old man's hand — his sombrero was one of the few prized possessions the old man had left — then turned to the door.

But a quiet voice echoed from the doorway separating the two rooms. "You would leave without embracing your mother?" she asked.

Juan paused, then walked to where she stood in her ragged nightgown — tall enough that he was face to face with her. "No, Mama, not if you are awake."

But she brushed by him and went to the

cupboard and shuffled through the meager things there for a moment before she turned back. "Give me the tortillas you took," she commanded.

Knowing that he would be in serious trouble without them, still Juan obediently opened the sack and dug them out for her.

Carefully, she took the last of the chocolate she had hidden away and spread it on two of the tortillas and rolled them up, then added a spoonful of leftover beans to each of the other two and rolled them. She wrapped them all in a cloth and handed them back. He stuffed them away, then moved into her open arms and felt her shudder slightly as she hugged him.

"*Vaya con Dios,* and return to your family soon," she said quietly, but she thought, *I will never see my son again. He will become a vaquero, far away, and never return. He will have no children, for the land and the cattle will become his mistress, and the reata and a tall stallion his pride.* She turned, went back to bed, and to worrying about her remaining four children.

With an empty feeling in the pit of his stomach, barefoot, and with four filled tortillas and a handful of raw beans in the cloth sack along with his prized possession, an eight-inch iron knife his father had left him, he walked out without looking back.

A corked goatskin bag with a shoulder strap hung from a peg alongside Tío Jorge's sombrero on the outside wall, and Juan picked it up as he went by — leaving his uncle's prized sombrero, for he could not bring himself to take it. He could not imagine seeing his uncle outside without the hat proudly perched on his head.

Stopping at one of the few sinkholes left in the Salinas River, a mile upriver from where his father had built their adobe just before Juan had been born, he filtered the stagnant water through his jerga shirt to fill the goatskin. He would have enough for two days, even in the heat of summer.

Carving a pole from the river willows growing on the dry riverbed, he hung the goat gut bag and the cloth one from one end. Placing the pole and his meager belongings across his shoulder he set out into the rising sun.

Before he had walked half the morning, climbing the low hills, bearing south to pick up the old Indian trading trail to the valley, the sun beat down in earnest. He wondered, as he rubbed the back of his neck, if he had made a mistake not accepting his uncle's generosity and taking the sombrero.

The *lomarias* lay covered with oaks, underlain with sparse wild oats gone golden in the summer heat. Specks of dark green oaks dappled the golden hillsides. Meadowlarks flew before him and an occasional hawk circled above, easily riding the currents of rising hot air. In the distance, when he could see far enough through the low hills, false lakes wavered, teasing him with feigned reprieve from the heat. By the afternoon, he had not eaten; had only stopped twice to take a couple of mouthfuls of water, but now, even as tough as they were, his feet began to burn on the hot baked soil of the trail.

He had walked at least fifteen miles, he thought. He could rest, and eat something.

He turned off the trail and made his way forty feet up a low hillside to a wide oak and plopped down below it on a variegated lichen-covered rock. He dug into the cloth sack and pulled out one of the tortillas and slowly ate half of it, savoring each chocolate-filled bite for a long time in his mouth before he swallowed it. A blue-bellied lizard watched him from a nearby rock, doing push-ups in the sun. Just as Juan was about to decide to go on, he heard the sounds of hoofbeats. He stayed in the shade until he saw them approach.

Five riders, vaqueros, each well mounted

and one with silver trim on his saddle. As they drew even with where he had left the trail, he stepped out from under the spreading branches and called out, *"Hola!"*

To his surprise, two of the vaqueros whipped sidearms up and leveled them at him.

"Quien es?" one called out.

He sunk back into the shadows of the tree. "Only Juan Ochoa of Paso Robles!" he answered, his voice timid.

The man in the lead, the vaquero with the fine silver trim on his saddle, reined his tall gray stallion off the trail and spurred him up the hillside. He pulled rein and the horse sidestepped and danced as he spoke. "Step out, Juan Ochoa, so you can be seen. You have put a terrible fright into my amigos," he said, and laughed.

Juan stepped out into the sunlight. "I did not mean —"

"They will live to be frightened again," he said. The vaquero was thin faced and he too wore a sidearm as well as carried a long arm in a saddle scabbard. His sombrero was laced with silver thread to match his saddle trim and he wore silver conchos down the sides of his tight fitting *calzonevas.* He was as handsome a vaquero as Juan had ever seen. "Where are you going, Juan Ochoa?"

he asked.

"To the San Joaquin Valley, to become a vaquero," Juan said, and stood taller as he did so, throwing his shoulders back.

"It is many miles to the San Joaquin, muchacho," the man said. "Have you seen other riders on the trail?"

"No, señor. No one since I left the pueblo of Paso Robles."

"That is good. The trail is not crowded."

"You are going to Paso Robles?" Juan asked.

"Where we are bound is not your concern, muchacho. You have a long journey, and I will not keep you."

Juan nodded, picked up his bundle and placed it over his shoulder, and strode out without looking back. He heard the men laugh and wondered what they found funny, but still did not look. He strode on to the sound of their hoofbeats fading in the distance.

That night, he finished the last of the tortilla he had eaten earlier, and with his stomach growling, managed to fall asleep under an oak tree — but the trees were becoming more scarce. Tomorrow night, he thought, he would be sleeping under the stars.

It was the middle of the next day while he

sat and finished his second tortilla when he noticed that his goat gut was leaking slowly. His water was well over half gone, and he wondered if he was halfway to the valley. He would have to find water before he came down out of the hills and started out across the long sage-covered flats. He had been told that it was another day across them before water could be found.

There was nothing to catch the leak in but his mouth. But he couldn't just sit and wait for the water to drip out, or he would be no closer to the water hole that he *must* find. So he walked, with the bag held in front of him, and every time a drip formed, he sucked it away. At least it kept his mouth wet as he traveled.

But by that night, the water bag was empty.

With the morning, his mouth tasted as fresh horse dung smelled, and by noon of the third day, like dung dust. Still he carried the bag, for if he found water, he would have to have it. And searching for water lengthened his trip. Each time he would see a patch of green willows or a grove of cottonwood, he would move away from the trail to check and see if a spring or seep was the source of the life color. But so far, it was not. Two hours later, in a cut in a hillside, he found a seep. But less than that, really. It was a slow drip. Again, he could not wait for the bag to fill. He slept there that night, drinking a few good mouthfuls, but only filling the bag a quarter full before he walked on. The mouthfuls had been enough to wash down the third tortilla. He carefully placed his handful of beans into the goat gut so they would soak, and even though he had nothing to cook them in, he could eat them raw if they were soft.

By noon, he thought this would be the longest day of his life.

By the late afternoon, he looked down across what must be the San Joaquin Valley. It stretched out before him as far as he could see in the hazy heat of summer. The trees were behind him now, and in front was only a broad savanna of low grass. And he knew that somewhere beyond that was a sage and greasewood desert until the bottom of the valley, where there was life-giving sloughs and swamps.

But where, nearby, would there be water?

He started down until he found a cut in the hillside that would offer some shelter. He had found he could keep the last of the water from leaking by turning the bag upside down, keeping the water away from the seam at the bottom. He drank half of what was left, only three good mouthfuls. He walked well into the night, then he slept, sung to sleep by the yapping of coyotes and the distant howl of a lonely wolf.

The next morning, he drained the last of the water, but still had the handful of soaked beans. As he dropped into the valley, he continued to upend the bag and drop a bean into his mouth, chewing, savoring, keeping his mouth at least damp.

It was hotter here and his feet burned continually, but still he walked on. There was nothing else to do. Hawks and turkey vultures and an occasional condor circled overhead. Once, a bush rabbit bolted in front of him, teasing him with its promise of succulent roast meat — but he did not have even a rock to throw at the sassy little beast.

His beans were gone by noon, and by mid-afternoon, with the *lomarias* far behind him, and the wet beans only a memory, his tongue began to thicken.

He had been wrong the day before — this was the longest day in his life.

Finally, with the sun at his back and his shadow stretched out before him, he sank to his butt and sat in the trail. And with darkness, sleep swept over him like a shroud. He did not move from where he had sat, only lay over, and slept.

He awoke, wondering if he had died in the night. He felt as if he had died — his joints ached, his eyes ached and seemed to be rubbed raw with the dust and dryness. His feet felt as if they had blistered, but he found none rising and soft to the touch. It was as if they were burned below the thick calluses.

But the dawn was ahead of him, golden and promising of water in the valley bottom, but also threatening of the heat to come and the miles he must cross. He struggled to his feet and strode out with new strength, but within the hour, had begun to stagger. Again he sat, then lay on his back and watched with interest as the vultures wheeled overhead. He curled in a fetal position and waited.

He dreamed of home, and the Salinas River, when it ran full and joyous.

The splash of water was like a slap. He coughed and sputtered and managed to rise to the laughter of a group of men. Then he realized it was water and opened his mouth like a baby sparrow and soon realized more — the man upon whom his blurred vision focused, the man who held a canteen of water and splashed it into his mouth, was the same vaquero he had seen on the trail, what seemed so many days before.

A man who now seemed a savior.

The men laughed and joked as he managed to gulp the water.

"Juan. . . . Juan was your name, right, muchacho?" the vaquero asked.

"Sí, señor," he managed with swollen tongue. "Juan Ochoa."

Juan looked around him, and to his surprise, the men now drove a herd of over fifty horses. Fine horses, tall and straight. And lathered, from a hard run.

"Well, Juan Ochoa," he said, "my name is Enrico Zaragosa."

"Sí," Juan managed. Enrico put a strong arm under his and helped him to his feet.

"You have made it to the San Joaquin, Juan. Have you found a job yet?" Enrico asked, and the men sitting their horses nearby guffawed loudly.

Juan, exhausted and confused, just looked at the tall thin-faced vaquero.

"Well, I guess not. We are riding near Baker's Field, muchacho. There are a few farms and ranches nearby. Would you prefer to walk the next forty miles, or would you consider the loan of a mount to take you that far?"

"Ride," Juan managed.

"Inocente," Enrico called to one of the

men. "Take a lead rope and tie a hackamore for our young friend." Then he turned to another. "Paco, see if your loop can find a gentle horse broke to the rein . . . try one of those mares with the headstalls."

Juan stood quietly as the men went to their tasks.

"When have you last eaten, muchacho?" Enrico asked.

"A few bites yesterday."

"Here," he tossed a chunk of thick jerky to the boy, then followed it with his canteen. "Don't drink too much too fast, muchacho. You'll swell up like a toad and pop." He laughed and swung his horse away. The fat vaquero they had called Paco led over a small dun-colored horse he had roped out of the herd, and the other vaquero, Inocente, slipped a hackamore over the mare's nose, tied so the ends of the lead rope hung on either side and became reins.

Juan tried to mount, but bareback with no stirrups, he could not. With a laugh, Inocente reined his horse around and leaned down and caught him by the seat of his pants and lifted him, almost throwing him over the little horse.

"He is a runt horse," Inocente said with a snarl, "you should give him to the runt boy."

"His price may be far too high," Enrico

said, "at least if we don't ride on. Yee haa!" he yelled, and they were away with a leap, circling behind the herd, pushing them to a lope again.

Juan reined the little horse away from the herd to the side, trying his best to hang on without stirrups or forks and cantle, and while trying to hang on to the canteen and the jerky. Soon he settled into the little animal's easy stride.

He was not a tall horse, this horse, but he rode easy. And it was so much better than lying in the wide dry plain, drying your bones in the scorching sun waiting for the vultures.

A ride. A ride to Baker's Field, or at least nearby.

He could not believe his good fortune.

At a lope, he reined the mare over next to the fat vaquero, Paco. "Señor Paco, is it far to this place . . . Baker's Field?"

The man scowled at him. "A few miles. You should earn your way, *chingadero.* Get behind this herd and push them."

Obediently, Juan pulled up the mare and let the herd pound past, then reined in behind them. The dust immediately coated him so he looked like an apparition. His mouth caught the flying dirt, tasting gritty on his teeth, and his eyes cramped and burned. He wished he had a bandana to tie around his face, but he did not. Eventually, he got wise and reined over to the side and out of the stream of dust that billowed behind the pounding herd.

In the next few hours he covered many more miles than he ever could have on foot, even when he had water. After only a few miles, they began to have to pick their way around marshy tule-lined areas, some of which were spotted with willows and cotton-woods. Just the sight and smell of the green foliage and water made him happy — but nothing made him so happy as riding the horse. He could not believe his good fortune — even though the little mare was hardly his idea of what a true vaquero should ride.

When the sun was low at their back, they had to rein up at a river's edge. The horses immediately moved to the bank and lined up and lowered their heads to drink. The bank lay grass- and brush-lined, but the horses managed to wade out knee deep and line the edge behind until all found a spot.

Juan caught his breath, then reined over close to where the men had gathered. He was tired, bone tired, and filthy. He hoped they would stop and camp.

"It is too soon, jefe." Paco referred to Enrico as boss.

"Possibly, amigo, but I don't want to push them across while they are winded. The bed of the Kern is soft here and has quicksand. We may lose many of them, and that would make this a wasted week. We will wait until morning when the horses and we are fresh."

Paco shook his head in disgust, but Juan sighed in relief. The men reined away from the horse herd and dropped from their saddles, then pulled their tack away from the lathered animals.

Enrico instructed two of the vaqueros. "Hobble that tall sorrel stallion and the big roan mare. They are the leaders and the others will not leave them."

Juan watched intently, eager to help, but not wanting to do something the men would consider silly. After a few moments, he dismounted and pulled the lead rope that had been tied as a hackamore off the mare and let her join the other horses. He watched as Enrico roped another tall dappled-gray stallion from the bunch and resaddled, but he did not pull the cinch tight. He obviously was not going to mount the horse, only keep it at the ready. He tied it to a nearby cottonwood sapling.

Juan found a spot at the river's edge and brushed the dust away as best he could, then washed his bare feet tenderly as they were very sore, then his hands and arms, and lastly, his face and hair — his hair was long, and suddenly the thought came to him: who would cut his hair now? His mother had always cut his hair. But then, other vaqueros did not have their mother to cut their hair. There must be a *barbero* among the vaqueros? It was something he must ask, when he is among vaqueros he would work with. Then again, maybe he could find work here with Enrico and his men. They must be in the horse business?

It was still hot, even though the sun had ducked below the horizon. Pulling the shirt off, he dried with it, then pulled it back on. It would dry quickly.

Paco snapped at him to gather wood, and he did so and soon, even as weary as he was, he had a large stack of driftwood gathered from the riverside in a pile in a clearing where the men were centered.

Paco built a small fire and one of the men produced a pot, which an end of his bedroll had been stuffed into, and in minutes, coffee boiled.

"Keep that fire low," Enrico cautioned.

Paco looked at him with a glare, but said nothing. Each of the men produced his own cup and soon had coffee to complement hard biscuits and jerky they pulled from pockets and bedrolls. Juan sat aside quietly as darkness fell, until Enrico noticed him and called him over. He dumped the dredges from his cup and handed it to him.

"Take coffee, and I have a biscuit and chunk of jerky for you. Tomorrow, you will go your own way."

Juan paused. "I cannot ride any more?"

"No, muchacho. It is for your own good."

Juan wondered at that, and wondered if it was a good time to ask for work with Enrico, but decided against it; instead he went to the pot and poured himself a cup of the black grunge from its bottom. "Should I add water to this pot?" he asked Inocente, who sat nearby.

"Only if you want more," he said, then smiled at the boy. "Set the pot off the fire and smother it with some dirt. We want no glow from it." Juan looked at him curiously, but did as instructed. Inocente seemed pleased with him "You watched me tie the hackamore today. Can you tie your own tomorrow?"

Juan smiled, knowing the man was teasing him. "No, but I could learn to if you would teach me."

"After you finish your coffee."

Juan hurried through the scant dinner offering, then joined Inocente, who spent the next thirty minutes working with him, showing him the intricacies of the Spanish hackamore while the rest of the men smoked, worked on their tack, or cleaned their guns.

At full dusk, Inocente tired of the instruction. "I'm going to roll out and bed down now, amigo. Why don't you do the same."

Juan noticed that the rest of the men were asleep, except for one who sat his horse quietly out at the edge of the herd where the horses grazed. He found a spot in the grass, only a few feet from Enrico, and curled up. He had no trouble finding the respite of sleep.

Juan sat up with a bolt, wondering what had caused him to, and rubbed his eyes in the predawn light — then another shot rang out close by. Juan flinched, startled at the muzzle flash and the clap of sound that made his ears ring.

"Every hombre for himself," he heard Enrico shout and watched his back disappear toward the dappled gray he had tied to the sapling the night before. Without bothering to bridle up — the bridle hung on the saddle horn — or to tighten the cinch, Enrico vaulted in the saddle and gave his heels to the big gray. Chunks of dirt flew from the big horse's hooves as his powerful legs bolted to a gallop. He pounded away into the underbrush and shadows. More shots rang out and Juan sunk as deeply as he could into the grass.

"Get that'un ridin' off," a man shouted. A man whose voice Juan had not heard before. A gringo.

Men were running everywhere and shots split the night like thunderclaps.

Then the sounds seemed to fade as the voices — gringo voices — rang from farther out in the darkness, and the shooting stopped.

Juan slowly, cautiously, climbed to his feet, standing with his head canted to the side, listening, trying to figure out what was happening.

"Greaser!" he heard the shout from behind him and spun only to receive the butt of a rifle across the side of his head. He collapsed in a heap.

When he awoke, the sun told him it was midmorning and his aching wrists and shoulders told him he was trussed. He could not move, tied by both wrists and ankles. His own heartbeat tortured him with a continued throb like an anvil being pounded in his head. Paco lay beside him in the grass, blood worming its way out of his thick black mane that was his hair, seeking respite from the hot sun below his collar.

"What happened?" Juan asked groggily.

"They caught us, muchacho *estúpido,*" Paco said angrily. Juan could see that the big man lay hog-tied with rawhide biting into his fat wrists.

"Shut your face," a voice rang out, and Juan tried to sit up to see who was speaking from close behind them. "Stay down, greaser," the voice commanded.

"I want to go home," Juan managed.

"I'll bet," the voice said, then Juan could hear pounding hooves as more than one horse rode into camp and four mounted men came into view and slid to a stop in the clearing.

"Couldn't catch 'em?" the voice behind him asked, as the men began to dismount.

A thick-shouldered man with a full black beard walked over and leaned over Paco and Juan, his knotted fingers on his thick knees. "Where's home for you boys?" he asked in a gravelly voice.

Paco spat onto the ground near the man's booted feet. "In hell, amigo," Paco said, and received a hard kick to the ribs for his trouble.

"Don't knock him out, Striker," another of the men said. "We want ol' *gordo* there to know he's being hung."

The man with the beard, Striker, snarled back over his shoulder. "I want to know where the rest of those bloody horse thieves are headed, then we'll hang these'uns and get after the others."

Them? thought Juan. Surely they did not think he was involved in this, whatever this was. Even though his head hurt terribly, and his thoughts were scrambled, he spoke up. "I do not know these hombres, señor. I was in the desert, coming to Baker's Field and to San Emigdio ranch to find work. I was very sick with no water and they offered me the loan of a horse."

"You borrowed a horse all right," Striker snarled. "You and these other greasers borrowed half a hundred of them."

"He's only a boy," one of the men said, stepping forward to stand beside Striker.

Juan could see the man was a little older than he was.

"Bull dung," Striker snapped. "He rode a Oso's Ranch horse to get here an' that's good enough for me."

The man who had been behind them while they lay tied spoke up. "The fat one said 'they caught us,' to the boy when the boy woke up. Us means the both of 'em. That's good enough for me."

"The muchacho tells the truth, señor,"

Paco said, "I meant the other men and I when I said us . . . Why would you harm this whelp of a muchacho?" and received another boot toe deep in his stomach for his trouble. He coughed and spat, then kept silent.

Juan could feel the tears well in his eyes, then overcame it, refusing to show them he was only a child. "I have only just left my home in Paso Robles . . . I was going to find work."

"Throw a couple of loops over that cottonwood limb," Striker commanded.

"But, Striker —" the young cowhand started to complain again.

"Don't cross me, McKenna, or you'll find yersef' carryin' yer tack flung over yer shoulder, and it's still a fer piece into Baker's Field."

"Yes, sir," the young man said, but did not participate as the others tied simple slip knots in the tails, then flung the pair of hemp ropes over a thick limb.

"What can I do?" Juan asked Paco in desperation.

"You can die with dignity," Paco said, "and curse gringos to hell with every breath."

The men came over and bent down and jerked them to their feet.

"Holy Christ," the young cowhand said. "That boy don't even have no boots. He weren't one of this band."

"I was walking across the desert and they offered me a horse," Juan said, hopefully. "I have only thirteen years."

"Old enough to steal, old enough to hang," Striker said with finality, as the men walked them to the cottonwood.

They had tied off the tails of the ropes to the tree trunk. One of them lifted Juan onto the back of the little mare he had been riding. Juan sat in stunned silence while three men fought to lift a kicking, squirming Paco up on another horse until one of the men brought his gun butt hard across the vaquero's head, dazing him, and with the help of Striker, the four of them got him into the saddle.

"You got any last words, greasers?" Striker asked.

"He ain't tall enough," one of them observed. They had tied the rope off and the loop did not hang low enough to drop over Juan's head.

"Get my horse," Striker instructed.

One of the men hurried across the clearing and picked up the reins of a tall palomino and led him over.

In less than a minute, Juan was off the

mare and astride the horse, and had the rough hemp rope fitted around his neck.

"Now, again, any last words?" Striker asked.

"He ain't even got no boots, not even no sandals," the young cowhand repeated.

"Shut the hell up, McKenna, or you'll be takin' shank's mare to town to look for work."

"Then by your leave and by all that's holy, I will!" The young cowhand moved to a dappled strawberry roan in three strides and stripped the saddle and bridle away, flung his tack over his shoulder, and strode out of camp mumbling that he would abide no outfit that hung children.

"I'll be damned," Striker managed, watching him stomp away.

"I think there is no question about that, gringo *puerco*," Paco said, then spat into the dirt.

"Don't change things," Striker said, ignoring Paco's prediction, and the fact he had called him a pig. "Any of the rest of ya'll squeamish about hangin' horse thieves?"

He got no complaint from the others, but two of the remaining three men hung their heads and would not look at him.

Striker pulled his Colt and fired into the air.

Juan still did not believe what was happening to him as the tall horse bolted. He tried to cry out that he was only thirteen, and that his mother and brothers and sisters needed him to send money home, and that his uncle wanted him to sit tall in the saddle, and that he wanted to become a true vaquero, and above all *that he was no horse thief* — but words would not come as he heard the much heavier Paco's neck break, and kicked his own bare feet. Until they stilled.

It had been much too short a time, astride a tall horse.

Later that afternoon, while Striker and the three cowhands followed Enrico Zaragosa's trail, one of them turned to the burly trail boss of the Oso Ranch. "I hear'd the railroad was surveying up north?"

"Yep. Sure as the sun rises, they'll be blowing steam down here in the south end of the valley sometime next year."

"Do you think that'll be good for things?"

Striker spat a long stream of tobacco juice into the dust where the tracks of the tall gray horse ridden by the escaping vaquero marked the ground. "It'll bring trade, but it'll also bring a bunch a' thievin' John Chinamen. We'll be chasing them next. By God,

I wish they'd leave this country to those of us who took it by rightful means."

Striker spat again. "I just want to get this done, get this greaser strung up and get on back to San Luis Obispo."

They rode a few more strides before the cowhand spoke again. "Striker, what the hell does San Luis Obispo mean anyways. That's no proper name for a town."

"Don't matter. Keep yer mind on yer business, we got a horse thief to catch."

■ ■ ■ ■

L. J. Martin is the author of more than forty western, thriller, and mystery novels and several nonfiction works. He lives in Montana with his wife, Kat Martin, also a novelist. The Martins travel extensively researching their work, and winter on the coast in central California. For more info, contact ljmartin@ljmartin.com.

■ ■ ■ ■

HALFWAY TO HELL
BY GREGORY LALIRE

■ ■ ■ ■

Folks in Halfway, Montana, said town marshal Charlie Truslow was too tough to die — or maybe just too stubborn. They were right, for better than four tempestuous years, anyway. He had showed up in the territory in the middle of the War Between the States, prematurely white-haired, hobbling, tormented by dark recollections, and fully alone. Talk was, he long ago lost a wife to childbirth in the backwoods of Virginia and sometime later abandoned the twin daughters who made it out alive.

In Halfway, halfway between the gold mining towns of Bannack and Virginia City, he put on a dusty six-point star nobody else was willing to wear and never once took it off — either because he viewed it as a badge of honor or because he wasn't partial to bathing. He had no deputy, no close friend, and more enemies, subtle or otherwise, than he could shake his horsehead cane at. He

501

was a limping target on Main Street and a sitting prairie chicken in his bare-boned office, where he took his meals at his desk and slept in the lone cell with only one eye shut. He had taken the job "for life." Somehow, he survived three shootings, two knifings, a pickaxe ambush, an attempted scalping, a dozen one-man posse pursuits, every little fuss at the saloon, and the three-hundred-pound presence of Terrance Goodman, who owned at least half of everyone and everything in town except for the marshal and the jailhouse.

Charlie Truslow's luck ran out on a bleak winter day, a few ticks short of noon, in the alley behind Goodman's Saloon/Hotel/Hurdy-Gurdy. He knew the good-for-nothing twin sons of Goodman were road agents that shot first whenever a lawman asked a question, but this time he hadn't even opened his mouth when George put a .44 slug in his good leg and Pete put another in his bad leg. As he lay squirming on his back in the red clay, someone poked a shotgun out an upstairs window and plugged the marshal in the belly.

Everyone figured the shooter must have been the twin brothers' daddy, Terrance Goodman himself, but nobody was prepared to object, let alone make a citizen's arrest. The mortally wounded Charlie Truslow, the only man in town who didn't fear "Big Belt" Goodman, took more than a week to die when it would have taken an ordinary man less than twenty-four hours. Townsfolk agreed it was just like him, not only refusing to go when Doc Stone said his time was up but also insisting on going it alone. That wasn't exactly true, though. After Doc declared Truslow a lost cause, the marshal spent his last days in the jailhouse lying on a new cot with extra blankets and a soft pillow provided by an unlikely caretaker, the young stagecoach driver, Dan Buck.

Travelers and men transporting gold between Bannack and Virginia City knew Buck, by sight if not by name. He handled four or six horses right well on the almost daily round trips and never risked his own life or that of his passengers when road agents halted the coach, which was still a common enough occurrence in the mostly bare hills on either side of Halfway.

Buck was a slight, closed-mouthed fellow, and nobody bothered to ask him where he was from or anything else about his past. It was hard to tell whether he had sided with the Yanks or the Rebs because he never talked about such things, but in any case, he would have been too young to fight in the war and was anything but a fighting man now. He believed that self-preservation was the first law of nature, and the citizens of Halfway shared that sentiment.

The Bannack & Virginia City Express stopped running regular for better than a week during the marshal's last days. That wasn't unusual for winter. Heavy snows were known to box in for weeks or months at a time the residents of the two mining towns and of the little way-station town halfway between. Actually, at the time, the snowfall had been only moderate. Still, nobody wondered where the driver was or that he might have other matters on his mind besides the transportation of passengers and gold.

After he had taken care of the burial business at Halfway's grave patch, Dan Buck went back to work. Not being one to carry a pistol, he had seen no reason *not* to bury the marshal's .42-caliber LeMat revolver with the lawman. Though young and spry enough, he elected to hang on to the marshal's horsehead walking cane. He kept it in the boot under the driver's seat. He also kept the marshal's badge, tucking it away in the pocket of his sheepskin coat, but that was his own little secret.

On his third day out on the familiar road, four masked road agents stopped the stage at the steep climb over Beaverhead Butte and demanded Bing Taylor's $10,000 in gold, having learned of the shipment ahead of time as usual. "Up with your hands!" two of the ruffians shouted at once. Bing protested with his mouth and took a pistol butt to the face that made his split lips look like a gutted fish and cost him a tooth and a half. His two private guards protested by reaching for their weapons and were instantly disabled — one permanently — by bullets and buckshot. The only other passenger, a three-town drunk known only as Boosy, laughed through the entire holdup, even as he lost a pocket watch he himself had stolen, suspenders inherited from a father he hardly knew, and a half bottle of rye.

Driver Dan Buck raised his hands and stood perfectly still like the veteran driver victim he was. Two of the robbers, wearing blankets over their clothes, slid off their mounts and kept him and the wounded guard covered with shotguns, the barrels cut down short. The other two never dismounted; they wore identical black outfits and black cloth masks with slits for eyeholes.

These, Buck knew, were the leaders — the Goodman twins — but he pretended they were strangers and deserving of any man's respect. They didn't have to pretend back; they held the .44-caliber Colts.

"You ain't holdin' out on us is you, Buckaroo?" asked one of the twins.

"No, sir," Dan Buck replied. "No, sirs," he quickly added as not to leave out the other Goodman.

"Best show us what you got in the boot, you sonofabitch," the other said, anyway.

All Buck had in the boot was the horsehead walking cane. He produced it and tapped his own head with it as if to show the outlaws it was harmless.

"That sonofabitch was gonna cane us like the old man done . . ."

"No, not Buckaroo. What you aim to do with that there stick, Buckaroo?"

"Lay it back down to rest till I feel my old age comin' on."

The one Goodman laughed. "Good man," he said.

"Give it here," said the other, his face dead serious.

Maybe Dan thought of the late Marshal Truslow and what he might have done in such a fix, but not for more than a second. He tossed the cane to the meaner twin, who tried to catch it with one hand but dropped it. That made him meaner; he cursed Buck and thrust the barrel of his pistol toward the driver.

"Not that," the other Goodman said. "Old man's liable to cane you again. We don't want nothing to happen to Buckaroo. He knows how to be obliging. Besides, he got a pretty face for a jehu."

"I'd as soon shoot the sonofabitch as look at him," yelled the mean Goodman. But he shot at the horsehead cane on the ground instead — four times. The first shot was a clean miss. The second missed by a hair. On the third shot he nicked one of the wooden ears. But his fourth was wide left — he was clearly squeezing too hard on the trigger — and he didn't risk a fifth one. His flesh flushed splotchy red above his mask. He galloped off without even a second glance at Bing Taylor's gold.

The other twin ordered the two lesser ruffians to fill his saddlebags with gold, and when that was done he tipped his hat to Dan Buck and rode leisurely away. Robbers three and four grinned at each other, loaded up the rest of the plunder, and followed the leaders, spurring on their horses while firing pistol shots in the air and hollering like old Rebels.

Dan Buck stepped down and put the one-eared horsehead cane back in the boot before helping the first guard into the coach and dressing his wounds. Ignoring Bing Taylor, who condemned him and both guards right through his pained lips, Buck broke out the company shovel to dig a shallow roadside grave. Boosy stopped cackling but was of no help with the nursing or grave digging. He was too busy mourning his missing rye and trying to hold up his trousers. Bing Taylor finally hobbled his lip, but then buried his face in his hands and sniffled over his lost treasure instead of saying a word over the dead guard.

Once back in Virginia City, Bing Taylor talked again about his horrible loss and Dan Buck's gun-shy behavior, but the Bannack & Virginia City Express Company didn't expect its drivers to go out of their way to risk their own lives, and the general sentiment was that close-fisted Bing should have shelled out more gold to hire better guards. The Virginia City vigilantes showed restraint. They were convinced they had hanged all the road agents and banished all the hard cases, including Boosy, in the Alder Gulch area, and that the robbery/murder at Beaverhead Butte was the concern of Halfway, where the law wore a badge and looked upon the vigilantes with disdain.

"The marshal is dead," Bing Taylor reminded the silver-haired vigilante captain.

"That's also Halfway's affair," the captain said. "Halfway don't believe there was ever such a thing as a road agent band. They told us we was unnecessary. The fools."

"All I know is I am a citizen of Virginia City and the victim of a high-handed outrage against the laws of God and man."

"The outrage occurred in the vicinity of Halfway. You have my sympathy."

"I don't need sympathy. I need my gold back. Those four highwaymen must *not* escape punishment."

"They'll have to answer to God on Judgment Day."

"That's not good enough, Captain. You call yourself a vigilante?"

"You see 'em in Virginia, point 'em out to me, and the Vigilance Committee will make sure they never trouble anybody again."

Over in Bannack, vigilantes had also been active at one time, even stringing up a sheriff suspected of directing outlaw outrages on the side. But with most of the bloodstained miscreants dealt with, things had grown quiet on gallows hill.

In Halfway, no vigilante group had ever stepped up when Marshal Truslow served as the lone law enforcer, and none appeared now that the town lacked a lawman. Terrance Goodman was big all over, and that included his brain. Big Belt was too smart to allow his twin boys and the rest of the gang to rob or harm the locals who minded their own business. As for those locals who opened their mouths about what they might know, they had short life expectancies. For their own safety, the citizens of Halfway could easily look the other way when the alleged Goodman gang made a greedy, overly fortunate Virginia City man poor again.

Marshal Truslow had never overlooked lawbreakers, but he had never been able to pin anything on the Goodman family that would hold up in a Halfway people's court. And he had been as opposed to vigilante action as much as Big Belt was — for different reasons, of course. Not that the marshal ever gave up in his effort to give the town boss a taste of legal justice. It was that unabated persistence that finally did in Charlie Truslow.

"Anyone want to pin on a badge, I'll see to it that he gets fair wages and will personally back him to the end," the boss man announced in his saloon the day after the Beaverhead Butte robbery/murder and four days after Charlie Truslow was laid to rest.

It was not entirely a disingenuous offer. A town marshal, even one as hard to handle as Charlie, at least gave Halfway the appearance of having law and order, which might even discourage those tempted to form an organization bent on imposing its own brand of morality.

The men froze with their glasses raised, as if afraid to either put them down on the bar or bring them to their parched lips. In the adjacent room, the piano music died, and the hurdy-gurdies and their male partners stopped dancing. Nobody was willing to break the silence; they all waited for Big Belt to say more.

"What — no takers?" he finally said, smoothly manufacturing surprise. "Oh, well. It's nothing to fret about, friends. When you get right down to it, we're a damn peaceful, law-abiding community unplagued by the gold fever to the east and west of us." The town boss paused as if daring anyone to argue the point. Nobody did, and Big Belt smiled and patted his belly as if he had feasted on a plate of lamb and spring vegetables.

"As you all know or should know," he continued, "our old marshal let his badge go to his head. Without question he brought on most of our troubles his own self with his pigheaded sense of justice and heavy-handed methods. If he had had his way, not a man amongst us would have been allowed a drink of whiskey in my saloon or a whirl with one of my girls on the dance floor. Why, that marshal would of arrested his own mother for spitting in the street. Now he and his game leg are at full rest in our peaceful little grave patch. I'm not saying that his demise calls for us to dance an Irish jig, but we all know our community is none the worse for being shut of him. Don't let anyone tell you, friends, that Terrance Goodman isn't a fair man, a reasonable man, a just man. I look after you as I do my own two sons. You show me a four-flusher here in Halfway who truly needs to be behind bars and I won't dillydally around; by gum, I'll toss him in our little calaboose my own self. That's the end of my jawing, friends. Strike up the music. I want to hear gaiety and laughter. So, bend an elbow, boys, your next drink is on me."

Nobody clapped or cheered, but every man in the saloon stepped up to the bar for his free shot of rye, and those in the next room tried to get back in step with the working girls in their low-necked dresses with scarlet waists.

■ ■ ■

Without a man occupying the marshal's office, nothing much changed in Halfway except, of course, nobody was arrested for public intoxication, creating a disturbance, or interfering with a peace officer in the execution of his duties. Terrance Goodman chose not to put a single soul behind bars. He did have a Virginia City gambler suspected of marking a deck beaten half to death, and he banished a traveling medicine show whose "miracle cure" in a brown bottle was cutting into his whiskey sales.

Holdups of stagecoaches, freight wagons, and men on horseback continued periodically, always near enough to town to be considered Halfway business. Halfway folks traveled freely, never getting robbed or harassed on the road. The road agent king was also their great protector. When outsiders representing the law, lynch law or otherwise, came around to make inquiries into the Beaverhead Butte robbery/murder and other misdeeds, no citizen pointed a finger at Goodman and sons or even acknowledged witnessing a crime. Terrance Goodman might not have been a good man, but he was good enough for the undemanding citizens to feel safe and reasonably content in a hard, dangerous country halfway to hell.

Soon the snow was falling steady in the mountain passes and even in the valleys below, piling up faster than nuggets of gold ever did over in Alder Gulch. The placer mines shut down and the roads became impassable, which meant no transportation in or out but also no holdups of any kind. In Halfway, the citizens' one and only concern became starvation, and Terrance Goodman was good enough to share some of his stockpile of canned goods with the people in need. Marshal Charlie Truslow, who had served perhaps too diligently for over four years and had died in the line of duty, faded fast from their collective memory that winter.

When the snow melted and the sagebrush buttercups appeared on the dry, open slopes that surrounded Halfway, the Bannack & Virginia City Express began operating regularly again. It didn't take long for a pair of road agents to halt the first coach carrying anything substantial out of Virginia City. They tied their horses out of sight and struck in a willow grove where the road made a sharp turn before the final long straightaway into Halfway. The masked duo waved around their Colts as their signature greeting. Dan Buck happened to be the driver. As usual the little unarmed man quietly submitted to this latest villainy, as did three of his passengers, men who in short order were separated from their money belts and watches.

Not so the fourth passenger, a vivacious woman in a blue dress and bonnet who bounced lively off the coach and craned her neck to get a closer look at the two men in black masks and high-crowned black hats. After she failed to engage them in small talk and they demanded she remove her silver ring, she put her hands on her rather full hips and dressed down the ruffians. By standing on her tiptoes she nearly matched their height, and her tongue was sharp enough to cut at least a surface wound.

"You ain't from around here, miss," remarked one of the bandits, yanking down hard on the brim of his hat and then adjusting his mask. "You speak your mind."

"I'm Mrs. Howlett, a widow woman."

"Is that right? We met previously?"

"Never been in these parts before. None of the men I know wear masks."

"I see you right fine. Something familiar about your . . . your facial features, miss . . . I mean, ma'am. You know, you'd look even better in a golden ring."

"My husband is gone but this ring he gave me is staying."

"We'll decide that," said the other road agent, reaching for her left hand.

She turned her hip and he caught only the dust the coach had kicked up.

"You got anything else of value, ma'am?" asked the first robber.

"Of value only to myself. Nothing you'd want."

The second robber grunted and grinned. "We don't see it that way." This time he reached for her left shoulder, but she gave it a twist, and he missed again.

"I have no money or jewelry hidden on me or in my trunk up there. Used most everything I had to get by after Mr. Howlett passed on before his time. You'll have to take my word on that. I won't allow you to search my person or my trunk."

"She won't allow!" said the second robber. "Ain't this she-devil got some nerve, George!"

"Shut up, you talk too much," said the first.

"Well, I'm done talking. I need me a better look." This time the robber moved his hand as if pulling a six-gun, latched onto her blue bonnet, and ripped it off her head.

A mass of golden brown hair flew freely in all directions as if a quarrel of sparrows had been released from a cage. "I seen better, but none out here!" He tried to touch the hair at her neck, but she slapped his hand like it was a fat mosquito.

"None of that now," the first robber said, but the second one held his ground menacingly close to the female passenger. "Tell me, Mrs. Howlett, where do you happen to be headed? To Bannack to catch the coach for Salt Lake, I suspect."

"Wrong. If it's any business of yours, my final destination is Halfway."

"Halfway, Montana Territory?"

"You know of another Halfway?"

Her three fellow passengers tittered or cracked crooked smiles despite their predicament. The second road agent turned his fierce attention to them and his six-gun, too. Their faces flashed fear and then froze with mouths partially open.

"You know someone in Halfway?" the first robber, the one who had been called George, asked the woman.

"I did. He is dead and buried there."

"You don't say. And would that be Mr. Howlett?"

"No. Mr. Howlett died in St. Louis better than a year ago. That's where we lived."

"I see. Another man, then. If you don't mind me asking, ma'am, who do you happen to know that's buried in our little . . . that is to say, the Halfway cemetery?"

"Charles Purcell Truslow. Know him, do you?"

"I . . . I know he was the town marshal."

"Murdered on the street in cold blood, I heard."

"That's a damn lie," said the second robber.

"In a back alley would be more accurate. His killers all escaped punishment, I heard."

"Who you been listening to? That's mighty loose talk!"

"As highwaymen, I imagine you two prefer to be more tight-lipped about the marshal's murder."

"What made you pass that last remark, she-devil?"

"Maybe you prefer to be called road agents? Or perhaps plain outlaws?"

The second robber turned his pistol away from the three male passengers and pointed it between the woman's hazel eyes. He settled for touching her nose with the barrel tip and then running it across her left cheek.

"None of that, either," the first robber said, but the other one used his weapon to prod the high neckline of the woman's blue dress. "Now, Mrs. Howlett, you best tell us what connection you have with the late marshal?"

"Back in Virginia, I called him Daddy for a while."

"Daddy? You mean . . ."

"My full name, gentlemen, is Charlotte Truslow Howlett. My friends call me Char."

"You ain't no friend of ours!" shouted the second robber. "I ain't never blowed the head off a woman before, but there's always a first . . ."

"Don't mean to interrupt," said Dan Buck, who had kept his hands properly raised through the entire conversation. Now he clambered down from the driver's seat and then raised his hands again. "But there's nothing else of value aboard, and I need to get a wiggle on or I'll be an hour late into Halfway and then be driving the last leg into Bannack in the pitch black. If you don't mind, lady, please step back inside the coach. You other passengers, too."

"Shut your bone box!" yelled the second robber, shifting his pistol again so that it was off the woman and pointed at the driver's chest. "You ain't running this show, you damned sonofabitch!"

"That's no way to talk to Buckaroo," the first robber scolded. "If we make him late too many times the Bannack & Virginia City Express Company is liable to send him packing. We can't have that. He's been good to us. So, everyone back in the coach, please, and do proceed, Buckaroo." The polite robber picked the blue bonnet off the ground and handed it to the female passenger. "You can keep your silver ring," he said. "Maybe I'll get you a golden one later on."

"One ring is all I need, mister."

"Is that so? Anyhow, I do hope your stay in Halfway is a pleasant one, Char, eh . . . Mrs. Howlett."

When Charlotte Truslow Howlett visited her father's grave, the curious citizens of Halfway took notice, some offering their condolences and a few providing kind, if not heartfelt, words about the late marshal's dedication to duty and sense of justice. Nobody volunteered any information about how he died or who might have shot him, and everyone was grateful the daughter asked no questions.

When she took up temporary residence in the marshal's office, it seemed reasonable because the town had no suitable accommodations for a respectable single woman and that was as good a place as any for her to grieve and get her bearings. Terrance Goodman soon sent word that she was welcome to check in to the hotel portion of his establishment for the remainder of her stay in Halfway, but she politely declined in writing.

Instead of sleeping on the hard cot in the lone cell or the bloodstained cot the marshal had died on, she fell asleep each night in the same chair where the marshal used to nod off. She stuck close to the office but stepped out to walk up and down Main Street three times a day. She was friendly enough, greeting everyone she passed and introducing herself to those she hadn't yet met. She didn't cross paths with Terrance Goodman at first. For one thing, she never walked into Goodman's Saloon/Hotel/Hurdy-Gurdy or tried to visit the alleyway in back where her father had been silenced by three different guns. For another, Big Belt didn't go on walks and had no reason yet to visit the marshal's office. The fact was, Charlotte never entered any residence or business, not even the general store. How she ate was a mystery to the community until someone saw stagecoach driver Dan Buck deliver two boxes of provisions through the back door of the jailhouse early one morning. Buck was seen going in and out other times, too, once carrying yellow bells, which naturally caused citizens to suspect that a romance was brewing if not blossoming.

After a month, she was still there. Dan Buck was visiting her in the office regular enough to be a suitor and then some. Talk on the street and in the tonsorial parlor was that the young driver was doing extra driving and rearranging his stage schedule so he could spend full nights in the unlocked cell. Charlotte kept up her thrice-a-day constitutionals up and down Main Street, but now she always appeared using a horsehead walking stick. Clearly, Dan Buck had given it to her, no doubt telling her it had belonged to her daddy. He gave her something else, too — the marshal's star badge. He never would have worn it himself in a million years, so she asked him to pin it on her, as if that somehow made everything official.

Of course, there was nothing official about her wearing the badge. But the whole town noted how her once unassuming walk became, even with the cane, a strut and how dusty sunlight, both in the morning and the afternoon, reflected off that dented star on her chest. No citizen told her she shouldn't be wearing the badge. After all, it was an inheritance, nobody else wanted it, the town marshal's position was vacant, and she wasn't actually going around arresting anybody. Even the owner of Goodman's Saloon/Hotel/Hurdy-Gurdy was heard to comment to his steady customers that he found the behavior of the little woman in the blue dress and bonnet quite amusing. Meanwhile, the robberies on the roads outside of town continued unabated.

Come June, the widow woman wearing the star made several other striking changes. Dan Buck gave her a wide-brimmed white hat that sat on her head like a mountain goat, and she took to it instantly. She put her blue bonnet in a drawer, telling herself she might bring it out if she ever went to church again. Halfway didn't yet have one of those. Buck brought her some pants, but she didn't find them a practical necessity while going about her business in town, so she stuck to her blue dress.

Although he shunned weapons of any kind himself, Buck apologized for burying the old marshal's LeMat revolver and bought her a .32-caliber Smith & Wesson with a large supply of metallic cartridges. The rounded bird's head grip fit her hand perfectly, and she took up target practicing in the weeds behind the jailhouse. Halfway had no ordinance against carrying or shooting off guns within the town limits. All that regular gunfire was hard to ignore, though, and inquisitive men came out to observe her and mark her progress. George Goodman, without mask but still wearing his usual dark clothes, even showed up one day to help her squeeze the trigger. He appeared in the weeds the next two days, too. On the day after that he showed up at her office.

"It smells better in here," he commented, making himself at home by sitting on the desk and twiddling his itchy thumbs. "Not that I ever spent much time . . ."

"Daddy never arrested you?" she said, leaning back in her chair, crossing her legs, adjusting the Smith & Wesson in her belt, and tipping back her big white hat.

"What? Oh, you mean Marshal Truslow. Of course not. Why would he do a fool thing like that! My own daddy is Halfway's leading citizen, and I'm following in his mighty large footsteps."

"I see. More so than your brother, Pete?"

"Huh? Look, I ain't here to talk about no daddies or brothers. You ain't half bad to look at, you know, even if you're a mite older than me. I hear you're looking for a man."

"I was. I think I found him."

"You mean the stage driver? I call him Buckaroo. He's a nice enough fellow if all you want is nice. You can do better. You already shoot better than him."

"I hear he doesn't shoot at all."

"Sure. That's why he's still alive — but barely! He's no man in my book."

"You don't say." Charlotte smiled. "Not like you, a genuine pistoleer."

"I can handle a Colt all right, or your Smith & Wesson, as I've already demonstrated."

"Yes, you have. George Goodman is a real bad man."

"Hey, let's not get personal."

"I don't aim to. What else you got on your mind, George Goodman?"

"Nothing. But my father was wondering some things about you."

"Too shy to ask me himself, I reckon."

"He don't have a shy bone in his body, and it's a big body. The people hereabouts call him Big Belt, you know, but that's only 'cause he likes it."

"I wouldn't call him that."

"Too much a lady, huh? That's one of the things my father was wondering about."

"Whether or not I'm a lady?"

"Like, why a widow lady would wear that

old badge and that new hat and that little pistol?"

"It's not so little. I thought we weren't going to talk about daddies."

"I'm talking about what you're doing here in Halfway, acting the way you do."

"You don't like me? Maybe you and your daddy want to run me out of town?"

"Not me. I like you this way. I like ladies who can shoot. We'd make a hell of a team, you and me. Course you'll have to tell Buckaroo to hit the road."

"But what you don't understand, Georgie . . . You don't mind me calling you Georgie, do you? What you don't understand is I'm not acting at all. I really and truly want to be marshal of this town."

"What the hell for?"

"To make sure justice is served, Georgie."

"Don't call me that. My mother's the only one who can call me that and she died when I was four. Pete, my twin brother, don't even remember having a mama."

"Sorry to hear that, George. I didn't have one, either. Is that all right, me calling you George?"

"Sure. I'm George. My old man calls me that."

"And you call him Big Belt?"

"Hell no. He don't like for Pete and me to

call him that or *old man,* either. It's best for
us to call him *sir* if we don't want a whipping."

"A whipping at your age?"

"Never mind him. He's the boss around
here, in case you hadn't noticed. And it's
best *not* to forget it. But I'd rather talk
about you, Mrs. Howlett . . . Charlotte . . .
Char. So, what do you think?"

"About justice? I'm all for it."

"I meant about you and me."

"Sorry, George. There's no justice in that.
I'm simply a widow woman who believes in
upholding the law."

"Like father, like daughter, I suppose."

"Something like that."

"Not sure how wise that is. But beauty
can sometimes make up for brains."

"That's not much of a compliment,
George. I could be smarter than I look."

"I reckon. But you really think you, a
widow woman, can keep the peace?"

"Peace? I never said I wanted to keep
that."

"And you won't, not with that little Smith
& Wesson."

"Thanks for the advice, George. Now, if
you don't mind. It's time for my afternoon
stroll."

"Huh? Oh, that. I'll walk with you . . . at

least partway."

"No thanks, George. I'm all talked out and tired of listening. Goodbye, George."

"Sure, I'll go. But I can tell you one thing, my old man will be talking to you."

"I can hardly wait."

Pete Goodman came to talk to her first. Not that he did much talking. It wasn't apparent what he hoped to accomplish. It was near midnight, and he had come from his father's saloon, clearly full as a tick. He barged into the marshal's office, ripped apart a copy of *The Daily Montana Post* that he found on the desktop, kicked over a chair, waved his Army Colt around, rattled some keys, and demanded that she lock him up in the cell. Sitting in the marshal's chair, Charlotte calmly told him he best go home and sleep off whatever was ailing him.

"Don't tell me what to do, she-devil," he said, but he holstered his revolver and raised his hands. "My brother come here. Now, it be my turn."

"Yes, I can see that. And I see you both came without your masks on."

"All right. You know I'm a *bad man*. What you gonna do about it?"

"I'm not sure. You said you wanted to be arrested?"

"Your old man buffaloed me twice, put me in the cell them two times, and a half-dozen other times more gentle," Pete confessed, bending down so that his stale whiskey breath blew in Charlotte's face. "Don't expect you to hit me over the head with the butt of your Smith & Wesson, even if you be a damned she-devil, but the least you can do is jail me pronto."

"For the bad things you've done?"

"For what I'm bound to do to you 'less you lock me up real tight for the night."

He put a hand on each of her shoulders and lowered himself slowly so that he was all but seated in her lap, face to face. When he nuzzled her face, she never felt more like a she-devil. She kneed him in the privates. He grinned even as he yelped, but he did stand off, giving her the room to nudge him toward the cell door. He went like a lamb, but once the key was turned behind him, he noticed Dan Buck lying there on the cot and turned mountain lion.

"You dare lock me up with this sonofabitch!" he screamed.

"I forgot he was there. He was resting. He's not a prisoner, you know."

"I know what he is — a sonofabitch driver! I hate Bannack & Virginia City Express men. Only thing I hate worse are vigilantes and lawmen."

Next thing Charlotte knew her prisoner had pounced on Dan Buck and while sitting on his belly began wailing away at the prone man's face. Dan woke up to the nightmare but was helpless to do anything about it. Pete Goodman was a mean drunk, that is to say, even meaner than he was when sober, and he kept punching long after Buck's body went limp and his eyes rolled back in his head. Charlotte screamed for help but realized she was the only one who could do anything about the situation. She opened the cell door and considered shooting Pete Goodman in the back. She wasn't yet an expert marksman, but she couldn't miss at this range. Instead she grasped her Smith & Wesson by the barrel and brought the pretty bird's head butt down on the crazed man's skull. It took her three whacks, each one progressively harder, but she got the job done. She had buffaloed Pete Goodman like her daddy had done.

Dan Buck gained his senses first, and he helped Charlotte drag Pete Goodman outside and down the street. They propped him into a sitting position and left him on the plank sidewalk in front of Goodman's Saloon/Hotel/ Hurdy-Gurdy and quickly retreated back to the jailhouse. They worried about Pete waking up mad enough to kill. Charlotte was the one with the gun, but Dan stayed with her all night for moral support and suggested she forgo her usual Main Street strolls the next day to keep from running into Pete. Charlotte refused.

"Folks expect the marshal to make the rounds," she said first thing in the morning.

"You're letting that badge go to your head, Char," Dan said as he held a wet cloth over his bruised eye sockets.

"It's still over my heart where you pinned it."

"I know, but nobody elected or appointed you marshal."

"Same with Daddy. He made this star his own."

"I got to go make my stage run. You watch out for the Goodmans, especially that Pete. He punches harder than a mule kicks."

"You sure you're up to driving today?"

"How do I look?"

"Like hell. How do you feel?"

" 'Bout the same. But I'll be fine. It's what I do; it's what I've been doing here for three years. It's you I'm worried about, Char."

"We'll worry about each other. I got to do what . . ."

"I know, what a Truslow girl gots to do.

One Truslow girl, anyway."

"See you later, Danny boy."

"Real soon, sister."

They hugged, and then Dan Buck tossed aside the wet cloth and left.

When Charlotte went out for her first walk an hour later, she only made it two blocks before two young tawny-haired women, half dressed and half awake, intercepted her. They had orders to escort her to Terrance Goodman's office in the hotel part of his establishment. They touched her elbows to guide her in the right direction.

"I know where it is," Charlotte said. "You saloon gals gonna strong-arm me?"

"We're dance hall girls," said the shorter one. "There's a difference, you know."

"No, I didn't. I'm not from these parts."

"Nobody's from these parts," said the other one, the sleepier one. "Why anyone comes to Halfway, I swear I . . ." She interrupted herself with a yawn.

Charlotte adjusted the Smith & Wesson in her belt but went willingly. It was high time she faced the town boss.

The two hurdy-gurdies led her through the batwing doors of the saloon. It was too early for customers. The barkeep was sedately wiping glasses with a rag, and a surprisingly energetic toothless man was sweeping one corner as if digging for gold. They both paused in their work to stare, mostly at the one with the gun, as the three females passed quickly through to the small hotel lobby, where a wagon wheel with kerosene lamps hung so low from the ceiling that Charlotte instinctively ducked her head. Near the front desk was a thick oak door with "Goodman" on the nameplate.

The girls directed Charlotte to an armless straight-back chair and both said "please" when they asked her to sit. Terrance Goodman dismissed the two employees by waving a fork without looking at them. His great bulk was squeezed into his armed desk chair, and he was finishing off a plate of steak and eggs. He greeted his invited guest with his mouth full.

"Marshal Truslow, I presume."

"Howlett, that's my last name."

"Marshal Howlett, then?" Staring at her badge, he smirked but not enough to dislodge the stringy egg particle pasted to his lower lip.

She played it straight. "You don't mind, I mean, me being marshal?"

"No, no. Call yourself anything you want, my dear. Sometimes I call myself king!" When he roared with sustained laughter, the particle broke free and danced all the way to his plate. "King Goodman of Half-way," he added when his jowls stopped flut-tering.

"I'm glad you approve, Mr. Goodman. Did you also approve of my late father?"

"He wasn't as pretty as you. That's an aw-fully big white hat you have on."

"You approved of him most after he was dead?"

"Now, now. Is that any way to talk to a king in his castle? Your father was a hard man, a difficult man, and we had our differ-ences, but . . ."

"Such as him trying to bring law and order to Halfway."

"We have law and order in Halfway whether or not anyone is sitting in the marshal's chair. I see to that."

"And have you seen to my father's mur-derers?"

"We don't know that it was murder. Out here in the West, men often must kill in self-defense. And whoever did the shooting must have seen the badge and fled. No doubt it was the work of an outsider."

"That's how you see it?"

"Exactly. That's how we all see it here in our peaceful community."

"I heard my father was shot three times, once in each leg and the fatal third slug was fired into his belly from above. I also heard that he hadn't fired a single shot from his LeMat revolver."

"I wouldn't know. I understand his weapon was buried with him. Anything else on your mind, Mrs. Howlett?"

"You asked to see me, remember?"

"Yes, of course. Would you like an egg, Mrs. Howlett, hard boiled, perhaps?"

"I've had my breakfast, thank you."

"And Dan Buck, too, I presume? You've been keeping company with him in the jailhouse. Of course, you are a widow woman. I understand."

"I don't think you understand anything, Mr. Goodman."

"But I do. I didn't get to where I am by *not* understanding the way things are. I beseech you, Mrs. Howlett: Don't let anyone tell you that Terrance Goodman isn't a fair man, a reasonable man, a just man."

"As a rule, I form my own opinions. Like my father did."

"You must have a low opinion of my sons. You rejected one and buffaloed the other. Of course, they do sometimes come on a little strong, especially boisterous Pete. They have plenty to learn about women, too, I mean, respectable women. My only excuse is that they grew up without a mother and, as you might have noticed, Halfway is still young and suffering from an absence of good female society. So, I do understand how the twins might seem a bit unpolished, and I do understand you, Mrs. Howlett."

"So, you must understand that I want to bring my father's murderers to justice."

"I understand why you are discomposed over what happened to him, even if you had lost touch with him and hadn't seen him in years. Blood ties are that powerful."

"Especially in the Goodman family?"

"All I can say, Mrs. Howlett, is that it is fine by me if you want my twin sons to leave you alone. I would only ask that you leave them alone, as well."

"And you, too, Mr. Goodman?"

"I think we understand each other, Mrs. Howlett."

"Hurry up, gal," said Dan Buck from the driver's box of the Bannack & Virginia City Express. "I got a rear boot full of mail and a schedule to keep."

"I'm not going to leave him alone," Charlotte said, hesitating at the coach step and tapping the front wheel spokes with the horsehead cane. An impolite thin man in a hurry threw his satchel over the top railing and brushed past her to get inside, where

536

one of the tawny-haired hurdy-gurdies waited impatiently for him.

"Never figured you would," Buck replied. "You're nothing like me. Isn't that funny?"

"Ha. Ha. Why we going again?"

"You've never seen Bannack, and even a town marshal needs a day off. Don't worry. Terrance Goodman will still be here when you get back."

"What does Bannack have that Halfway doesn't?"

"People — lots of people. And some of them are vigilantes."

"I'm not asking for help."

"But you'll be needing plenty if you keep getting under Goodman's skin."

"I got you. Don't laugh. You're not as much of a coward as you think."

"Sure I am. Must take after my poor unfortunate mama. Get inside, will you? Plenty of room this trip — only a traveling gambler and his lady friend. No gold."

"Had some, lost it," the thin man said, before he spit a stream of chunky tobacco juice out the coach window. "Luck of the draw. But I won a bigger prize."

Right on cue, his woman poked her head out next to his. She must have been sitting on his lap. "I'm that lady," she said. "Remember me, marshal woman? I'm Dottie, from the dance hall. I'm showing Halfway my heels and my backside to boot. Slim and me are going to town!" She wiped tobacco juice off the gambler's chin, perhaps to show how committed she was to her decision to leave with him.

"Bannack?" Charlotte asked, rubbing her own chin.

"For starters. Slim's promised to buy me a new dress there. Looks like you could use a new one yourself."

Charlotte looked down at the hard wrinkles in her rumpled blue dress, the same one she had on the day she first rode the stage to Halfway, except now the dusty dress was belted and the brown belt was accentuated with a Smith & Wesson.

"Step right in, marshal woman," Dottie said while she smoothed out her gambler's chin whiskers. "We don't plan on breaking any laws in here unless you got one against love making in a public conveyance?"

Charlotte didn't move. She began picturing the late Mr. Howlett, who had chewed tobacco even after the consumption caused his body to waste away at a speed that stunned the doctors and denied him enough time for a "good death." Clean, mountain air might have done him some good, but he had never wanted to leave their St. Louis home. Now she was out west alone. The hill air she inhaled during her Halfway walks never seemed quite clean enough, yet she might have done herself some good by coming out here sooner — when her daddy was alive.

That would have meant choosing a father who had deserted her when she was still a girl over a husband who promised to stick with her in sickness and in health for as long as they both shall live, with him assuming, of course, that they would do *all* their living together in the Gateway to the West. She hadn't given him a child, but she hadn't died in childbirth, either. That was something. She had always feared dying that way, like her mother. But was that really any worse than being consumed by consumption or for that matter being shot down in cold blood in an alleyway of this no-account one-horse town?

"I'll be riding outside," she finally told Dottie. "Protecting the driver." She turned her back on the gambler and his dance hall lady and climbed onto the seat next to Dan Buck. She held the cane tight across her lap while Dan called each of the four horses by name, clutched the reins, released the brake lever, and exhorted his four-legged friends to make up for lost time. Buck tipped his small black hat and Charlotte held her big white hat over her badge when they passed the Halfway cemetery's most recent grave, that of Marshal Charlie Truslow. The stagecoach lurched and jounced to Beaverhead Butte, where the coach and everything else in the world seemed to slow down.

"Can't go any faster on the ascent," Buck said. "It's a damn good spot for a holdup, as you know. But you can bet the road agents know the strongbox is empty. All we have on today's run is mail and the two runaway lovers."

"And me."

"Right. My protector."

"You bet, Danny boy."

"But who's going to protect you, sister?"

Charlotte smiled and tapped the cane's horsehead against the hammer of her Smith & Wesson.

It was clear rolling and pleasant conversation until they reached Grasshopper Creek Crossing six miles from Bannack. At least one fallen tree trunk, broken limbs, and ungrounded bushes obstructed the wooden bridge.

"Windstorm?" Charlotte asked.

"No," Buck said. "It ain't natural."

"Man-made? Maybe we can plow through it."

"Don't want to do that. Might damage the coach. No telling if the bridge is intact."

Buck pulled in on the reins and pushed hard on the brake lever with his foot until the team stopped twenty feet before the obstacle. One masked man immediately popped his head out from behind the fallen tree trunk. His Colt showed next, and then he fought his way out of the brush. Dan froze. Charlotte started to reach to her belt but then noticed another man walking up slowly to her side of the coach. His Colt was holstered, but he carried a Henry rifle and wore a black cloth mask like the first man.

"Step on down, Buckaroo, and the lady, too . . . slow like," the second bandit said.

Charlotte handed Dan the cane and obeyed. The bandit even lent her a hand, as if it was important to him to show off his good manners. Buck tied the lines around the handle of the brakes and followed her down, but the bandit paid no attention to him. He was pointing his Henry elsewhere. "You, in the coach, do the same."

Dottie, the former hurdy-gurdy, and Slim, the gambler, came out reluctantly, but they had enough sense to have their hands raised before their feet hit the ground.

"Took you long enough to get here,"

complained the first bandit as he finally joined the others, loose leaves and twigs falling off his shoulders and back. He glared at the driver.

"Yes, sir . . . sirs. But there must be some mistake. No gold this time."

"Shut your bone box, sonofabitch driver! Nobody asked you nothing."

"Rest easy, Buckaroo," said the other bandit. "All we want is the card sharper's greenbacks."

"You have been misinformed, gentlemen," Slim said. "I have no money at all."

He produced a wallet from a vest pocket and showed them it was empty. "Even lost my pocket watch."

"You're a goddamned liar!" shouted the first bandit.

Dottie jerked her head to the side, studied her man's poker face for a moment, and then blurted out, "How was you gonna buy me my new dress, Slim?"

"Don't you fret none, sugar," the politer bandit said. "He has a wad on him somewhere. Do me a favor, sugar, and take a look for me."

"Sure, I will," Dottie said, but she turned away from Slim and stared at the bandit closest to her as if she could read his lips through his mask. "That's you, isn't it, George? George Goodman. I'd know your voice anywhere. I wasn't sure at first, but . . ."

"Jesus Christ!" shouted the other bandit. "She knows us."

"Brother Pete, too. I suppose I shouldn't be surprised. I heard the hushed rumors. You two look smaller out here, away from Papa."

"And you look like the trash you are," Pete shouted back. "It figures you'd take up with this card cheat."

"Don't need to cheat to beat the likes of you boys," Slim said. "All I need to do is stay sober and watch your nervous blue eyes."

"You're the one who best be nervous. Your money or your life, gambler man!"

"Don't mind him," Pete's brother said. "We're on the rob, not the kill."

"Damn it, George!" snapped Pete. "They know who we are." He yanked his mask off in frustration. "If we want to ever show our faces in Halfway again, we need to kill 'em all!"

"Nonsense. Buckaroo has always known who we are. He's had the good sense to keep his mouth shut. Dottie and Slim are cutting loose of Halfway. They won't be back if they know what's good for them."

"Sure," Dottie said. "Big Belt would take it out of my hide for leaving him."

"What about her?" Pete ripped the star off the front of Charlotte Howlett's blue dress. He threw the badge in the dirt and stomped on it twice. "She buffaloed me once; now she'll want to hang me . . . hang us."

"Wanting and doing ain't the same. My brother's running out of patience, folks. Hand over the wad, gambler man, and we'll go our separate ways without anyone getting hurt."

"Sounds reasonable," Dan Buck said. "Best to cooperate, mister."

"Buckaroo talks from experience. He's a good man."

"It's in my left boot," Slim said. "Can I lower my hands to get it?"

"Sure," Pete Goodman said. "I got you in my sights."

The gambler dropped to a knee and began removing his left boot. He had quick hands, and instead of pulling out a wad of greenbacks he produced an over-under derringer. Without hesitation, he pulled the trigger and by luck put a .41-caliber slug in Pete Goodman's chest. George Goodman raised his Henry and aimed for the gambler, but

Dan Buck thought he was about to shoot Charlotte so he tried to knock the barrel away with the horsehead cane. He managed to alter the direction of the barrel only slightly but that was enough to save Slim — the .44 slug lodged in his left shoulder instead of his heart.

From a prone position on the ground, the fatally wounded Pete Goodman performed his final mean act on earth — firing off a shot from his Colt. Whether he was aiming at anyone in particular or not is uncertain, but Dan Buck again believed that Charlotte was the intended target. He hurled the cane like a spear at the shooter as he stepped in front of the marshal without a star and took a slug traveling upward right between the eyes. Dan died on the spot. Charlotte gasped, pulled the Smith & Wesson out of her belt, and fired quickly at Pete, who had already made his last gasp. She missed him, but hit his brother in the right ankle. George dropped his Henry and danced around in pain on one foot. Soon Dottie was busy attending to Slim's shoulder and Charlotte was on her knees mourning over the body of the kindhearted stagecoach driver. She hadn't protected him in the end, but he had protected her — probably saving her life at the cost of his own.

Maybe George Goodman could have stood the leg pain enough to pick up his Henry and cause more damage, but he apparently had seen enough killing for one day. He simply limped away in the direction of his hidden horse, perhaps wondering if he would be crippled for life and what he could possibly tell his father.

Pete Goodman was left where he lay, but Dottie helped Charlotte pull Dan Buck's body up into the coach. Between the two of them, it was a surprisingly easy job. Dan didn't weigh much. It was a wonder how such a slight man with not a mean bone in his body could handle a team of four, sometimes even six, horses so well. Slim was no help because he fainted from loss of blood, but the two women roused him afterward, and he managed to get himself back inside the coach before collapsing again.

Charlotte and Dottie cleared off the bridge at Grasshopper Creek Crossing as best they could, succeeding after much labor in getting the fallen tree trunk to roll just enough to drop into the shallow water below. All the sweat and aching muscles kept Charlotte from thinking too much about Dan Buck back in the coach, but when she sat in the driver's box and held the lines tightly, her eyes opened up like a gully washer. Regardless, she got the horses moving, and they knew how to do the rest. Charlotte remembered her badge half buried in the dirt, but she wasn't about to try turning the coach around and going back for it. Dottie sat beside her, continually praising her driving and occasionally throwing pebbles at the horses' hindquarters. At the moment, she told the driver, it seemed far more important for her to do that than to go back in the coach to tend to her lover, who, after all, only had a shoulder wound.

The vigilantes in Bannack decided to act again at last. They were surprisingly nice about it, apologizing for past inaction. Marshal Charlie Truslow had been a loner who had never come to them for assistance, while Terrance Goodman had always come across as a big bug in an insignificant town, too well off to get himself mixed up with a road agent gang. Maybe the death of the reliable, good-natured longtime driver for the Bannack & Virginia City Express had struck a nerve with the vigilantes. And maybe they were impressed with Charlotte Truslow Howlett for coming all the way to Montana Territory to seek justice in the name of her late father. There was also the matter of now having clear-cut evidence — Pete Goodman was unmasked and dead at the scene of the attempted holdup while George Goodman wouldn't be able to conceal his bullet wound to the ankle while he tried to lay low in Halfway. On top of that, some of the vigilantes were itching for another necktie party.

"We are starting to get a clearer picture of the Goodmans' operation," the vigilante leader told Charlotte in the lobby of the Goodrich House. "Terrance has been pulling the wool over our eyes for too long. Shame on us! He is hardly the first two-faced citizen we've had to deal with. If anyone needs hanging, it's him and the surviving twin. Rest assured, Mrs. Howlett, we shall attend to the burial of the dead twin, recover your prized badge, and then proceed to Halfway to make a surprise visit to Terrance Goodman's establishment."

Charlotte thought that it might be all right if the vigilantes decided to spare George Goodman the gallows and allowed him to wander the West with a permanent limp and without the support of a twin or a father. But she said nothing. She went to the doctor's office, where Slim was quickly recovering from his shoulder wound while Dottie was proudly wearing a new yellow dress with a high lace collar; buttons down the front; full, bell-shaped skirt; and wide flaring sleeves. Slim did have the wad of greenbacks after all, but in his right boot.

"It came up from Salt Lake this spring," Dottie told Charlotte, preening like a parrot. "It might even still be in fashion among the respectable ladies down there. Do you think it covers me up too much, Char?"

"No, no, Dottie. I think your nice form still shows through, exactly the right amount."

"Slim and the doctor seem to think so. I mean I'm not a dance hall gal anymore, but I still want to, you know, be appreciated."

The doctor told Dottie she had nothing to worry about in that regard, especially not in Bannack where men still outnumbered women twenty-five to one. He then took hold of Charlotte's elbow and ushered her into another room where the body of Dan Buck was stretched out under a clean sheet waiting for burial. Charlotte again found it impossible to hold back her tears, and the doctor handed her a wadded handkerchief. But he didn't give her time to wipe her eyes.

"Speaking of form, Mrs. Howlett, you do know about Dan Buck, don't you?" the doctor asked.

"Naturally," she said, sniffling. "But I may

be the only one who does. Not even Marshal Truslow knew, except maybe at the very end when my father was dying."

"I see. And do you want the body transported to Halfway for burial, perhaps next to your father?"

"I think not. Whatever cemetery you got here will be fine."

"As you wish. We do, on occasion, have funeral services in Bannack, you know."

"Not this time. But thanks."

"I completely understand. You don't want others to know?"

"Not if it can be helped. It would only cause talk and confusion."

"Your secret is safe with me. But who, might I ask, was Dan Buck?"

"Theresa Truslow, my dear twin."

"I see."

"We don't even look like sisters, do we?"

"Well, you are both very pretty . . . I mean . . ."

"We were only beginning to know each other again."

"I offer you my most heartfelt condolences, Mrs. Howlett."

"Thank you. You see, Doctor, she came out here to find our father. She wanted to be close to him without letting him know. Don't ask me why. It was her way. We long-lost daughters don't always act like regular folks. And by disguising herself as a man she could get the work she wanted."

"Driving the stage?"

"Exactly. And by concealing her true sex in this wild country, Theresa figured it would be safer for her. Well, I suppose it was for a while."

"Thank you. No need to say anything more. I know you are grieving and you want to take the next stagecoach to Salt Lake."

"That's true. I believe I have fulfilled my marshal duties in Halfway."

"I understand. Rest assured, Mrs. Howlett, I shall see to it that Dan Buck receives a nice, quiet, and safe burial."

■ ■ ■ ■

Gregory Lalire of Leesburg, Virginia, is the editor of *Wild West* magazine and the author of the offbeat historical novel *Captured: From the Frontier Diary of Infant Danny Duly* (Five Star, 2014).